Mon Amour, Friend or Foe

a novel of WW II Occupied France

Mon Amour, Friend or Foe

a novel of WW II Occupied France

Elizabeth Pye

Mon Amour, Friend or Foe
Elizabeth Pye
Copyright February 2020

ISBN: 978-0-9982130-2-6

Original watercolor cover art by Barbara Parish

Edited and formatted by Jenny Margotta,
  editorjennymargotta@mail.com

Printed in the United States of America

DEDICATION

For my daughter, Paula—who embraced the name of my heroine, Paulette—and her family; David, Bryan, and Blake.

For my son David , and his family, Karyn, Kate, and Parker, who traveled with me to France and endured a four-hour walking tour of WW II Paris, as well as a wonderful timeout at Monet's home in Normandy at Giverny, the chateaux of the Loire Valley, and Nice and the Gold Coast in the South of France.

For my son, Mark, who loves the kiss of the ocean breeze on his face and the warmth of sand on his feet.

ACKNOWLEDGMENTS

I'm indebted to the High Desert Branch of the California Writers Club for their critique groups, and many other sponsored events. A heartfelt thanks to Roberta Smith for her encouragement and to Lorelei Kay, Marilyn Ramirez, and Ann Miner for their savvy suggestions for improvements in the story.

I am beholden to Jenny Margotta, my editor par excellence, for editing the first two novels in my French Connection series, and again this third one, *Mon Amour, Friend or Foe*. Her extensive knowledge of WW II history is a fortunate bonus. Her help and guidance throughout the journey to publication is much appreciated.

I'm most grateful to Dave Thompson for his generosity in the sharing of his technical skills.

Many thanks to beta readers, Kathleen Puffer, who read each of the three novels in this series, and Anita Anderson, who shares my passion for France. She and her family lived there for ten years— 1969 to 1979—when her husband's work took him to Morocco, Martinique, Paris, and Lille. The people in Lille often spoke of the Occupation as if it had just happened.

I'm most grateful to Barbara Parish for another beautiful, original watercolor cover design for *Mon Amour, Friend or Foe* and for the continuity it provides with the first two books in the series.

AUTHOR'S NOTES

Mon Amour, Friend or Foe is a work of fiction set in World War II-occupied France. Through the characters, I write of a people whose country and way of life are under siege and of how their morals and instincts direct their behavior. Some chose to collaborate with the enemy and others to fight to the death to defend their sovereignty for future generations and to protect those most vulnerable in their society.

I have taken care to represent actual historical people and events as accurately as possible. All other characters are entirely products of my imagination, some of whom appeared in the first and/or second books of this *French Connection* series.

Research included primary and secondary sources such as memoir accounts, historical reports, and other writings, including many well-written novels set in the time period.

In *Mon Amour, Friend or Foe*, I focus on the French Resistance workers rather than the horrors of the German concentration camps, although many Resistance workers were sent to the camps and died there after having been brutally tortured while imprisoned in France, either by the collaborative French Vichy Government or Nazis such as the ruthless Klaus Barbie, known as the Butcher of Lyon at the Montluc Prison in Lyon, France.

Members of the French Resistance in World War II came from all levels of French society—students, aristocrats, academicians, clergy— as well as liberals, anarchists, and communists. They not only carried out both clandestine and brazen acts of sabotage against the Nazis who occupied their country, but they also provided detailed intelligence to Allied forces, published underground newspapers, and ran escape networks that helped hundreds of Allied airmen and soldiers trapped behind enemy lines. The Cross of Lorraine, also known as the Patriarchal Cross, which I have used to indicate section breaks, was personally chosen by General Charles De Gaulle as the symbol of the Resistance.

Chapter One

August 1, 1939 – Claremont, California

I remember well the hot, dry heat of the sunny Southern California day when I said goodbye to Mama. We sat on the back patio of our Mission-style home, drenched in the perfume of lemon blossoms from our citrus groves.

"Paulette, what am I going to do without you?" Mama said, more tears in her tear-weary eyes, as she brushed strands of my blonde pageboy from my face.

"I'll be back. It won't be forever," I said with little emotion, as she had done when I cried as she and Daddy left for months at a time to sail to France on the SS *Paris* and later the SS *Normandie*, while I stayed home with a nanny. Mama, poor-little-rich-girl Camille, "Descended from the French aristocracy," as she would say. She always expected someone to take care of her.

"How can my own daughter be so cruel?" Mama cried, her face distorted with no vain attempt to hide the lines that marred her beauty since we'd lost Daddy, two months after they'd returned home from their cruise on the new, faster SS *Normandie*. "You know I miss Jean-Paul. You are all I have left."

My father, Jean-Paul Rousseau, had flown a tiny Nieuport 11, a single-seat fighter aircraft, for the French Air Force against the German Fokker E. III during the Great War, before the United States had its own air force. Daddy had then accepted a job with Douglas Aircraft Company, soon after my unplanned arrival in 1921.

My parents continued their exclusive love affair until Daddy died in an airplane accident in 1935, when I was fourteen. So why should I devote my life to my widowed mother, when I yearned for the attention of my daddy, a man who revered everything French? No. I would assert myself and go to France to study at the Sorbonne—and maybe gain a deeper understanding of my value as a person.

Sometimes, I felt as though I had nothing to offer the world. Daddy hadn't seemed to think I did. Now, Chris, my high school boyfriend, was another matter. Daddy had praised him and thought that he was "the cat's whiskers" so to speak. He once said to me,

"Chris is the son I never had. You better hope he wants to marry you and take care of you. Your mother and I have many good years ahead of us and want to travel as we did before you were born."

✝

September 1, 1939 – Paris

The world remembers the date as the day Germany invaded Poland, the start of what would become World War II. But for me, it was the day my life in France began.

I recall awakening in my third-floor apartment at five in the morning to the loud, clear song of a pair of chimney swallows positioned high between the neighboring buildings outside my floor-to-ceiling bedroom window. The window looked out onto soot-blackened limestone walls and three chimney pots of varying heights, lined up like so many nutcrackers. It was a glorious autumn day in 1939—my first day at the Sorbonne. I hadn't seen anything like that in California, and I watched the birds with interest until I felt energized enough to get ready for school. I wore a light blue sweater set with a gray wool skirt for my first day at the Sorbonne, and took the Cluny-La Sorbonne Metro Line 10 to the college.

While students walked around me, I paused in the square, facing the Chapelle de la Sorbonne, the iconic face of French higher education. Green-leafed trees lined the square, casting shadows around me like huge ink-stamp imprints. I took a deep breath and started inside to begin the study of European history that I hoped to teach after college. I turned suddenly and bumped into a tall, slender, dark-haired young man.

"*Pardon,* mademoiselle," he said. His enchanting cornflower-blue eyes matched his sweater and contrasted with his polished, jet-black hair.

"I'm sorry. The fault is mine," I said in English, my command of French having deserted me as I stood mesmerized by his jewel-colored, lavender-blue eyes.

"American?"

"Oui. I am Paulette Rousseau from California."

"Enchanté. I'm Guy de Laval. *À beintôt!*" he said and left me gawking at the man of my dreams, one who was charismatic and exuded confidence. One I aspired to share a life with in France. My daddy loved France, and I had a feeling that I'd stay rather than return home. Of course, I would *not* tell Mama about my dreams.

I followed Guy at a discreet distance until we were in the rotunda. He stopped there to talk to a group of students, and when he saw me, he said, "Paulette, come and get acquainted."

And that's when I met and was befriended by Aline de Fleury, a willowy-figured beauty with black hair and soft golden eyes, and Renee Greenberg, a petite, soft-spoken girl with a mop of curly brown hair atop her head.

Aline said, "If you're enrolled in chemistry, you might want to join Guy's study group."

"Sign me up," I said to Guy.

"Not so fast. What makes you think it'll help you?"

I couldn't let him brush me off so easily. "I'm not very good at science. My daddy warned me that chemistry wasn't one of my strengths."

"Did he now?" He seemed engaged, as if he were seeing me in a different light. "That wasn't helpful. You're in. We'll start meeting two weeks from now."

"Merci, I promise to benefit from your help."

He turned to Aline. "I'd like you to keep Paulette informed of our schedule."

"My pleasure," she said and walked with me to my first class.

Eight months later, after the German Army had defeated many European countries, I hadn't changed my mind about my dream man and making a life for myself in France, as I'm sure Daddy would have liked.

May 10, 1940 – Paris

The pristine sky promised a beautiful day. It lied!

The relaxed setting of Montmartre, the butte, as the old bohemian area of Paris was known, suddenly changed. We were shaken from our inertia when eerie sirens wailed their forlorn warning for everyone to rush to the nearest bomb shelter. Scraping metal sounded as black, wrought iron chairs and tables were pushed aside in front of the Café de Montmarte, our pleasant red-and-white awning-covered gathering place. Brown trails of spilt coffee snaked around our feet as people from every direction moved as if in a choreographed rhythm, like waves rolling to shore.

As the leader of our study group, Guy de Laval took charge of the nine of us. "Follow Paulette and me." He linked arms with me and led us past the ancient chestnut tree, down the narrow winding street to a friend's house where a bunker awaited in the basement. Apparently, he wasn't the only one to know of its existence. There must have been about twenty of us crowded in as the door closed. We pressed together in the musty, 15 foot x 15 foot space as if we'd gone through a giant waffle iron. I didn't mind, because I was crushed against Guy's chest. Our hearts echoed each other. I know it's strange, but I would endure anything to be with him. He fulfilled my dreams of my ideal man—charming, handsome, and one of the smartest students in our Sorbonne chemistry class. I was an average science student, but I conspired for him to tutor me by feigning ignorance. It worked, and I persuaded him to tutor me two days a week in addition to our group study sessions.

"It's going to be okay, Renee. You'll be safe," Aline de Fleury said in a low voice.

I knew why Renee was in tears. She came from a Jewish family, and there were rumors that the Germans had begun to round up Jews. People of their heritage disappeared into the night and were never heard from again.

I prayed that Aline's sixth sense was attuned. She had a way of knowing things before they happened. I disregarded them when she'd say there was no future for me with Guy, that my life would be with another. She must be *wrong*. In no way would she discourage me.

I glanced at Chris Forbes, my American high school ex-boyfriend and, from the dim lightbulb overhead, saw beads of sweat on his forehead. He frowned at me, and I averted my gaze. He'd asked me not leave California, but when I refused, he followed me to the Sorbonne, unbeknownst to me. He and my daddy had gotten along well, and he used that relationship to keep tabs on me, but when Daddy was killed, he began to talk of marriage after our graduation from high school. He'd been a football star at our school and couldn't believe I wasn't ready to nab him when given the chance. I wouldn't be surprised if Daddy had planted the idea.

"Eighteen years old is too young to make a lifetime commitment! We're just friends," I had told him. Time had not changed my mind.

Now, as the minutes crept slowly by, the stale, cramped quarters began to take a toll on our nerves. The odor of fear drifted into my nostrils, and my throat tickled. What was taking so long? I felt the tension in Guy's body and my own. Surely, this was just a drill. Why hadn't we heard the all-clear signal yet?

After waiting another ten minutes, the hoped-for blast released us from our underground confinement. Well-seasoned, we exited in an orderly manner, having gone through such air-raid drills for months.

Guy motioned us to the chestnut tree. "Over here." The nine of us formed a tight circle around him and waited. "Is everybody okay?" he asked and stared at Aline's pale face. Nine pairs of eyes followed his, but when no one replied, he said, "Well, what shall we do with the rest of our morning?"

There were shrugs and strained expressions but no suggestions until Ida spoke. "I'm going home."

"All right. Let's call it a day," Guy said, and he and Aline began to walk away.

I took Renee by the hand and caught up with them. I hoped we could stay with them for a while and, ultimately, that I would be alone with Guy after Aline met up with her Montmartre artist friends. I wondered why Ida hadn't volunteered to take Renee to the Silver Quill. Renee's father owned the bookstore and Ida worked part-time for him. Renee Greenberg was only fifteen and overprotected by her father. I couldn't just leave her alone. She was close to a nervous breakdown since she'd lost her mother to the Nazis in Poland.

Not to be thwarted, Chris joined us. "Renee, Paulette and I will see you home."

Chris, speak for yourself, I thought. Guilt immediately slapped me. Chris might be pushy, a holdover from his high school football days, but Renee looked relieved. She needed his broad shoulders to lean on. I understood.

"Thank you, Chris," she said in a whisper.

5

Pleased with himself, Chris said, "Swell."

We made our way up the cobblestone street toward the Sacré-Coeur, the white stone basilica built on the highest point in Paris. We stopped in our tracks when we heard an unflappable voice on a radio in a nearby shop announce: "Winston Churchill has been named Prime Minister of Great Britain, replacing the peace advocate, Neville Chamberlain." After a pause, we heard a catch in the announcer's voice as he continued: "German forces have invaded Belgium, the Netherlands, and Luxembourg, despite repeated pleas from the governments of those nations that they desired to remain neutral. France stands ready to defeat the enemy forces."

Four days later, May 14, 1940, we stood in stunned silence and disbelief as we once again gathered around a radio. As the radio blared, images of whining airplanes releasing destruction, tanks plowing over anything in their way, and munitions exploding whipped about in my head, like the wind-torn French flag on a nearby flagpole.

> *Luxembourg is now occupied by German forces. The government of the Netherlands has fled to Britain and has ordered all Dutch resistance to cease. Belgium forces are weakening and their capitulation is expected within the week. Yesterday, German paratroopers landed in northeast France and a division of German tanks crossed the Meuse River, splitting the French Ninth Army. Hope that France can remain free is fading."*

"We'll see about that," Guy said defiantly. "Our troops will defend the Maginot Line and drive them back." Indignation registered in his voice. "We learned from the Great War. They won't get far, given the fortifications we erected. Together with the impenetrable forests of the Ardennes, our French forces have created an impenetrable line."

I said a silent prayer that he was right.

Chris hugged Renee and said, "Let's get going."

We rode our bikes back to the Latin Quarter. The Greenberg's Left Bank home included the Silver Quill—a book lover's paradise—and their residence on the second floor in the back part above the bookstore, not far from the bridge across the Seine on the Ile de Saint Louis, the heart of the ancient city of Paris.

As soon as we arrived, Renee scampered inside like a frightened bunny seeking safety in its rabbit hole. We followed her just to be sure her father was okay. I imagined that the familiar scents of musty old leather and lemon-oil-polished wood of the bookstore comforted Renee, as did Monsieur Greenberg's protective embrace.

He lifted his eyes from his daughter, tears threatening. "Thank you. Your friendship is appreciated." He singled me out and said, "Merci, Mademoiselle Rousseau. Renee tells me you've been most kind."

"De rien. It's nothing. We're friends." I smiled at Renee.

Aline patted the middle-aged man's arm. "You know we'll always be here for you both in times of need."

He nodded. "I know that." He released Renee and forced a smile. "I've forgotten my manners. Do you have time for a cup of tea?"

"Come on, Renee, I'll help you." Aline slipped her arm around Renee's waist while they went to the back of the store. I followed along a few steps behind to the familiar area where the hot plate, cups, tea, and sugar were kept on the old zinc countertop. Nearby, a small refrigerator was filled with a supply of milk, cold cuts, and cheese to go with a large, bakery-fresh baguette.

By the time the water boiled, Aline and I had assembled lunch and taken the tray to the front of the store. Renee arrived with the tea service as soon as the tea, generously packed in a metal tea ball, had steeped sufficiently. The French, like the English, liked their tea quite strong.

Guy started in on why there was no need to worry about the Germans over-running France. "You know as well as I do that we learned from the Great War," he lectured. "The country has spent the last ten years constructing the Maginot Line, a defensive fortification with bunkers and gun emplacements unlike anything else in the world. It stretches for two hundred and eighty miles across our eastern border with Germany. The Germans will not be able to break through it, you will see."

Chris's tone sounded doubtful as he replied, "Well, the Germans have defeated country after country and nothing has stopped them yet. The French defenses *better* be good." He did not point out that the Germans appeared to be coming from the northeast, through Belgium, and that the French's much vaunted Maginot Line stopped at the French/Belgian border.

"If our guns, mortars, and machine gun nests aren't enough, our engineers have added other obstacles," Guy continued.

"Swell. Such as?" Chris pressed.

"There are minefields, iron girders that protrude vertically from the ground to stop the advance of enemy tanks, and bunkers with forward-facing, twelve-foot-thick concrete walls, but thinner in the rear, so that any positions captured in frontal assaults can be easily retaken by counterattack."

Monsieur Greenberg stood and straightened a group of precariously stacked books. "No matter what happens, I will not leave Paris!"

"Fortunately, you won't have to make that call," Guy said.

I felt the need to change the subject from the German threat. "Are you ready for your exams?" I asked Renee.

"I am." A confident smile brightened her sad face. "I keep up with my work and don't leave my studies to the last minute."

"That you do," Guy said. "After that good lunch, we'd better get to work."

When we left the Greenberg's store, Guy stepped beside me and held my gaze.

I melted inside.

"I won't be able to tutor you until tomorrow."

"What time tomorrow?" I asked.

"Meet me at the library at ten thirty."

"I'll be there." Had I blushed, revealing my emotions?

Chris kept his cool and suggested we stroll through the Tuileries Gardens—one of my favorite spots.

"Okay. I need some peace and quiet in my life right now."

We rode our bikes to the gardens and, once there, began a slow walk. Chris reached for my hand and raised it to his lips. "I don't think Guy knows what he's talking about. There's no assurance the Germans won't get to Paris, one way or another."

"Don't say such a thing!" I snapped.

"You better wake up and be ready to leave the country while you can."

"Don't you trust me to do so?" I asked.

"How can I? You believe everything Guy de Laval says just because he's a French aristocrat."

"That's not so!" I said, rather too emphatically

"His pedigree doesn't assure that he has good sense."

"I'll think about it," I said to appease Chris. "I really need to get to the books now. See you in class tomorrow."

"We should leave for the States right after our exams are completed," he called to my receding back. "What do you say?"

"Absolutely not!" I stopped and faced him. "Calm down. We don't know what's going to happen."

"I know one thing for sure. You don't need to have Guy tutor you tomorrow. I'll do it today. I have a strong B in chemistry."

We'd see about that. He wasn't going to cut in to my time with Guy. "That won't be necessary. I really need to work on my Lit paper this afternoon."

Chapter Two

Wednesday, May 15, 1940

An eerie silence shrouded the city, reminding me of what it had felt like when I was a child and found myself alone in the house. Groggy from lack of sleep, I forced myself to dress, and dashed down the three creaky flights of stairs in my apartment building. I shared the small, third-floor walk-up with two other American girls, and although it was crowded, I loved the location—the Montparnasse district, a favorite haunt of Ernest Hemmingway during his early years in Paris.

I was the only one who had the early morning chemistry class, and could not afford the luxury of being absent. I felt the pressure of my upcoming final exam. Unspoken dread taxed my nerves. It wasn't just the rigors of my classes that threatened my peace; it was the threat of the German army and also the war Chris threatened to wage against Guy.

Chris had been steamed when we'd parted the day before. Guy would be blindsided if the ferocious attack took place, and I could think of no way to forestall the brewing melee. I couldn't begin to guess which one would come out the winner if such a thing happened—and didn't want to find out. Chris had the solid build of a football tackle, while Guy had a runner's physique: tall, slender, and muscular. Although wrong, Chris felt justified in defending his American territory—me—at the risk of alienating both his and my French friends.

The moment I entered the classroom, I breathed a sigh of relief. Guy, Aline, and Chris stood in the back of the room, engaged in what appeared to be an amiable conversation—but there was no sign of Renee. It was almost impossible to concentrate on the lecture as my mind wandered to the two young men seated somewhere behind me, both of whom were dear to me.

Immediately after class, Guy suggested the four of us go to the Silver Quill to check on Renee. When we arrived, a new student assistant, busy shelving books, turned at the sound of the door opening. *"Bonjour, ça va?"*

Guy stepped forward. *"Ça va bien.* I'm doing well, thanks.

Are Renee and Monsieur Greenberg here?"

She blushed—Guy had that effect on girls—and stammered, "They're in the back room. I don't know what's wrong, but something strange is happening."

Chris moved closer. "What do you mean?"

That's when I noticed that our friend, Ida, the other assistant, had removed valuable books from the rare-volumes cabinet. My heart sank because I always liked to peruse them.

"I don't know. Go and ask them." The girl didn't break her rhythm—up the ladder, return books to the shelves, and down again to repeat the pattern, all without another word.

In a hushed reverence we made our way to the kitchen. Renee and her father sat huddled around a radio and didn't glance up.

"Excusez-moi, monsieur," Aline said in her gentle, nurse's voice. "Are we disturbing you?" Her empathic personality and experience at the American Hospital helped to calm frightened people.

Renee gazed at us with glazed eyes until she focused on Aline.

"Please, join us," her father said, his mouth tight and grim.

The radio commentator's words shocked me as he spoke. "Word has it that Prime Minister Reynaud informed British Prime Minister Churchill by telephone, 'We have lost the battle!' And no wonder, Belgium is all but defeated." The somber voice went on. "Now, Hitler turns his attention to France!"

Mr. Greenberg shook his head. "This means I have to get Renee out of the country right away—before the Germans get to Paris. I lost my wife to them. I'll be damned if they're going to take my daughter, too."

"Papa, let me at least finish this school term before you send me away," Renee pleaded with him.

"I will not have you question my judgment. This is not a time to be like your mother. Look at what it got her," Mr. Greenberg said with finality.

Renee's face paled. She jumped up but caught the toe of her shoe on the chair. Guy caught her as she pushed the chair aside and stumbled toward him. He whispered something to her and stroked her hair while her sobbing subsided.

11

"Monsieur, I agree that events have taken a frightful turn for the worse," Guy said to the distraught father. "But I'm still confident our troops will defeat the Nazis before they can get a foothold inside our borders."

"And, if for any reason, you believe your daughter is in imminent danger, I agree you should send her to safety. But I also believe you want Renee prepared to make her way in life, and that means completing her work at the university, this term at least. I feel there's ample time for her to do so."

"Right now, in the face of this threat, what we need is a plan of action. She'll be better off that way. Don't you agree?" Guy said.

Renee cast a pleading look at her father. "Say something, Papa."

Mr. Greenberg turned off the radio, stood, and opened his arms to his daughter.

She rushed to him and buried her face against his chest. "Please say yes."

The monotonous tick-tock of the wall clock broke the heavy silence that hung in the air. Finally, Mr. Greenberg's emotion-choked voice granted his daughter's request. His eyes blazed as he pointed at Guy. "I'll hold you responsible if anything happens to her!"

Guy held the man's gaze. "I am not God and do not accept your terms. You'll just have to trust me and know I'll do everything in my power to protect Renee. But you have to do your part as well. It's self-defeating to get worked up before it's necessary."

"Of course. I shouldn't have spoken in the heat of the moment," Monsieur Greenberg said. "What steps can we take to prepare ourselves?"

"Let's begin at my house—Hôtel de Laval. Can you come with me now?"

Monsieur Greenberg nodded.

"Good. What about the rest of you?" Guy's gaze settled on each person in the room.

"Yes," I said, and my affirmative was echoed by everyone except Chris. Of course, I was going to say yes. Despite the less than desirable circumstances, I was thrilled to be invited to the de Laval's *hôtel particular*. The term *hôtel* did not pertain to the size of the mansion, but rather to its owner's rank. When I'd first arrived in

Paris, I'd thought it odd, but as I learned more about French history, it made sense. Intrigued by everything I'd heard about the *ancien régime* townhouse—it had been built in 1769, a decade prior to the beginning of the French Revolution—I'd been trying to figure out how to wangle an invitation to visit.

Chris edged toward the door, appearing to have forgotten his concern for Renee. "Not now. I thought you knew I have a class this afternoon," he grumbled at Guy.

"You can come tomorrow," Guy said as he walked to the door with him. "I'll fill you in on what you've missed."

"Swell." The one-word reply was laden with sarcasm.

"I'll come tomorrow too," Aline said and placed her hand on Chris' shoulder.

Thank goodness for the peacemakers among us.

At the last minute, Monsieur Greenberg changed his mind about riding with us. "You go ahead. We'll be there within the half hour," he said.

Things were looking up. Guy and I—just the two of us—rode our bikes the short distance to the huge limestone home in the St-Germain-des-Prés Quarter. There were other similar homes along the way.

As I followed Guy through the open, wrought iron gates in front of the mansion, he told me, "Now that the Germans threaten us again, it's too bad we tore down the wall and solid doors that enclosed the courtyard. As it is, everyone can look through the wrought iron gate directly to the house," Guy got off his bike and waited for me to park beside him. "I need to talk to you before the others get here." He unlocked the heavy entry door with a super-sized key. "*Entrez.* Make yourself comfortable. Wine?"

I had him to myself and couldn't think of a clever response, so I just said, "Please," although I knew wine probably wasn't a good idea.

He brought a bottle and poured each of us a glass after he sat down beside me. My hand shook as I accepted it. I noticed he seemed at ease with the whole thing.

He leaned close and I delighted in his fresh woodland scent. I

13

wondered whether he would kiss me. If he tried, I wouldn't object. I turned my face toward him, but to my chagrin, he started to talk in a hushed tone as though the walls might have ears.

"You know I've assured my friends there is no reason for alarm about our defenses here. I still believe it . . . but no longer with certainty. I need your help. There may be German sneak attacks and, God forbid the *Luftwaffe* breaches our defenses and heads for Paris. If so, we'll need ready access to bomb shelters in a hurry."

Sobered by his serious commentary, I set aside my half-empty glass. All my senses were on full alert. What did he want me to do about it?

"Yes, the newspapers report daily on the German air force victories," I whispered.

Guy reached into his pocket and pulled out a ring with several keys attached, one of which was a duplicate for the large front door. "No one is to know you have these, nor should you use them unless necessary."

I kept my hands firmly clasped in my lap and stared at him in shock. "You . . . you trust me with them? Why me?"

"I'm an astute judge of character. I've observed you in many situations and believe you are the one for this job."

"Job? What about Aline? Why not her?"

"I have my reasons. You wouldn't understand, so I won't burden you with them. What do you say?"

Chapter Three

Frozen in place like an ice sculpture, I tried to speak. No words came.

Since I'd first laid eyes on Guy, I'd tried to get his attention in any acceptable way I could. Now I was scared. He trusted me above all others? *No!* What was he thinking? I wasn't the person he imagined to accept the risk. I was the American girl who dreamed of an idyllic life in beautiful France, the home of my ancestors.

"I'm sorry. I can't accept your keys," I told him.

Guy placed his hands on my shoulders. "You can and you will, because your friends' lives might well rest on your decision."

"What are you talking about?"

He lowered his hands and took a step back. "I've downplayed the threat of war, but the blunt truth is that the Germans will bomb Paris to make way for their troops to capture the city. We have to be ready for an attack at a moment's notice."

"But you said . . ."

"I know. That's what I've been telling everyone. But the truth is what I just told you—the Germans will come."

I shook my head. "I can't believe they'll get this far inland."

A knock sounded on the front door and Guy thrust the keys into my hand before he responded.

The cold metal weighed heavily against my clenched fist. Could I do what might be required of me? I didn't want to face the awful possibilities.

Guy returned to the salon, followed by Renee and Monsieur Greenberg. "Come with me. I'll show you the way to the bomb shelter and explain how it's set up." He took me by the hand and said in a whisper, "Where will you keep the keys?"

"For now they're in my pocket," I said.

He nodded. "We'll have to remedy that."

The four of us passed several rooms before we reached a large kitchen. Guy opened a wide but nondescript door at the center of the room and led us down a flight of stairs to a huge basement. We walked past a wine cellar, supply room, and storage room before reaching the bomb shelter that occupied at least one fourth of the basement.

I was amazed to see so many folded cots and chairs along one wall. Five large tables with lamps and radios were sprinkled around the room. "How many can you accommodate here?" I asked, surprised that the de Lavals had stored provisions for such a large group.

"Fifty. In the nineteen twenties, after our experience with the bombings during the Great War, Father commissioned the design and building of this safe space. Come along, I'll show you where the supplies are kept," he said as we approached a wall of enclosed shelves. "Here, in these cabinets."

Feeling the weight of the responsibility he'd thrust at me, I drew alongside him and followed him to the wall like a mechanical soldier. It was most likely an exterior wall, I presumed. Guy's demand had so overcome me that I couldn't enjoy our close proximity. My thoughts turned to Chris. Our time together always seemed so carefree—no life or death issues depended on our decisions. We needed someone like Guy to think of our safety in such uncertain times.

"Pay attention, Paulette!" Guy's intense blue eyes, the rich color of blue delphiniums in June, flickered with exasperation as he took me by the arm. "Where are the batteries?"

I felt like a naughty little girl and shook my head in shame. "Did you show me?"

"Oui, I most certainly did." He let go of my arm. A swath of wavy black hair fell casually on his forehead. "Right there on the other side of the canned goods."

How could I defend myself? He seemed to have some sort of magnetism I couldn't resist. I focused on the well-stocked shelves. Indeed, jars of various sizes were neatly arranged. Others held bedding, towels, first aid supplies, and various flashlights, lanterns, and jugs of water, to mention just some of the supplies.

I instinctively took a step away from him and moved to stand by Renee and her father.

"This is astonishing!" Mr. Greenberg exclaimed.

"It takes a lot of planning to keep it ready for use." Guy replied, turning to the Greenbergs. "I wanted you to know of these protective quarters. You're welcome to shelter here, if the need arises."

Renee asked me with a shaky voice, "Is there an immediate

danger?"

"I don't know," Guy replied softly. "But thank you for coming. I think that will do it for today." He turned off the lights when we reached the top of the stairs and opened the door leading to the ground level.

Mr. Greenberg cleared his throat. "I couldn't help noticing that most of your valuable furnishings and works of art have been removed for safe storage."

"That's right. After France joined with the Allies and declared war on Germany, my family removed our most valuable items from Paris. As you know, the Louvre has relocated many of their collections to various undisclosed locations, as well."

"I've begun taking my valuable books out of Paris," the bookstore owner confided. He paused in the gallery and said, "That's an original Picasso, isn't it? You better get it out of town."

Guy nodded. "I plan to, but there are only twenty-four hours in a day. I'm doing everything as quickly as possible. The safety of the citizens of Paris is my top priority."

I questioned why Guy seemed to feel the weight of all of Paris rested on his shoulders. Sometimes, he confused me. I knew that his father had been an officer in the Great War. I didn't know much about Monsieur de Laval's current role in the French government. Was Guy acting on his father's behalf? He was still a university student, after all, although he displayed wisdom far beyond his years.

"Of course," Mr. Greenberg agreed, pulling my thoughts back to the conversation at hand. "Thank you for the generous offer, Monsieur de Laval." Then to his daughter he said, "Come, Renee."

Guy walked with them to the door while I sat on the sofa and tried to think of a way to discourage his confidence in me. When he returned and gave me his full attention, I steeled myself to insist he be forthright. "You gave me a responsibility without giving me any sense of what it entails." I stood up. "Either you tell me, or my answer is no!" I took the keys out of my pocket, set them on the table, and made a halfhearted move toward the door.

"I'm proud of the backbone you've shown. I'll bet you didn't know you had it in you." Guy reached for my hand and pulled me toward him. "You're going to have to sit here beside me."

I came willingly and put the keys back in my pocket.

He slipped his arm around my shoulders. "*Cherie*, I need you on my team. I realize I'm asking a lot. I wouldn't do it if circumstances weren't so perilous. A German attack is all but certain. If—when—that should happen, I may have to leave Paris occasionally and will need a trusted assistant to work closely with me to protect our interests here."

I was dismayed at what I thought he meant. "What sort of things would you ask of me?"

"I'm part of a group that has vowed to fight the Nazis any way we can. I want you to be a part of that. As the occasions arise, you'll receive specific orders from me. I repeat, I need for you to be part of my team."

I stared at him, speechless. I didn't know how to be a spy or an underground agent. Overwhelmed, I laid my head against his chest and tried to take it all in.

He cupped his warm hand under my chin and kissed me on the cheek. "War is ugly. Think it over, and let me know tomorrow." He watched as I fought to control the tears that brimmed in my eyes, ready to flow, and drew me closer.

I don't know how long I stayed there, taking comfort from his strength before we heard a quick tap and Chris burst through the unlocked front door.

"I left class early and saw your bikes. I came for the tour," he said, fire in his eyes.

Guy stood and met him "No. We've finished for today. Come back tomorrow as we agreed."

I had to separate them any way I could. I stood and took Chris's hand. "Let's go." The last thing I wanted was to find out how well Guy could defend himself. He was certainly no pushover. His slender, muscular frame suggested agility and strength, but Chris outweighed him by at least thirty pounds, and he'd played tackle on our high school football team.

When Chris didn't move, the lines of Guy's mouth tightened a fraction. "Chris, get out of my house. Now," he commanded. "Come back tomorrow if you're thinking straight. You'll want to see what I have to show you."

Chris turned and allowed me to guide him to the door, slamming it on the way out. We mounted our bikes and rode in silence, each lost in our own tormented thoughts. When we arrived at my apartment, Chris followed me inside. "We need to talk," he muttered.

After the door closed, I regretted that neither of my roommates were there to defuse his tirade.

"What's the matter with you?" he scolded, glaring at me.

"It's not what you think," I said. "Guy confessed that the war situation is much more serious than we thought. I was disconcerted over the danger we face. That's when he tried to reassure me we'd be okay."

"Swell. He took advantage of your vulnerability. Don't you understand that? Wake up. The next step will be to comfort you in his bed."

"Chris, I'm shocked at you. You owe Guy and me an apology."

"I find that hard to believe. If I hadn't come in when I did . . . God only knows what he would have done."

"Believe it. In no way did he behave other than as a gentleman. I was distraught and he sought to calm me."

"My dear Paulette, I hope so." Chris drew me to him and started to kiss me. He stopped and grabbed at my pocket. "What's this?" he growled as he pulled out the keys.

Chapter Four

I gasped at the sight of long, raven black hair entwined like a vine around an ivory female figure reclined on the artist's table.

The man set aside his paintbrush and stepped forward, extending a hand that reeked of spirits of turpentine. "Roberto Santoni," he said.

Dumbfounded, I wanted to run but, instead, allowed him to grasp my dead-fish hand. "Paulette Rousseau, Aline's friend."

"Cherie, what are you doing here?" Aline nonchalantly wrapped the sheet around her bare torso.

"I came to see you. Sorry, your roommate said I might find you here." I couldn't look at either of them.

She motioned with her hand. "Don't go. Tell me, is Roberto doing me justice?"

"All right." Heat crept up my face as I forced my eyes to his canvas. I'm no art connoisseur, but at least I tried to recall what I'd learned in my art appreciation class last semester. As I focused, I perceived a yearning in the expression of the languid figure.

"Don't keep the lady waiting." Roberto lighted a Gauloise cigarette and put his arm around my waist, drawing me against him. "Out with it."

"It's . . . stunning. "It's like a sculpture . . . poised and balanced."

I glanced at Aline and saw that the model's longing was for the artist.

Propped on one elbow, she said, "Is your visit urgent? Do you need to talk to me today, or did you just pop in to say hello?"

I shook my head. "No, it's not urgent. How about tomorrow? Can we meet, perhaps for coffee?"

"That's better, if you're sure it can wait." She studied my demeanor while she spoke then returned her attention to the artist. She looked soulfully at Roberto, who had returned his attention to his work. He was mixing paint on his palette, the cigarette still dangling from his mouth.

I'd started for the door when she called me back. "Look at

me," she insisted. She must have seen the tears in my eyes, a reflection of how alone I felt at the moment. Her golden eyes were gentle and contemplative. She always seemed to sense when something was wrong. "I needed to take a break in a few minutes, but now is as good a time as any." She hopped off the table and slipped into a robe. "You need a glass of wine." She linked arms with me and led me to a table with a view of the Montmartre vineyard and beyond toward the well-known haunt of Pablo Picasso, Au Lapin Agile, a cabaret theater.

I reached for the glass she offered and helped myself to one of the cheap wines on the table. But when her gaze seemed to question me, I shook my head, afraid to speak until I had my emotions in check. After taking a large sip of wine, I said, "I haven't seen Chris for a week."

"So? Is that unusual?"

"Come on, Aline, you know how he hovers. Never a day goes by that he doesn't make an appearance."

"It's near the end of the term. He's always worried about his grades, so I'll bet he's hitting the books."

"No, that's not it."

"Did you two have a tiff?" Aline stilled and set her glass on the table. She seemed to look through me.

I breathed out slowly. "It's worse than that. He thinks Guy and I are having an affair."

She chuckled and, with a wave of her hand, dismissed the idea. "That's ridiculous! Guy is still grieving."

"What do you mean?"

"I'm sorry. I shouldn't have said anything. Forget I said it. Just rest assured, he's not going to make a move on you."

"He gave me keys to his house!"

"Gave them to you?" Aline's face brightened. "So you accepted them without discussion?"

"He talked to me about the bomb shelter after the Greenbergs left. He swore me to secrecy."

"Then I suggest you honor his request." Her voice carried an authoritative certainty. "If you cannot, you must return the keys immediately!"

"You speak as if you know what he told me."

"I do know. Now, about Chris. Is he going to make trouble?"

"I hope not."

"That's not good enough. You must find Guy and tell him what you've told me."

I nodded and stood. "I will."

Aline swallowed the last of her wine and rose. "These are dangerous times. It's hard to know who to trust, so be careful." She hugged me and resumed her pose for Roberto.

I hurried down the stairs and out into the brilliant light of day. I hopped on my bike and wondered whether to look for Chris while on my way to Guy's. Aline's words about warning Guy about Chris and returning the keys if I couldn't keep a confidence reverberated in my mind. I rode to the de Laval mansion without delay.

I parked my bike and, after pounding quite loudly several times on the door without an answer, I unlocked it and entered. An eerie quiet greeted around me. "Guy?" I called and listened. "Guy, it's Paulette." No answer.

I'll leave a cryptic note about tutoring.

"Paulette! What are you doing here?" Guy had slipped up behind me so quietly that I jumped at the sound of his voice. I turned to see him smooth his rumpled hair and brush his hand across his unshaven face.

"Guy . . . Chris found your keys in my pocket . . . and unfortunately, jumped to the wrong conclusion." When Guy didn't say anything, my anxiety increased. What if Chris was in trouble? "I haven't seen him since the afternoon I was here." I tried to decipher Guy's blank expression. What was he thinking? Did he blame me for being careless with the keys? I so desperately wanted him to see me as a trustworthy woman—and maybe even one he could grow to love.

Perhaps he saw the desperation in my eyes, because he said softly, "It's going to be all right." He took my hand and led me to the sofa. He appeared to have momentarily set aside his own torment, and now his full attention was on me. "I share the blame," he said. "Chris is insecure, but he's an honorable man. I'll have to chance asking him to take part in our work."

He had put me at ease, and I couldn't resist wondering why

he was grieving. "You don't look as though you've slept in days. What troubles you so?"

He gently turned my face toward him. "You've caught me in a moment of weakness. I recently lost my wife in an automobile accident." Moisture glistened in his eyes. "I've been with my two-year-old son this weekend. His name is Claude," he said with tenderness.

Oh, my God. I couldn't believe my ears. He'd been married and was a father! How could it be? It was my turn to be silent.

"He's without a mother and has the misfortune of an absentee father. How can I be joyful?" Guy turned from me, his sorrow palpable.

In spite of my jumbled emotions, I felt his intense pain. At the moment, my only thought was to comfort him. I wrapped my arms around him and whispered. "I'm here for you. You can trust me."

"Thank you, Paulette. It seems you are the strong, compassionate woman I judged you to be."

"You've taught me a lot about myself already. I know I can do this."

He managed a small tentative smile and gave me a congenial kiss on the cheek before standing. "I look forward to partnering with you."

A loud knock at the door jarred my nerves. Guy answered it directly.

"She's here." Chris snarled as he followed Guy back into the room. "I'm surprised a smooth operator like you didn't have her hide her bike somewhere."

"Yes, she's here, and I'm glad you are too. She's been worried about you."

Chris stopped walking and looked around until he saw me. "She has?"

I got up and hugged him. "Yes, I have. I've been looking everywhere for you. I went to see Aline and now Guy. No one knew where you were. I've been so worried."

"Chris and Paulette, I want to talk to the two of you together. Please be seated." Guy took a chair across from the sofa. Chris and I sat together, holding hands. I was genuinely relieved to be with him. I felt terrible about the distress I'd caused.

"Prime Minister Reynaud has appointed a respected military man, Maréchal Pétain, as Vice Council of Ministers. Things are looking up now that there's a war hero watching out for us. But still, the battles in Belgium are going poorly. The Allied troops may not hold the lines much longer." Guy's brow furrowed.

Chris squeezed my hand. "That's ominous for France." He looked at me. "We have to leave after the term ends."

"No, Chris. I'm going to stay and help fight the Nazis." I spoke with more confidence than I felt; my heart rather than my head won this round.

Guy pinned his gaze on Chris. "I hope you will consider staying with Paulette. We can use all the help we can get."

Chris slid away from me. "My hope is she'll come to her senses." He stood and glared at me. "Come on, we need to talk."

"All right," I said, relieved to have time to reflect on my hasty decision. It wasn't a political decision on my part. The chatter from the satanic Stalinists and the rabid far-right activists did not resonate with me, given my modern views. My main consideration centered on Guy.

I realized Chris had made the rational decision. We rode in silence to my apartment only because serious conversation was impossible.

He lost no time after we started up the stairs. "Paulette, I have two Pan Am tickets for tomorrow in my pocket—one for you and one for me."

"What?"

"Don't act surprised. I care about you, and the way things are going, you may not have a choice to leave later."

"I'm an American citizen. I can leave when I want."

"Do you think Hitler cares about that?"

"America is a neutral nation. Of course, I can leave."

"You may find that is not the case. What if there are no flights out, for example?"

"Chris, I can't leave yet."

"Our flight is at noon. Meet me at the airport by eleven tomorrow morning." When I didn't answer, he continued, "If you aren't there, I'm going to leave without you!"

He wouldn't do that. He's bluffing.

Chris rose and walked to the door. Hand on the knob, he said,

"I'm leaving to pack and close down my apartment." He paused, seemingly to wait for me to say something. When I did not, he closed the door with a thud as he departed.

After he left, I regretted not having thanked him.

Chapter Five

Monday, June 10, 1940 – Paris

The cracks in our world turned into gaping fissures as tattered and disorganized groups of exhausted French soldiers straggled into Paris, and throngs of civilians pushed past them to escape the city.

Guy shook my arm. "Paulette, sleepy head, wake up. Have a cup of coffee. It'll help." He sat down on the edge of the sofa where I'd spent the night alone. I bolted up with a start and tried to straighten my skirt and tame my hair.

"Where were you?" I asked. "Surely, Prime Minister Reynaud didn't require your presence all night." I shivered although it wasn't cold inside.

"Cherie, the Prime Minister and the officials of the entire French government have left Paris. They're on their way to Tours in the Loire Valley."

"Guy! That's a pretty feeble excuse." I surprised myself by how emboldened I'd become after working closely with him for a little over two weeks.

He shrugged in resignation. "I only wish you were right. But unfortunately, you are not. Italy has declared war on France and Great Britain."

The enormity of his words began to penetrate my groggy brain. I realized our resistance work would now begin in earnest. I felt alone, abandoned. Chris had returned to America, and Guy was a father, grieving for his dead wife. I might not be able to keep my promise to be there for him. And who would be there for me? I was a frightened teenager, for heaven's sake, with no one from whom to draw strength. I'm ashamed to admit I began to cry right in front of Guy.

He held me in his arms until I quieted and so disarmed me that I told him how I felt.

"My sweet Paulette. I am going to tell you things that should be left unsaid. I will speak frankly so you will understand." He reached for my hand and kissed it. "My marriage took place to please my family. My wife did her part and bore a son for the de Lavals. Neither of us really wanted to be a couple, so we agreed to

26

lead separate lives. She died in the car with her lover. The pain I feel is for my son. He won't have a childhood much different from my own."

All of my internal inhibitions vanished. I wrapped my arms around him and kissed him on the lips—a long pent-up, passionate kiss. Lord knows, I'd daydreamed about it often enough. Guy returned it with restrained affection as he sought to defuse the outcome of my impulsive behavior.

"I must go to the Loire Valley within the next day or so. I'd like you to come with me," he said as he gently disengaged from my bear hug.

I wanted to be with Guy wherever he went. "Is your invitation for training purposes?"

A thoughtful smile curved his lips. "Not entirely. But as a citizen of a neutral nation, you'll be able to travel more freely than French citizens after the Germans arrive. There is no denying that may come in handy. Just in case, I want to introduce you to Prime Minister Reynaud."

"Whatever you think best." I tried to calm my pounding heart and sound casual.

"My family home is in the Loire Valley. We'll stay there, and you can meet my family, especially little Claude."

"I'd like that." I pondered for a moment before I remarked, "You must have been a child groom."

A devilish smile graced his mouth. "Probably about your age."

"I thought you *were* about my age. How old are you?"

"Twenty-two."

"You're not dumb. How come you were in our class?"

"I went to military school first and then attended university."

I persisted. "I still don't understand why you were in my class."

"Enough questions for now." He kissed my nose. "Be advised it's better not to be too well informed."

27

Wednesday, June 12, 1940 – Paris,

I dragged my largest piece of luggage down the three flights of stairs from my apartment. Somehow, I felt I had to take everything I could because I might not get another chance. I stood outside the building and weighed my decision to lug my suitcase and walk the two miles to Guy's house when I could travel light and ride my bike.

For me, everything was uncertain, including life itself. Apparently, others felt the same way. The streets of the city were like a ghost town, deserted, with no evidence of a living soul in view. How many people had stayed behind in the houses with boarded up windows? The absence of motorcars on the wide Boulevard Raspail allowed me to hear the birds' joyful songs of welcome to another picture-perfect day. I envied their ignorance of the dreadful events that were befalling us.

As I drew closer to Guy's house, anticipation overcame my feelings of desperation. I'd be a guest at Lamont, the de Lavals' historic chateau in the Loire Valley, free for a few days from worry about the war. Most specially, I'd be with Guy! By the time I knocked on his door, my arms ached from carrying my overstuffed bag. I waited for a few moments before I unlocked the door with the key he'd given me. After hoisting my bag inside the house, I heard the sound of the radio and went to look in on him.

I found him in the study. A revolver and a glass of wine sat on his desk. He seemed to be intent on listening to the radio commentator. His elbows rested on the arms of the chair, his back to me. When I entered the room, he turned and shook his head. "Paris is now officially an 'open' city, which means we will not try to defend it. The U.S. ambassador is in charge and is the closest thing we have to a mayor."

"Ambassador William Bullitt?"

Guy nodded. "He and the Prefect of Police, Roger Langeron, are responsible for keeping the peace. Soon, the German Wehrmacht will enter Paris. I never thought I'd see this day, and probably, neither did they."

"Have your plans changed?" I asked with a sinking feeling as I moved to his side.

"Not in the least." He stood, reached for my hands, and

covered them with his own. "I'll know more after I've spoken with Reynaud again."

"When will we leave?"

"Within the hour. *Café et croissants*? If so, in the kitchen."

"I'm not hungry."

"You may not have another chance to eat for a while. I'll bring what I can to eat and drink, but we could be delayed along the way. The roads are filled with refugees and Frenchmen headed for safety in the south."

"Oh," I murmured. "I hadn't anticipated such a complication." Without another word, I left him and went in search of beverages and solid food. I had misjudged what the trip involved. I'd looked on it as an exciting adventure.

My heels tapped with each step I took on the green-and-white-tiled floor of the kitchen—rubber soles would have come in handy. I found the coffee pot still hot on a gorgeous, orange, La Cornue range surrounded by white tile counters and white cabinets. An oversized refrigerator stood some distance from the stove. That seemed logical to me—hot and cold functions wouldn't mix well. I poured coffee into the extra cup set on the counter, helped myself to two croissants, butter, and jam. Little did I know what a luxury I enjoyed, for upon our return to Paris, everything would already be in short supply.

Forty-five minutes later the blue Renault was loaded to the hilt, with just enough room for Guy and me in the front seat. At the time I didn't suspect, but the Picasso was in Guy's luggage, tucked between layers of clothes. When I saw the gas gauge at "full," I appreciated Guy's careful planning for the trip.

"Is gasoline in short supply yet?" I asked.

"I believe so, but we don't have to be concerned about it."

"Why not?"

"This car has been retrofitted to burn a liquefied coal fuel."

We zipped along the open streets of the city, only to come upon crowded roads as far ahead as could be seen. Refugees of all sorts—some from Paris, some from Belgium and other countries, as well as French soldiers—trudged along the dusty, hot road. They had brought along as many belongings as possible in carts, wagons, cars, and other motorized modes of transportation. Others rode bicycles or walked with packs on their backs. Babies cried, and children clung to their mother's skirts.

It was dreadful. The progress was next to nothing. Stoic, Guy inched the car along.

"Isn't there a way we can get around this?" I moaned.

"Non." He kept his eyes straight ahead. I couldn't read his expression so I closed my eyes and tried not to think at all.

After driving the entire day, Guy pulled into a field for the night, as had many others. Our meal consisted of bread, cheese, and wine. Guy slept, but I stayed awake for hours, watching the shadow figures of humanity struggle to make it through the night just to face another day of the same. When most of the activity subsided, I slipped out of the car and relieved myself in its cover before returning and drifting off to sleep.

Thursday and Friday, June 13 and 14, 1940 – on the road to Orléans,

As soon as Guy started the car, I awoke in darkness and sat up with a start. "What's happened?"

"Not much. Go back to sleep if you can."

"Not until you tell me why we're leaving."

"We should make better time while most people wait for daylight." He patted my hand. "Are you okay?"

"So far," I said without looking at him. Resigned to my fate, I slipped into a semi-conscious sleep for most of the day as an escape until such time as I could wash up and change my clothes. I certainly didn't want to draw attention to myself. We stopped with the crowds at dusk and pulled to the side of the road again. Thank heaven for the faded sky. I could see his shadowy two-day beard. He must have had circles under his eyes from lack of sleep, but I couldn't tell. We repeated the ritual of the previous night—eat, drink, and sleep.

By the time we got underway again, there were fewer cars to contend with because many had run out of petrol and had no way of getting more. "Where will we be able to stop and get more supplies?" I asked.

"Within the hour we'll arrive in a small village. A general

store and café are there. Maybe we can pick up supplies and have a real lunch."

By the time we saw the signs to the village, people congested the roads again, but now more small groups of French soldiers were among them, all retreating from the enemy. My heart bled for them. I felt helpless to do anything to assist. At least they would soon reach the town where they could eat, drink, and get out of the heat.

"We're here. Let's hope they haven't run out of wine and cheese," Guy said as he turned from the road and followed the narrow street to the center of town.

I wanted to scream when I saw the boarded windows, doors standing open, and broken glass and other debris littering the sidewalks, with no sign of life in sight. Guy's shocked expression matched that which I felt. "Who did this? The refugees or the Germans?" I whispered.

Guy swiped his hand across his whiskers, now clearly evident. "Probably, the refugees when they found the townspeople had abandoned their shops, and in desperation they helped themselves."

"What are we going to do?"

"Get to Orléans as soon as we can." Guy gunned the engine and turned toward the road.

Suddenly, airplanes roared overhead. They flew low along the road ahead of us and swooped down. Bombs exploded all around, far and near. The car shuddered, bounced, and landed upright on the ground again.

On impact I bumped my head on the dashboard, and the taste of blood filled my mouth. *Oh God*! The sound was deafening and the dust blinded me. I panicked when I smelled smoke. Something was burning. "Guy! Guy!" I screamed in terror.

Chapter Six

I'm dead, but where is heaven?

Gradually, I emerged from my vertigo state and found myself cradled in Guy's arms—a heaven of sorts. The roar in my ears subsided enough that I could hear him say, "*Mon Dieu,* you gave me a scare when I saw the blood. Open your mouth so I can take a look."

I opened my mouth as wide as I could.

"That's it. The bleeding has stopped, but your mouth is going to be raw for a few days."

"The Germans bombed us!" It was all coming back to me. "Are the planes gone?" I asked as my head cleared. I squinted as I looked to see if Guy was hurt. His face looked the same as I remembered, so I concluded the blood on his shirt was mine since my face had rested there.

"They're gone for the time being. We can't assume they won't be back." He handed me a canteen of water. "Take a little, and see if it's okay to swallow. "We must get past Orléans and cut across to the Loire Valley. The Nazis follow the roads and rivers to locate their targets. The sooner we're off the streets the better."

The sound of his mellow voice soothed me into a tranquil limbo while he drove. I couldn't tell if there were many people on the road, because I paid it no mind. I trusted my safety to Guy. Maybe, my brain was addled, because later, when I thought about it, I realized the two of us were at the mercy of the Germans. Warplanes could appear on the horizon without warning. We might not be so lucky the next time—but at least we'd be together, which brought some comfort. I concluded one must live in the present, for this moment, and I ran my index finger along the flesh of his arm, seeking a tactile bond. He returned my gesture with a tender expression that amazed me. He must have felt as I did.

The damaged road was clogged with people and animals, some alive and others dead by this time; the bombs hadn't been selective about who was injured or killed along the way. The chaos slowed progress considerably.

"There's still hope in spite of these crater-scarred roads," Guy said. "We can choose to trust that the enemy met resistance in

Orléans and has been unable to inflict irreparable damage there."

Sunday and Monday, June 16-17, 1940 – Orléans,

Orléans had been bombed the night before we arrived. Rubble from destroyed buildings littered the streets. Guy slowly inched the car along as best he could until stopped by a brown truck and road barriers straight ahead of us. A soldier with a French uniform approached and spoke to him. Guy flashed an ID card. "Will we be able to get to Tours?"

"Follow me and pray we're in time before our troops blow up the bridge," the man called as he sprinted toward the truck.

As we neared the bridge, I saw hordes of panicked people headed toward it. Guy glanced at me. "We'll have to chance it."

I nodded. "I'm okay. Everything happens according to divine plan, so my mother says."

A glint of wonder lit his deep blue eyes as he glanced at me and nodded. "I'm not surprised."

"Do you think so too?" I asked.

"I do." He didn't elaborate, and I didn't want to distract him further.

The truck ahead began to move again, and we followed it to the other side. An audible sigh escaped my lips. Until that time, I'd been controlled, although frightened out of my wits all the while. The worst thing was the realization that this was probably just the beginning of the close calls we'd experience.

We hadn't gone far before we came to another roadblock manned by French soldiers. They stopped us and looked in the car as they had done with those ahead of us. They asked for our IDs and destination. I showed my passport and Guy again showed his identification papers. Rather than waving us on, however, one of the men yanked open the back door of the car and another one pulled out Guy's luggage but left mine undisturbed.

Guy got out of the car. "Hold on. What do you think you're doing?"

"Orders," one of them said. He opened the suitcase and meticulously searched until he found the Picasso. "We had a report that this painting was stolen in Paris and that we should watch for a blue Renault." The second soldier put the other items back into the bag and shoved it into the car. "Go on, get out of here. We don't have time to arrest you."

"You'll answer for this," Guy said. But seeing no alternative, he climbed back into the car and accelerated away from the soldiers.

It didn't make sense. Guy's ID had drawn respect from the soldier in the truck. Besides, how did the man know he was coming there with the painting? Could the soldiers be Germans in French uniforms? Would Guy have answers to my questions?

"Unfortunately, I didn't have time to get their IDs because of the rush to get across the bridge. I'm sure the Germans were behind it, but they had inside help," Guy said by way of an explanation.

"I wonder how they knew we'd come this way?"

Guy shook his head but seemed relieved to be on the outskirts of Orléans and on our way to Tours. "Another fifteen miles, and we'll stop for the night."

I looked at him in surprise. "What makes you so sure we can find a place that's open for business?"

I thought it must be wishful thinking on his part. Surely, fatigue must be getting the better of him after having driven through most of the last twenty-four hours. On top of that, the loss of the Picasso and the bizarre circumstance of the theft must weigh heavily on him. I said a silent prayer for our safety.

"It's their calling." Guy didn't leave me in the dark much longer. "There's a small monastery up the road. I went to school with Brother Roger. He'll take good care of us."

"Does that mean we can wash up and finally change clothes?"

"Oui. It's not Paris. Their lifestyle is rather primitive, but it covers the essentials. I admire their dedication."

"How many permanent residents are there?"

"Nine or ten *frères*, but the numbers of those not in the order vary."

Satisfied that I had something to look forward to, I fell silent the rest of the way.

We left the highway a short time later and entered a dirt road that ran through a wooded area. The monastery sat straight ahead and consisted of a few small, timber buildings that blended into the natural landscape. The surrounding pine trees and smaller, leafy green growth gave the peaceful impression of seclusion from the rest of the turbulent world. The trees extended around it for as far as I could see. The tension in my shoulders seemed to melt away, and I glanced at Guy. His tight expression had relaxed into a smile as he parked the car.

"Wait here while I go in and speak with Roger," he said, giving my hand a squeeze.

He hadn't been gone more than five minutes before he returned with a man who wore a long brown robe and had a round face with rosy cheeks.

"Paulette, say hello to Brother Roger."

"It's nice to meet you," I said and extended my hand, not sure of the proper response in this situation. I doubted the French *bise* would apply in this case. Even an air-blown kiss didn't seem to be appropriate, to my way of thinking.

Roger accepted my outstretched hand. "Welcome, Paulette. Come in and join us for supper."

"Merci." As I thanked him, I wondered what Guy had told him about me. Would we be able to stay the night?

Guy and Roger talked about the war and the French Government's abandonment of Paris on our way into the building. We entered a large open room and passed through to a dining area. A huge tureen of soup sat on one end of a long, wooden table. The men sat on one side of the table and the women on the other. I sat with six other women, and Guy sat with the men, some robed and others in civilian dress. Brother Roger led us in a prayer of thanksgiving before ladling bowls of savory beef stew. I didn't have time to be concerned with the seating arrangements after a bowl of stew and plate of crusty bread were passed to me. They smelled heavenly. Another brother poured glasses of red wine for each of us.

"I suppose you're safe for the time being." The woman who sat beside me looked me in the eye.

"And you're not because you're British?" I said in response because of her accent.

"That's right, but my French husband and I have no intentions of leaving Brother Roger."

"How long have you been here?" I asked after I finished chewing and swallowing a piece of delicious beef. I hadn't realized how hungry I was.

"Six years. Monsieur de Laval is a benefactor and stops in often. We all hold him in high regard." She paused and looked expectantly, as if I should explain why I was with him.

"Do any of the women here have children?" I asked.

"Yes, I have a boy and a girl. There are two other boys and one girl who belong to one of the women and her husband."

"Why aren't the children eating with us?"

"They eat separately at an earlier hour."

I thought it odd but didn't pursue it. I hoped the evening would soon draw to a close, as exhaustion threatened to claim me now that my appetite was sated. I cast a weary glance at Guy. He looked as tired as I felt, and when Brother Roger stood, as did Guy, and started for the door, I rose and met them.

Brother Roger said to the English woman, "Please show this young lady to her room. Monsieur de Laval and I will fetch the bags." He looked at me. "Breakfast is at six sharp. Be there on time, or you may go hungry." The words were stern, but there was a twinkle in his eye.

The woman led me to one of the long, low buildings, each with numerous doors, that surrounded the main building. As we passed the first door, she said, "This door goes to the toilet facilities." We went by it and moved along until we reached the fourth door. The English woman opened it and escorted me inside. One side of the room contained a small bed, and the other side housed a dresser with an attached mirror next to a washstand and basin. "Is there anything I can do before I leave?" she asked.

"Nothing more, thank you." I sat on the bed after she left and waited the few minutes before Guy arrived with my bag.

"I'll see you at breakfast at six," he said as he sat my bag on the floor inside my door. "Then we'll be on our way."

"Where will you sleep tonight?" I asked.

"In a room very similar to this . . . in another building down the way." He pointed toward it on his way out.

I don't know what I had expected, but at the least I thought

36

he'd be within shouting distance, maybe in the room next door. Well, it would just be for one night. Too weary to battle with myself, I washed up and went to sleep as soon as my head hit the pillow.

The next morning, I splashed water on my face, brushed my hair, and put on clean clothes. It felt so good to feel presentable when I went to breakfast. By the time I made my entrance, I seemed to be the last person to arrive of those I'd seen the previous evening.

"Bonjour," I greeted Roger and Guy before taking my seat by the English lady.

"I trust you slept well," she said, before Roger gave the morning blessing and we all partook of boiled eggs and freshly baked bread with butter and strawberry jam.

After breakfast we gathered around the radio and heard the commentator announce, *"The German army entered Orléans a few hours ago. Refugees are not to go any farther. Trains will be available to repatriate everyone."*

Guy lingered and talked privately with Roger while I gathered my things and tidied the room. I went to meet him and found the others huddled around the radio. A different voice proclaimed, *"This is Marshall Pétain speaking to you. French citizens, by order of the President of the Republic, I am, as of today, assuming the direction of the French Government.*

"My heart is heavy, for I say to you today, we have to cease the combat and find a way to end hostilities."

The initial hush in the room became a controlled buzz as everyone sought confirmation of what they had just heard.

A solemn Guy gave Roger a hug, picked up our bags, and loaded the dusty Renault. He opened the car door and held me close for a long moment before I slid onto the seat. When he came around and got behind the wheel, he said, "First thing when we get to Tours, you and I will stop by to find out from Reynaud what has happened . . . what is going on."

Thus, we began a long journey together into uncharted territory. Little did I know of the heartache mixed with joy, the manic-depressive experiences that lay ahead.

Chapter Seven

Monday, June 17, 1940 – Tours

Billows of smoke assaulted my nostrils and burned my eager eyes on our approach to the city of Tours.

"The Germans are coming," I screeched. "Where will we go?"

"Looks like the Luftwaffe has already been here." Guy's brows drew together in an agonized expression. "But perhaps the Germans haven't actually occupied the city. Let's hope we're not too late."

As we crossed the Loire River into the heart of the city of Tours and headed toward Prime Minister Reynaud's office, we saw in the distance city block after block leveled, leaving only smoldering rubble where buildings once stood.

"Mon Dieu!" Guy muttered under his breath and took the next corner a little too fast.

"Take it easy," I said, dictated by my instinctive need for self-preservation.

He glanced at me as if he'd forgotten I was there. "Sorry."

After an uneventful, two-block drive, Guy parked the car and got out. He came around and opened my door then ran up the steps of the building with me not far behind.

As far as I could see, the only damage to the building was a few shattered windowpanes. When we entered the lobby, I saw cracks in the walls, paintings hanging crookedly, toppled bookcases, and other things that had fallen to the floor or were broken.

A dark-haired man with a neat moustache and wearing a gray suit came to meet us. "Monsieur de Laval, I'm glad to see you. All hell has broken loose since we last spoke."

"I can see that."

"Non, you cannot see it all. There's more. I rushed up from Bordeaux just to meet with you," Reynaud said. He looked my way. "Pardon, Mademoiselle. You must be Paulette. Guy told me you were accompanying him."

"I'm pleased to present Mademoiselle Paulette Rousseau," Guy said belatedly. "Paulette, this is Prime Minister Paul Renaud."

"Mademoiselle, *c'est un plaisir,*" Renaud said graciously. Turning to Guy he added, "Let's go into my office where we can talk," and he escorted us to a room at the end of a long hallway.

I sat in a chair across from Guy and the Prime Minister as Renaud began, "Three days ago the Germans bombed the roads in Parçay-Meslay, just north of here. The roads were filled with refugees. Many were injured or killed."

"And the Saint Symphorien Bridge, too?" Guy asked.

"No, our defending army did that. A defensive action."

Guy stood and walked to a window. "What chance do we have to stop the enemy?"

I knew I shouldn't follow him, so I got up and went to a different window, but not so far that I couldn't hear the conversation. I wondered how resistance groups could sabotage the occupying army that was sure to arrive at any time.

Reynaud rose and went to stand with Guy. "The warring factions within our government have crippled our response to handle German aggression. Our military leaders were ill-prepared. Our soldiers cannot fight the powerful new German Panzer tanks with only the outdated weapons of the Great War.

"I had one small victory when Charles de Gaulle was promoted to brigadier general and named Undersecretary of War. He and I are in accord that France must fight on. At the cabinet meeting on Sunday in Bordeaux, I made it clear I was not in favor of an armistice, but General Pétain argued for one." Reynaud paused and stared out of the window before finally saying, "I submitted my resignation, and it was accepted!"

"You should not have done that." Guy turned to face Reynaud. "What now?"

"We'll have to wait and see who's appointed in my stead. Meanwhile, I'll make sure de Gaulle flies to London. Let your father know how quickly things are happening. I have to get back to Bordeaux now that the government is there, and who knows, I may need to leave the country . . . and not to North Africa."

"I'm confident you'll do what you can for France," Guy said and came to me. "Paulette, it's time we get to Lamont and talk to Père."

By the time we left Reynaud, the wind had picked up and blown cinders all over our car and everything in sight. It reminded me of a volcanic landscape I'd seen on the island of Hawaii. The car was already filthy from our trip, and I had thought it couldn't get more so. But it had. We dusted off the ash and soot as best we could and climbed into the car.

Guy didn't start the engine right away; instead, he turned to me. "You'll begin work as soon as we return to Paris," he said and studied my response.

"What will my job involve?"

"You'll be a messenger until further notice. The various resistance factions that have been operating independently are now organizing into a serious resistance effort. I want you to be a go-between among the various cells that will be operating in the Paris area. Communication is key, but it is important that the actual members of various cells do not know each other. In case the Germans capture one of them and . . ." Guy's voice trailed off, but I knew enough to know what he'd been going to say. Already, even this early in the war, the Germans were not known for their gentle treatment of their enemies.

My head spun. One bit of bad luck, or a mistake on my part, could cost my life—and possibly, the lives of others. Would I be strong enough to withstand the relentless interrogations that would result or God only knows what else should I be caught? I remained in serious silence on the ride to Lamont-sur-la-Loire. The highway we drove along had escaped German bombs. I supposed that boded well for Chateau Lamont, for which I was grateful.

Before long Guy turned from the road into a lane that curved between the wooded hills. The car moved quickly along the winding road until the chateau appeared on the horizon—a storybook castle with towers and a drawbridge. Such beauty as yet untouched by the terrible bombings all over France. Caustic tears formed in my eyes. Were they from the fumes of war or from the ache in my heart for the devastation of this beautiful land? At least for the time being, Guy's home appeared tranquil "The chateau escaped the bombings," I said in a lame attempt to be positive.

"Oui. That's because it's not in the industrialized area of Tours. Most of the damage is in the western and northern regions of the town." He shook his head. "No telling what's next."

As we came out of the woods, I saw gardeners working on a gorgeous, formal French garden to my left. Guy drove the car across the drawbridge and parked it in a courtyard that was enclosed on three sides by the central block and two wings of the chateau. The low wall at the far end allowed a panoramic view of the Loire River and the valley to the north.

A black Lab bounded toward Guy, followed by a boy in work clothes who looked to be about fourteen. The dog jumped up on Guy while the boy reached for the car keys and took them. "Your car needs a good washing. I'll see to it."

"Mystique." Guy leaned down, stroked the dog's back, and was rewarded with a wet kiss before he stood and patted her on the head. He held his hand in the halt position. The dog sat and tilted her head, not taking her eyes off of her master.

"The dog's name is Mystique?" I asked.

"Oui."

"What an unusual name. A female, I'd guess,' I said.

"Yes, to both remarks." Guy patted her on the head.

"Why did you name her Mystique?"

"She appeared out of the blue one day and followed me everywhere I went all day. She was skin and bones—either lost or abandoned by her owner. I put notices in stores and cafes, but no one claimed her. So she's my mystery girl now."

Guy addressed the eager boy, who stood on one foot and then the other, clearly impatient for the word to wash the car. "You can wash the car as soon as we get our luggage." Clearly, mutual regard existed between Guy and the boy.

Here, in this setting, I saw Guy in a different light than in Paris. In the countryside, with Mystique and workers who knew him so well, he seemed more contented. He seemed equally comfortable both here and in Paris, but in the city his demeanor changed and he appeared as cosmopolitan as anyone.

No one else came to meet us, so I concluded we were not expected. We'd taken our luggage into the house before a young woman appeared. A lilt in her voice, she said, "Monsieur, I'll get those." She stopped and did a double take when she saw me.

"Paulette, this is Yvette. She is indispensable around here. She helps Claude's nanny, Greta, in addition to her regular responsibilities. If you have any questions, just ask her. She knows everything that goes on around here."

Yvette eyed me with interest. "Mademoiselle, I'll take your

bag to your room, and when you're ready, show you to it."

"Merci, Yvette."

Guy and I left our bags and continued through the "fortress room," as I named it, given its display of weaponry, including several suits of armor. With the exception of the massive, slanted, outside door and a smaller interior oak door, the room was built of large blocks of stone.

When we stepped into the next room, bright daylight flooded through a bank of full-length, crystal, diamond-shaped panes and stained-glass windows. I couldn't believe my eyes; the chateau had morphed into a beautiful Renaissance palace. A majestic spiral staircase lay straight ahead of us. Along the grand curving stairwell, carved motifs on the limestone wall changed from late Gothic to Italian Renaissance. The interior walls, the pilasters, and ogee arches contained exquisite scrolls of classical acanthus leaves, carrying the eye to the de Laval family armorial shield.

Instead of starting up the stairs, Guy led me to the left into a casual sitting room. A man with black silver-streaked hair, sat intent on the floor model radio in front of him, his back to us. When he turned toward us, I saw a handsome man with a neatly groomed, silver moustache. He broke into a broad smile and rose when he saw Guy.

"Papa, we've been on the road for three days now. I wanted to get here sooner," Guy said by way of greeting.

Guy's father placed his hands on his son's shoulders. "You're here now. That's what's important." His deep blue eyes glistened as he turned to me. "Who have we here?"

"Papa, please meet Mademoiselle Rousseau, a colleague of mine from Paris." He reached for my hand and added, "Paulette, this is my father, Mathieu de Laval."

"Bienvenue," Monsieur de Laval said. Further conversation was delayed by the pattering of the feet of a toddler, which preceded the entrance of a very small boy and a strikingly beautiful, blonde-haired woman with kind blue eyes. I saw tears in the woman's eyes as she swooped down, picked up the boy, and ran to Guy. There was no doubt the little boy was Guy's son.

"Papa! Papa!" The toddler flung his chubby arms around Guy's neck.

Guy held him in the air and twirled him around to the

delighted squeals of the child.

"Take me horseback riding," the boy demanded.

"In a little while." Guy set him down and said, "Maman, please say hello to Mademoiselle Paulette Rousseau."

Madame de Laval did not immediately acknowledge the introduction, as all her attention was on her fussy grandson. "The horseback ride will have to wait, Claude. It's time for your nap. Nanny Greta will be here for you any minute now," she said. Then she turned her attention to me. "I'm happy to make your acquaintance. You're a brave soul to have traveled at a time like this." Madame de Laval watched Guy as he relinquished his son to a stern, gray-haired woman. "Where did you and Mademoiselle Rousseau meet?"

I thought I understood the reason for her question. She wondered whether I was a new love interest of his.

"At the Sorbonne." Guy came to my side and put his arm around my waist. "Paulette is indispensable to me at this time in my life."

"In that case, I imagine she's indispensable to all of us."

Guy kissed me on the cheek and then affectionately kissed his mother.

"It's good to see you so playful." She ruffled his hair as if he were a little boy.

"Pardon, I must sit," Monsieur de Laval said after the introductions concluded. He returned to his chair by of the radio and lowered the volume. "Pétain has just been named President of the Council of Ministers, and already, he has requested an armistice with the Germans!" he called to us.

Guy sat across from his father. "We'll talk more later after we've freshened up."

I slid onto a chair next to the sofa where Guy sat and waited for his next move. I didn't have to wait long. He reached out and pressed an intercom button. "We're ready for you, Yvette," he called into the speaker. Then he glanced at his watch. "Meet me back here at four o'clock," he said to me.

Yvette must have been nearby, because she appeared at the door almost immediately. "Mademoiselle, come with me. I'll show you to your room."

As I followed her to the staircase, I could not believe what I saw. Six men dressed in coveralls had begun the removal of the colorful, stained glass panels from the windows. Shocked, I asked, "What are they doing?"

Yvette shrugged. "Monsieur de Laval's orders."

I could have kicked myself. I shouldn't have been surprised, for hadn't the Louvre removed their priceless paintings? This was a time of war, and I better change my usual way of thinking. Reminders of the reality of war were becoming more and more numerous with each passing day.

Yvette stayed close to the interior wall on our way up the stairs, and so did I, not wanting to risk getting in the workmen's way. At the top of the stairs, we stepped into a spacious anteroom. She opened one of three, heavy wooden doors and led me along a hallway with an oriental carpet runner extending as far as I could see. We passed fifteen to twenty doors. I drew comfort from seeing we had gone the length of the hallway. How could my room be much farther?

She stopped at the last door on the right and turned the well-worn brass doorknob that was embellished with a carved hunting scene. "Your luggage is here. Is there anything more I can do for you?"

"Oui. Is there warm water in the bathroom, or do I need to ask you for it?"

She smiled. "Chateau Lamont is modern. There is both hot and cold water in the bathroom." She didn't wait for any more of my questions.

"Well, you never know about these country homes," I mumbled in my defense.

My room reminded me of one of Norma Shearer's movie sets. The bed was fit for a queen, with two carved wooden angels, cheek to cheek, perched above the headboard, which was a tapestry of lovers frolicking in the woods. A real antique if ever I had seen one.

I went to the window. What a view! The Loire River was a glistening silver ribbon as the sun reflected on it, and beyond it lay more of the countryside. And then I noticed dark clouds. Was a storm brewing? "No! It's smoke," I said to myself and jerked the drapery closed.

I found the bathroom, and as Yvette had indicated, a turn of the hot water faucet handle delivered lukewarm water within a few minutes. I washed my face, patted it dry, and applied lipstick. After giving my long hair a thorough brushing, I parted it, pulled it to the side, and rolled up one fourth of the front section before I fastened it with hairpins. I certainly wasn't ready for a party, but it would have to do. Anyway, this was not a time to celebrate.

I had over an hour before Guy and I were to meet. Would he discuss the Resistance with his parents while I wasn't present? At any rate, I decided to go back downstairs and wait. Maybe listen to the radio.

On the way there, Yvette came running toward me, fear in her eyes. "Have you seen a little boy up here?"

"No, I haven't seen anybody."

"Little Claude is missing. One minute he was watching the men work and the next he'd vanished!"

Chapter Eight

June 17-25, 1940 – Loire Valley

My heart went out to Guy and his parents as they returned from directing the search team on the vast grounds of the chateau. Furthering the group's dark mood, the radio brought no good news from the battlefront, but we listened anyway.

Guy stood and addressed his parents. "I have to turn this house upside down again. Are you coming with me?" He turned to me. "Paulette, monitor the radio while we're gone."

"I will." Of course they couldn't rest until they retraced their steps in the vain hope that somehow the child was in the house.

I desperately wanted to be useful, yet there was little I could do other than be a contact in the sitting room. After hours of sitting and listening to various radio commentators drone on and on, I needed a break. I got up and went to look out the window—no sign of success in sight. As the clock chimed seven, I turned the radio dial until I found the BBC.

To my amazement General de Gaulle, now in London, was speaking to the French people. I had to make notes. After grabbing the first things I saw—the major's crossword puzzle and a pen—I jotted down as many highlights of the speech as the white space permitted. I wrote quickly:

"I, General de Gaulle, currently in London, invite the officers and the French soldiers . . .

"But has the last word been said? Must hope disappear? Is defeat final? No!

"Whatever happens, the flame of the French Resistance must not be extinguished and will not be extinguished."

Guy returned just in time to hear the end of the speech. "Tours and Bordeaux lost." He sighed. "But we will resist. The general is right about that."

Without asking, I already knew by Guy's expression that they had not found Claude. I wanted to hug him, but something held me back. And then he came to me and I rose and opened my arms, my heart aching along with his. We stood together for a long moment, our thoughts unspoken.

He broke the silence. "At least General de Gaulle gives us hope. Now we must do our part."

"I know."

He patted the sofa. "Come, sit with me." He leaned forward and pressed his hands on his knees while arching his back, his head down. Momentarily, he straightened and gave me a resigned smile. "I cannot do any more tonight. This waiting is the worst kind of torture!"

Madame de Laval rushed into the room, breathless. "In all the confusion, I didn't realize that Nanny Greta didn't come to work this morning. Your father is on his way to her house now to see why and find out what she might know. She's been fearful about Claude's safety. It never occurred to me that she might have taken any kind of action without our permission."

Guy rose. "I'm going over there now."

"Would you like me to come too?" I asked.

"No need. There's no guarantee it'll lead to anything."

I nodded. "If you need me, I'll be in my room." I paused by the stairs to watch Guy and Madame drive from the courtyard. Alone in the reception hall, I turned, climbed the stairs, and went to my room. The day, filled with anxiety about the child's safety, combined with the barrage of war news, had drained my energy. I undressed, got into my pajamas, and settled down into the comfortable bed.

The next morning I awoke to voices from below in the courtyard. I slipped out of bed, ran to the window, and saw Claude in Guy's arms. *They found him!* Relief washed over me like cool waters on a hot day. A group of men surrounded them, including the boy who had offered to wash the car when we first arrived.

I hurriedly dressed and ran down the stairs to the courtyard. "Is he okay?"

Guy's wide smile told the story. "Oui." He gazed down at his son. "Claude, say bonjour to Mademoiselle Rousseau."

"Bonjour," Claude said and gave me a smile like his father's before he looked away and snuggled against Guy's chest.

An older man with leather-like skin said, "If there's nothing more we need to do, we'll get back to work now."

"Thank you for your help." Guy patted him on the shoulder. "Paulette, have you had breakfast?" he asked, turning to me. "I've neglected you shamefully. Please forgive me."

"Under the circumstances, there's nothing to forgive. But now that Claude has been found, I'm ready to eat."

On our way to the breakfast room, I asked, "Did Nanny Greta take Claude without telling anyone?"

"She panicked when she overheard two of the stained-glass-removal workers say, in German, that if they abducted Claude, they could receive a lot of money in return. She took him from the house through a back door and went to her home. Greta told us she thought the men might be involved with the German soldiers."

"Will she still be Claude's nanny?"

"No. Yvette will take care of him for the time being. The responsibility to protect Claude seemed to overwhelm Greta. It's a good thing she asked to spend time with her daughter and grandchild. I'm afraid she's on the verge of a nervous breakdown. She and her family fled from Germany soon after Hitler came to power."

When we arrived in the breakfast room, Guy's parents were in deep conversation over their meal. Yvette kept a watchful eye on Claude as he romped around the room. The butler poured coffee and brought plates for Guy and me.

"I think Maréchal Pétain has made the right decision to seek an armistice," Major de Laval said. "The Germans have powerful new weapons that we cannot hope to win against. No one thought such military development possible under the terms of the Versailles Treaty. Somehow, the Germans developed and built them in secret."

"They deceived us once. Why should we think they'd honor a new agreement?" Guy asked.

"What is the alternative?" his father shot back.

Guy didn't say anything, but the stubborn set of his jaw took issue with his father's assessment. He would resist to the very end. And I had committed to help him.

"Guy, I know what that look means," his father said. "General Pétain has our best interests at heart. We must trust him to make wise decisions."

"Is it wise to abandon Paris and run like cowards?" Guy rose and paced back and forth. "Pétain was part of that decision, no doubt."

Monsieur de Laval pointed his index finger at his son. "I served under his command during the Battle of Verdun during the

Great War. He was the one who changed procedures and rotated our troops out after only two weeks on the front lines." He reached for his cane and stood. "I owe my life to his military genius!"

Madame de Laval placed her cup on its saucer. "Those poor people who wait for the trains to leave for Paris. They've been stranded in the stations for days, and not one train has departed." She sighed. "The desire to go home is powerful."

"Speaking of leaving for Paris, Paulette and I will wait until morning to start out. Claude gets my attention today."

His mother frowned. "You're leaving so soon? Claude needs more than a day of your time. Stay over the weekend."

"Maman, you know that I would if I could, but I cannot. There's no telling how long the journey will take, and I must get back to Paris as soon as possible."

"I do understand." Guy's mother smiled at him. "While Paulette is here, why don't you show her around the grounds? A walk will do you both good."

"Good idea. And when Claude gets up from his nap, we'll have a picnic at the river."

☩

Guy appeared relieved with the idea of a change of scene—I certainly was. He rose and led me from the room. We climbed the stairs to the landing and entered through another one of the carved, wooden doors I had seen when we first arrived. It took us into the library, an inviting room with a huge fireplace at one end. Two walls were dedicated to bookshelves filled with beautiful, leather-bound books. I would have liked to sink into the soft leather sofa with one of them.

"This way," Guy said as he took my hand and guided me to the French doors which, I found, overlooked vast gardens that seemed to go on forever. As soon as we stepped onto the stone terrace, I did a quick search for airplanes or smoke around the panoramic view. I relaxed when I saw neither. My heart beat a little faster for this beautiful land and, especially, for the little boy inside the house, who represented all the children whose futures hung in the balance of this war.

Then and there, I committed myself without reservation to

work with Guy and the Resistance. Something had changed in me; it was as though a bolt of lightning had delivered an epiphany. If everyone thought like I had in the past, the next generation would surely be lost. I felt a responsibility for the outcome. I was at peace with my resolve to fight. When I came out of my reverie, I saw Guy watching me. "Let's go down to the gardens," I suggested.

"I didn't want to disturb you. You seemed far away, lost in thought. But now that I have your attention, I'll tell you a bit about them. The formal gardens are the work of Andre La Notre, King Louis the Fourteenth's chief landscape designer at Versailles."

"Yes, I know of him. When was this garden designed?" We began to descend the horseshoe-shaped double staircase. On the way down, misty spray from the gurgling mouths of the fountain's mythical beasts cooled me as heat from the June sun blazed above us.

"In seventeen twenty-one," he said as we stepped from the stairs into the grand parterre with its boxwood-hedge-defined rectangular flowerbeds and emerald areas of grass. The formality of the extensive ornamental gardens gave way to small shrubs and progressively larger ones, leading into the forest.

"I love this garden. It's beautiful! It's an escape from the terrible destruction I've seen the last few days," I said.

Guy nodded. "I know. It's a place I like to come to contemplate the tough decisions I must make. Life seems to be filled with challenges to which we must respond. No action is an action in itself, so there you have it."

I looked up at him. "Did you just give me a pep talk?"

"Not planned, but probably so. When we return to Paris, I'd like for you to attend social events with me—not for frivolous reasons. So I expect you want to know why."

"You're right. It doesn't make sense. We have important work to do, and we need to get started. Attending social events doesn't seem productive to that work."

Before I knew it, Guy literally swept me off my feet and twirled me around. "You don't know how much that means to me."

"I think I do. You've had reason to question my commitment, but since being here and seeing Claude, I understand what's at stake. I'm with you one hundred percent."

Guy reached for my hand and held it as we moved along.

"Our work is dangerous, but it must be done. France is now a divided country. There will be French citizens who welcome the Germans, and then there's the rest of us." He stopped walking and looked me in the eye. "One of our tasks will be to identify those who may betray the homeland. If we are discovered, it may well cost us our lives."

I saw determination and pain in his eyes. Was his pain for Claude or what he was asking of me? It didn't matter, because I felt it too and said nothing.

He drew me close and kissed my forehead. "I won't blame you if you're not ready to take the chance."

"I've already told you, I'm with you all the way." I put my arms around him and leaned against him.

His lips brushed against mine as he spoke, "Paulette Rousseau, if these were happier times, I'd ask you to marry me."

Speechless, I stared at him. His black hair glistened in the sun in contrast to his beautiful blue eyes that held me spellbound. I wanted to cry because I had grown to love and admire him, but he hadn't asked me to marry him. "I pledge to you, Guy de Laval, I'll treasure your words the rest of my life—whether long or brief."

He grew silent and my mind began to question his motives. Did he really mean what he said? Or did he want to let me down gently? Had I made a fool of myself with my response?

Chapter Nine

July, 1940 – Paris

Swastika shrouds strangle Paris!

The German army had marched into Paris on June 14 and the Wehrmacht wasted no time subduing their beautiful conquest. I cringed when I saw the evidence of their presence. A swastika fluttered atop the Eiffel Tower, one of the most recognizable symbols of the City of Love. I shuddered at the sight of German soldiers in gray-green uniforms standing guard in front of Nazi-flag-draped buildings. As far as I could tell, they were trying hard to remove the French identity of Paris and to replace it with their powerful German presence by sheer numbers and their powerful tanks and machine guns.

One week later, on June 21, France officially surrendered to Germany at Compiegne in the very same railway car where Germany had surrendered 22 years previously. I think all of France listened in stunned silence in front of their radios as Marchal Pétain solemnly proclaimed, "Too few children, too few arms, too few allies. These are the causes of our defeat."

"Let's hope *les boches* don't requisition the house," Guy said, as if thinking out loud.

"Who?"

"The Germans. It's an offensive term from the Great War days."

A cold sweat chilled me. "Let's hope they leave us alone."

When we were a block from the de Laval residence, two German soldiers stopped us. One of them approached me and in fluent French demanded, "*Soeur*, present your identification,"

In spite of his relatively polite manner, I trembled as I pulled my passport from my handbag. I didn't speak, because I didn't want him to hear my voice break.

"American citizen. Hum. It seems your papers are in order." He returned my passport.

Relieved, I looked at Guy and heard the other German say to him, "Have you been out of the city?"

"Oui, I've been with my family in the Loire Valley."

"How long do you expect to be in Paris?" The soldier tipped his head toward me. "With your . . . friend?" he asked with a smirk.

I felt my cheeks burn. His insinuation riled me.

"She is a fellow student at the Sorbonne," Guy said without hesitation.

"That's all for now." The guard clicked his heels and returned to his companion.

Guy drove on to the house on Rue Notre Dame des Champs. As he unlocked the door to the house, we could hear the incessant ringing of the telephone. He hurried ahead into his study and answered it. "Don't worry, Gaston. You did a good job keeping an eye on the place. Everything's just as I left it."

I thought about how lucky Guy was to have Gaston on his team. They'd been friends for years. I went back to the salon and settled onto the sofa to wait for him. I knew he needed to be guarded in everything he said in front of others. Each day brought new challenges, but I felt safe inside the substantial building that had endured through the various French revolutions and many wars thereafter. Of course, Guy's presence made a huge difference to my peace of mind.

"Le repas," Guy said. He set a tray of coffee and almond croissants on the table by the sofa and sat beside me.

"Where did you get the coffee and croissants?"

"A welcome home from Gaston, or maybe he bought them for himself."

I filled a cup for each of us and selected a croissant with lots of almonds on top. "This is good. I didn't realize I was hungry." I quickly finished the pastry and although I wanted more, thought better of taking another croissant. "What's our next move?"

"I'm glad you asked. I'll explain in the office."

We went by way of the kitchen so Guy could drop off the tray and then we continued on to my favorite room. "You see those window seats over there?" He pointed toward to the tall bank of windows that faced the side garden.

"Yes. How could I have missed them?" The inviting, cushioned seats and colorful throw pillows below the high-arched windows had caught my eye on my first visit to the study. I loved the rich woodwork and fabric accents of tan, brown, and red. And the book-lined shelves were an added bonus. "It's a handsome room."

"Take a closer look," He accompanied me, removed one of the long cushions that covered the window seat, and lifted the wooden top to reveal a storage space. "This could be a lifesaver should we need to hide papers, your typewriter, or ourselves in a hurry."

"My typewriter?" I peered inside. Storage was always a bonus.

"You do know how to type, don't you? I saw a typewriter at your apartment."

"Well, I do, yes, but . . ."

"Good."

When Guy removed the floorboard below the bench and revealed a ladder into a lower level, I said, "You're full of surprises. Where does that go?"

"To the lower-level cellar area. Just extra insurance in case anyone needs to hide for a prolonged time."

His line of thinking alarmed me. Why had he anticipated and prepared for such drastic measures?

The thought of being a fugitive on the run was one I hadn't taken seriously. Beads of perspiration broke out along my upper lip. The reality of the danger I had innocently embraced sank its icy talons into my consciousness. I'd never imagined myself in such a situation when I had gleefully anticipated studying at the Sorbonne.

Guy seemed focused on preparing me for the days to come. "Come on." He took one look at my face and hastened to say, "There'll be time for questions later."

I shook my head. "No. I need to know what else. Now!" I couldn't bear wondering what might be next.

"All right. I suppose it's for the best." He rose and I followed him to the top level of the house, just below the eaves. "As you can see, this is a storage room. And another place to hide, if necessary." He pushed on a paneled section of the wall until it opened into an unfinished space about the same size as the storage room. "Questions?"

"Not right now," I managed to say.

"Okay. How about a glass of wine downstairs while I fill you in on some of our upcoming activities?"

"Fine." I had asked for it, and now more than one of glass of wine might very well be required.

As we descended down the steep stairs from the attic area of the house, he said, "As of tomorrow you will be known to the team members as Maria Simmons. Only Gaston and I will know your real identity." After we returned to the study, he handed me a sack with a copper-red wig and gray trench coat inside. "Remember, these belong to Maria—not Paulette."

"Maria Simmons." I repeated my Resistance name to get used to saying it. I'd have to practice until I could respond without thought. I'd never used an alias before.

Guy set two glasses on the desk and waved his hand toward the collection of bottles. "What can I get you?" he asked as he opened a bottle of Côtes Du Ventoux, a fresh and fragrant wine, perfect for drinking early in the day.

My eyes fastened on the Dom Perignon champagne. I rose and picked it up. "This one." *Why not me rather than leave it for the Germans*? I rationalized.

He opened the bottle and set it on the side table. "You'll receive instructions each day from either Gaston or me."

"I thought you and I were a team. Aren't we?" I asked. My hand shook as I poured myself a glass of champagne.

"Yes, for the most part, but for now I'll be on the move, organizing and overseeing the work of various teams."

"So you're sort of a coordinator of many teams, not just ours?"

He ignored my remark. "You'll have typing and delivery work each day and other assignments as the situation dictates. Also, you'll work on a team with two or three others. Some of the time you may work here but most of the time from your own apartment, as long as it remains safe to do so."

"As soon as you're ready, we better check out your place before any more plans are made. Let's hope German soldiers aren't already billeted there."

As we drove toward my apartment, we passed building after building marked with huge, black-and-red swastika flags, guards posted at the doors. I began to lose all hope of having a place of my own, and goodness knows what they'd do with my belongings. When we rounded a bend in the street, I breathed a sigh of relief. Nothing seemed to have changed at my home. I could only hope I'd find the apartment as I left it.

Guy parked the car a few houses down the street. "We don't want to draw attention to ourselves," he said as he removed my luggage from the trunk. I led the way and waited for him and my luggage before starting up the creaky stairs.

The landlady stuck her head out of her apartment and called, "You decided to come back after all. You're one of the first."

"Am I? How has it been here?"

"It's not the same. I just stay inside as much as I can. But it's not our Paris anymore. The food shortages get worse every day. You'll see. Your roommates fled the day the Germans arrived and told me they wouldn't be back, so you'll have the apartment to yourself."

"I'm sure I'll be fine," I said as I continued up the stairs. At least she hadn't said that anyone had disturbed my apartment or asked about me. Still, I worried what I might find. My hand trembled when I tried to fit the key into the lock. Guy waited without a word or a suggestion that he try it. Success on the third try! The open door revealed things just as I had left them. My familiar brown Emerson radio and Royal typewriter were on the table. My blue sweater remained slipped over the back of a chair. "I don't have much to offer you to drink, but I can make some coffee," I said to Guy.

He sat down at the table. "I accept, and then I'll be on my way. I'll have to work late into the night."

I turned on the radio to hear the latest news, as had become our habit, since each day brought new developments.

The solemn voice of the reporter began: *After failed negotiations for surrender of the French Naval Fleet, the British Royal Navy has today attacked the Vichy Government's fleet at Mers-el-Kébir on the coast of French Algeria. So far, reports are one battleship sunk, two others damaged. The French death toll is unknown at this time, although many are lost.*

Although the terms of the Vichy Government's armistice with the Germans state that the German government 'solemnly and firmly declares that it has no intention of making demands regarding the French fleet during the peace negotiations,' Churchill ordered that a demand be made that the French Navy either join with the Royal Navy or be neutralized in a manner guaranteed to prevent the ships falling into Axis hands, for should the French fleet be annexed by

Italy or Germany, it would tip the balance of naval power in favor of the enemy and might lead to the Allies' total defeat.

For a moment we sat in stunned silence, Guy's face a frozen, pale profile. He didn't look at me. He shook his head and sighed. "What went wrong?"

I didn't know, but I shared his sense of loss. *What would this mean for the war effort?* I wondered, but I didn't dare intrude on Guy's clear distress.

I'd refilled his cup when a knock on the door interrupted us. I panicked at the thought of an extended German interrogation. Guy and I were already both in shock at the dreadful news we'd just listened to. What else could go wrong?

"Go on, answer it." Guy motioned to the door. "They may have been watching and know you're here."

My legs felt as though they might collapse as I stood. After a deep breath to compose myself, I turned the knob. I thought I was hallucinating when I saw Chris, but when he swooped me up into his arms, it felt so natural and familiar. "You're back!"

He smothered me in kisses and murmured. "Couldn't stay away—like always."

Then I remembered Guy and turned to speak to him, but he was gone. How had he gotten out without me seeing him? "Coffee?" I said to Chris. His presence was like a breath of fresh air. For just a moment he'd taken me back to carefree times. And then the nagging dread of the morning's work returned with a vengeance.

The sound of Chris's voice brought me to the moment. "I'm sorry I left without you, but at least it brought me to my senses. I went home and tried to forget about you. I couldn't. All the familiar places where we used to go reminded me of us. I suppose, if I went to the ends of the earth, I still couldn't forget you."

"Oh, Chris, I've missed you so much. I didn't realize how much a part of my life you are."

"I love you and I'm willing to wait for you, Paulette—even if you insist on working for the French Resistance. If you do, so will I."

I looked at him through a vale of tears. "I don't deserve you." I clung to him and kissed him. We sat together in silence until I broke the spell. "Resistance groups will work independently so everyone knows as little as possible about the identity of those in other groups. But there needs to be some communication between them. Guy has asked me to be one of those people. I have agreed.

"Oh, Chris, so much has happened since you were here last. I don't have to tell you that. You can see it for yourself. You probably heard it on the news, too."

"I haven't listened to the news," Chris said.

"Starting tomorrow I'll be assigned each day's work. I hope we can be partners. We'll need to let Guy know you want to join us when he stops by in the morning."

"I certainly hope he agrees. That's what I'm here to do."

"Good. Be here by seven."

"If I can. Paulette, I don't have anywhere to stay yet. All of my buddies are gone from my building. It's become a German enclave!"

"Stay here. There's an extra bed now. My roommates have taken their belongings and gone."

"I don't think staying here's a good idea," Chris said.

I kissed his cheek and said, "I insist! Just until you find another room. No arguing so soon after our reunion. Promise?"

He let out a long, audible sigh. "You win. I'll stay."

In spite of my exhaustion, Chris fell asleep hours before I did. Still, my reliable internal alarm awoke me at six o'clock after only five hours of sleep. Without disturbing Chris, I managed to dress and make coffee. Then I sat down to wait for Guy's arrival with my first official assignment as a member of the French Resistance.

After two cups of coffee, I began to wonder what was delaying Guy. The clock said he was half an hour late. And Chris hadn't gotten up either. I concluded that males of the species slept more soundly than their female counterparts.

The sound of footsteps outside the door preceded Guy's quick three taps on the door before he opened it. "Sorry I'm late. Lots of stops to make today," he said between breaths.

"I understand." I poured a cup of coffee and handed it to him.

"It'll go more smoothly as soon as I assign others to this job." He took a swallow of coffee. "This hits the spot. I didn't take time to make any. Thanks." He reached into his pocket and pulled out a folded sheet of paper. "Read the instructions and then destroy it."

I had just enough time to see that typing was my first assignment when Chris staggered out of the bedroom, his hair rumpled.

Oh, no. I hope this doesn't ruin Chris's chances to work with us. I held my breath until Guy spoke without showing emotion of any kind.

"Chris, you've returned. Have you had a change of heart about working with us?"

"As a matter of fact, I have."

"*Bon.* You're here in time to be partnered with Paulette." Guy shook Chris's hand. "Welcome to the team. I must be on my way, but I'll have further instructions for you both tomorrow."

I was relieved that there was no posturing by either of them, but it irked me that Guy seemed to embrace relinquishing me to Chris—not that Chris and I didn't need the time together. I had grown fonder of him during his absence, but I couldn't deny that I idolized Guy. I drew courage from his strength.

I pondered the dichotomy of being happy and sad at the same time.

Chapter Ten

August 1940 – Paris

August blindsided me like a winter whiteout blizzard, leaving only darkness.

By six o'clock in the morning, the summer heat prompted me to turn on the fan while Chris and I had a cup of coffee. I sensed his tension as we awaited Guy and our first joint assignment.

Chris reached for my hand. "Let's go someplace where we can relax and talk this afternoon." His voice slowed and dropped an octave. "If we finish up in time."

"I'd like that." I tried to sound confident.

"Swell. We have so much catching up to do."

"Yes, we do."

"I haven't asked about home yet because I don't want any interruptions when we reminisce. Guy will be here anytime."

"It's better to get away from everything that's going on around here. I can hardly wait to tell you about it."

A single rap on the door startled me. It wasn't Guy's signature, three quick taps. I steeled myself as I opened the door. "Gaston? What happened? Where's Guy?" I asked with alarm before recovering enough to say, "Come in."

"I'm your contact now." Gaston stepped inside. "Guy's taken another section of the city."

Whoa! I took a deep breath before I spoke. "Oh, he didn't say anything about that."

"He decided last night. I'm sorry he didn't tell you." Gaston looked at the floor. "That's all I can say. I have your assignments—Paulette, get this typed up and secured in this," he said as he pushed an envelope into my hand. "After that you and Chris will take the Métro to the little café on the corner of Rue Saint Antoine and Rue de Turenne. Give the envelope to the man with the black moustache behind the counter."

"Understood," I assured him.

"Excellent. Until tomorrow," Gaston said on his way out without any cautions or guidance on how to be safe.

Guy had let us down. He'd promised to prepare us for our work. Chris had received no guidance, and all I had was a quick summary of how things worked. However, my brooding about Guy's sudden departure and careless disregard for our safety would have to wait until we'd completed the day's work. I started to type at a furious pace. The nonsense combination of letters and numbers meant nothing to me but would relay valuable information to those who knew how to decipher them.

Chris watched over my shoulder as I worked. "Do you know what you're writing?"

"No, Chris, I don't," I snapped, irritated at the interruption.

"Calm down. I just wondered. You realize I don't know what's going on."

"I'm sorry." I stopped work. "Guy should have come and prepared us, as he promised."

"That's what I heard him say last night."

"Okay. I'll tell you what he told me. The less we know of the overall plans and activities, the better for the groups as a whole. We cannot reveal what we do not know. When we make deliveries, we must be sure we're not being followed. The mission must be aborted if we have any doubts about it."

I didn't mention code names to Chris or tell him that he'd be asked to take an oath to choose death rather than provide names of anyone in the Resistance.

"We'll have to take it on faith that our work makes a difference?" Chris grumbled, clearly skeptical.

"I'm afraid so." What else could I say? I had my own doubts.

Chris patted my arm. "Tell you what. After we're free this afternoon, we're going to your favorite place."

"Yes, the Tuileries! I'd love to go there with you and talk of pleasant things. I really need that. But at the moment, I have to get back to work."

"And I'll take a look outside. Be back in thirty minutes."

Chris came in before I'd finished typing. "Not much going on out there. I hope it stays that way," he said.

"I'm almost done." I drank the last drops of my cold coffee.

"Please, sit down. Your pacing makes me nervous."

I didn't bother to object when Chris disappeared into the bedroom. I'd work faster without him watching me. This first run had both of us jittery. I worked quickly, reviewed the pages, and decided we could get them on their way. "Chris, let's go," I called and slipped the envelope into my handbag.

Most of the residents of the apartment had not returned to Paris, and we didn't see a soul until we came to the *propriétaire's* apartment. Her door stood open and her eagle eye spotted and acknowledged us with a knowing nod as we went on our way.

"Let's walk," I said. "It's not far. And German guards ride the Métro."

Chris agreed. "I'm for that after being cooped up in your apartment."

"Watch it, buddy. You don't have a bed of your own?"

Chris took my hand and led me around a corner. "This way," he said in an even tone.

"What is it?" I mumbled.

"Probably nothing. I didn't like the way that man kept behind us, even when we slowed."

"How did you know he was there?"

"I noticed that the odor of cigarette smoke kept pace with us."

"Know what?" I said.

"What?"

"You're a good partner." We walked hand in hand quite a distance out of our way before circling back toward the Pont Neuf across the Seine and then the short distance to the cafe. There weren't many people there at that hour, so I was able to hand the envelope to the man behind the counter without hesitation.

"Godspeed," he said as he handed each of us a coffee and croissant.

We thanked him and started back toward the Jardin des Tuileries. I felt as if a great weight had been lifted from our shoulders. I knew that tomorrow the tensions would build again, but the rest of today belonged to us. I hoped Chris would get a bike soon so we could ride together. Our own time would be in short supply.

"I stopped by to see your mother when I was home."

"What did she say?"

"She asked why I didn't insist you come back. She's worried about you and can't understand why you want to stay in France."

"It's been so crazy here, I haven't made time to write to her. To tell you the truth, I don't know how to explain my reasons."

"You mean Guy de Laval?"

"No!" I slapped Chris on the arm for emphasis—or maybe because I felt Guy had abandoned me at a critical moment.

"Well, at least I can tell you why I'm here," Chris said. "It's because I care about you."

"Oh, Chris, I don't deserve you. I wish I had my act together as well as you do. Sometimes, I'm so confused."

"I think everyone is. President Roosevelt says he's not willing to involve the United States in European affairs."

"Isolationism," I hissed. "Can't they see the danger Hitler poses for the entire world?"

Chris shook his head as we passed the Palais Royal, the Duke d' Orleans' hot bed of unrest during the French Revolution, and later, an arcaded ribbon of shops and gardens, an island of tranquility in the heart of Paris.

"It's a difficult decision to make," he said as we crossed the street and walked along the side of the Louvre Museum and on to an entrance into the Tuileries.

Although the evening hours approached, little of the afternoon heat had dissipated. I looked forward to sitting with my back to the sun and listening to the water splash from the fountains in the park.

I took the first available chair. Chris sat beside me and wiped his brow with a handkerchief he'd pulled from his pocket. "It's too hot to stay here long."

"After we rest and cool down, let's leave by way of the Orangerie Museum. I never tire of Monet's panorama, 'Water Lilies.'"

Chris stretched and shrugged his shoulders. "There's only one way out of here as far as you're concerned." He yawned. "I'm ready anytime you are. I'm beat."

"So am I. This hasn't been the best visit I've had here." I stood and prayed none of the Germans would single us out for interrogation, whether to amuse themselves or because something had triggered their suspicions. Neither Chris nor I were in peak form.

I didn't calm down until we'd closed the apartment door behind us. So much for my relaxed day with Chris. It was anything but relaxed—the new norm, I had to admit.

The following morning Gaston arrived at seven thirty. He set my envelope on the table. "You know what to do. This will be the last day that you need to accompany Chris on the run."

"I think he needs a couple more days of experience before he's on his own," I protested.

"Time and personnel are luxuries we can't squander. Chris, I brought a bike for you. I'll show you where it is. Come with me now."

"Just a minute." I blocked Gaston at the door. "What do you hear from Guy? When can I expect to hear from him?"

"He hasn't been in touch. Now step aside."

When I didn't move, Chris frowned at me. I turned away and let them leave. A nagging fear for Guy's safety surfaced. I forced myself to open the envelope and begin typing. Chris didn't need unnecessary obstacles with the delivery today. I'd go with him for support, but this would be his run. Then we'd talk about it when we got back to the apartment. I felt responsible for putting him at risk. If only I could talk to Guy. I stopped typing and pondered whether I should try to contact Madame de Laval in Tours but made no determination.

Chris didn't return until I was almost finished working. He stood behind my chair and massaged my shoulders as he had when we were dating in high school and I was tense about an important exam or some minor thing with my parents. It always worked wonders. "That's better," he said and stepped away.

Renewed optimism allowed me to finish the last few lines.

We made the delivery and stopped at a market to replenish our meager supplies. We were shocked to find most of the shelves empty. My usual brand of coffee was gone. We found one stale loaf of bread in the baker's display case, although he worked feverishly over his ovens. My mouth watered as the aroma of freshly baked bread filled the shop.

"When will the fresh bread be ready?"

His white moustache twitched as his lips moved. "In a few minutes. But it's not for you. It's all been requisitioned by the German Army. I work from dawn to dusk and still have no bread for my regular customers. I'm sorry."

"Do you know where we can get bread?" Chris asked.

"I don't. If I did, I get it for myself."

I nodded and clung to the hard, stale loaf under my arm. "Let's go," I said to Chris.

"I have heard the government will start issuing ration books to everyone soon," Chris told me.

"But what good will rationing do if there's nothing to ration?" I moaned.

On the way home neither of us spoke of going anywhere except to the apartment. Tomorrow would be another day like this one, if not worse.

As we ate our evening meal of bread and cheese, a light tap on the door interrupted us. I hurriedly looked around the room to be sure the typewriter and paper were out of sight and opened the door with caution.

"Cherie, I'm glad I found you here," Aline greeted me. Dark circles under her eyes testified to sleepless nights.

"Come in." I pulled out a chair for her. "Where have you been? You look exhausted."

"I am. I've been at the hospital since I last saw you. There are so many casualties brought in every day that we can't take care of all of them. We do what we can, grab a couple hours of sleep there, and go back to work."

"You can't go on that way," I said. "Would you like some bread and cheese?" In spite of planning to limit coffee to mornings, when she wearily shook her head, I offered, "Coffee or tea?"

"No, I can't stay long. I've come by to ask for your help at the hospital."

"I don't know anything about nursing. Besides, I'm working with Guy's network."

"You don't have to know about nursing to be a lifesaver for us. Any free time you can give will be helpful. Please come when you can."

"I will," I promised. "What about Roberto Santoni? Does he help you?"

"No, he's gone home to Italy to be with his family. There's so much unrest and repercussions from the Mussolini government." Aline stood and hugged Chris and then me. Her usual slender frame was just skin and bones now. She'd lost a noticeable amount of weight in the last month.

I knew I had to go to the hospital every free moment to help. How long we could keep going in the face of unthinkable demands remained unknown.

Chapter Eleven

Early September 1940 – Paris

The Germans owned all of Paris within a brief three months, or so it appeared.

I'd given up any hope that General Pétain, at the helm of the French government, would be the salvation of France. True, he was a French war hero from the Great War, but now he'd sold out his countrymen. Under his leadership, or I should say lack of leadership, the Third Republic of France had voted itself out of existence in mid-July. A new *État Francais* was established, with Pétain as chief executive, and Pierre Laval as vice president of the Council of Ministers and Pétain's designated successor. Laval lost no time in cooperating with the Germans, nor did he hesitate to arrest French citizens suspected of any minor infraction.

Finally, after two months without speaking to Guy, I was summoned to the de Laval Paris house via a letter delivered by Lawless, the current courier of daily assignments from the Resistance. "What time shall I expect you tomorrow?" I asked as I read the letter requesting I be at Guy's by eight o'clock the next morning.

"Monsieur de Laval will take care of that." Lawless gave the crisp response and immediately took his leave.

I awoke early the next morning and lay in bed while pondering the meaning of the change in our routine. To make matters worse, not only had Guy disappeared from my life, but for the past seven weeks, Chris had also been absent. Our paths had crossed only once, and that one time I had seen him he'd said, "I can't talk about it—my assignment is top secret."

"When will I see you again?" I'd asked, although I knew he couldn't give me an answer.

He shook his head and put his arms around me. "I wish I knew."

I simply said, "I miss you," and turned away so he couldn't see the emotional storm brewing. "Please, go now." I kept my back to him until I heard the door close. Each time we parted could well be our last time.

Fortunately, my busy schedule numbed me. I had little time to think about either Guy or Chris, given my greatly increased workload for the Resistance and the many hours I spent at the hospital, caring for the wounded soldiers.

✝

As I stopped outside the de Laval house the next morning, nothing seemed to have changed, but I felt strange being there again after having avoided the Rue Notre Dame des Champs in response to Guy's sudden exit from my life.

After some hesitation I knocked at the door. When Guy opened the door, he kissed me on both cheeks as if nothing had changed. Stepping back, he looked at me. "You're as lovely as always."

I wasn't deceived by his effort to charm. "Looks are deceiving," I insisted, and then I confronted him about the invitation in his letter.

"Please, take a seat while I get coffee and croissants."

I didn't object, since coffee and other breakfast items were in short supply in my apartment. He returned so quickly with a teacart that I deduced he'd had everything ready. After he poured the coffee, he passed the croissants and jams. I savored the freshly ground coffee and made a concerted effort to chew slowly and wait between bites of the flaky, jam-drenched croissant.

Guy sipped his beverage before catching my eye and focusing on me so completely that I felt he could look into my soul. I broke eye contact to reclaim control of my feelings. I couldn't afford to slip under his spell.

"Paulette, I want you to know I'm deeply pained that a sudden change of circumstances forced me not to see you." He paused as if he expected a response, but I was too hurt to talk about it and made no response. "For the past six weeks, I was forced to host top German military officers in my home."

"You what?" I said, shaken to the core.

"They arrived and announced they would be staying while they looked for permanent quarters to requisition. My home was one they were considering. And if they chose it, I could cooperate and

68

entertain them, or I could leave the fully-staffed house to them. Needless to say, I chose to stay, hoping I'd be able to monitor them."

"I never thought I'd hear that from you."

"Of course, it's as distasteful to me as it is to you. I had to put my personal feelings aside for the cause for which we both work. Fortunately, they finally chose a residence on the right bank, close to the German headquarters at the Hotel Maurice and the Ritz, where their top brass gathers. The last of them left only yesterday."

"It could have been dangerous to have them in your home. They could have watched you as easily as you watched them."

"It'll be much more difficult now to infiltrate their circle and glean valuable information. But it could save the lives of innocent people, and that brings me to what I ask of you. I want you to accompany me to an event at the Ritz that will be attended by high-ranking German officers, as well as some of the French rich and famous."

I set down my cup, stood, and stamped my foot. His suggestion was unthinkable. "I won't go to the Ritz event and fraternize with German officers for *any* cause. For all I know, you're a collaborator!"

He rose and took my hands—as if that would change my mind—and spoke with a velveteen voice. "I've tried to explain to you why I seemed to abandon you. While the German officers were my uninvited guests, I couldn't risk endangering you."

"You don't seem worried about my safety now." I removed my hands from his. "Why the change?"

"Listen to me, Paulette. The Germans didn't choose to requisition my house. Perhaps, I wasn't a good enough host, although I did the best I could to convince them, but I failed without the cooperation of my parents. Don't you see the information-gathering I could have accomplished if they'd stayed?"

My response was a blank stare. I wasn't convinced.

He sought to clarify. "I would have been aware of their movements and some of their thoughts and plans."

"So they went elsewhere. Why don't you let it go rather than joining them at their celebrations at the Ritz?"

"It's the next best way to keep an eye on them. It's inevitable that tongues loosen after too much alcohol."

"And that's not all," I snapped. It was no secret the Nazis

fancied Parisian women.

Guy's mouth was tight and grim. "If you don't think you can handle such situations, you shouldn't go." His expression softened. "You're doing valuable work for us every day, and I appreciate it."

The question for me was whether I wanted him to work with another female to accomplish his goal. The answer was stunningly clear. I wouldn't relinquish him to another woman. "I'll go and judge for myself whether it's a good plan." This time I was the one to reach out to him and lay my head against his shoulder.

"Thank you." He kissed my forehead.

Our eyes met and I saw a tenderness that amazed me. At that moment, I knew I'd follow him to the ends the earth and believed he'd do the same for me. A twinge of regret about Chris nagged at my conscience. I'd led him to believe Guy was out of my system. I had tried to convince myself that Chris was the one for me while Guy was out of my life. I hoped I hadn't misled him too terribly.

"Come and sit with me," Guy invited and led me to the sofa, his arm casually around my shoulder. "Pétain's Vichy Government is working on behalf of the Germans at lightning speed. I'm sure you have been keeping up with it on the radio."

I shook my head. "No. Resistance work takes most of the day, and then I go to the hospital to help the wounded, who arrive daily."

"Well, then, you need to be brought up to date. In the Free Zone, Vichy law forbids employment for those not born of French parents, and they have enacted anti-Semitic laws. The Germans also forbid Jews to reenter the Occupied Zones."

"Oh my God. I wonder whether Renee Greenberg left the country?"

It was Guy's turn to have a long face. "No, she won't leave her father, and he won't leave Paris. They're here and are in danger."

"We have to help her." I rose and paced around the room.

"She enrolled in classes for this semester at the Sorbonne. You might see her there . . . if you go back this term."

"*I* might see her!" My voice rose an octave. "What about you? You're better able to assist her than I am."

Guy stood. "Calm down. Don't unnecessarily waste your energy. She needs all the help we can muster."

I nodded, my arms crossed. "And where's Chris? I haven't

seen or heard from him in weeks."

"He's fulfilling his assignments with great skill."

"Are you responsible for separating him from my team?"

"Yes." Guy paused. "Each person is assigned according to his or her strengths, including Chris."

Grudgingly, I had to acknowledge that Guy's response made sense, but it didn't make me feel any better. "Is he still in Paris?" I asked, hopeful we'd meet by chance one day.

"Paulette, you know better than to ask."

So he's going to play by the rules rather than put my mind at ease. I understood the reason as well as he did. In this case he seemed to care more about my life than I did. I controlled my desire to make a snide response and asked, "Aren't all of the prestigious hotels taken over by the Germans and closed to the public? How come the Ritz is still open?"

"The hotel owner, Marie-Louise Ritz, is Swiss. The establishment will be allowed to stay open to the public while it is requisitioned by the Nazis."

"How does that work? Are French guests there with the Nazis?"

"Germans occupy most of the rooms, but there are suites available to wealthy patrons who don't mind rubbing shoulders with the occupying forces."

"What's the occasion for the event we'll be attending?"

"It's in honor of Reichsmarschall Hermann Göring, who will take up residence in the imperial suite. It occupies an entire floor and he's taken it all, just for himself, so I'm told."

"What sort of French person wishes to welcome him?"

"You'd be surprised. Some people want to make the best of an unpleasant situation, while others struggle against it. You might see Coco Chanel, Josée Laval de Chambrun—the daughter of Pierre Laval, Petain's right-hand man—as well as journalists."

"Laval?" I let the name roll slowly off my tongue. "A relative of yours?"

"That socialist! No relation." Guy swatted the air as if banishing a fly. "He comes from the Auvergne region. His father ran the village café."

"Just wondered."

"I'll pick you up at seven thirty tomorrow evening. It's semi-

71

formal, so dress accordingly. We won't stay long if you're uncomfortable. If you find it's worthwhile, we'll work together on the same team. There'll be no typing, and there'll be more free time to work at the hospital or attend university. All I'll ask is that you coordinate with me."

"Let's hope all goes well tomorrow evening," I said. I tried to process how things would change if Guy and I worked together again. I knew there were no guarantees in times like these. "If you're finished with me today, I'd like to get to the hospital. There's so much to be done there."

"That's all for now. I'll see you tomorrow," he said as he walked me to the door.

The next morning I awoke a little before noon and still felt tired. I'd stayed late at the hospital the night before, but I believed that most of the fatigue stemmed from anxiety about my first evening at the Ritz. I knew what I'd wear—my little black dress and pearls—it was my only choice. Fortunately, I had two pairs of silk stockings I hadn't worn at all while in Paris. I'd have been out of luck had I not brought them from home. Women had hoarded them since May, and the stores had not restocked.

The afternoon was torment. In the past few months, I'd been too busy to plan ahead much, so to keep occupied, I took an extra-long time getting ready. Even so, I was dressed and ready to go by three o'clock. After that I stewed about what ifs. What if I made a blunder that jeopardized Guy's cover? What if Guy and I were not a believable couple? What if . . . ad nauseam?

I had too much time on my hands and began to drive myself crazy, going back and forth in my mind whether to take my typewriter to Guy's for safekeeping and whether my mother's French ancestor's heirloom gold locket was safer on me or in my apartment. Finally, I removed my pearls and fastened the heavy locket around my neck.

Right on schedule at seven thirty Guy's signature taps sounded on my door. I glanced in the mirror, approved of what I saw, and answered the door.

He took one look at me and whistled. "Are you out to

impress?"

"This is the only suitable dress I have."

"It's lovely, but I don't recommend you advertise that you own such an elegant locket. Why don't you wear your pearls instead?"

"I've thought about it and decided the locket will be safer around my neck than in this empty apartment."

"We can put in the safe at my house."

"That'll make us late. Maybe later, but I'll wear it tonight. Oh, yes, I'd like to leave my typewriter at your house, too."

Chapter Twelve

September 1940 – Paris

"The bronze spiral wrapped around Napoleon Bonaparte's huge stone column that dominates the Place Vendôme was made from the 1,200 cannons captured in 1805 at the Battle of Austerlitz," Guy told me as we passed it.

A calm replaced the jitters as Guy and I arrived at the spacious square, home to the Ritz Hotel and, tonight—I found it ironic—the Department of Justice. An austere feeling pervaded the rectangular space, minus its corners, dominated by Napoleon's overpowering green column. A cool breeze swept us along to the unorthodox event in the multistoried, stone building decorated with wrought iron balconies that repeated the Ritz's seventeenth-century design. The luminescent façade appeared to welcome us.

Guy glanced at me. "Take a deep breath. Everyone will be on their best behavior."

I nodded and did as he asked while pressing my hand to the gold locket, heavy on my skin that, for some reason, I'd felt compelled to wear this evening. I put my thoughts into words. "My mother, Camille, insisted I bring this locket to France— 'from whence it came,'" she'd said.

"She must have a lot of confidence in you to trust a young student with such a valuable piece of history."

"I didn't want to be entrusted with the safekeeping of it, but she wouldn't take no for an answer." I kicked at a paper wrapper that fluttered in front of me. "Maybe she hoped I'd be invited to some gala event!"

"Given the turn of events, she most likely regrets her decision," Guy said, just before we arrived at the door.

"Bonsoir, Monsieur de Laval," the doorman greeted us and opened the door.

When we stepped inside, my senses were overwhelmed by the elegant ambiance. Myriad lights held high by the arms of gigantic chandeliers illuminated the room and cast golden ripples along the window dressings and the large, round tables awaiting their odd mix of guests. The soft music in the background was hardly discernible over the din of voices. It sounded as if alcohol had been flowing for hours. Whiffs of delightful scents of expensive perfumes filled the air.

Guy took my hand and led me toward a nice-looking blond man wearing a white tie and neat uniform who was making his way toward us. When he reached us, Guy said to me, "Mademoiselle Rousseau, please meet Colonel Dietrich."

I greeted him and offered my hand. He lifted it to his lips and said in impeccable French, "What a pleasure to make your acquaintance." His eyes met mine briefly but lingered on my gold necklace. I immediately realized my grave error—wearing it was a terrible mistake. I should have listened to Guy or shipped it home before the German troops reached Paris.

Guy slipped his arm around my waist and said to the colonel, "Mademoiselle Rousseau is my fiancée."

I was grateful to Guy for intercession in what could have been an evening of unwelcome attention. I couldn't resist the urge to try to read his expression but saw no clues as to whether he thought of me in a romantic way. Upon reflection, I concluded he had said it to protect me.

The German locked eyes with Guy. "Monsieur, you're to be envied," the colonel said and moved toward a woman with dark hair. When she turned toward us, I recognized her as a well-known French actress. Apparently, she discouraged the colonel, because a few minutes later I saw her on the arm of another German officer. Guy guided me toward them and introduced me to the actress and her German, Lieutenant Oehringher.

Much to my relief, Guy suggested we find a table as soon as people began to be seated at the white-linen-adorned tables. All but two of the ten chairs at the table Guy pointed to were taken. On our way to the table, a slender woman with dark hair stopped us. The first thing I noticed was that her teeth were a dominant feature of her face. She fixed her eyes on me but spoke to Guy. "Marquis de Laval, what a surprise to find you here, and with a beautiful young lady no less."

"Countess de Chambrun, please say hello to my American fiancée, Paulette Rousseau."

"Paulette, to you I'm Josée de Chambrun. I know titles don't mean much to Americans," she replied graciously. She peered at

Guy and added, "I had no idea you were engaged. Where have you been keeping her?"

"Madame de Chambrun, you're one of the first to know."

"Well, Paulette, my husband and I have a special place in our hearts for Americans. I hope to see more of you," Josée said. With that, she turned and headed for the table at the front of the room where the actress and the German officer were sitting beside the guest of honor, Herrmann Goring, Adolph Hitler's second in command.

I leaned toward Guy and lowered my voice. "Josée's title suggests she's a member of the French aristocracy."

"Yes, she married Count René de Chambrun, a captain in the French Army. Also, you might be interested to know that his American mother is a member of the Roosevelt family. His sphere of influence is extensive."

I was dismayed when Guy led me to the table at which Colonel Dietrich was seated with two German officers, who greeted Guy as a long-lost brother. They introduced two Frenchmen and a satin-draped woman who held an ornate, cigarette holder between her manicured fingers. I was again introduced as Guy's fiancée. Unless Guy was serious about me, I felt that his announcement raised expectations about our future behavior. No doubt any missteps by one of us would impact the other.

My face burned when I sensed Colonel Dietrich's arctic-blue eyes focused on me. I didn't dare glance up to see his expression. Was I still of interest to him, or was it just my locket or cleavage? Either way, the evening couldn't end soon enough. I couldn't eat a bite of the excellent, gourmet meal. I, who hadn't had a steak since the Germans had arrived in Paris.

An animated conversation in French ensued—some of which was difficult to understand because of the heavy accents. It became clear that these officers had been guests at the de Laval home on the Rue Notre Dame des Champs. Guy made comments now and again, enough to elicit a continuation of subjects of interest to the Resistance. I remained silent, as did the other two women at the table, each of whom sipped champagne and smoked, while nodding approval when their companions raved about the service at the Ritz. The German officers did most of the talking about the warm welcome they had received from the Parisians and the beauty of the city. I listened intently to the conversation while keeping my eyes off the colonel.

"Fräulein Rousseau, what do you think about our accommodations at the Ritz?"

I quickly discarded my thought of kicking Colonel Dietrich under the table. That would be a battle I'd lose. "The Ritz is top of the line. You couldn't ask for better service," I said and forced myself to make brief eye contact.

Guy patted my leg, a reassuring gesture. Clearly, the Germans showed neither of us any respect. I couldn't bear to think of these obnoxious men in Guy's house.

After another excruciating hour of small talk with Colonel Dietrich, the aging, corpulent Reichsmarschall Goring made a few remarks before he left the event.

One of the officers at our table said, "As is his habit, he'll retire to the Imperial Suite and be entertained by a bevy of beauties."

The orchestra warmed up, and soon the music began in earnest. Couples streamed onto the dance floor.

"We're engaged now, so we're obliged to dance at least once tonight," Guy said. "After that I'll take you home."

I saw the logic of his reasoning and allowed him to lead me to the floor. The song, "Smoke Gets in Your Eyes," was one of my favorites. We danced cheek to cheek. I didn't want the moment to end, but it did.

The orchestra segued into "Whispering," and Guy asked, "Shall we dance again, or shall we get some fresh air?"

A chill ran down my spine when the colonel appeared from nowhere. "May I have this dance?" he asked, holding out his hand.

The thought of dancing with the enemy made me sick, but I knew better than to object, so I yielded to his request. As I took his hand, my stomach began to churn. When he tried to steady me, I lurched forward and heaved on his shirt before I realized what was happening. Mortified, I apologized profusely and ran to the ladies room. As I tried to clean up a bit and figure out my next move, I heard a voice behind me. I glanced in the mirror and saw Josée.

She put her arm around me. "I'm sorry you had such a terrible experience. I'll take you out the back way. Guy is waiting for us outside. I know you're upset, but just think of these young soldiers as spoiled puppies. They're lonely, away from their

77

sweethearts, and have been drinking too much."

"That doesn't excuse their predatory actions."

"I know." Josée kept a protective arm around me as she slowly opened the powder room door, peeked outside, and hustled me around the corner to an outside exit. I thought my legs would collapse by the time she transferred me into Guy's arms.

"Thank you, my dear friend," Guy told her.

I added my profound appreciation for her help and watched her disappear behind the closing door.

"You're trembling." Guy removed his jacket and wrapped it around my shoulders. We took a roundabout way to the car and drove back across the Seine. "You shouldn't be alone tonight. Not that I think you're in any danger, but you've been through an unpleasant ordeal with Dietrich. I want you to stay with me tonight."

"Emotions and thoughts raced by at a dizzying speed. I no longer felt capable of making the right decision. I doubted my ability to think clearly at the moment. Finally, I murmured, "Yes, I think I should. Thank you." But little by little my head began to clear and questions arose that needed answers.

As an extra precaution, Guy pulled the car into the garage rather than leave it in the courtyard, as he usually did.

Nina, the gardener's wife, apparently heard us coming, as she met us at the door. "You're back early. Can I get you anything?"

"Hot tea and a shawl for Mademoiselle. Double check that the rose guest room is ready. She'll be our guest for a day or two."

If surprised, she didn't let on. "Oui, Monsieur."

"Merci, Nina."

Guy's attentiveness, together with the tea and shawl, worked wonders. I held his gaze as I put my thoughts into words. "We can't consider this evening a success. I'm afraid we're going to have trouble with Dietrich. He's been a guest in your home and showed blatant disregard for our announced engagement. His behavior is unforgivable. He doesn't know that the announcement isn't true."

"He's a cad, I agree, but I think you misinterpreted his intentions when he asked you to dance."

"You didn't see the way he leered at me and took note of my locket."

"It is an awkward situation. I'm sorry to have put you in that position. At the time I thought it would be helpful."

"Well, now what are we going to do. You told Josée and everyone at our table we were to be married."

"I wanted them to expect to see us together, especially if you and I continue to attend their social events."

"It's a sham. I don't know if I can pull it off."

"I could say, yes, it is, but I won't, because as far as I'm concerned, it's not a sham. You're a beautiful woman—just the kind I've dreamed about over the past weeks we've been apart."

"Come on, do you expect me to believe that?"

He stood. "You don't believe me? Wait here." He went to the study, returning a few minutes later with a small box. He removed a square-cut diamond ring and softly asked, "Paulette, will you marry me?"

I cast my eyes downward so he wouldn't see the moisture gather in them. "I don't understand. You told me you wouldn't consider marrying, because of the war."

"That shouldn't stop us from being engaged. Surely, this war will end."

I lost control. "What does the war have to do with it?" Tears streamed down my cheeks. Guy handed me his handkerchief and held me in his arms. "Well, what do you say?"

"If you're sure, my answer is yes." I didn't really have to think about it. I dabbed my eyes. "I just don't want to wake up one day and find it isn't so."

He slipped the ring onto my finger and kissed me. "I want you to know that you and little Claude give meaning to my life. I don't want any complications about your citizenship rights. As an American you're not subject to many of the restrictions that French citizens are."

"I'm a believer in the idea that love conquers all." Snuggling closer to him, I said, "I know we'll be happy." I couldn't stop gazing at the ring. "It's beautiful."

"It's been in the family for several generations. It belonged to my grandmother. I spent many happy hours with her and miss her to this day."

"I know what you mean. I miss my Grandma Emily Smith. She doesn't sound very French, does she? You see this locket? It's a French heirloom from her side of the family. You were correct, I shouldn't be wearing it. I'll to send it back to Mamma for

79

safekeeping. I didn't like the way Dietrich stared at it, and I'm aware that the Germans take what they want."

"By all means, you should keep it out of sight. And I'm having second thoughts about exposing you to the unwelcome advances of German officers. I'd like for you to consider visiting with my parents until your classes begin at the end of the month. It would give you a much-needed respite from the pressure of our work, as well as time to think about whether you want to continue with it. And best yet, you could get better acquainted with little Claude. What do you think?"

"Why do I get the impression that you would stay in Paris?"

"I'll go with you for a few days, but I can't be away longer than that. Things are changing here every day, and I have to keep my ear to the ground."

"I know, and I *would* like time away. It's just that there's so much that needs to done at the hospital. But I guess I won't be much help to them if I'm constantly looking over my shoulder and afraid to go home."

"You need the time away. It'll give you clarity of thought. I'll know more at the end of that time. Maybe, you'll want to stay here, or maybe, you'll want to keep your apartment. Those are possibilities you need to consider."

"Time away sounds wonderful. When do we leave for Lamont?"

"As soon as possible . . . no more than a couple of days."

"Good. That'll give me time to let Aline know I can't be at the hospital for a while. I don't want to go back to my apartment alone. Will you take me to pick up the things I'll need? My rent is paid through the end of the month."

"Of course, cherie. Now, you need to get some sleep before the sun comes up. I'll show you to your bedroom, since Nina has retired for the night. She and her husband, Hugh, are back with me full-time. They're trusted friends as well as employees."

Guy and I climbed the stairs to the rose bedroom. He opened the door and said, "Is there anything I can get you?"

"No, thank you." I wondered whether he would come in, but when he kissed me and said, *"Bonne nuit, amour,"* I had my answer.

Chapter Thirteen

September 1940 – Loire Valley

Although safely away from the Ritz and Colonel Dietrich, I'd still managed to land in a German beehive.

As it turned out, Guy and I didn't travel together to the Touraine. Rather, Aline and I made the journey on short notice to attend the wedding—her arranged marriage to the twice-married, sixty-year-old Marquis de Maille. Her father, Count de Fleury, had somehow negotiated for immediate transport for us to Chateau Fleury in the Loire Valley.

Two days after the Ritz fiasco, I'd gone to the hospital to work, where I planned to let Aline and the doctors know I'd be away for a while. When I arrived I didn't find Aline walking the halls or attending to patients. "Have you seen Aline today?" I asked the first nurse I saw.

She nodded as she hurried along the hall and called back to me, "In the storeroom."

"Good." I mouthed to myself. We'd have a chance to talk while we unpacked newly arrived medical supplies and put them in their places on the shelves.

Aline looked around as I approached. "Where have you been the last couple of days?"

I sighed. "It's a long story."

"Not as long as mine. I was afraid I'd be gone before I could get word to you."

Oh my God. My pulse weakened and my mind raced. She been so busy at the hospital, how could she have offended the Germans? "Gone where?"

She whispered in a husky voice, "My father has sent for me immediately. He's promised me to an old man I've never seen—but I have heard about his womanizing."

"What do you mean 'promised?'"

She looked at the floor. "The wedding will take place at the end of the week."

"That's awful! What about Roberto?"

She shook her head. "I don't know—he's probably in Italy." She turned from me and stacked the last of the much-needed bandages on the shelves while I stowed rolls of tape in their designated place. "Anyway, it doesn't matter. I'll be married soon."

"I'm so sorry." I hugged her to let her know I cared but couldn't find the words to express my feelings.

She looked into my eyes for a moment before she spoke. "What I want is for you to be my maid of honor. Please say you will."

"I'd be happy to." I paused. "If I can get there."

"Merci, *mon amie.* You can ride with me . . . I think Guy will see that you get back to Paris after the wedding."

"I don't know if I have anything appropriate to wear."

"Any dress you have will do—with the war and all, the ceremony will be short and simple. I expect a wedding dress of sorts has already been selected for me."

I'd never seen Aline give up so easily. She'd always been an independent spirit, and now I wasn't so sure. I needed to respond. "I'll be honored," I said and let go it at that. No point in telling her about Guy and me or that I'd soon be at Lamont.

Rapid footsteps interrupted the awkward silence and one of the nurses stuck her head in the door. "Hurry. Another group of casualties has arrived."

Dread as to what I'd see registered as pressure in my chest. It took all the willpower I could muster to control my natural reaction to the sight of blood and cries of pain that surely awaited me.

"You'll need to be ready to leave tomorrow morning," Aline said in a calm voice. She grabbed at a bottle of antiseptic and two others fell to the floor.

The pungent odor from the broken vessels filled my nostrils. I grabbed a towel, covered the spill, and pushed it all toward the shelves before I followed her. *Maybe she isn't so calm after all.*

As we both ran down the hall, I wondered whether her sixth sense had deserted her or whether she knew things she hadn't told me. I felt satisfaction that I could go with her and, hopefully, make the ordeal less painful.

Some of the wounded moaned and others looked to be near death. I swallowed hard to keep the bile in my throat from exploding. My pulse weakened as I applied a tourniquet to a patient who looked to be no more than sixteen years old. He was losing a lot of blood—there was no time to delay. My heart broke for him and his comrades.

War stinks! What a waste.

I moved on to another who moaned and struggled with Aline. I reached for his hand and held it. It seemed to calm him and he mumbled something about his mother.

Aline spent the rest of the afternoon in surgery while I rendered aid in any way I could. After what seemed an eternity, she returned from surgery, and we were relieved by a couple of other nurses. We went into the break room and sat in silence for a long while. Finally, I glanced at my friend, but her eyes were closed. I couldn't tell from which nightmare she sought to escape or whether sheer exhaustion had overcome her. I asked in a whisper, "Where will you live after your marriage?"

When minutes passed without a response, I thought she hadn't heard me, but eventually she said, "If I'm lucky, my new husband will bring me to his apartment here in Paris—at least for a while. Given his reputation, I have no doubt his desire for my body won't last long. He'll want the apartment for a new mistress or his current one. Of course, he'd like to impregnate me with his heir. I'm certain he's already extracted a generous dowry from my father in exchange for giving me his name."

The whole thing repulsed me. "If you don't live in his apartment, where will you live?"

"His ancient, ancestral chateau is somewhere near Lyon. It's likely I'll be relegated to it."

"Let's hope not anytime soon," I said, at a loss for words.

"I'll find a way to work at the hospital, if and when I return to Paris. There's so much need. I've accepted that I won't be able to resume my studies at the Sorbonne, but I assure you, no matter where I am, I'll find a way to continue my work," she said with passion.

"I know you will. That's the kind of person you are."

Aline nodded. "Thank you. My advice for you, my friend, is not to let anything get in the way of completing your studies. After which, you'll return to America—and be glad you did so."

Goosebumps rose on my arms. "I don't plan to leave France."

"Not right away," she said dismissively. "In any case, be ready by eight sharp tomorrow morning. We'll pick you up at your apartment."

"No," I said with emphasis. "I'm not staying at the apartment right now."

"Oh? Why not?"

I paused a moment before I decided to tell her my good news. "Guy and I are engaged." I watched her brow crinkle, but other than that, her expression remained blank. I stared at her until she acknowledged my presence.

"Congratulations," she said and glanced at the ring finger of my left hand. There was nothing there to see, simply because I hesitated to wear the beautiful ring on the streets of Paris. I wanted to lock it in the safe and only wear it on special occasions, maybe because it intimidated me.

"When will you marry?"

"We haven't set a date. Guy doesn't want to endanger my status as an American citizen." I couldn't resist telling her about my engagement ring. "He gave me a beautiful diamond ring that had belonged to his grandmother."

"Oh my God, then it's for real." She took a deep breath. "I was afraid you'd misunderstood something he said." She frowned. "Oops, that didn't come out right. He does know a good thing when he sees it." She gave me a prolonged hug. "I wish you both many joyful years of marriage. So, I take it you'll be with Guy, ready and waiting for me in the morning."

"By all means."

I left the hospital, grabbed my bike, and rode to my temporary quarters. Not until I saw Guy did my fatigue vanish. His presence replaced the disturbing images of the day. My only thought was of him. I eagerly retreated into the safe bubble of just the two of us that closed out the rest of the world and its tragedies.

That evening Nina served a beautiful dinner of fresh greens from the back-yard garden—allowed to flourish while the Germans were there. I can't imagine where she got the fresh salmon, but it was delicious. Doubtless, the Germans would have confiscated it had they known she had it.

Neither of us asked the other about their day. "On way here I noticed the leaves on some of the trees have begun to change color,"

I said.

Guy smiled at me. "Yes, I'll speak to the gardener about planting some cool-weather vegetables. Any special requests?"

Resting my elbows on the table, poor manners be damned, I pondered a moment. "I don't know . . . cabbage, radishes, and lettuce? Oh, before I forget, I need to ask you to take me by my apartment after dinner to pick up some of my things."

"Can't it wait until morning? I had other plans for tonight."

"No, I wish it could. It's just that Aline's father has arranged for her to be married on Friday. She asked me to be her maid of honor. The wedding will be at Chateau Fleury."

"Yes, I received an invitation today, as well. I'll get you there in time. We'll leave Wednesday afternoon."

"I want to go with you, but Aline isn't herself. She seems so vulnerable now. I promised to accompany her tomorrow morning. I believe my presence will help."

Guy didn't respond for some minutes and then all he said was, "I understand."

"Thank you."

"I'll stop by Chateau Fleury on my way to Lamont and see how things are going."

"Why do you suppose Aline is going along with this marriage that is so repugnant to her?"

"Paulette, Aline and I are duty bound by certain traditions of which Americans have little knowledge. Fortunately for you and me, I've honored the family tradition of marriage and from now on I am free to make my own decisions in that regard." Guy rose. "Let's get over to your apartment."

Two Germans soldiers emerged from the shadows as Guy and I started up the walkway to my apartment building. "What is your business here?" one asked and clicked his heels in impatience.

I noted the double-S insignia on his jacket, identifying him as one of the dreaded secret police. "I live here. Has something happened?"

"Your identification," he demanded and held out his hand

I dug around in my purse and handed him my passport.

He perused it. "Paulette Rousseau?"

"That's correct."

He handed it to the other soldier, who scanned a sheet of paper and nodded.

"Go," he said and walked forward.

As soon as we entered the front door and stepped into the vestibule, the landlady opened her door enough for me to see her face. "I'm glad there's no trouble. They've been watching the house for a few days. It makes me nervous . . . and frightens away prospective tenants. At least you're back."

"I'll be away for a week or so. Don't worry, though, I'll be back before my rent is due."

She looked me up and down. "Where does anyone have to go these days with the city locked down?"

I shrugged and, following Guy's lead, started up the stairs.

She called, "With all the male companions you have, it's no wonder you can get away for a few days."

As soon as I walked in the apartment, I sensed that something wasn't right. The musty odor didn't explain it. I couldn't put my finger on what it was until I looked at the coffee canister on the stove shelf. It had been moved—just off enough to touch the clock. Its placement on the shelf had to be exact. I looked at Guy and whispered, "Somebody has been here."

"How do you know?"

I pointed to the canister and adjusted it. "See? Now it fits exactly between the fan and the clock, without touching either of them."

Guy reached for the tin and looked inside, stirring the meager bit of coffee in the bottom of the container. "Look around and see what else has been disturbed while I check for hidden recording devices."

I couldn't be sure but suspected that things weren't exactly as I had left them in my jewelry case. I sighed. "Thank God, I didn't leave my locket here after the party."

After setting my suitcase on the bed, I turned my attention to the clothes I wanted to take with me. First off, I carefully folded my lavender dress for the wedding and then added enough other clothes for a two-week stay in the Loire Valley.

Guy made a thorough examination of the bedroom after

looking through the kitchen and bathroom. "Nothing found here. Ready to leave?" he asked as he picked up my suitcase.

"Yes" One final glance around put my mind at ease. Everything was again in its specific place. I'd know if anyone moved something while I was away.

Upon our arrival back at the house on Rue Notre Dame des Champs, Guy brought my suitcase inside and set it by the front door. He poured each of us a glass of berry-flavored Chambord liqueur. "I wish we were going together to the Loire Valley this time." He raised his glass. "*Santé*. To better days to come." We touched glasses and drank to our mutual dream. I snuggled against his chest, not wanting the moment to end. "To your health" was especially apropos, given there seemed to be no end in sight for the dreadful war.

Guy ran his fingers along my arm. "For sure, we'll have that picnic with Claude while we're at Lamont. Remember, he didn't want you to leave the last time?"

"I do. I can't wait to see him. He's a charmer . . . just like his father." I felt Guy's body relax against mine.

"That little fellow needs more than part-time love from his father. With both of us there, he'll get double the amount of attention." He kissed me with tempered passion.

An urgent pounding at the door interrupted our contentment. "*Nom d'un chien*," he muttered as he came to full attention and went to answer it.

He'd been surprised. I understood the expression he had used—"name of a dog"—as I would say something like "for goodness sakes."

Chapter Fourteen

September 1940 – Loire Valley

German guards milled around the outside of Aline's magnificent Italian Renaissance-style home and sullied the image of Chateau Fleury.

Why hadn't she warned me that Chateau Fleury was no better than the Ritz Hotel in Paris—overrun with Germans? I regretted that I had agreed to come with her. Had Guy known it was a hotbed of Nazis? I felt betrayed and trapped as the car pulled to a stop.

Aline leaned close to my ear and whispered. "I didn't know. I swear I didn't."

One look at her ashen face convinced me she was telling the truth. Poor dear, having to come to terms with the old marquis and the Germans on what should be the happiest day of her life. I rued my luck that found me caught up in her personal tragedy, but I had to stick by my promise to her. At least I took some comfort that, unlike Aline, it would end for me in three days' time.

The chauffeur came around and opened the doors for us and fetched the luggage from the trunk of the car.

"The chateau is spectacular. You must have loved growing up here," I said to Aline to lessen the concerns she might have for me.

She nodded as we approached the steps to the house. "I have some good memories."

"Mademoiselle de Fleury and her friend, Mademoiselle Rousseau," one of the two guards said to the other as they stepped aside to allow us to enter the spacious, limestone gallery. And I mean *completely* limestone: floors, walls, and barrel vault ceiling. The room was absolutely stunning. A beautiful chapel lay to our left and to the right a blue salon in which sparse, tired furnishings had seen better days.

A gray-haired man came forward. "I see you've returned and brought a friend," he said to Aline.

"Oui. Papa, please say hello to Paulette Rousseau, my maid of honor."

"Bonjour," he said to me and turned to his daughter. "Bon, you've taken care of your part of the wedding arrangements. Sonya will make the necessary alterations to your mother's wedding gown.

"Merci, Papa." She gave him a bleak, tight-lipped smile.

"As you can see, we have guests. Dinner is served promptly at seven o'clock. Sonya will show you to your rooms."

My heart broke for her when her father turned on his heel and walked away in the direction he'd come without any sign of affection for beautiful, caring Aline.

A plump, dark-haired woman seemed to appear from nowhere. "I am Sonya and I will show you to your rooms. Mademoiselle de Fleury, things has changed since you was last here. Our new guests are housed in the west wing." She pursed her lips. "And it's now off limits," she said as she picked up my suitcase and started toward the smaller of the two staircases, each topped with horse-head finales.

"What about Maman's and my rooms?" Aline picked up her luggage.

"Your maman's room was cleared out after she died. I packed some of her things for you and took them to the attic. A month later your papa told me to do the same with your room. He sold some of the furniture from the two rooms." She lowered her voice and added, "Now the Germans are in there and the other folks over here." Sonya spread her arms and gestured. "Men on the right and women on the left."

"When do you expect the Marquis de Maille to arrive?" Aline asked as we walked down the hall.

"Thursday, or so I've been told." The woman pointed across the room toward an opaque garment bag visible through the open door of an armoire. "I bring your maman's gown from the attic for you to try on tomorrow morning."

I realized that Aline would be busy much of the day, and I would be on my own to try to keep clear of the Germans. If ever this was one of those times, I needed Guy to run interference for me, this had to be it. My fervent hope was that Guy would arrive early and spend the two nights at the chateau so we could be together. Of course, he would go to Lamont first to see little Claude, and if I were lucky, he and I could spend the afternoon there on Thursday after the groom arrived. I didn't suppose Aline would miss me, given all the wedding plans to be finalized.

"I be sorry, Mademoiselle, we make you wait," Sonya said. She picked up my suitcase and started for the door. "Your room is next door." Aline and I followed.

Right away, I noticed the disconnect. *What Spartan furnishings in a beautiful room with fine bone structure.* In my opinion the art deco-style bedroom set looked as if it could have been purchased at a Parisian flea market.

Aline moaned. "Papa must have moved the furniture from this room. Sonya, where is it?"

"West wing." The corner of her mouth twisted upward. "As befits our new guest, your papa say." She turned toward the door, "I go now, if there's nothing more."

"Look back in on us in a couple of hours," Aline said.

"Don't fret, I have everything I need here," I said. The last thing Aline needed was to worry about me.

"Now I know why I left here in the first place. Papa disappoints me." Aline sighed. "And I don't hold out much hope for my soon-to-be husband." I saw the tears in her eyes before she turned and said, "I'm going to lie down for a while and get a little rest before Sonya returns."

A wise decision, I thought and set about hanging up my clothes, including the dress I'd wear at her wedding. I prayed that by some miracle Aline could find happiness in her future. My thoughts turned to Guy and me. What did our future hold? Would I ever be Mrs. Guy de Laval? It was my turn to suppress misty eyes. I lay down on the bed, mostly because I didn't have much else to do before dinner. But my mind refused to use the time for relaxation. The glorious Chateau Fleury occupied by Germans. What a shame.

I sensed that Aline felt as uncomfortable as I did in such alien territory. The world was turned on its head. Dinner loomed as a nightmare to be endured. As the hours ticked by, I could no longer postpone the inevitable; I freshened up and slipped into my light green, two-piece suit—the shantung outfit. It was the only one suitable for dinner and would also have to be worn again the next day. I went next door to look in on Aline and found her ready. She had changed into a yellow taffeta dress that looked lovely with her dark hair and complemented her golden eyes. I shivered at the thought of the rogue marquis ravaging her.

"Where do the Germans eat?" I asked on our way to dinner. Before she could answer, we met her father and a younger man as we stepped into the gallery on the way to the dining room.

"Paulette, I would like for you to meet my brother, Louis," Aline said. "Louis, this is my American friend from college."

I extended my hand and Louis grasped my fingertips. "Bonjour," he said with little enthusiasm. He returned his attention to his father and continued, "You were saying that we should limit the hours we go to the stables. His men need to have uninterrupted time to plan their activities there."

Aline ignored the snub and took my arm. "While we wait for dinner, let's take a look into the chapel. I want to be sure it's set up for the ceremony."

"Yes, I'd like that. I've wanted to go inside ever since we arrived."

As soon as we passed from the *salle des gardes* into the *chapelle*, I felt at peace. The chapel was a modest-sized, limestone space with a high, vaulted ceiling and pilasters sculpted with acanthus leaves and cockleshells. High above the altar, light poured in from three, stained glass windows. Within the walls, a reverent dignity prevailed in spite of the tension outside its doors.

Aline walked slowly along the aisle and stopped to rub her finger over one of the pews. A distinctive line appeared in the layer of dust. "Heavens. When was this place last dusted? I must speak to Sonya about it in the morning. She'll need to sweep and dust. And make sure we have candles for the holders."

"Will you need a guestbook and a pen and paper for the priest in case he needs them?" I asked.

"I need to speak to Papa. He hasn't told me what he expects me to do." Aline's sad face revealed the deep pain she felt. "Maybe we can catch him now. We haven't talked at all about the wedding plans."

"Do you think he has planned a reception?" I asked as we retraced our steps in the gallery toward the grand staircase.

"I'm not sure. He may have." She paused. "He has if he wants to impress my groom, the Marquis de Maille!" Aline hesitated in front of a closed door and then gave a feather-fingered tap on it. After receiving no response, she opened it a crack.

Her father sat at a large desk made of dark wood. "What do

you want now?" he snapped.

"I won't take long. What do you need me to do to get ready for the reception?"

"I have already given you instructions. All you have to do is get yourself to the wedding. And don't be late for dinner."

"All right, Papa." Aline turned to me and we returned to the entry gallery. "We better get dressed for dinner. I'm sorry to ask this of you."

"And don't be late for dinner," he called to us.

I was more concerned about Aline than myself having to dine with the Germans—the unwelcome occupation army in her native country. Guy had already prepared me at the Ritz for such an affront.

The first thing that struck me when I entered the salon on our way to the dining room was that Aline's glum brother, Louis, had transformed into a patronizing conversationalist when it came to the Germans.

"As mayor of Cléré, I assure you we'll apprehend the scoundrels who defaced your headquarters," Louis said to the *Kommandantur*, the German commander of the military office in the region.

So he was collaborating with Germans against the citizens of his village. I considered pleading a headache and begging to be excused but succumbed to the rumbles of my empty stomach. I hadn't been exposed to such delectable aromas since in the dining room at the Ritz. However, after months of limited rations, once we were seated and the meal began, I was unable to finish the food on my plate. I noticed Aline's meal went untouched.

Fortunately, the Germans were occupied among themselves, trying to outdo each other's tales. They talked of a new census that required the registration of all Jews, communists, prostitutes, Free Masons, and other "undesirables" in the occupied zone.

One of the officers bragged, "We rounded up a group of Catholic youths. Their leader seemed surprised that they fell under the ban of twenty-eight August prohibiting all uniformed movements. I soon convinced him."

"What, with the butt of your rifle?" Another officer quipped and the group laughed.

A third one said, "I'll bet you did. We need a ban on the nomads. Those Gypsies sneak around and steal anything not fastened down."

"Yeah, but some of those girls are delicious and easy." Again, peals of laughter filled the room.

The first light of day peeked in through the tall window. *What day is it?* I rolled over on the lumpy mattress. Thursday. One more day until the wedding, I realized. I slid from under the sheet and dressed to await Guy's arrival at Chateau Fleury, spurred on by the hope that he would come early. The thought of his presence calmed my frayed nerves. If I'd known Germans were billeted at the chateau, I wouldn't have come here with Aline. Why hadn't Guy warned me? I'd ask him just as soon as we were out of earshot of the swarm of enemies—German and French.

Fretting about my predicament, I sat by the window and waited and waited until Sonya tapped on my door and called, "You awake, Mademoiselle Rousseau?"

"Oui. Come in."

She carried a tray with coffee and two croissants. "*Petit déjeuner.*" She set the tray on the nightstand. "Monsieur de Laval be here," she added on her way out.

Needless to say, I wolfed down breakfast and dashed downstairs to look for Guy. He stepped from behind one of two large potted plants as I made for the salon. "Were you hiding from me?" I teased while allowing myself to be enfolded in his embrace. His lips met mine just as I started to warn him about the Germans.

"I know," he whispered.

"Why are you whispering?"

"Eavesdropping while I waited for you," he continued in a soft tone. With a glint in his eye, he added, "Now that you're here, let's take a stroll to the stables."

"Only the animals will know we're there?" I gave his arm a playful smack and teased. "Aren't you the sly one?"

Guy steered me through the blue salon and out a side door and through the walled rose garden. We came to a huge, three-tiered formal fountain that could be seen from the approach at the front of the chateau. In spite of the fountain's beauty, the horsehead finial atop it created a jarring effect as it spewed water from its mouth and nostrils. Beyond the fountain, the garden beckoned; I looked forward to exploring its nooks and crannies. "I wonder where this goes," I said as I started to follow a path toward the inner wall.

Guy took my hand. "We'll come back later after we've checked out the stables."

"Why come back when we're here now?" I pointed out.

A quick kiss to the cheek was my answer as he put his arm around my shoulder and led me through the open garden gate and across the vast expanse of graveled parking area in front of the chateau. We had continued on toward a vegetable garden when a group of soldiers came from the house and got into cars or on motorcycles.

"Where are they going?" I asked.

Before Guy could answer, Aline's brother, the mayor, rushed from the chateau and approached one of the cars.

"They'll disburse to their various posts. I don't need to remind you that the Nazis are regulated down to the last detail." Guy sighed. "God help the villagers."

We followed the path along the length of the kitchen garden and continued toward the large, brick, stable complex. As we came close to the building, my body tingled with anticipation at being alone with Guy where we could express our pent-up passion. My hopes were dashed when I saw the door ajar and heard the low hum of German voices. Guy stopped and listened. I looked at him, and he shook his head at me.

Without warning a gruff German officer came out and confronted us. "You're strangers around here. What are you doing skulking around the premises?" he demanded in broken French.

I hadn't seen him at dinner the night before and wondered if he was billeted at the chateau.

"Guten Morgen, mein herr," Guy said, which brought about a congenial demeanor from the soldier. The two men carried on a conversation in German. I could make out Guy's name, my name, the Ritz, and the names of some of the people we'd met there.

After several minutes, the German turned and spoke to me in broken English. "Miss, you are bridesmaid?"

"Yes," I said, disconcerted to speak with him in my native language—he had a better mastery of English than of French.

"Passe une bonne journée," he said in French. He clicked his

heels and went back to the stables.

"Have a nice day, indeed," Guy said to me.

Impressed with Guy's ability to defuse a tense situation, I said, "He didn't ask for our papers. What did you say to him?"

"It was important to put him off guard. He's ruthless and I intend to keep an eye on him while I'm here."

His response raised more questions in my mind. "How do you know about him?"

"I've been keeping track of him, as well as Aline's father. They're too cozy to be coincidental. The Count de Fleury is not to be trusted either."

"Poor Aline. I'm worried. Will you stay here tonight?"

"I'll stay until she's safely married. Then we'll go to Lamont and announce our engagement."

I breathed deeply, ashamed I had doubted Guy's sincerity when he proposed.

As we walked along the driveway, the crunch of gravel led us closer to the public highway. Upon our arrival there, I tugged on Guy's arm. "Let's start back. That sun gets hotter by the minute," I said with a pat to my hot cheeks. Guy stepped back from the shoulder of the road and looked at me. "Of course. Things are quiet out here."

"So? What did you expect?"

He didn't say anything, so I fell into step with him as we headed back to the chateau. When we reached a curve in the drive, the trees cast shadows on the road and provided blessed relief from the relentless, scorching sun. As eager as I was to go inside, I couldn't resist the sound of splashing water coming from the walled garden. I wanted to dash water on my face, and then bathe my tender feet in the coolness of the fountain. I picked up my pace and hurried through the garden gate. "Come on. You promised."

Guy caught up with me and drew me to him. I forgot cool water and everything except being in the arms of the man I loved. He maneuvered our bodies as one to the soft bed of leaves beneath the umbrella of a plane tree. As well as sheltered from the sun, we were out of sight of any prying eyes that might approach. I lay back on the leaves, and every time his eyes met mine, my heart turned over in response to the passion I saw. His steady gaze bore into my silent expectation. Suddenly, he sat up and helped me to my feet.

"What's the matter?" I moaned.

"We're not alone."

And then I heard it too. Mournful sobs. Guy and I struck a pose to suggest an interest in the peculiar pattern formed by the tree's uneven bark. The weeping neared. I gasped when Aline came into view. "Oh my God! Aline! What's wrong?" I asked as I flung my arms around her without a thought of my disheveled appearance.

She blotted her tears with a lace-trimmed handkerchief. "Nothing is going right. The groom has been delayed until tomorrow morning. And that's not the worst of it. Papa has made arrangements for the mayor to perform the civil ceremony in the blue salon. He says that's the only thing required and there will be no religious ceremony."

I stepped back to look into her eyes. "But it's your wedding. Why would he disregard your wishes?"

"You don't know him."

Guy took Aline's arm, "Come. I'll speak to him," he said. And I linked arms with her free arm.

She shook her head. "It won't do any good, I'm afraid." Her body stiffened and her voice grew strong. "I won't feel truly married unless a priest conducts a ceremony in the chapel!"

"In that case, the Marquis de Maille may not have a bride after all." Guy turned to Aline. "I suggest we wait until morning and hope the marquis arrives early. Maybe he can persuade your father to change his mind."

I doubted that the marquis would be Aline's gallant knight to the rescue, but I kept my thoughts to myself. What would become of my friend?

Chapter Fifteen

September 1940 – Loire Valley

Wedding or no wedding? An oppressive uncertainty hung heavy around the maid of honor.

I awoke at three o'clock, well before the first light of day, although the full moon shone brightly, illuminating the mismatched furniture in my bedroom. I dangled my feet off the bed while I pondered how to best serve Aline as her friend and, perhaps, her attendant. Actually, I had little control over the events of the day. Poor Aline, she had to meet her groom for the first time and hope that by some miracle he would agree to being married by a priest as well as the mayor.

A tap on my door startled me. Who could it be? "Go away. No, not at this time of day!" I muttered.

Another tap sounded, followed by another louder one. "Paulette, open the door." Aline said it twice before I responded.

"What's going on?"

"The wedding will take place."

"You agreed to only the civil ceremony?"

She shook her head. "The marquis and I spoke briefly after he arrived late last evening and spoke to my father. He told Papa that just the civil marriage ceremony was not acceptable to him and he preferred to include the second, religious one as well."

"Your father agreed?"

"Reluctantly. He said it was a waste of time. But Papa is trying to stay in the marquis' good graces. I don't know why this marriage is so important to him." She sighed. "Anyway, when I told Guy, he kindly volunteered to find a priest for us on such short notice."

Overcome with relief, I hugged Aline. "The groom agreed. That's a good omen."

She pursed her lips. "I hope so."

"We have a wedding to get ready for today." I saw that she had her doubts and wanted to take her mind off things that might never come to pass. At least this wedding was not in that category. "What can I do to help you?"

After a bite of breakfast, we need to help Sonya set things up in the chapel. There's so much to do in so little time. We can't hope to have everything done in time."

"It'll be okay. We'll get the most important things done first," I said.

"That's all we can do. Sonya is dusting and mopping as we speak."

"Good."

"As soon as we get to the chapel, we'll get to work. We have time for a croissant and coffee in the kitchen before it becomes a beehive of activity with the onslaught of our German *guests* clamoring for their morning feast. At least their presence here means they brought along good things to eat. Otherwise, I don't know how we would be able to provide a wedding meal today."

"Okay," I said rapid fire. "I'll meet you at your room in fifteen minutes." As I slipped into a simple cotton dress, my thoughts turned to Guy. He'd been there for Aline at a critical time and might well have enabled the wedding to take place. I couldn't wait to hear the details from him.

By the time I was ready and stepped into the hall, I still had five minutes to make it to Aline's room in spite of the woolgathering I had indulged in as I had brushed my hair. Guilt dogged me because I just wanted the wedding to be over so I could leave this place.

Aline opened the door at my knock. "I'm not ready yet, as you can see." She stood in front of her wedding dress on the fitting form and wiped an errant tear from her cheek. "I'm missing Maman. She could be stern, but I always knew she loved me."

I knew I had caught an unusually strong woman in a moment of vulnerability. "I'm sorry it has to be this way." At that moment I was humbled to be there to take away some of the sting of having so few friendly faces present on such an important day.

She didn't say anything while she hurried to dress in clothes suitable for cleaning. We left the room, each of us lost in our own thoughts. After a small breakfast, we headed toward the chapel.

"Where will you change into your gown?"

She looked happy for a moment. "I'm going to wear my teal silk suit for the civil ceremony. Then I'll change into Maman's wedding gown in a small private room next to the chapel for the religious ceremony." Aline took a deep breath. "I can't imagine what

I'd do without Sonya. She'll bring my gown downstairs while we're at the civil ceremony and then make sure everything is in order so I can change without delay."

By the time we walked into the chapel, Sonya had worked her magic there and not a dust mite survived her attention. The wood glowed and gave off an orange-blossom aroma, and the rich colors of the stained-glass windows sparkled—it was a place fit for the wedding of a princess. Sonya had placed candles and flower arrangements on each side of a large Bible centered on the altar.

"It's beautiful!" I said and stared in awe.

"C'est magnifique," Aline said. "Just as I dreamed of when I was a little girl." She paused. "Sonya thought of everything. We don't have anything more to do here. You're free to do as you like for the next three hours."

I felt light on my feet as I headed for the blue salon in search of Guy, but my hopes were dashed when I arrived and found an empty room. Well, it was still early in the morning—maybe he had slept longer than usual. "No," I told myself out loud. I didn't believe it. And then I heard a voice behind me.

"Paulette, I didn't expect to see you before the wedding."

I whirled around and came face to face with, by the looks of him, a too-well-fed man with salt-and-pepper hair.

"Cherie, I've heard a lot about you already this morning," he said in a seductive tone as his eyes roamed the length of my body.

Beside him, Guy chuckled.

Embarrassed and angry, at that moment I wished the floor would open up and swallow me. My anger vanished when Guy put his arm around me and said in his most charming way, "Paulette, please say hello to the Marquis de Maille."

"The marquis responded to my greeting, "Enchanté. You're a rare woman to have stolen the heart of Guy de Laval."

My opinion of him softened. Maybe he wasn't a rake after all.

The marquis' eyes burned into mine. "Why are you looking at me that way?"

"I . . . I didn't expect to like you."

"Mademoiselle, I understand your wish for the best for your friend."

"My wish is for Aline to have a fulfilling marriage."

"Let me put your mind at ease. Aline is important to me. I will bestow upon her today the de Maille name and a family ring that belonged to my mother. A ring that will be passed on to the heirs of our union." He came closer to me. "You still look doubtful. You need to know I'm not one to break with tradition. I was tempted to sell the ring but found I couldn't bring myself to do so. Lord knows I could have used the money for repairs to the Maille chateau, but I had to let that idea go because I hadn't given up hope that a woman would enter my life who was worthy to wear that ring and be the mother of my children."

I hoped he'd say those words to Aline. It suggested that he wanted a successful marriage, at least. "Thank you for sharing your plans."

"My pleasure, mademoiselle." He caught sight of Aline's father. "I best see whether everything is in order for today." He disappeared through the open door in pursuit of the count.

"I'm glad I got to talk to the marquis. He seems to want a good marriage this time."

Guy hesitated for a moment. "I wouldn't be so sure about that if I were you."

"Why not? You heard what he said."

"But you didn't hear what he said to me earlier."

I stood my ground. "Oh, what did he say?"

"He can't wait to get back to life in Paris."

"With his new wife, of course. There's nothing wrong with that."

"Cherie, he means the glamorous life at the Ritz."

"You don't think he's a Nazi sympathizer, do you?"

"Non, I don't. I think he's apolitical."

"He's marrying a young woman in hopes of producing an heir?"

"Not for that reason. He already has three children. I think the wedding is a financial transaction—I doubt he has any true feelings for Aline whatsoever."

Aghast at the deception, I muttered, "Oh, no, I don't want to believe it."

Guy reached into his pocket and took out a small box. "The groom let drop that he received a generous dowry from the de Fleury family—worth lots more than a diamond-studded wedding band and old chateau." He handed the box to me. "The marquis told me that Aline's father was desperate to make the deal in order to impress the Germans—they place a high premium on pedigrees. And the Maille name certainly has that."

"Why do you have the ring?"

"Think! You know the answer."

After a moment's reflection, I knew. "You're the best man?"

"Stand-in best man. His first choice hasn't arrived."

I felt my cheeks flame with indignation that Aline was being treated like a piece of property put up for auction and that Guy would agree to stand with the purchaser. And then I took comfort that at least her husband would probably allow his wife a good deal of freedom, and maybe Robert Santoni would add artistic zest to the life of a sensuous woman trapped in a sterile marriage.

The mantel clock chimed on the half-hour. I'd lost track of time and quickly excused myself from the conversation in the salon. The civil ceremony had been brief and businesslike. Hopefully, the ceremony in the chapel would feel more like the happy occasion a wedding should be.

Fortunately, I'd applied makeup in the morning, so all I had to do when I reached my bedroom was change into my lavender dress and have Sonya redo my hair. I was already wearing my precious silk stockings, and beige high heels. By the time I left my room, I had fifteen minutes to get to the chapel dressing room and see what assistance Aline might need.

Upon my arrival I found her dressed and waiting for me. Sonya handed me a small nosegay of pink roses and blue bachelor buttons accented with tiny fern fronds. Aline's bridal bouquet consisted of yellow roses and sprigs of deep blue lavender. Her lovely facial features gave no suggestion of the trepidation she must be feeling.

Music sounded in the chapel as we made our way to the back of the room. The priest, Marquis de Maille, and Guy stood by the altar. Since I was Aline's only attendant, I made my way down the aisle, noting there were only a handful of guests—many seemed to have departed after the civil ceremony. I glanced at her brother with disgust. He sat between two German soldiers! I must admit, my pace down the aisle increased the rest of the way. There could be no acceptable reason for Nazis to blemish this sacred ceremony. I took my place with the wedding party and willed myself not to let anything overshadow the breathtaking beauty of the bride, who glided down the aisle on the arm of her cold-hearted father. She deserved better!

Apparently, the white-haired priest had his orders to keep the ceremony to a minimum because his brief remarks and the wedding vows were completed within fifteen minutes. I later learned it was to accommodate a rushed reception—cake and champagne only—for the bride and groom and the remaining few guests before the Nazis were served a full dinner in the dining room.

Sonya served the cake and champagne and then Guy raised his glass. "Aline and Jacques, may God bless your union."

Those of us who remained in the room clinked glasses and called, "Santé!"

I congratulated Aline and her new husband while Guy spoke in a low voice to the priest, a longtime friend of the de Laval family.

I hugged Aline and turned to the Marquis de Maille. "Will you return to Paris soon?"

"We have little choice. There is constant turmoil in Lyon these days since Herr Klaus Barbie has been the chief of the Gestapo in Lyon. He is ruthless in rooting out Allied sympathizers. Most of them are tortured before they are murdered. I have lost several of my friends and neighbors to the Butcher of Lyon. Everyone lives in constant fear that they will be his next victim."

"Oh, I thought your chateau was quite some distance from the city," I said.

"Not far enough. When I left, travel was uncertain. German troops were maneuvering along the roads and searching cars at random. All in service to Herr Barbie, no doubt."

"That's a shame."

"Such is life in these times. They bring it on themselves. If they accepted that Germany now controls France, they would be allowed to live in peace." He shrugged. "We'll leave for Paris in the morning."

"I hope we can visit with you while you're there," I said,

keeping eye contact with the marquis.

"*Certainment*! No doubt my wife knows how to contact you," he said and patted Aline on the arm. "We'll have Guy and you over for dinner."

Before the clock struck eleven, Guy and I were in the car and on our way to Lamont. Guy glanced away from the road long enough to see the troubled look on my face. "What's wrong?" he asked, concern in his voice.

"Nothing. Why do you ask?"

"You haven't said a word since we got into the car."

"I'm sorry. The situation depresses me. Aline's father is awful, and I'm worried that her husband may not be much better."

"Stop imagining their life. Aline is strong and resilient. She'll make the best of the situation." Guy reached for my hand and squeezed it. "As soon as you get back to Paris, we'll contact them. You'll see they will have adjusted to married life."

Chapter Sixteen

September 1940 – Chateau Lamont-sur-Loire

Friday the thirteenth, not an auspicious day for marriage—or, for that matter, for an engagement announcement—if one is the least bit superstitious.

The effects of the dark clouds of Chateau Fleury and the German troops dissipated as the blue Renault chugged up the wooded drive to Chateau Lamont. A smattering of autumn color reminded me that the Master Creator of the universe had not abandoned us entirely. Hope displaced nagging fears about the future.

Guy's hand brushed my cheek. "I know Aline's family shocked you, but your presence made it easier for her."

"Sophie and you were wonderful," I said. "Because of you, Aline's wish to be married in the sight of God was realized."

"I'm glad I could help." He nodded. "She'll be okay with the marriage."

My jaw clenched. "You think so?" I had serious doubts.

"Of course, I do. Aline draws on a vast inner strength."

A twinge of insecurity surfaced. Would Guy say the same about me?

As the forest gave way to the manicured lawns of Lamont, the fortress-castle, perched on the edge of a cliff for centuries, took my breath away—just as it had the first time I saw it. Soon the car rumbled between the two round towers, across the drawbridge, and into the enclosed courtyard.

Guy parked the car, opened the door for me, and removed our luggage from the trunk. I reached for mine, but he waved me away. "I've got it." I didn't protest, because neither of us had brought more than one bag, and when inside, the butler would take them up to our rooms. I breathed slowly to calm my churning stomach. What would Guy's father and mother think . . . and say . . . about our engagement?

This time Guy took me a different way, by a door that led directly into the large gallery, bypassing the armory and its extensive weapons display. The new way brought us more directly to the casual sitting room. The dark-haired major sat alone, much as he had done the first time I'd met him. The volume of the floor-model radio carried through the open door. Upon seeing us, he turned down the volume and stood with effort.

"Papa, wait there, we'll come to you." Guy rushed forward and hugged his father. I stood a polite distance away. "I can see that your leg is giving you trouble today," Guy said as he stepped to his father's side.

Monsieur de Laval turned to me, "Welcome. I know little Claude will be happy to see you again."

"Papa, wouldn't you think he'd be looking forward to his father's visit?" Guy chided.

"Cheer up, that goes without saying, but Mademoiselle Rousseau wouldn't know how she's been missed."

"How much is that?" I asked.

"Little Claude talks about the picnic and horseback rides 'the lady' promised him."

I saw that Guy was displeased that his father gave him little credit for the plans we'd both shared with the little boy.

"Oh, yes, Claude and I both were excited about Guy's plans for the three of us to spend time together," I replied.

"Be that as it may, he is fond of you and speaks of you often." The major moved toward his chair, Guy's offered arm summarily dismissed. "Get comfortable while we catch up on things," he said and waved Guy away before gingerly lowering himself into the chair.

"Where is Claude? Napping?" After looking around as if expecting his son to appear, Guy finally sat beside me, apparently accepting that his reunion with the little boy would be postponed.

"I think so. He should be up pretty soon. Your mother is around here somewhere, though."

Guy's father annoyed me with the way he tried to control and diminish Guy.

A long silence followed before the major spoke, his brow furrowed. "The Germans announced a new policy yesterday. Hostages will be imprisoned or executed if violent actions are taken against the Nazis." Monsieur de Laval's eyes locked on his son. "Don't minimize the danger. It's already happening, here and all around the occupied zone. God only knows what's going on in the

Free Zone."

"Papa, you of all people should know that, as a military man, I must do what needs to be done to protect France."

The major's face had turned red. "That argument won't convince me. I know what your work involves, as well as your misguided political views. You think you have all the answers. I say to you, leave it to the experienced men who fought and won the Great War. At great sacrifice, I might add."

"Men like Marshal General Philippe Pétain, our new prime minister of France, who lays down arms and declares Paris an open city? The man who negotiated an armistice with the Nazis?" Guy's voice was filled with disgust. "How can you expect me to crawl under a rock and pretend all is well?"

"I can assure you that you won't be spared if you're arrested."

"That's a chance I'll have to take!"

"You talk like that after the British murdered more than a thousand French sailors in the Mers-el-Kébir attack?"

Guy's expression stilled and grew pensive. "It grieves me deeply that the French government's representative, Admiral Darlan, couldn't be located to negotiate with the British, which resulted in the death of my countrymen, killed during the shelling of our fleet. I cannot condone what happened, but I know it would have been disastrous if the French Navy had been taken over by the Germans. It could have brought them victory in short order. And the end of an independent France!"

"Papa, Papa and Mam'selle." Claude jumped from his grandmother's arms and ran to Guy. Once in his father's arms, he lowered his eyes as he looked at me. I wondered if his sudden shyness was because I differed from his memory. The next moment I was forgotten by father and son until, after several minutes, the little boy twisted out of his father's arms.

By that time I had seated myself next to Madame de Laval.

"How was Aline's wedding?" she asked me.

"It went well, considering the circumstances." I sighed. "She was married by a priest in the beautiful Chateau Fleury chapel."

"I'm pleased to hear it."

"It meant a lot to her."

Claude looked at each of us as we spoke. After we fell silent, he leaned against his grandmother while studying me.

I held out my arms to him, but he made no gesture of acceptance. Not to be defeated, I asked him, "Do you remember what your papa promised you on my last visit?"

His face brightened and he jumped down to the floor. "Ride the pony." He stood between the two of us, but I had his full attention. With a clap of his hands, he said, "Go now?" and tugged on my sleeve.

No way could I ignore his request, although Guy and his father couldn't seem to agree to disagree. At least their voices sounded normal.

"General Pétain is a war hero," Monsieur de Laval repeated. "If anyone can save our nation, he's the one."

"Papa, Pétain is no longer the man you served under during the Great War. Age has weakened him, clouded his thinking."

"Guy, you're not doing your own thinking. You're listening to others."

"You're wrong! I observe events as they take place. Allowing the enemy to take possession of our country without resisting is unthinkable. General de Gaulle is the voice of honor."

"General Pétain has not abandoned us and fled to another country. He stayed to negotiate and save lives and honor—and perhaps, find a way to defeat the Germans."

Little Claude in his unfettered enthusiasm broke free and ran to his father. "Papa."

Guy's face lit up as he lifted his son into his arms again. "Here's my boy," he said, his father no longer the object of his attention.

"Papa, pony ride."

"Pretty soon."

"Now. You promised."

Guy stood and looked at his father. "Here's the real French negotiator. We're going to find the pony."

Monsieur de Laval's expression softened. "Yes, you better do as he says."

My shoulders relaxed. The shared love for that little boy

eclipsed their political differences—for the time being.

When Guy and I started to leave the room, Madame de Laval said, "I'll expect you back in time for wine and cheese at five."

"Oui, Maman." Guy restrained the rambunctious boy. "You hear that Claude? Mamie wants us back before five. We better hurry."

When Guy lifted his son onto his shoulders, Claude squealed in delight. "We better hurry," he mimicked.

I followed them out a side door and past the largest tower at the back of the house. In the distance the Loire River shimmered like a silver ribbon as the sunlight danced on it.

"Water." Claude pointed.

"Yes." Guy turned onto a gravel path that led to a stand of trees rather than the river.

"Non, Non. I want water." Claude pounded his father's shoulders.

Guy lifted him from his shoulders and held him with one arm so they faced one another. "You want water or pony?" he asked with a note of irritation.

Claude began to cry and rub his eyes.

"Son, life is full of choices. You might as well get used to it."

I held out my arms to the child. "Come. Let's talk about the pony." Claude wrapped his arms around my neck.

"What's the pony's name," I asked him.

"Jacques."

"I want to meet Jacques. Will you show me?"

Claude nodded, and with that, the sun shone in his smile again.

Guy walked two paces ahead of us. I wondered whether he was displeased with himself or me. I could find myself in an awkward position. Had I offended Guy by interfering with his method of discipline of his son?

A fenced pasture lay to the side of a long, low building—the stables, I gathered, after having seen the grand ones at Chateau Fleury.

Guy slowed until we caught up. "Thank you for thinking of Claude. I'm afraid all this talk of politics has affected my ability to be a patient father."

"De rien." Goodness knows, I'd help him in any way I could.

He took Claude from my arms. "I love you, Paulette Rousseau." He leaned close and kissed me.

I reached for his free hand. "Guy de Laval, you make me very happy."

"I try," he said and squeezed my hand. "We'll share our good news with my parents when we return this afternoon, if we can keep politics out of it."

I assumed he meant our engagement. Would we be questioned about wedding plans?

Claude's voice put an end to further reveries. "Jacques, I'm coming," he called as we drew near the stone-clad building that housed the chateau's horses.

I saw that the stable was not as low as I had thought; rather, it was at least one and a half stories high.

By the time we went inside, Claude was dragging his father in his eagerness to reach his pony. They hurried along a row of stalls on the right, stopping at the fourth one. I had to hurry to catch up.

When I got there, they had the little Shetland pony saddled. Claude was already seated on his back, Guy's hands folded over his son's on the reins. Once outside, we walked along the fence and watched the horses frolic in the pasture.

"Look." Claude pointed and giggled as two horses chased each other to the fence.

Guy reached out and patted the chestnut one on the head.

"I want to ride him," Claude said.

"Tomorrow, we ride. It's time to go to the house now. Papi and Mamie are waiting."

The little boy pouted. "I don't care."

His father ignored him and led the pony to his stall.

We headed back the way we had come and would arrive in ample time for wine and cheese with Monsieur and Madame. As the time drew closer, I prepared myself for whatever reaction they would have to our engagement. Earlier in the day I'd witnessed how blunt the major could be. I hoped he'd show more restraint this afternoon, whether or not he was pleased.

"Noir." The child pointed at a crow.

"That's right." Guy touched my blouse. "What color?"

"Bleu."

"Good," I said. "You're bright like your papa." Turning to

Guy, I asked, "Do you think your parents will be happy for us?"

"I think so. They realize that two parents are better than one for a child. They take Claude's best interests seriously."

"Who? Me?" Claude said.

"Oui, you. Papi and Mamie want the very best for you."

After we changed and arrived at the salon for wine and cheese, we found a messenger waiting for Guy. "Monsieur de Laval, I have an important message for you," the man said.

Guy took the envelope from the man's hand, opened it, and read it. "Thank you." His face was expressionless. "You may leave now."

I knew what that meant—another emergency needed his attention right away. He'd leave within a day, most likely before we announced our engagement.

Confirming my suspicions, Guy addressed his parents. "My apologies, but I must leave. However, I have asked Paulette to stay at Lamont for a week before her classes start so that she and Claude can get better acquainted. How does that sound to you?"

Madame de Laval gave him a knowing smile. "That's wonderful."

The major nodded. "And what will you do?"

Guy didn't give a direct answer. "I must return to Paris, but I will purchase a train ticket for Paulette before I go." Guy stood and took my hand. "Walk me to the car."

After we were out of earshot, he said, "I'm sorry we didn't get to announce our engagement, but I don't want it to be a rush job. I promise we'll spend at least two weeks together at Lamont with Claude during the Christmas holidays."

"Does your mother know about our engagement already?"

"She guessed and I didn't deny it. Why do you ask?"

"I saw how she looked at you when you mentioned you wanted me to spend time with Claude."

"When you return to Paris, go to your apartment. It will be safer than my house."

"Will you be there?"

"It's not likely. I'll be going to various locations and will be away most of the time." He turned abruptly. "I have to get going. I'll have someone bring your ticket by for you." He gave me a quick kiss and climbed into the car.

I watched him drive away until he disappeared from view. Unwelcome doubts replaced the joyful feelings of an hour ago. Our plans had evaporated instantaneously with the arrival of that special communiqué. I couldn't live my life this way. I wondered whether he'd arranged the whole thing. Maybe he regretted all the engagement talk and realized that wasn't what he wanted. Why should he tell me to go to my apartment when I returned to Paris? His work with the Resistance gave him the perfect excuse to not tell me where he was going or what he would be doing. At the moment, however, there was little I could do about it, so I might as well make the best of my time at Lamont with Claude.

My week at the chateau passed more quickly than I would have liked. I dreaded going back to my apartment and could only hope that Aline had returned to Paris.

Madame and I sat in the salon, each of us with a glass of wine, the evening before I was to catch the train out of Tours for Paris. Given the erratic train schedules, I worried I might not be back by the time my classes began at the Sorbonne.

Yvette came into the room with pajama-clad Claude. "He won't go to bed until he says goodbye to Paulette."

I gave him a hug. "Sweetheart, you'll see me in the morning."

"Not at bed time tomorrow night?"

"Ah, you're right. Let me give you a goodnight kiss," I said as I held him in my arms. "I wish I could stay longer, but I have to go back to school in Paris."

He sat on my lap, facing me, his legs one on each side toward my back. His eyes locked onto me. "Mystique thinks you should stay here."

"We had a lot of fun, didn't we?"

"Oui."

"Of all the things we did, what did you like the best?"

"The boat rides."

"That was fun. Come on now, and I'll tuck you into bed." I picked him up and took him to his room. Afterward, I returned to the salon to say goodnight to Madame de Laval.

"Did you get him settled?" Madame asked.

"Yes. He's ready for bed. I think he's tired after everything we did today. He didn't even want to stop for dinner."

She smiled. "You're wonderful with him. I'm so happy that you will be part of this family."

"Thank you. It's impossible not to love Claude."

"I suppose we won't see you and Guy until Christmas. That's too long for Claude to have to wait."

"I know, but you're probably right. I doubt either Guy or I will have time to visit before then." I set down my glass of wine and sighed. "I better get to bed too. I have a long, uncertain journey ahead of me tomorrow."

"Bonne nuit, cherie," Madame said.

She had given me the encouragement I needed. How well did she know the man her son had become?

Only time would tell.

Chapter Seventeen

Autumn 1940 – Paris

My only companion was uncertainty as I made the return trip to Paris in time to begin my second year of studies at the Sorbonne.

I had arrived at the Tours train station an hour early for the trip, ever mindful that, should a large group of German soldiers need to be transported, civilian ticketholders would be bumped as necessary to accommodate them. My upgraded ticket offered some comfort that at least I wouldn't one of the first to give up my seat.

Crowds of people gathered around me on the platform as we awaited the opening of the outside gate by the depot. As I stood there I noticed three men in work clothes and hats. One of them seemed to do all the talking, while the other two every so often surveyed the crowd as if watching for someone. I soon lost interest when a woman holding a baby approached me.

"I've been here for two days, waiting to get to Paris," she said, her eyes drawn with fatigue.

"You had a ticket but weren't allowed to board?"

"They held me for questioning and caused me to miss the train."

"Did it have to do with your papers?"

"At first they said it did. After the train left they said they mistook me for someone else and that I was free to board. A lot of good that did. The train had already gone."

I lost sight of her when a crush of people made room for a group of German soldiers as they moved to the head of the line.

Two hours later, I heard the train whistle long before I saw the black puffs of smoke as the train pulled into the station.

The gates opened and everyone began pushing. I was jostled along with everyone else, but I managed to hold my place in line. At least I wouldn't have to worry about the Germans; they'd have their own first-class compartments.

After the arriving passengers had disembarked and the soldiers had boarded, the line moved slowly while each passenger's papers were checked. My American passport and Sorbonne student card ensured my prompt entry, and I was allowed to board the train.

Partway down the car, I slid open the door to a compartment that appeared to be almost empty. An elderly man and woman, the only occupants, sat in the window seats across from each other, the drawn blinds darkening the space considerably. They did not look at me as I took a seat close to the door.

Sometime later, the three men I had noticed on the platform entered our compartment, filling it to capacity. One of the men had pale skin, unlike the other two, who had Mediterranean olive skin. The pale one kept his eyes down except when he took furtive looks around. He swiped at the beads of perspiration as they accumulated on his face.

I closed my eyes, hoping to catch up on my sleep rather than clock-watch. Who knew how long we might be delayed?

Loud German voices awoke me just before the compartment door flew open. Three German soldiers with bayonets drawn entered and removed the three workmen. The elderly woman gasped and clutched her chest. I said a prayer for them. I had already guessed what they were: two members of the Resistance attempting to get an Allied serviceman to safety.

We arrived in Paris mid-morning, twenty-four hours later, without further incidents.

By the time I reached my apartment, I was utterly exhausted, physically and mentally. I forced myself up the stairs and collapsed on top of my bed after I set the alarm clock for seven.

I opened my eyes at six the next morning but waited until the last minute to dress for school. I guess I wanted to delay the inevitable reprimand for missing the first day of class. When I started down the stairs, I saw the landlady outside her door.

Her hands on her hips, she said as I approached, "You're up early. Off to school already."

"Yes," I said as I slipped past her. "I don't want to be late."

"We need to …"

I didn't hear the rest of what she said. Usually, I would talk as long as she wanted, but today, I was in no mood to worry about my manners.

The bike ride in the crisp autumn air invigorated me. I would face the day reasonably well, I assured myself on my approach to the campus. I always felt humbled when the Chapelle de la Sorbonne came into view and I realized afresh that I was a student at the renowned institution of learning. I glanced at the clock nestled beneath the landmark tower. Whoa. On time—a good beginning.

This day appeared no different than the others. Nevertheless, I braced myself for the changes I might find inside. I parked my bike and moved along the pleasantly shaded courtyard and passed between the portico pillars on my way to the lecture amphitheater. The halls were eerily devoid of students as I headed for my first class of the day—French Literature. Only a handful of students were there, including Renee Greenberg. I took the seat next to hers. In a modulated tone, I said, "I didn't think I'd see you here."

She looked through me without a word.

"Why didn't you go to New York?" I persisted.

Renee pursed her lips. "I said I wouldn't leave my father . . . and he is still here."

"You disobeyed him?"

"I love my father enough to disobey him." She turned her back on me again.

After class I'll make it up to her, I thought.

Things did not go as planned.

"Mademoiselle Rousseau, you're American, aren't you?" Professor Charpentier asked as he caught up with me after class.

"Oui, why do you ask?"

"At the Sorbonne, even in times of war, we don't do things as you might do in America. This course requires an inordinate amount of reading. Are you confident that your French language skills are sufficient for you to perform satisfactorily in this class?"

"Oui, monsieur le professeur. I wouldn't be here if I had doubts."

"Presumptive on your part to be absent from the first class meeting."

"I was delayed in the Loire Valley. Travel is a nightmare these days."

"In this troubled time, you will have many stresses unrelated to your studies. Do consider my words before you make a final decision about continuing in my class."

By the time he finished scolding me, I couldn't find Renee.

Frustrated, I climbed on my bike and rode around in circles while weighing the wisdom of heading to the Greenberg's bookstore.

"Mademoiselle Rousseau," a male voice called.

Colonel Dietrich! I whirled around. "Colonel, what can I do for you?"

He came closer. "What a beautiful autumn day. *S'il vous plait,* join me for a cup of coffee, and I will explain."

I wondered whether I dared decline. Was I in serious trouble—or could it have to do with Guy or Chris? Their safety always hovered in the back of my mind. "I'd like to, but I have another class in an hour. Can we make it another time?"

He was not to be put off. "I won't keep you long," he said, placing his hand firmly on my arm. "There's a little café just across the street."

I did not want to be seen in public with him, but I also did not want to anger him and be arrested. Accepting the inevitable, I forced a half smile and went with him.

"Bonjour. *Deux cafés,*" Dietrich said to the man behind the counter when we entered the café.

"Bonjour. I will bring it to you *dans un instant.*"

"It'll be here in just a moment," the colonel assured me as he sat down across from me.

I nodded, wondering what came next.

The proprietor arrived before the silence became awkward. "Enjoy this nice weather. In Paris you never know when it will turn cold," he said as he placed the steaming cups of coffee, along with a pitcher of cream and a sugar bowl, on the blue-and-white oilcloth that covered the table.

I breathed in the aroma of real coffee as I eyed the cream and sugar. I knew they were reserved for Germans frequenting the café. Had I been alone, I would have been served a far less appetizing beverage, and the cream and sugar most assuredly would have been absent.

As soon as the proprietor was out of earshot, the colonel said, "I'd be honored if you would attend my birthday celebration at the Ritz. It's two weeks from today."

I had to answer him without time to weigh the pros and cons. One thing for sure, if I wanted to help the Resistance know what was going on at the Ritz, this would give me the perfect opportunity.

Still smarting from Guy's apparent lack of candor about what he would be doing for an unspecified length of time, I slipped in to the role he had given me to play. "With pleasure," I said with a smile.

"I hope it meets your expectations."

I breathed a sigh of relief when he showed better sense than I had—he did not let on that he was pleased and gave no indication of the nature of our conversation. "I'm sure they will be exceeded."

He stood. "I hope I haven't delayed you unduly."

"Not at all." I rose and picked up my handbag "*À bientôt.*"

"See you soon," he said in English as he strode away.

What have I done? The fat was in the fire, as Mother would say. By the time I climbed on my bike, my stomach was churning like an angry ocean during a hurricane. I just wanted to go home and climb into bed, but I had to talk to Renee. I took off toward the Silver Quill and hoped to goodness she would be there.

On my arrival I saw a yellow sign in the window, but I could not read it until I drew closer. *Entreprise Juive.* Why would the Greenbergs have a bright sign saying the store was a Jewish business?

Uncertainty as to whether I should leave delayed my entry, and I stood transfixed for several minutes before I ventured inside. Finally, after a deep breath, I opened the door. At least everything looked normal inside.

Ida, the student assistant, was stacking books. She turned and saw me. "*Allô, comment ça va*? she said as she climbed down from the ladder.

I kissed her on both cheeks. "I'm well, thank you."

She shook her head. "I'm angry that our government does the Nazis' bidding."

"Is the sign in the window on their orders?"

"Oui. I'm worried sick for the Greenbergs."

"Where are they now?" I asked.

"In the kitchen, listening to the radio."

"Do you think it's okay for me to peek in on them?"

"Oui."

"One more question. Who put up the sign—the French or the Germans?"

"Mr. Greenberg put it up soon after it was delivered with an explanation of the new policy."

"Why?"

She looked at the floor. "The French police have begun taking a census of Jews, but I don't know if that's why. Mr. Greenberg just mumbled, 'It's better this way,' and walked away."

I shook my head. "I'm going to say hello to them." The kitchen door was closed. I tapped on it and called out, "It's Paulette. May I come in?"

A sliver-sized opening appeared at the edge of the door. Renee looked through it. "What are you doing here? You've startled my father." And then meek Renee hissed, "Go away!"

Before I could react, the door opened wider. Monsieur Greenberg stood behind his daughter. "Paulette, my dear. *Ça va bien?*" His appearance shocked me. His stooped shoulders suggested the heavy burden he carried.

"Very well, thank you," I said softly. "I'm sorry to find things deteriorating so rapidly."

Renee's father's put his arm around his ashen-faced daughter. "Thank you for your concern."

"I'm alarmed to hear that the police demanded you display that obnoxious sign in your window."

"It doesn't bode well for the future." His eyes misted. "I complied because I want to stay in business and hope to do so by not drawing attention to us." He paused as he coughed and gasped for breath. "Those who do not comply will most likely be dealt with immediately." After a long moment he continued, "Each day we're here is a victory of sorts."

Renee stepped from her father's side "Papa, you need to rest. Paulette, please excuse me. I have to study."

"Renee," he said. "Paulette came to see you, too."

I shook my head. "Take care of yourself. I must be on my way, but I will look in on you again. You know I want to help in any way I can."

Renee returned to her father's side as I exited with a heavy heart.

I hurried back to the apartment to get to work on my French Lit assignment. After working for two hours, I rationalized that I'd stretch out for a few minutes before getting back to my studies. It felt so good to slip into a rag-doll position on the bed. After some time I slowly stirred, struggling against the remnants of a vivid nightmare in which I was being choked. Had the irritation in my throat caused the dream? *Wouldn't you know I'd catch a cold on that train?* I thought. I lay still in the dark, swallowing again and again to lubricate my mouth and throat.

More than five minutes passed before I glanced at the clock on the nightstand and realized I had slept more than five hours. Rousing my foggy brain, I went in search of a remedy for my throat. *I can't get sick. I have to work through the night*! I drank two glasses of water and sat down at my multi-purpose kitchen table. It also served as my office desk for my Resistance work and study desk for my classes.

Forcing myself to ignore my scratchy throat, I soon lost myself in my studies again. Fortunately, I got a few more hours sleep in the wee hours of the morning before it was time to get ready for school.

Professor Charpentier did not single me out for attention during class, so he must have decided to accept my presence in his class. I sat two rows behind Renee so I could follow her at the conclusion of the class. I would feign confusion about the details of our next assignment and ask her understanding of it. Nevertheless, I kept copious notes on the lecture. Minutes seemed to advance in slow motion, and I made an effort to limit the number of glances at the clock. Nevertheless, I gave my complete attention to the professor's lecture, which cemented my decision to write the assigned term paper on the author Andre Gide's writing style. When the professor concluded his remarks, I wished he had lectured longer and given more information.

I kept my eyes glued on Renee as she started to leave the hall. She stopped outside the door, took a handkerchief from her bag, and blew her nose. I edged nearer. "The hall was chilly. I hope you're not catching a cold," I said softly.

She seemed surprised to see me. "No," she said in a breathless voice.

"I'd like to talk to you about the lecture. Let's get a cup of hot coffee at the café. It'll warm us up."

She nodded. "I can't stay long. Papa needs me at the store."

"I understand. How is he?" I asked as we walked our bikes across the street.

"His cold is going into his chest. I worry about him. Just think what would become of him if I'd let him send me away?"

"He worries about you too. You're young and should have opportunities to realize your potential—just not here under Nazi rule."

"I'm all he has." Renee shook her head. "I can't think only of myself."

"Think of how many sleepless nights he'll have worrying about you while you're here."

We parked our bikes and went inside the café. After we sat down, I tried again to tell Renee she should leave France. During a moment of silence, she stood. "I forbid you to speak of this again if you want to remain my friend. It's not your choice to make. I have to live with myself."

"I'm sorry. Please forgive me for being insensitive. Truce?" I opened my arms to her.

She accepted my gesture and clung to me. "I know you mean well," she said, her voice muffled against my shoulder.

"You wait here; I'll get the coffee." I went to the counter and placed our order, fully expecting to get the usual watered-down version served to the public. I returned with the cups and set one in front of her.

She lifted hers and sipped. Her eye opened wide. How can they serve coffee like this?" She stared at me.

"What's wrong?" I took a whiff of the questionable beverage and was startled at the delightful aroma. I took a small sip from my cup. Real, full-bodied coffee—like Colonel Dietrich had received— not the awful excuse for coffee served in most places, and also, to most of the patrons.

"I can't imagine. It must be a mistake," I said.

By the time I arrived back at my apartment, I had little motivation to start on homework. My mind went everywhere but to Andre Gide. Some of Renee's angst had infected my mood. I dwelled on Guy's unexplained absences. To his credit, he had confirmed our relationship to his mother, who seemed pleased. But he had been evasive when I asked him about wedding plans. With little Claude and me, he talked about our family and the future children we might have. I wondered why he asked me to take the train back to Paris and, more than that, why he insisted I return to my own apartment. Had he been responsible for keeping Chris and me apart? I needed a friendly ear to help me sort out my feelings. Was I being unreasonable?

Reluctantly, I opened my book and began reading and jotting notes for my assignment. After an hour of little progress, I knew what I had to do—go to Guy's and ask Nina if she knew where Aline lived. It was a long shot, but it was the only thing I could think of.

I brushed my hair and applied lipstick, just in case I saw Guy. My heart hammered and my throat burned as I pedaled along Haussmann's grand Boulevard St.-Germain—part of Napoleon III's modernization and beautification of Paris—toward Rue Notre Dame des Champs. Trembling as I stepped off my bike, I paused, took a deep breath, and slowly exhaled before starting toward the door. What would I find inside the house?

The heavy metal knocker reverberated as I lifted and lowered it a second time. *What's taking so long?* I waited and realized I wanted answers from or about Guy that had not yet been forthcoming.

After a long moment Nina opened the door. She took a step back when she saw me. "Mademoiselle! What are you doing here?"

"May I come in?"

"Well, of course."

That was good enough for me. "Is Monsieur de Laval here?"

"No. No, he isn't."

"Do you know when he'll return?"

"Désolé. I do not. You know how secretive everyone has to be these days." She broke eye contact. "May I pour a glass of wine for you?"

"Thank you, I'd like that." While she poured, I asked, "Do you by chance have the Paris address for Marquis de Maille, who recently married Aline de Fleury?"

She set down the crystal decanter and replaced the stopper. "I can be of help. Madame de Maille stopped by, left her address, and asked that I share it with you when I saw you again. She said something about a dinner date." She turned toward Guy's office. "I'll get it for you right away."

I followed her and peered inside. After all, I was Guy's fiancée, not a rude stranger. Tears scalded my eyes as they swept around the room, resting first on the equestrian trophy that meant so much to him and then the chessboard, set up ready to test the skill of an opponent. Neatly stacked papers sat to one side of the desk—not his usual habit of completing projects and filing them. He must have left in a hurry for some reason.

I stood my ground and faced Nina when she raised an eyebrow at my presence. *Guy neglects me, and now Aline doesn't even stop by the apartment to see me or leave a note. Do I mean that little?* But all I said was, "Thank you. I must be on my way." I folded the monogrammed piece of notepaper Nina gave me and returned to my apartment.

Chapter Eighteen

October 1940 – Paris

André Gide . . . Russia . . . French Equatorial Africa . . . Marc Allégret . . .

Immobilized by a high-pitched sound, my awareness slowly returned. I found myself lying on a wet sheet in a cold place. *Where? Date? Place?* The sound faded to a low-pitched hum. *American student at the Sorbonne in Paris. Oh my God, my Lit paper.*

Almost a week had passed since I'd last attended class. A raging temperature and chest congestion kept me from venturing out. I worked on my French Lit project but did little else other than sleep and worried about how I'd manage without replenishing my supplies. I prayed that Guy or Aline would stop by to see me. Or maybe Chris would materialize in Paris and check on me. Feeling sorry for myself served no useful purpose, and I tried to focus on positive thoughts. Each day I hoped to have the strength to go to the pharmacy to pick up aspirin, cough drops, and menthol rub—an assembled medicine chest of sorts.

A slight tap at my door interrupted my thoughts . . . or was I hallucinating? Yes. There it is again. *My prayer is answered*!

"Just a moment," I managed to call before a fit of coughing struck. I clung to the dressing table with one hand. My fingernails skidded along the white enameled finish while I tried to fluff my sweat-soaked hair with the other hand. A glance in the attached swivel mirror assured me I needed no rouge for my lobster-colored cheeks. On the way to the door, I struggled into one sleeve and then the other of my old chenille robe, ready to throw my arms around my savior.

A jaw-dropping shock awaited me. German Colonel Lorenz Dietrich stood there—polite, proper, and confident in his power. Today, dressed in a charcoal gray pullover sweater and slacks—no beret or uniform, thankfully—he appeared to be young, like one of the students at the Sorbonne.

I didn't invite him in, and he didn't make a move toward me. "You are unwell? Can I get you anything?" His voice was solicitous.

I didn't want him outside where my nosey landlady might

hear us; neither did I want to have him inside. My need for supplies outweighed my reticence. "Oui. Come in."

Stepping through the door, he said, "I stopped by the college to see you, and when you weren't there, I decided to look in on you. I hope you don't mind."

Under normal circumstances I would mind, but at the moment I did not. "I need something for this fever and cough." I tried to give an ambiguous answer that wouldn't offend him. I expected he'd leave when he saw that I was sick. I'd heard that the German soldiers were fanatical about their health.

"I'll see that you receive the care you need. Rest now. I'll show myself out."

Receive the care I needed? What an open-ended assurance. I'd been taken by surprise, but before I could ask, he disappeared through the door. I went back to the bedroom, pulled off the wet sheet, and lay on top of the blanket, my mind whirling while I tried to figure out how to solve my dilemma. I had to admit I was worried about the deterioration of my health. On each of the last four days, my breathing had become increasingly labored, and my temperature had risen a degree, reaching one hundred and four this morning.

After a time that seemed to be little more than a few minutes—the clock had a different take; it indicated more than half an hour had past—I heard another rap on the door. Without a thought about my hair, I slipped into my robe and opened the door.

Dietrich carried a sack in each hand. "May I?" He gestured to the table.

"Of course." I wondered what Guy would think if he could see us. It probably wouldn't faze him—he'd hosted Dietrich and other German officers at his home time after time. I put the thought out of my mind and focused on the first aid kit the colonel set on the table. I steadied myself on the edge of the table and sat.

He removed a bottle of red syrup from the kit. "Take a teaspoon of this now and another tonight. Twice a day for five days."

"What is it?"

"Prontosil . . . you probably know it as sulfa drug."

I took a dose and looked at the contents of the kit. It contained a variety of items, among them lozenges, menthol rub, and aspirin—all things needed.

By the time I looked up, he had removed a round-shaped

container from the other bag.

"Another elixir?"

"I can't tell you. It's a secret formula." He laughed and waited for my reaction before he said, "Chicken broth. It's good for you." He removed the lid and poured a small amount in a coffee cup on the table. I hadn't been pampered like this since I had come to France, and I had to admit it comforted me, in spite of my distrust of him. The aroma of the steaming bouillon stimulated my appetite. My mouth watered. I hadn't realized how hungry I was. Also, he'd brought freshly baked bread, butter, and real coffee—hard to come by unless you were German. "Thank you," I said with gratitude.

"You're welcome." He handed me two books: *Paris, France,* by Gertrude Stein, and *The Complete Works of Bulwer Lytton* that included *The Parisians* and *Pilgrims of the Rhine.*

"*Merci.*" I averted my eyes and leafed through *Paris, France.* "What a joy to read for pleasure . . . for a change."

His brow crinkled. "What do you mean?"

"I have little time for optional reading. I'm behind in my French Lit assignment and have been working on it every spare minute."

His expression brightened. "Tell me more."

"The author André Gide is the subject of my research paper. I still haven't settled on the focus." I gestured toward the stack of books on the floor by my chair. "It wearies me just thinking about it."

"Perhaps I can be of help. During my student days at Leipzig University, I studied some of Gide's works, and while in Paris I have been reading more of his writings. I'm especially interested in his brief foray as a communist."

Wouldn't you know a Nazi would want to peer into the soul of a communist? I thought. "What aspects of it?" I was well aware that psychological warfare was included in the German arsenal of weapons used to ravage the human spirit.

"Too many to enumerate, but I could share some of my notes with you."

"I don't want to trouble you, I'll keep plugging away on my own."

"It's no bother."

"What did you major in at the university?" I had to

discourage him from another visit to my apartment. He was like a dog with a rabbit in its mouth. How could I hold his interest at bay—at least until his birthday party at the Ritz?

"My father was a mathematics professor there but despaired at my lack of interest in science. Instead, I studied philosophy. Music and religion interested me, also. You may not know that Leipzig University has a long association with religious leaders."

Why is he telling me that? I wondered. In reply I said, "Many of my favorite composers are German—Bach, Beethoven, Brahms." Their names rolled off my tongue. "I love music." Although beset by many questions, I forced a yawn. Had I already lost control of the situation? This man was the enemy! An officer in Hitler's dreaded Nazi army—a member of the occupation troops that brought the proud city of Paris, and all of France for that matter, to its knees while Hitler and his soldiers marched through Napoleon's Arc de Triomphe. "I'm sorry. You'll have to excuse me. I need to rest now. Thank you for your help."

After he left I felt as if I'd been drained of energy. I managed to change the bedsheets before I crawled between them, and I was asleep before my head dented the feather pillow.

When I awoke in the dark, I wondered how long I had slept. The sheets were still dry, and I felt a little better. After turning on the lamp, I gave the thermometer several sharp snaps of my wrist until the mercury line reached ninety-eight degrees before I put it under my tongue. Four minutes later, it registered one hundred. Hallelujah! That's better. I'd be able to work on my paper.

My strength returned more slowly that I had hoped. Two days later, I knew there was no way I'd have a decent expository essay to turn in the next day. No matter the outcome, I'd have to go to class and surrender it to Charpentier.

As I pondered my situation, a tap on the door saved me from my unproductive what-if thinking.

"You're looking much better today." Dietrich handed me a bag and a large envelope.

"Come in," I said and turned to set the bag on the table while gripping the envelope with trepidation. "Thank you."

"Merci, but not today." He stood arrow straight. He did not click his heels but was still very much the German officer in his uniform. "I have a full schedule today."

"I understand." I shuddered at the thought of what he'd do after he left me.

"I'll stop back later this week," he said and was gone.

Figuratively speaking, the envelope seared the flesh it touched; yet I held onto it and fingered the clasp, conflicted by its promise. I felt sure it contained missing pieces for my less-than-stellar essay. My paper should be my work and mine alone. Reading the notes wouldn't be wrong—yet, sharing an interest with a Nazi, I couldn't deny, was dangerous! I had to be careful he didn't lull me into betrayal of my code of ethics. I thrust the envelope beneath the stack of books under my chair to read after I'd turned in the paper. I reasoned that I had to review his notes so I might gain insight into his way of thinking. My knowledge might be useful to the Resistance. I would appeal to his ego and probe for information useful to our cause. That night I rested easy, my conscience clear.

☦

The next morning my sweaty palms gripped the handlebars on my bike as I pulled into the Sorbonne courtyard, parked, and raised my eyes to the clock midway up the domed chapel before I went inside.

I arrived early for class, paper in hand, eager to turn it in for better or worse. Professor Charpentier rose as I approached his large oak desk at the front of the lecture hall. His eyes, shaded by craggy eyebrows, searched mine. "Mademoiselle Paulette Rousseau, you're looking a bit wan this morning," he said as he reached for the folder.

"Oui, I'm recovering from a pulmonary infection. My paper may have suffered too," I said and released my grip.

"I wouldn't want your grade to suffer because of your illness," he said with emphasis on my choice of words. "You have two additional days to polish it and have it back to me."

By this time groups of students had begun to take their seats. The professor returned to his desk, and I took a seat midway up the aisle in my usual row. Renee Greenberg wasn't there yet. I hoped she wasn't ill and that her father had recovered from his cold. When the lecture began, a sinking feeling lodged in the pit of my stomach. I realized I was further behind than I'd expected. There wasn't enough time to develop my paper and to catch up with the class. I'd have to ask Charpentier how I could make up for what I'd missed.

He had meant what he said about the risk of falling behind in one's assignments.

During the professor's lecture, my mind began to wander and I found it hard to keep my eyes open. I had planned to stop by the Greenberg's bookstore before going home to study, but as I struggled to stay alert until class ended, I concluded I couldn't take the time to stop at the Silver Quill.

When I got home my lunch consisted of the spoils from Dietrich—a slice of buttered bread with cheese and ham, served with real coffee. While enjoying my *repas*, I turned on the radio and, without success—too much static—I tried to pick up the BBC. I settled for the Radio-Paris broadcast. The commentator's voice came in as clearly as if in the next room.

The Vichy Government has published the Statut des Juifs, effective in all of France, its colonies and protectorates. The legislation specifies who is to be regarded as a Jew, based on the Nuremberg Laws, and expels Jews from the civil service and professions associated with culture.

He changed topics without a pause for me to process his words.

Gaullist tags have been discovered on Parisian walls.

I sat in stunned silence. "Outrageous. This has to stop," I said out loud and prayed that Guy wasn't involved with the Resistance group responsible for the graffiti. If caught, their lives would be at stake, whether they participated or not. There was no doubt about the threat to the Greenbergs. Dejected, I turned off the radio. *The Resistance needs me!* I had waffled about whether to go to Dietrich's celebration at the Ritz. Now I knew I had no choice.

Dietrich stopped by later in the afternoon. "How did your paper turn out?"

"I think Professor Charpentier will be pleasantly surprised." I smiled.

He looked pleased. *"C'est bon."* His mood changed and he said, "I'm sorry, I wish I could stay and talk about Gide, but my duties prevent it. A limousine will pick you up at five o'clock next Thursday for the party." He shook his head. "I may not see you before then."

Alone again, I took my essay from the folder and stared at it. I had two choices—turn it in without change or read Dietrich's notes and improve it. I reasoned that reviewing his notes was part of my research. I opened the envelope and pulled out at least twenty sheets of paper—twice the number of my essay. I followed his conclusions about Gide from page to page, written in his meticulous penmanship. *If I insert some of his conclusions . . .*

The next morning I pedaled by stately limestone buildings marred by huge, red-and-black Nazi flags and applauded my decision to hand in my original paper with no changes.

A small victory for me!

Chapter Nineteen

October - December 1940 – Paris

Instead of studying to catch up with the Lit class, my thoughts strayed to Renee Greenberg. She gave the impression of timidness but had a determined streak—that could be dangerous in the current anti-Jewish environment. I felt compelled to go to the bookstore and bundled up in my well-worn green winter coat and woolen scarf. While listening to the radio as I dressed, I had heard that the Vichy French police had rounded up a group of French communists. *Why? Were they involved in the Resistance?* I wondered.

I was struggling to catch my breath by the time I reached the Silver Quill. The objectionable yellow sign remained in the store window, but there were no other indications of change. Somewhat composed, I went in.

Ida flung her arms around me. "Thank God you're here."

Cold fear rippled through me. "What's happened?"

Her voice quavered. "Renee has been arrested."

"What? Why?" I'm sure my eyes flashed for freedom.

"She's accused of tagging disparaging Nazi slogans on walls at the Tuileries Gardens."

"I don't believe it." I left Ida and knocked on the wall by the open kitchen door.

Mr. Greenberg looked up. "Now you know why I wanted her to go to her uncle in New York."

"Where is she now?"

"I haven't been able to find out . . . yet. I hope you can help me."

Worried, I thought, *I really need Guy's help, but where is he?* "Is there anything more you can tell me about it?"

The stooped-shouldered man stared at the newspaper on the table and shook his head.

"I'll see what I can find out and let you know as soon as possible," I said and left the grieving man still staring at the paper. I could offer little comfort until I had news of his daughter.

An adrenaline rush took over as I retreated from the store, jumped on my bike, and rode straight to Guy's house. Surely, Nina or someone there would know something about when Guy would return or at least how to get word to him. I lifted the metal ring and brought it down with a thud. The noise startled me and would surely attract the attention of anyone in the house. A slight crack of the door appeared before it was flung open like a breached dam overwhelmed by floodwaters.

Gaston, Guy's assistant, glared at me. "You were told to stay at your apartment. I was on my way to check on you."

"Fine lot of good that would do," I said. Who did he think he was anyway? I'd have a word with Guy about his assistant as soon as I saw him. "I needed help last week. Where were you?"

"Out of the city. There's no reason to be hysterical."

I wanted to say go to hell but bit my tongue because of Renee. If I expected a modicum of cooperation, I had to indulge him. "When will Guy be back?"

Filled with self-importance, he preened and shrugged. "By the end of the month."

"Three more weeks?" My voice rose an octave.

"Or before."

Did the jerk know what he was talking about? "Let him know I need to talk to him right away. It's urgent!"

He smirked. "You can talk to me about anything."

I didn't trust him. "No, I can't. Some things are between Guy and me. You should know that!"

"You'll just have to wait then." He shut the door without a reply.

"What a waste of time," I mumbled and climbed on my bike. *Where to now? Aline—she's a wise woman.* I'd been irritated that she'd left a note with Nina for me with her new address rather than stop by my apartment to see me. Gosh, where had I put the slip of paper, given all the confusion of the last week and a half? I fumed. I'd planned to visit her before I got sick. And so much had happened in the intervening time.

The walls of my apartment seemed to close in around me. The discreet inquires during the last few days had not provided information about Renee's whereabouts, and my search for Aline's address had been fruitless. I chose to try to keep up with my schoolwork and wait a few more days before returning to Guy's house to confess to Nina that I'd misplaced the address.

The next morning I left early for school. I knew I couldn't contain myself; I would stop at the de Laval mansion before class. I had already thought it through. If Gaston answered the door, I would tell him a thing or two. He had not come by to see how I was or to bring word from Guy. I rang the bell rather than use the knocker, fully prepared for a battle. The door opened, and I found myself swept into the arms of the man of my dreams.

"*Mon rayon de soleil*, I've missed you." Guy covered my lips with kisses and held me tightly.

Ray of sunshine! He sure knew how to get to a girl. "I've missed you too," I managed to say between kisses and ran my fingers through his thick black hair. His deep blue eyes reminded me of jewels in a night sky, promising the dawn of a happier day. The last vestiges of frustration faded. I clung to him while my heart thundered. *Don't let go.*

"I'm sorry I was away so long. General de Gaulle needed me on a special assignment. You must understand that I couldn't tell you."

"I know. I guess that means you aren't going to tell me where you were?"

"That's right." He cupped my face in his hands and looked deeply into my eyes. "Do you have time for a cup of coffee and a croissant before your first class?"

I nodded and followed him to the brightly lit kitchen, where I turned to face him. That's when I noticed his prominent cheekbones. He'd lost a noticeable amount of weight. Wherever he'd been had exacted a toll! Had he been held hostage and starved? I stammered, uncertain if I should trouble him further, "I need your help." I knew I couldn't abandon our friend. "Renee Greenberg has been arrested."

His brows drew together. "How did that happen?"

"She's accused of being at the scene of anti-Nazi graffiti."

"Where is she now?"

"The police station, I think. When I inquired about seeing her, a young French officer asked whether I was family. I said I was not but was a classmate of hers. He responded that I needed to leave and get back to my studies."

Guy shook his head. "Good advice." His expression stilled and grew serious. "I'll see what I can find out."

I sat at the table, taking in every detail about him—how he held the coffee carafe, how his long, graceful fingers steadied the cup as he poured the coffee, his full lips that had kissed me when I came in, the way his hair fell across his forehead as he placed a croissant on a plate and set it in front of me.

He seemed to sense the intensity of my expression. "What is it?"

I cleared my throat. "Aren't you having anything?"

"Non, not now." He sat across from me and watched me with contemplative eyes.

"You look deep in thought. What are you thinking?" I asked.

"About you . . . and Renee."

His mood worried me. I broke off a piece of the croissant and held it for a moment. I was no longer hungry. I didn't want to eat or be alone without him. I worried that he was sick. He'd always eaten with me before.

"I have to get started for school. I'll take this with me," I said and wrapped the rest of the croissant in my handkerchief."

He nodded. "I'm sorry not to be better company this morning. I haven't slept for thirty-six hours." He stood and offered me his hand.

I put my arms around him. "When will I see you again?"

He caressed me and stroked my hair. "Soon, *mon trésor*. I'll stop by your apartment in a day or two."

"You don't have to do that. I'll stop by here."

"Non! It's too dangerous."

I couldn't accept such a vague warning. "What do you mean?"

"The Vichy Government is hell-bent on proving to the Nazis that they can control the population. We are in a life-or-death struggle for freedom."

I opened my mouth to protest, but he silenced me with kisses. And just as quickly released me. "You'll just have to trust me for a while."

I left with a sense of impending doom. I could only hope that a few days at home would restore his body and soul.

The next two days passed in classes or working on homework. I made a concerted effort not to think about Guy or Renee. I'd done what I could, and waiting seemed the only reasonable option.

Finally, the suspense ended when Guy stopped by the apartment late in the afternoon. Three rapid taps on the door and I knew before I opened it that Guy was there. It reflected his approach to life—courteous impatience. Much to my relief, I saw he looked rested and relaxed. I did wonder why he'd worn a nice suit to the police station.

"L'amour de ma vie," he whispered into my hair as he hugged me. Our lips met ever so gently as if I were as fragile as a newborn—such tenderness touched my vulnerable heart. Time stood still in the moment, unwilling to break the spell until a siren pulled us apart.

Guy released me and clasped my hands. "How would you like to have a real dinner tonight at La Tour d'Argent?"

"I'd love to." I had waited a year to hear such words. "What's the occasion?" In fairness to him, I had to admit ours was not a typical courtship—if you could call it one at all.

"We'll celebrate our time together."

"Give me five minutes and I'll be ready," I said with joy in my heart. I selected my black sheath dress and pearls to wear on this special occasion.

I don't remember much about leaving the apartment or the ride to the restaurant along St.-Germain and Quai de le Tournelle. It really hit me that we were on a dinner date when I saw the sign, *Tour d'Argent* and beneath it, *Maison fondée en 1582,* on the blue front of the establishment. Wow. The reflection of green leaves on the window glass created a colorful overlay on the golden drapery from inside the restaurant.

When we entered, Andre, the maitre d', greeted us. "Monsieur de Laval, what a pleasure to see you again. It's been too long."

"Indeed it has. More than a year."

"I still remember your table," Andre said and escorted us to a secluded table by a window.

I felt like a princess with Guy at his table with its spectacular view of Notre Dame Cathedral. It reminded me of a glorious ship under sail on the Seine. For the time being I indulged in the moment. This night we'd eat some of the rations set aside for the Germans.

Of course, we both ordered the specialty of the house— pressed duck served with white asparagus and mini, oblong rolls of bread—fine wine flowed until I seemed to float on a cloud after two refills. I don't remember if I ate the dessert.

Guy set his fork and knife on his plate. "I do love you, Paulette, even when I'm preoccupied." He paused. "I know we haven't spent much time together, and I regret it."

I basked in his words—the words I needed to hear from him.

He smiled. "I look forward to our time together during the Christmas holidays at Lamont with you and my family. It'll be a happy time for us . . . a respite from our usual activities."

"That's wonderful." I reached for his hand and squeezed it. "I miss you terribly when we're apart. You mean the world to me," I said, because I knew I wouldn't be seeing him much if the past weeks were any indication of the future.

Guy waited until we'd finished the main course to tell me that Renee had been questioned at the police prefecture and released.

"Where did she go?" I asked, as soft accordion music filled the air.

"Home or a friend's, I'd think."

While we ate our way through course after course, the sky had changed from a cerulean blue to ultramarine to black. We said our thanks and left the restaurant ten minutes before the night curfew took effect at nine o'clock.

Guy parked in front of my apartment fifteen minutes later, opened the car door for me and escorted me inside.

I heard the dead giveaway squeak of the landlady's door opening. She must not have oiled the hinges on schedule.

"*Bonsoir*, Madame," Guy said and put his finger to his lips. The door shut with a thud.

"Why did you do that?"

He chuckled. "To surprise her. I'll knock on her door on the way out."

"But I want you to come in for a while."

"You want me to be out long after curfew?"

"No, I don't. It's just that I don't get to talk to you much anymore."

"Never mind, my sweet, I'll stay the night."

At that moment I didn't care what the landlady thought. "Yes, you shouldn't be wandering the streets during the wee hours."

When we went into the apartment, I decided to invite him to sit on the loveseat in the bedroom—the hard wooden kitchen chairs were not the way to cap the evening. "We can sit in here. It will be more comfortable," I said as I led him into the bedroom.

We reminisced about dinner and how our life together should be in the future. Of course I neglected to mention that I had been sick or that Dietrich had tried to ingratiate himself, let alone that I planned to go his birthday party at the Ritz. I'd cross that bridge with Guy when the time came —if he were in Paris.

He slipped his arm around my shoulders and turned to face me. "Every minute with you is precious. I hope your landlady doesn't give you any problem about entertaining a gentleman."

"It'll be all right. I will have guests when I choose. Besides, I'm sure she knows who you are and that we are engaged." *Oh God, I have to put a stop to Dietrich's visits.*

Guy nodded. "She won't see me for a while. I leave in two days for Lyon and on to places yet to be determined."

I slumped against his chest. "You wouldn't leave the country?" Tears scalded my eyes.

He cradled my head against his chest. "I'm needed to help plan the Free French strategy for victory."

"How long will you be gone?"

"As long as it takes, up to a week before Christmas. But I *will* be back for Christmas. That's a promise."

I pulled away from him and flopped onto the bed, tears flowing freely, releasing the built-up tensions of the last six months.

So lost in feelings of hopelessness, I gasped when Guy lay down beside me and held me in his arms. He didn't say anything. We must have stayed that way for an hour as my mind raced and tried to make sense of the muddle I'd made of things. I relaxed, comforted by his presence, and began to doze.

"Keep thinking of the holidays." He gently removed his arms from around me and placed my head on the pillow. "Keep thinking about the holidays," he repeated.

"Don't go." I sat up and grabbed his arm. "Stay with me while you can. Nothing is certain these days."

Chapter Twenty

Mid-October - End December 1940 – Paris

The time of reckoning loomed on the horizon while I dressed with care for Dietrich's birthday party at the Ritz. I had less than an hour before the limousine would arrive to deliver me to Dietrich. A sense of betrayal plagued me as I slipped into my black sheath dress—the one I'd had worn three days ago with Guy for dinner at La Tour d'Argent. My reflection pouted back at me as I tried to rationalize my actions. I would endure an evening with Dietrich and his cronies for the Resistance. That's what Guy does—sacrifices our together time for the sake of France. I tried to tell myself it was the same thing . . . without success. I doubted that Guy was attending events with another woman.

I fastened my pearls and convinced myself that Guy would applaud my ingenuity when I brought back secrets let slip in moments of Nazi celebratory exuberance. Anxious, I went downstairs to wait in front of my building, and in about five minutes the car arrived.

"Bonsoir, Mademoiselle Rousseau." The chauffeur climbed from behind the steering wheel and opened the rear door. "May I pour you a glass of champagne before we get underway?" The man regarded me with evident curiosity.

Although I could use a drink to settle my nerves, I had to be careful. I'd be expected to drink champagne at the event. "Merci, non," I said and slid onto the smooth leather seat.

The driver spoke perfect French; I couldn't detect any trace of an accent. After we were underway, my curiosity got the best of me because I had a good ear for accents. "How long have you been in Paris? Your command of French is excellent."

He laughed. "It should be, I was born here."

"How long have you worked for the Ritz?" I thought I had disguised the motive for my question—to find out whether the Nazis or the hotel employed him.

"Two months."

Wasn't he clever? His answer was matter of fact but confirmed nothing about his employer. Not to be stymied, I would ask Dietrich about him.

We drove across Pont Saint Michel to the other side of the Seine and picked up Rue de Rivoli most of the way to the Place Vendôme. Lights—lights in abundance—twinkled a mesmerizing welcome to the hotel's pampered guests, just as it had done for almost forty years. I didn't have to walk across the square as Guy and I had on my first time at the Ritz; the driver delivered me to the front door. The doorman greeted me by name and ushered me inside.

Dietrich wore a black suit, white shirt, and black bow tie, and waited for me just inside the door. "*Bienvenue.* You look lovely this evening."

He looked spectacular in his black suit and white shirt, and I could easily imagine an innocuous evening with him. That thought didn't last long when I saw some of the Germans officers had come in military dress. Had he dressed to impress me, or was it a ploy to lower my defenses?

"Let's check your coat and celebrate," he said, his good humor evident.

I didn't share his festive mood. Frankly, the thought of his uniform and what it symbolized terrified me, a member of a Resistance group. When he ushered me into a large, smoke-filled, private dining room full of Germans, I felt sure I'd made a fatal mistake by coming to the Ritz a second time. The first had been bad enough, but that time I'd had Guy by my side. Around the room I saw familiar faces from that first event—officers and their female companions. A quick head count suggested about fifty in attendance.

"Champagne? Or would you like something else?" asked a waiter who balanced a tray of filled champagne glasses.

I took a glass and said, "Please bring me a brandy on the rocks." I needed to be numb as quickly as possible if I were to survive the evening.

Dietrich seemed to be aware of my feelings and led me to the head table. But after his experience with me at our first meeting, no wonder caution prevailed. "Let's sit for a moment and relax with our drinks," he suggested.

I was grateful for his sensitivity to my feelings; still, I couldn't help worrying about the tightness in my chest. *It's the smoke*, I thought. I didn't want to draw attention to myself this time. My idea was to be the fly on the wall.

Dietrich spoke softly, "This is an adjustment for you, here amongst strangers. I do understand and will wait to introduce you to some of my friends until after dinner." He stayed with me a while longer then announced, "I'm going to make the rounds before dinner."

"Of course, I'm sorry I've taken your attention from your friends."

"Not at all. I'll be back as soon as I can."

One of the women I'd seen at my first visit came and sat beside me. I'm Francine Deoui," she said as smoke billowed from her cigarette holder. "We weren't formally introduced last time. You were with Guy de Laval then."

I nodded. "Nice to meet you. I'm Paulette Rousseau. Do you come to many events here?"

"Oh, yes, I spend a lot of time with Lieutenant Colonel Heller Artur. He is quite enjoyable company."

"I don't see Josée de Chambrun here tonight."

"No, I don't suppose Colonel Dietrich is friendly with her husband, the Count. Rene is a diplomat and spends much of his time in the United States, and he's also known as quite the activist. Colonel Dietrich is an intellectual and doesn't indulge in the social scene often."

"I saw her here the night we met."

That was a different kind of gathering." An enigmatic smile spread across her cherry-red lips. "When it comes to being in the right places, the count gets around. He even goes to Washington to meet with your American President, Franklin Roosevelt, so I hear."

I concluded she wasn't going to provide the sort of information I'd hoped to glean but was grateful for her company.

She swished the last of her champagne around the rim of her glass without looking at me. "Do you see the colonel often?"

"No, I don't."

"He's quite handsome, don't you think?"

"He is." I nodded.

I didn't like her probing for information. She could want to report to her friend, German officer, Artur Heller. Up to that time, I hadn't expected to need to justify my reason for being there. "Please excuse me," I said and stepped onto the balcony nearest our table to breathe smoke-free air away from prying eyes. I stood in the shadow of a potted tree and took a deep breath to clear my head, intending to pass the last half hour before the dinner—until I caught a whiff of cigarette smoke. Two men—one a German SS officer and the other apparently French, since he was in formal wear—stepped through the open door and sat at one of several, small, glass-top tables. I moved farther into the shadows.

"The Jewess didn't go home to the bookstore," the Frenchman said to the SS officer.

"You shouldn't have let her out of your sight. That one's a troublemaker. Find her and bring her in for questioning."

"Under what charge?"

"That's for you to determine." The SS officer rose. "I don't intend to miss dinner," he said and left the other man at the table.

The Frenchman—I'd now concluded he was an officer—lit another cigarette and took a drag, his brow furrowed.

If I didn't return for dinner, I'd be in deep trouble by raising Dietrich's suspicions. The last thing I wanted was for him to start looking for me and asking questions. I blotted my moist palms on my dress and prepared to go inside. From the shadows I could see Dietrich and Francine standing near the head table in conversation.

She pointed toward the balcony. Dietrich came outside, looked around, and saw the Frenchman, who ground the tip of his cigarette into an ashtray when he caught sight of him.

The man stood. "Colonel Dietrich, what a delightful evening."

"Are there other stray guests out here enjoying the evening with you?" Dietrich asked as he eyed the two empty glasses on the table.

"Not now. I'm on my way in for dinner."

Dietrich scowled, stood for a moment, and looked the length of the balcony. As he came back toward the tree by the door, I could have reached out and touched him. He paused for a moment, took a step backward, and breathed deeply of the night air.

I froze.

Darn it. I hope he doesn't get a whiff of my Midnight in Paris perfume! I said to myself.

I waited until he went in, took his seat at the table, and engaged in conversation with Lieutenant Von Petz, Francine's companion for the evening. Then I slipped back into the room and sat down beside him. "I hope I haven't kept you waiting," I murmured.

"No need for apologies. It was I who left you unattended." He resumed his conversation with his friend for the few minutes before the first of the five courses of dinner was served.

The warm onion soup and soft background music relaxed me and seemed to have the same effect on him. "I've greeted my guests, and now you'll receive my full attention."

I nodded. "Please feel free to enjoy each of your guests."

"I am doing so, but I want you to have fond memories of your time here."

"How could it be otherwise?" My eyes met his. "Every detail is beautifully planned."

Francine watched as the second course arrived. "Yum, that looks good." She picked up one of the tiny brioche toasts with peas and ricotta in a red sauce and nodded her approval as she took a second one.

As it turned out, Dietrich and Von Petz carried on a conversation while Francine engaged me throughout the other three courses of the meal.

After a large chocolate cake was brought to the table, Champagne was served. Von Petz rose. "Colonel Dietrich is an honored soldier, as most of you know. But are you aware that he is a talented and learned man whom we all can be proud to call our friend?

"May your life be long and your successes know no limits." He lifted his glass. "Santé." Glasses clinked and a chorus of voices repeated the toast.

After Dietrich's brief remarks, the cake was served and the flow of Champagne rivaled that of water in the Seine during a deluge.

Francine's inhibitions evaporated. "How o-old are you, Herr Dietrich?" she blurted, slurring her words.

Aghast, Von Petz said to Dietrich. "Ignore her. She's doesn't handle alcohol well."

"It's not top secret. I'm thirty years old today."

The lieutenant regained his composure and announced, "Before the dancing begins, our guest of honor will join the musical ensemble on the piano for Bach's 'Concerto for Two Pianos in C minor."

Astounded, I said to Colonel Dietrich, "You're going to play one of those pianos?"

He ignored my schoolgirl exuberance. He nodded and stood. "What better way to celebrate?" he said to me before he took his place at one of the gleaming black instruments.

I had no difference with him on that score. Music was a wonderful way to celebrate. The concerto started out with a happy, lively allegro. I soared with it and no longer thought about my everyday concerns. And then the piece slowed to a contemplative adagio. I marveled that music was one of the joyful places to which we could all go in such troubled times—a salve for the restless soul. The third and final movement began at a cheerful, jaunty pace. And when it ended, my rapid pulse returned to normal.

The performance concluded to a thunderous applause. Dietrich stopped along the way to accept congratulations as he worked his way to the head table.

"Bravo! Your true calling is in music," I said when he sat down by me.

"I'm glad you enjoyed it."

As bright as he was, I knew he understood my implied reference to his military service. In my opinion it was a travesty that he wasn't free to bring joy rather than pain to others. But as fate would have it, he had been born a German and was caught up in the Nazi fervor and the promises made to the decimated German population, who had suffered severe sanctions under the Versailles Treaty drawn up by the Allies after The Great War.

After the waiters had cleared the tables, soft music began. Von Petz announced a fifteen-minute intermission, during which time the tables were rearranged to open up the dance floor. Soon the orchestral ensemble returned and took their places. After tuning up, they segued into the "Blue Danube Waltz."

Dietrich reached for my hand. "We're expected to dance the first dance." I followed him, well aware that all eyes were on us. I knew they speculated among themselves about my relationship to the colonel. I had only myself to blame for rationalizing my reason for accepting his invitation. My cheeks burned with shame as I contemplated the mess I'd made. Why had I accepted—for the Resistance, or to send a message to Guy, or because I found Dietrich fascinating?

I found him as accomplished on the dance floor as he was on the keyboard. Although I could have danced the night away, I said—with confidence that his good manners would compel him to yield to my request—"Let's sit out the next one." I wondered whether it was just a game to him. No matter what, he had given a flawless performance. He made it too easy to be comfortable with him. I'd have to do whatever it took to put an end to it, but first I desperately needed Guy's presence and his reinforcement of my resolve.

"As you wish," Dietrich said and held my hand on the way to the table.

A server awaited our return. "May I pour more Champagne for you and the lady, Colonel Dietrich?"

"Oui, s'il vous plait."

I glanced at Dietrich. "Happy Birthday." We touched glasses and sipped the golden liquid. "Your party is different than I had imagined it."

"I prefer low-key celebrations—no fireworks or show girls necessary."

"I have a confession to make. I had feared that I'd hear unpleasant topics discussed tonight."

"I'd be unhappy if you were distressed and selected my guest list with great care to avoid such an occurrence."

"I'm sure you want to spend more time with your guests, and I am a student who is still behind in her class work." I fingered my champagne glass. "I'd appreciate being taken home now."

Without hesitation, he responded, "I'll have my chauffeur drive you home right away." He saw me to the coat-check desk and then accompanied me to the limousine. "Thank you for coming," he said. From the rear window I noted he waited until we moved away from the hotel.

Dietrich had surprised me that evening. He'd played his cards close to his chest for sure.

What does he want from me?

The next morning I awoke rested and confused. At the last minute I decided not to go to class so that by Monday morning I would have had three uninterrupted days to catch up on my studies.

Splendid! I started right away. After three hours of reading and notetaking, my mind turned to thoughts of Dietrich. How could he be capable of such extremes—give or carry out cruel Nazi orders and yet bring me such joy through his music and kindness? I knew I shouldn't waste precious time on a mystery I had no way of solving—and for that matter wasn't my concern.

"What's happening in the rest of the world?" I wondered out loud as I turned on the radio to the Vichy French station. The voice of the commentator came through, static free:

The Vichy Government has publicized its edict of October fourth and fifth that forbids Jewish ownership and management of enterprises and excludes Jews from the army and professions.

An audible intake of air accompanied my thought. The Greenbergs. I grabbed my sweater from the back of the chair and rushed downstairs. I had to get to the bookstore as soon as possible. Guilt plagued me as I pedaled along the wide avenue. I should have gone first thing after I awoke.

I rushed to the store door and tentatively turned the knob, half expecting that it wouldn't open. Thankful for small encouragements, I ventured inside. Mr. Greenberg moved the ladder along one of the shelves and climbed up on it. He paused and looked around at the sound of the door closing.

He presented a cheerful face. "Bonjour, Mademoiselle," he said, his usual greeting. "You're my first customer today."

"You're here alone?"

"He nodded. "I'm up to the challenge."

"Will Ida come in this afternoon?"

"Not today."

"I'm glad you're in better health than the last time I saw you."

"So am I. This is no time to be sick."

"How's Renee?" I asked as I gave a cursory look at *David Golder*, a book about a greedy Jewish banker written in 1929 by Irène Némirovsky, a Russian Jewish novelist who, ten years later in an interview, said she regretted writing it the way she had.

"Renee is confused and staying with a friend—says she can't stay with me." His eyes met mine and slid to the title in my hands. "I miss my girl, but it's best this way."

"I'm sorry. I'd like to see her?"

"Are you familiar with Némirovsky's writings?"

"Yes. She's a good author."

"I thought she'd be okay in France as the climate changed for Jews under the Vichy Government. She's a well-recognized author. But I don't know now," he said, almost under his breath.

"You didn't say where I could find Renee."

"My, you are tenacious. If I thought it advisable, I would tell, but it isn't."

"But . . ."

"No buts. You'll just have to trust me."

"I don't understand."

"None of us do. I'm sorry, Mademoiselle."

I left the bookstore confused. Mr. Greenberg didn't act as if he wanted my help for Renee. He seemed resigned somehow. I puzzled over his attitude. What could I do to ease their plight?

I rode by way of the Tuileries Gardens to take a break from the reality of the upside-down world in which we existed. After stopping beside a bench that overlooked the pond, I sat on it and let my mind drift with no conscious effort of thought. I couldn't tell you where my mind had gone, but when I finally left that bench, I felt at peace.

During the following two weeks, I made good headway toward catching up with my classes and had no pending assignments due. Most days revolved around school and homework. My thoughts focused on the holidays at Lamont with Guy and little Claude. At his age, the boy would be growing and changing almost daily. I looked forward to being with him and watching his wonder at each new experience. When I got out of class and started for home, I often daydreamed about decorating the Christmas tree and singing carols at Lamont while Guy looked on and Claude shrieked with delight. Perhaps, I wanted to relive my own childhood memories of the few holidays spent at home with my parents in California.

I'll never forget Tuesday, December 10, 1940. A cold wind whipped the long tail of my woolen scarf. My fleece-lined winter coat failed to withstand the ferocious attack. I started to sprint from the Sorbonne courtyard toward the shelter of the metro station, in a hurry to get out of the cold and see whether Guy had written again. A week ago he had written that we'd leave on the fifteenth for a three-week holiday at Lamont.

I paused when I heard my name called.

"Paulette." Colonel Dietrich stepped forward in lockstep by my side. "I trust you have worked diligently and successfully completed your course assignments."

What's with him? Isn't he cold? I wondered. "Fortunately, the answer is yes." I said. I tightened my grip on the flailing scarf and raised my eyes enough to see that he watched me.

"I'd be honored if you would have lunch with me where we can talk freely."

A chill ran down my spine. I'd thought he'd given up on me. I couldn't afford to be blunt and offend him, so I reluctantly replied, "I can spare a hour for lunch, but I have appointments this afternoon."

He raised an eyebrow. "Good. I consider myself fortunate to claim an hour of a busy lady's time."

He led me to the waiting limousine and we drove along Rue de Vaugirard and the driver dropped us at a small restaurant on Boulevard du Montparnasse, not far from my apartment. The long, narrow interior of the establishment contained several beautifully appointed private dining alcoves.

An attractive, middle-aged woman seemed to materialize from the shadows. "*Bienvenue,* Colonel Dietrich and Mademoiselle. Two for lunch?"

"Oui," Dietrich said, and she led the way to the last table that provided additional privacy, shielded by a woodland tapestry-covered screen.

She handed us the menu and said, "Our special today is a wonderful lamb stew."

It sounded so good that I said, "I'd like the stew."

"Make it two," Dietrich said in a dismissive tone. "And a bottle of your best red wine." He seemed impatient with her. "We're in a hurry today."

"Of course, it'll be right out." She left and returned within minutes with our orders.

"She likes to talk." He poured wine and watched me as I savored the first bite of the stew before he sampled it and nodded. "The food here is always good."

"It is today," I said.

"Did you enjoy yourself at my party?"

"Yes. I especially enjoyed the music. I had no idea you were an accomplished pianist."

His brow creased and he shook his head. "Music is a salve for the soul. If things were different, I would have pursued my interest, but the war changed all that and catapulted my life in another direction."

"But surely, you had a choice in the matter."

"You don't understand how the German people suffered from the inhumane constraints and penalties of the Versailles Treaty after The Great War. I care about our people. That's why I became a soldier.

"I've studied the terms of the Versailles Treaty," I said. "I know the Germans suffered."

"Before you say any more, I'm keenly aware of the pain that is happening across Europe now." He avoided eye contact. "Two wrongs do not make a right."

"No, they do not."

"If I could change it, I would. Don't think for a minute that I don't know how destructive war is."

"I'm sorry, for so many reasons, that you find yourself a part of this." I raised my eyes to his.

"Things will be different in the future."

"Let us hope so," I said.

"Germany will win this war. We have the superior military."

That wasn't the remark I expected, and I didn't bother to answer. Nothing would have been gained, and much could have been lost. I worried he'd press me for an answer, but instead, he caught me off guard by changing the subject. "Is your engagement to de Laval a sham?"

He'd hit a nerve! "Certainly not," I said, all the while doubting it myself.

"He isn't very attentive."

"You aren't in a position to know." I regretted my retort as soon as I said it. Of course he was able to keep tabs on our time together. He knew that Guy left me alone for long periods of time and that we didn't socialize with others.

"I asked because I don't want you to get hurt."

"How very kind of you, but I'll be all right."

He looked at his watch, "Our hour has passed quickly. Let's get you to your next appointment."

"Thank you. That will be to my apartment." I worried that he might intensify his surveillance of Guy and me because of what I'd revealed about my feelings.

Chapter Twenty-One

December 20, 1940 – Paris

Doubts battered my bruised ego like the waves of a hurricane thrash a small island.

When Guy left for Lyon in mid-October—and heaven knows where else—I fell hopelessly behind in my course work. So adrift was I that the idea of dropping out of school occurred to me.

I felt imprisoned in the quicksand of uncertainty from day to day. I began to question whether anything I did mattered. Guy's departure, for Lord knows how long, left me morose. So alone was I that I even missed conversations with Dietrich. I realized I'd alienated him, and I'd lost access to inside information about Nazi plans that would help the Resistance.

The B Charpentier gave me on my paper encouraged me enough to stay in school and keep up my grades—at least until after the holidays. I clung to the hope that my holiday at Lamont with Guy would clarify our relationship when—or if—he announced our engagement to his family. Maybe then I'd have something concrete to focus on.

The days crept along at a turtle's pace. I kept reminding myself that the turtle won the race rather that the swift hare.

Three weeks later, when I passed through the doors of the Sorbonne into the warmth of sunshine, I spotted Guy near the bike rack. I ran into his open arms as we met halfway. "You're back. Thank God."

"Mon trésor." He held me tightly. "I've missed you."

"And I you. But all that matters is that we're together now."

He reached for my hands and held them. "We'll leave in the morning for Lamont. Now let's get something to eat, and then I'll drop you off at your apartment to pack and take care of whatever else you need to do."

"It won't take long to pack." I gazed into his eyes. "What I need is to be with you."

"And so you shall be for three weeks. How's that for a beginning?"

I'd been lonely for too long. All of that changed with Guy's arrival, and at the moment I was giddy with the joy of being with him. I wondered whether he really felt the same need to be with me. "Pick me up about eight and take me to your place," I told him. "We can get an early start in the morning."

He hesitated as if torn by conflicting emotions. "My love, I wish I could, but I can't."

I pulled away and fought the urge to scream or cry. "I don't understand."

Softly, his breath fanned my face, and his lips brushed mine like a candied velvet whisper. "You know I'm involved in things I cannot share with you. Paulette, how many times have I told you, you must trust me?"

Early Saturday morning, just after dawn, Guy and I departed from Paris. As soon as we were on the highway, he reached for my hand. "I want you to know that the announcement of our engagement is important to me, and I intend to do so before we get caught up in the Christmas celebrations. I'll call my parents aside so that the four of us can have time together. A few guests will have been invited for the holiday, and some of them may already be there. Later, we'll share our good news with them after the Christmas Eve dinner."

My heart skipped a beat. Soon, Guy would make a proper announcement of our engagement for the entire world to know. I squeezed his hand. "That's as it should be."

"I'm sorry we have skipped many of the enjoyable aspects of a courtship, but these are not usual times."

"This awful war isn't your fault."

"You need and deserve more from me than I can give you now. One thing is certain, I love you, and much of what I do is to protect you."

What could I say? I made no response but wished I'd been able to get my engagement ring from his safe. It would have been a concrete symbol of our commitment to each other. Was that shallow of me to place such importance on a ring?

We rode in silence for quite some time before either of us spoke again. Perhaps our private thoughts would have made for poor conversation.

"Hungry?" he finally asked.

I nodded. "Little bit. But I no longer expect regular meals."

"I think there's time for a short detour by way of Brother Roger's table," Guy said and turned off onto a small country road. He drove for about an hour before turning onto a rough track in the woods, a back way to the monastery.

Guy and I stretched after we got out of the car. The wind whipped around us, carrying the scent of nearby pine trees. The odor of pine pitch grew stronger as Brother Roger came toward us with an axe in his hand. "Salut! Comment c'est va?" he said with a warm smile.

"We're on our way to Lamont for the holidays."

"Come in. We're about to have an early supper. The days are so short this time of year." Roger took two steps to Guy's one but kept up with him. "Will you stay the night and leave in the morning?"

"Non, not this time. I'm in a hurry to get home. Little Claude and the family expect us."

"Oh, yes, sometimes I forget you have a son. Children need their fathers . . . and mothers. Pardon, I shouldn't have reminded you."

"Don't worry, Claude looks forward to Paulette's visits. She made friends with him the first time they met." Guy beamed as he spoke. I knew he loved his little boy, but I hadn't realized how important it was to him that Claude and I connected.

Brother Roger regarded me with somber curiosity. I wondered whether he knew about our engagement. He led the way to the front door and on through the cozy gathering room that led through an archway into the dining room. A roaring fire in a potbellied stove kept the room cozy.

Roger gestured toward the far side of the room and said, "Paulette, I think you know some of those ladies seated by the fireplace. You're welcome to join them while we wait for dinner."

I took that as a polite but not so subtle invitation to leave Guy with him. I joined the women and listened to their conversation as they helped the children string popcorn garlands and balls on a small pine tree. Colorful paper chains for the tree lay in a box nearby.

Guy and Roger stood around the potbelly stove, their backs to us until the soup tureen was set in its place at the head of the rustic table. Three large baguettes and dishes of butter were strategically placed along the length of the table. I sat beside the British woman I'd met at the monastery in the summer, and Guy sat beside Roger.

Brother Roger waited for everyone to be seated before he bowed his head and said, "Let us pray. Father in heaven, hear our prayer. May there be bread for the hungry, love for the unlovable, healing for the sick, and protection for thy children. Bless this food for the nourishment of our bodies and the good health of those present. We pray for the forgiveness of sinners and an abundant life in Christ. In the name of Jesus Christ, we pray. Amen."

"Amen," those of us around the table echoed.

While bowls of chicken vegetable soup were passed to us, my lady friend asked, "Will you join your gentleman friend's family for the holidays?"

"Yes, they've graciously included me. And you, will see your family in England?"

"No, my family and I are estranged. They don't approve of our life choices."

"That's a shame."

She shook her head. "I had to choose between my husband and my parents' plans for me. I'm living the life I chose right here."

I glanced at Guy and Roger. When one of them took a bite of soup, the other talked and then took a sip of wine—an efficient use of their time together. There was a rhythm to it, and I wondered if it was a coordinated effort.

The meal concluded with fresh apple slices and cheese. Then it was time for Guy and me to say au revoir to our friends. Guy started out ahead to the car but Roger slowed by the door and placed a folded piece of letterhead paper in my hand. I opened and read it. *Should you need to get in touch with me by telephone, leave a message at this number.* I wondered whether he knew something I didn't about Guy. On our way across to the car, he said, "Take good care of him."

At the car Guy said to us in a teasing way, "It's cold out here. What's with you two slowpokes?"

Roger gave a hardy laugh. "You better learn to share her attention." He stepped away from the car and waved as we pulled away.

December 1940 – Chateau Lamont-sur-Loire

The entire drive from Paris had gone without a hitch, much to Guy's relief, and we arrived at Lamont late Monday afternoon, more than two hours after sunset. Darkness had surrounded us as we drove through the forest to the chateau. I suppose I should have expected to arrive in the dark, as the shortest day of the year had occurred the day before. The saving grace was the clear, star-studded sky overhead. However, it was still a relief when we reached the chateau's grounds and its well-lit courtyard.

I recognized the Marquis de Maille's 1934 green Austin-Healey with its oversized steering wheel parked near the chateau's front doors. "Aline's here," I exclaimed, surprised and thrilled that I'd get to visit with her.

"How do you know?" Guy pulled in beside their car.

I pointed to my right. "That's the marquis's car."

"What a nice surprise." He got out of our blue Renault—drab in comparison to the marquis's car—and opened my door. He reached into his pocket and handed me a familiar box—my engagement ring.

"Shall I wear it now?" I asked, my fingers crossed.

"It's up to you."

"Okay, I will."

Guy opened the box, slipped the ring on my finger, and kissed me. The joyful glow I felt outshone the full moon overhead as Guy pressed me next to his heart. The spirit of the season filled me in that magical setting. I wished our fairytale would never end, but I knew all too well the uncertainty that lay ahead.

"You're trembling. Let's get you inside where it's warm." Guy put his arm around my shoulders as we started toward the house. "I'll come back for our bags later."

"I didn't think you used this part of the house anymore," I said as, once inside, Guy led me past the grand staircase to the medieval part of the house.

"We don't very often."

A roaring fire in the floor-to-ceiling limestone fireplace in the great hall snapped and crackled a warm welcome as we stepped through the door of the medieval *la salle du conseil.*

He elaborated, "It's used for special occasions such as *Noël en Chateau Lamont-sur-Loire,* a centuries-old tradition that begins on December twenty-second or twenty-third with a banquet and gift exchange here in the hall for our staff and their families. On Christmas Eve, family and friends gather at nine o'clock for *le réveillon de Noël,* the celebration of Christmas dinner, and to open Christmas presents before midnight mass in the chateau's chapel.

"It's wonderful. I love it," I said. "I'm learning while living it." A magnificent cedar Christmas tree occupied one corner of the room beneath high mullioned windows and filled the room with the evergreen scent of Christmas. The tree almost reached to the strong-beamed ceiling. Rectangular rectory tables stretched along the opposite wall, at which I imagined the lord and lady of the manor had held many banquets throughout the centuries.

Across the room, strains of "Silent Night" came from an old, floor-model Victrola. Guy kept his arm around my shoulders as we sought the warmth of the roaring fire at the far end of the room.

"Look who's here, Guy . . . with Paulette!" Aline rushed forward, first kissing Guy and then me on each cheek. I wondered whether she greeted in the order of her affection. I knew she thought the world of Guy.

Monsieur and Madame de Laval gathered around us and introduced us to two other couples, one about their age and another, a young couple with two children. The priest who had performed Aline's wedding ceremony at Chateau Fleury carried on a conversation with the Marquis de Maille at some distance from the rest of us. We visited while the butler and his assistants scurried about, removing the last bits of Christmas wrap and ribbons remaining from the staff dinner and presentation of gifts.

Madame de Laval, elegant in a simple, deep green, velvet gown, greeted me. "Bienvenue. I'm pleased you're here with Guy." Her eyes lingered on my engagement ring. "The children have retired for the night. Your presence will be a wonderful Christmas gift for little Claude. He speaks of you often."

"He's precious. It'll be fun to watch his unabashed joy at Christmas."

"I'm sure he'll be excited. But I won't detain you. You both must be more than ready for dinner and to call it a day."

I looked around for Guy and saw that his father had joined him near the fireplace. By the time I worked my way there, they had vanished, so I decided to go to the powder room near the staircase before dinner. As I passed the morning room, I heard Aline's and Guy's voices. I paused and was pondering whether to go in before or after my main stop when I heard my name.

"You better find out what Paulette is up to with Colonel Dietrich," Aline said.

"What do you mean?" Guy's tone carried a challenge.

She and the colonel frequent a little café near the Sorbonne."

"Frequent? Come on, Aline."

"More than once, and that's not all. She sat at the head table beside him at his fancy Ritz birthday party."

"Wonder how she snagged that invitation?" Guy muttered with a chuckle. "She's scared to death of him."

"I warn you, don't make light of it. She danced with him several times and sat in rapture at his musical performance. People are beginning to talk."

"I'll speak to her about it," he said.

I ducked behind a curio cabinet before they saw me on their way out. I felt betrayed—that the woman I considered my best friend gossiped behind my back. *What are you trying to do to me, Aline?* After they were out of sight, I couldn't delay a visit to the powder room any longer.

By the time I reached the great hall, the de Lavals and most of their guests were already seated at the table. I slipped into my place beside Guy, not knowing how Aline's revelation had affected him. Would he change his mind about our engagement announcement?

He never failed to surprise me, and this was one of those times. He lifted my left hand and held it in front of his parents. "Paulette and I are engaged."

"That's wonderful," his mother said. "But I'll never understand why you kept it from us for so long."

"Congratulations to both of you," Major de Laval said. "It'll be good for you and Claude. Maybe we'll see more of you now."

"When will you marry?" Guy's mother asked. "Of course,

you'll wed here in the chapel," she added without waiting for an answer.

Guy shook his head. "We haven't set a wedding date. Paulette is an *Americaine*, and as such enjoys some protection during the occupation of our country. It would be selfish to take that from her."

"I see," Madame de Laval murmured and turned to her husband. "We'll have to wait and see."

What does that mean? I thought. *Has Guy announced other vague engagements?* My appetite vanished. The bowl of hardy vegetable beef stew no longer appealed to my churning stomach. I just wanted the evening to end so that Guy and I could sort out the significance of our relationship, probably, the next morning when clearer heads were sure to prevail. Efforts by Guy and his mother to draw me into the conversation garnered only, "Oui," "Non," or a nod.

"Please excuse me for the evening," I said at last. "I'm not very good company tonight after our long trip. Tomorrow, I'll be a new person."

"Of course, how thoughtless of me," Guy's mother turned to her husband. "Travel these days is quite an ordeal, I hear."

"It is," Guy responded. "Please excuse us both. Give our apologies to the guests."

"By all means. Have Yvette show Paulette to her room," Madame said.

Guy eased my chair from the table and hooked his arm through mine on our way out. I noticed Aline shake her head when Guy glanced in her direction.

"You should have told me you were tired," Guy chided me. "We didn't have to attend the dinner. The main events take place on Christmas Eve."

"I hope I didn't spoil the evening for you."

"Not at all. Remember, I've been on the road for days too."

I laughed. "So you have."

"Will you need Yvette's services tonight?" Guy asked.

"No, I don't know of anything I need, that is, if you know whether I'll be in the same room I had when I was here in September."

"You will. Maman thinks of it as your room now."

He accompanied me up the grand staircase and stopped by the door of my room. "Bonsoir, ma chérie." His lips touched mine as lightly as a summer breeze, and then he was gone.

Chapter Twenty-Two

Christmas 1940 – Chateau Lamont-sur-Loire

When I awoke Christmas Eve morning, I marveled at how well I'd slept. It should have been a perfect morning. Guy had announced our engagement and restored my confidence in his intentions, and his parents had been excited for us. But I couldn't get past Aline's attempt to drive a wedge between Guy and me. What had she hoped to accomplish? I'd already told Dietrich I wouldn't meet with him anymore.

Of course she hadn't known that, so what had I expected? I felt she should have asked me about it rather assume the worst. I tried to see it from her point of view and supposed that to her I seemed to be the one in the wrong. Worse yet, she might wonder whether Guy had a traitor in his midst. What power did I have to put her mind at ease? I could think of none.

I pulled myself together and dressed for the day, and Guy's familiar tap on the door buoyed my mood. It was Christmas Eve Day, and little Claude would be thrilled. My pulse raced at the thought of the holiday celebrations that lay ahead—just like it had when I was a child.

"It's ten o'clock," Guy said when I opened the door. "You've missed breakfast."

"At least I slept well." I shook my head. "I guess I'll have to wait for lunch."

"Non. I smuggled a croissant and coffee for you." He stepped outside the door and returned with a tray.

God bless him. He hasn't given up on me. "Thank you." I took it from him. "Come in and sit. I won't be long."

He sat across from me while I savored my *petit déjeuner*, the typical French breakfast. He had a glow of contentment that I hadn't seen since the German threat changed our lives.

"I promised Claude that you and I would help him decorate the Christmas tree. I think he's more excited about you than he is the tree."

"I can't wait to see him," I said as I contemplated the three of us together as a family. I took the last bit of the croissant and set the tray on the bedside table. "Let's go." We scampered down the stairs like two children, full of wonder, as I had been on Christmas mornings in California.

Yvette held Claude's hand at the bottom of the stairs as he strained to get away and meet us halfway. "Papa, Papa," he shrieked in delight. He broke free and Guy hoisted him onto his shoulders. Suddenly shy, Claude hid his face against the back of his father's head and peeked at me.

"What are you doing? Say hello to Paulette," Guy prompted.

The little boy regarded me from under long dark eyelashes. "Bonjour."

"Bonjour," I said. "Are you excited about Christmas?"

He nodded. "You can help with the tree."

"Merci. That'll be fun."

He squirmed and demanded, "Down. I want down."

"Okay," Guy said.

Claude took my hand and pulled me along the passage towards the great hall.

"Claude seems to know where he's taking us," I said as Guy and I linked arms.

"He does. I regret that I wasn't the one to teach him." His somber expression revealed the depth of the anguish he'd put into the words.

"You are a loving father. When things get better, you'll be with him and guide him."

Claude paid us no mind and continued to jabber about Christmas decorations for the tree. When we reached the great hall, we allowed the little boy to set the agenda.

Yvette called to us. "There you are." She had already laid out red ribbons for us to attach to the dark green cedar tree and red apple ornaments for Claude to hang, with the help of the two of us. We worked with Claude and finished hanging the red ornaments.

"Papa Noël," Claude shouted.

"Not now." Guy nabbed his son's hand. "Tonight, before you go to bed, I'll bring you back to leave your shoes filled with carrots by the fireplace for Père Noël's donkey."

"Time to get ready for lunch." Yvette took Claude by the hand. "Say bye to Papa and Paulette."

Claude followed without protest. Apparently, he knew better

than to argue—or was just looking forward to his lunch with his Papi and Mamie.

I continued to place ribbons on the lower part of the tree, and Guy climbed a sturdy stepladder to arrange other ribbons on the top branches.

He looked down at me, his eyebrows slanted in a frown. "I asked Aline to join us here at eleven thirty, but before she arrives, I want you to know she's worried about your association with Colonel Dietrich and spoke to me about it."

"I accepted an invitation from Dietrich in order to get inside information for the Resistance and, I must admit, partly because sometimes I feel you don't value my help."

"That was not a wise decision. When we went to the Ritz together, I had misgivings. I know you were uncomfortable. I can't understand why you would go there unaccompanied, especially after your strong reactions the first time."

"I wanted to prove to you that I could be useful to the Resistance."

Guy groaned and shook his head. "Oh, no. I take responsibility for getting you into this, but I must ask that you not do it again. I assured Aline that I had the utmost confidence you could be trusted."

"How could she question my loyalty?" I asked.

He sighed, climbed down from the ladder, and crossed the room to get another box of ornaments. "I'll let her explain."

Aline must have slipped into the room while I finished hanging the ribbons on the tree. I turned at the sound of her voice.

"So you want to know why. I'll be glad to tell you. Your intentions are dubious when you cavort with a Nazi officer. You can't have it both ways. It's an either/or proposition—with us or against us. And I have no doubt your German friend agrees with me. You're dancing a perilous gavotte."

The intensity of her remarks held a truth I was loath to hear. "I gather that, at best, all I proved is how desperate I am for Guy's attention."

Guy draped his arm around my shoulder and said to Aline, "You were pretty harsh. I trust Paulette." He drew me closer. "Blame me! I haven't been there for her nor kept her informed so that she knows what I'm doing. I understand how this could happen. Aline, you of all people should give her the benefit of the doubt. If ever, now is the time to put aside your indignation and rely on your psychic gift. You'll know what is in her heart, as well as I do."

"Guy, I don't want to argue with you," Aline replied. "I suppose you may be right. It's just that the stakes are so high. My gut feeling is that the outcome of this whole thing is bad."

Guy released me and took both of Aline's hands while he spoke to her. "I couldn't ask for a dearer friend, and I respect your view of things, but in this case I know Paulette loves me, and I love her. She wouldn't do anything deliberately to hurt me or the cause."

Aline bit her lip and nodded. She laid her head on his shoulder for a moment and looked up at him and then at me. "I trust your assessment and want what is best for you, Guy de Laval," she said.

"Merci, mon amie." Guy kissed her on the cheek and held her to his chest. "The four of us will sit together tonight at dinner."

"Thank you, but I can't. The marquis wants to get started to Lyon by noon. We'll stop at Chateau Fleury to leave gifts for the staff and Papa before we start home." Aline handed a red, tinsel-wrapped package to Guy. "For your son. He's adorable."

"Merci, that wrapping paper is sure to get Claude's attention."

"Before I leave, let's set the date for Paulette and you to have dinner with my husband and me when we all return to Paris."

"Oui, after the New Year. We'll be back around the twelfth, allowing for uncertain travel delays," Guy said. "I go on an assignment the eighteenth."

Aline removed a pen and a small calendar from her purse. "All right, dinner at seven on Wednesday, January fifteenth."

"We'll be there."

Guy and I accompanied the de Mailles to their car later that afternoon.

Aline hugged me and, when inside the Austin-Healey, said, "We'll make the most of our time together in Paris."

We said our goodbyes and waved to them as they drove away. Once back inside the chateau, Guy asked, "Ready for Claude, or do you want a sandwich first?"

"I'm hungry," I said sheepishly. I chided myself again for having missed brunch while I slept.

Guy rummaged around in the refrigerator and made a ham and cheese sandwich for me. He sat opposite me while I ate and enjoyed a second cup of coffee. "I fear Maman is giving us all her precious coffee, and who knows where she'll get more. But I am truly enjoying the luxury." He took another sip and sighed in pure enjoyment. "Yvette sat up most of the night with Claude. He had an earache, so he won't be going outside for a while."

"How is he this morning?"

"Much better, but all the more reason we'll have to insist he stays in for a few more days at least."

I shook my head. "He's going to be so disappointed. He always talks about the ponies and horses."

"I know. I think it hurts me to have to say no more than it does him." Guy took a deep breath. "Are you ready?"

"I think so," I said, a little afraid to share the indulged child's frustration.

"He'll be in the morning room with his mamie and papi." Guy said as we left the kitchen.

As soon as we arrived and sat down, Claude abandoned his grandfather and jumped onto my lap. Pleased to be the object of his attention, I welcomed him with open arms.

He reached up and ran his fingers along my cheek. "I want to see the horses," he said. "You promised."

"Non, not until you're better," Guy said with finality.

Claude clung to me and pleaded, "Tell Papa you want to see them too."

"It's too cold outside." Guy pointed to the window. "See, it's beginning to snow." He held out his arms to his son.

"Non," Claude said and clung to me.

I could tell that Guy was displeased at his son's preference. He stood and took Claude from me. "All right, but you'll have to bundle up and come right back inside after we see them."

He and Claude left the room and returned a few minutes later with Claude in several layers of clothing and a coat and hat. Guy held him inside his own long winter coat. "Do you want to come or stay where it's warm?" he asked me. "We won't be outside long."

I wanted to go but would have to go upstairs to get my coat and scarf. I knew Guy wanted to make a quick trip of it. "I'll wait. Maybe in a day or two, when we have nicer weather and Claude is better."

The child's big brown eyes watched me as he and his father left the room.

Madame de Laval sighed, tears glistening in her eyes. "That's what happens to a desperate father who loves his son too deeply. He'll do anything to try to make it right for him."

Guy returned a short time later without his son and sat beside me. "I took Claude to Yvette. He'll have time for a short nap before we take him back to the great hall."

I knew I'd done the right thing to give Guy time alone with his son. Claude was a clever child and had tried to play me against his father to get his own way. But I looked forward to sharing the Christmas Eve tradition with father and son—as an observer, for now. Perhaps, the future would bring a change.

"What traditional activities will Claude participate in this evening?" I asked.

"We'll take him to the great hall after his dinner to leave his shoes by the fireplace for Papa Noël. After that I'll read *Twas the Night Before Christmas* before Yvette takes him to bed."

"I love that story. On Christmas Eve when I was a child, I'd set my small chair by the hearth and then climb onto my mother's lap while she read it to me. By the time I could read, I'd memorized the words and would recite it for my daddy … My voice broke. "The Christmases he was home, that is." My efforts and love for my father were unrequited.

"Your memories of Christmas don't sound much different than mine," Guy said. "When Claude is older, he'll attend midnight mass with us in the chapel."

I turned to Guy. "Tonight is going to be such fun. I can hardly wait."

The last light of day had faded in the western sky by the time Claude finished his dinner and we began Christmas Eve with him. Guy and I each held one of the rambunctious child's hands to assure we all arrived in the same place.

"Let go," Claude said and struggled to break free when we entered the hall. I dropped his hand.

In one fell swoop, Guy lifted him to his shoulders and carried him beyond the Christmas tree to the hearth. "Now, what are you going to leave Papa Noël?" he asked his son.

"Some care-otts."

I laughed. "What? No cookies?"

"Non. I want toys. Papa Noël wants care-otts."

I concluded that someone must have told him to eat his carrots to be like Papa Noël.

You can imagine my surprise when Guy pulled out a small bunch of carrots from his jacket pocket and handed them to Claude.

Yvette stepped forward and gave Claude a small pair of shoes. The boy took them to the hearth and set them down. With much fanfare, he counted out, "*une, deux, trois*," two times as he placed three carrots in each of the shoes, to the delight of his onlookers.

Yvette started to pick him up, but Guy stepped between them and held fast to Claude's hand. "You stay here and watch the play," he said to her. "Paulette and I will take him to bed."

"Merci, Monsieur de Laval," she said with a big smile. "I helped the children practice for the play."

Claude reached for my free hand as the three of us left the festivities.

"Is the play part of the Christmas tradition?" I asked Guy.

"Yes, the children take an active role in the celebrations before dinner. Afterward, the younger ones retire for the night. Those ten or older take part in the rest of the activities, including the midnight mass."

As we approached Claude's room, he dashed ahead and jumped on his bed.

"Get off there! Where are your pajamas?" his father asked.

Claude unzipped the front of a stuffed tiger and pulled them out.

With feather touches, Guy helped his son get out of his clothes and into his pajama shirt and pants. He pulled back the covers and patted the sheet. "In you go." He glanced up and saw me watching.

"You're very good with him. He's lucky to have a father who takes an interest," I said, an ache in my heart for the love I hadn't received from my own daddy.

He nodded. "He keeps me going." He swallowed hard. "I want him to live in a better world than his grandfather and father have," he said in a whisper.

Unperturbed, Claude said, "Papa, read me a story."

After Claude was tucked into bed, Guy moved a chair next to the bed and began to read from *Twas the Night Before Christmas.* He paused to show Claude the illustrations on each page.

Claude's eyes gradually began to close, but when Guy finished the story, his eyes fluttered and popped open. "Again," he demanded.

Guy handed me the book. "Your turn."

I stood and closed the book. Guy frowned while Claude whimpered, but I placed a finger on my lips. "Do you want to hear the story or not?"

Claude's head bobbed up and down.

I'd done nothing to settle him for the night. But I had to continue with my ill-advised plan to dramatize the story from memory. I kept my eyes on Claude, afraid to find disapproval in Guy's eyes, but when I finished, he applauded my performance. Son, like father, clapped, "Merci, P'ette," Claude said and closed his eyes.

A thrill ran through me. Claude had spoken directly to me by name, albeit an abbreviated form. I liked the sound of it. I'd garnered the love and attention of both the father and son, whom I loved dearly.

"Pet is it?" Guy smiled at me. "It suits you well." He rubbed his son's back until the drowsy child slept then he kissed Claude's cheek, rose, and turned to me. "We have plenty of time to dress for dinner. I'll stop by for you in thirty minutes. Sound good?"

"Oui."

I was fully dressed and waiting when Guy came for me. On our way into the dining hall, he stepped in front of me and paused by the open door.

"Did you forget something?" I asked.

"Not exactly. I had to wait for the right time," he said, glancing upward.

My eyes followed his—mistletoe hung above our heads.

Before I could say a word, his lips silenced mine. I sensed eyes upon us, but when he released me, I saw nothing to confirm my suspicions.

Pushing away my suspicious nature, I smiled up at him. "Is this the way you intend to announce our engagement?"

"Mon trésor, there is a belief that a kiss under the mistletoe on New Year's Eve tells of happiness and prosperity in the New Year. That's my wish for us."

"That's beautiful. But it's not New Year's Eve yet."

"Good. We'll have lots of time to practice beforehand."

I thumped his arm. "Aren't you clever?"

After my senses returned to normal, the sights, sounds, and aromas in the hall thrilled me anew—I seemed to be transported to ages past. Red and white candles stood tall in their silver candelabra, casting pale shadows along the rectangular, monastery-style tables. The minimal lighting overhead illuminated the room just enough to avoid mishaps. Guests gathered around the fireplace began to move to the tables as if they'd been waiting for us, or I suppose it could have been for the clock to chime nine.

Guy and I greeted guests on our way to our places beside Major and Madame de Laval to partake of a bountiful feast. After devouring salad and soup, I chose turkey while Guy selected ham; however, we each took a serving of mashed potatoes and green beans, topped off with a slice of Yule log cake—*la bûche de Noël*—made of sponge cake and buttercream rather than the more colorful chocolate one.

After dessert, just before the guests gathered around the fireplace to share Christmas stories and legends, Guy said to his parents, "Paulette and I are going to look in on Claude." As we walked past one of the tables, a woman said, "The lovebirds want time alone."

Guy stopped a moment. "Madame, you are most perceptive."

I'd sensed his passion all evening and yearned to be joined with him in the sanctity of marriage. He'd known the freedom to love between man and wife. Why should he deny it to us?

Guy slipped his arm around my waist. "It's nice to get away for a while," he said as the din from the hall diminished the farther we moved away along the hallway.

"It is. But I like the group's festive mood, too."

When we reached Claude's room, he was sleeping, his breathing normal. Guy placed his hand on the child's forehead. "Thank God his temperature is normal." He smoothed his son's hair and turned to me. "There's plenty of time for us to enjoy a glass of wine before we rejoin the guests."

We headed to the small salon where afternoon tea or after-dinner liqueurs were usually served. Guy poured each of us a glass of Chambord berry liqueur and placed them on the table by the loveseat. We sat together and he slipped his arm around my shoulders. "I didn't want to say anything while we were in Claude's room about your reaction to my reading of the Christmas story and, later, your recitation of it."

"What do you mean?"

"You looked sad, like you were going to cry. What you said about Christmas and how you reacted were in conflict."

I sniffed. "I didn't think you noticed. I didn't want you to. It's just that it reminds me of Daddy."

"He died in an accident, didn't he?"

I nodded and wiped away the tears before they rolled down my cheeks. "It's not that. I tried everything I could to please him and always failed miserably. It makes me sad at times—times when I should be happy. I'm sorry to be a wet blanket on this beautiful Christmas Eve when you and Claude make me so happy. I felt your love and appreciation in Claude's room. It means everything in the world to me, and I love you so very much."

Guy kissed me on the cheek. "Mon trésor, I understand more than you might realize. Lay your head on my lap so I can look into your eyes while we talk about it."

I did as he asked. I knew I was the luckiest girl in the world and shouldn't allow the past to cast shadows on the present. "You're an amazing father. Oh, that every child had one like you."

"You think so?" Guy smiled. "My father didn't know how to show love to me when I was growing up. He only saw me as a continuation of the de Laval legacy. I often felt that I disappointed him, but I've had to learn to live with things as they are. When he sent me to military school, I became confident about my worth as a man and trusted my own decisions. I didn't crave his approval as I had earlier.

"If he had died, it might have made it more difficult for me. I

168

don't know, but for sure I want Claude to know I love him and appreciate him for who he is.

"And that brings me to you. It took courage to leave your homeland and come to France. It was a decision you must have been confident about. Don't sell yourself short. You're an amazing woman, and I love you for who you are."

I sat up, snuggled against his chest, and raised my lips to his. My heart raced as contentment banished all thoughts of Christmases past. I whispered in his ear, "I vow that I will live in the present and anticipate with joy our future together from this point forward."

"In that case, we better get back to the present Christmas celebrations."

I sat up and checked my hair and face in the mirror above the fireplace.

Guy stood behind me and watched. "No one will guess you've spent our time together soul searching."

I laughed. "Time well spent."

"I'm not sure the lady who imagined the escape of the lovebirds would agree," Guy said as we started back to the hall.

As we entered the great hall, Guy stopped under the mistletoe and kissed me. "We have to play the part of lovebirds," he teased.

A few minutes after the clock struck the half hour, Monsieur and Madame de Laval rose and led the guests through a sturdy oak door on one side of the fireplace. I'd been curious about it and concluded it went to a smaller meeting or storage room.

When I stood to wait in line, Guy said, "There's no hurry. Tradition requires that I'm the last one to enter the chapel before the procession begins."

"Why is that?" I asked somewhat impatiently.

"Because I'm the de Laval heir apparent."

"I see. It's all about protocol." I said as I settled down in my chair. "Where did all these extra people come from?"

"This isn't a normal Christmas, given the German patrols in Tours. Many of the citizens don't want to chance going to the cathedral."

"I don't blame them, but will we get to the chapel by

169

midnight?"

"I think so. If not, I'm sure the priest will wait for us."

I glanced at the clock when I estimated that more than half the room had emptied. "I guess there's no point standing just to inch along like centipedes."

Guy stood and pulled out my chair. "It's okay, considering we'll do a lot of sitting during Mass," he said and clasped my hand.

I leaned against his chest as we waited to step through the door onto the narrow, red tile-covered floor of a passage that seemed to go on forever. Every so often a torchlight sconce illuminated the limestone walls until we reached an oak door that opened into the chapel.

Guy led me to the front, where we took seats beside his parents—reserved seats. I focused on the three, narrow, stained glass windows that soared above the altar, relieved to be seated and less the focus of attention that I'd been while we made our way down the aisle past the twisted columns.

When the service began, I felt the group unity on a universal level. After the service of communal chanting and prayer, the true meaning of Christmas stayed with me while we departed.

On Christmas morning I awoke filled with the excitement of sharing Claude's wonder of this special day. I already felt a kinship with the family. It didn't take me long to dress, and once I was ready, I opened my door and waited in a chair by the window for Guy and Claude. We three would go together to the great hall, where Claude would open his gifts before the brunch, and the remaining packages would be distributed.

Father and son arrived about ten minutes later, heralded by Claude's voice carrying down the hallway. "Hurry, Papa."

Finally, I thought. I met them halfway. "Merry Christmas to my two favorite boys," I said. I kissed Claude on the cheek and Guy on the lips.

Guy looked as happy as I felt. "Merry Christmas to you, mon trésor."

Claude giggled. "Non, that's P'ette."

Guy patted his son. "One day you'll understand."

One day soon I hoped he'd also understand the love of *two* parents. And so it was at that moment that I knew I had to convince Guy we shouldn't delay our marriage. The question seemed to be whether to broach the subject during our happy time at Lamont or after our return to Paris.

Chapter Twenty-Three

January 1941 – Chateau Lamont

Guy and I stayed poised, hands joined, under a sprig of mistletoe hung from one of the rafters close to the door into the great hall. We waited for the signal, and at the stroke of midnight, we shared a prolonged kiss. I leaned back, Guy supporting me, lips locked, before we performed our oft-practiced love dance—our particular embellishment of the traditional ritual for happiness and prosperity in the coming year. A burst of applause from an appreciative audience and shouts of "Bravo, *bonne année!*" rewarded us. We joined in song with the guests and sang "Ce N'est Qu'un Au Revoir"—goodbye to the tune of "Auld Lang Syne." The words of the song were particularly sad, given the uncertainty of the separations I knew we would experience at the end of our holiday together. I dreaded time in Paris without Guy there too, and blinked back tears as we started to make the rounds, air kissing the guests and wishing them a Happy New Year.

By the end of the week, Claude appeared to be completely recovered from his congestion. His temperature had been normal for four days, and now he was demanding we take him outside for a trial run on his new sled, a gift from Père Noël.

"Today, Papa!" Claude stomped his foot. "Before snow all gone."

Guy looked at a loss as to how to refuse the little boy's demand. He turned to me. "What do you think?"

Claude's gaze held mine, pleading with me.

"Oui. Look at him. He's ready. Wait here, I'll get him bundled up in his coat, cap, and gloves," I said as I hustled Claude out of the room. Much to my surprise, Guy didn't protest. Needless to say, the child willingly accepted my assistance with his heavy outerwear, contrary to his usual insistence that he could dress himself—pretty good for a child who wouldn't turn three for another four months.

Guy met us by the door with the little red sled, ready to go. I put on my long green coat, bundled my head in a red wool cap, and worked my fingers into leather gloves. I hoped this first outing would be a short one.

"This way," Guy said as he handed me the sled before picking up his son. He took us across the drawbridge onto the sloped driveway in front of the chateau and selected a gently sloping portion that leveled out for a distance. "Ready?" he asked Claude as he lifted him, and the two of them sat on the sled. He grasped the pull rope and ran through how to steer and how to brake before they took the run. "You see, I can turn it this way and the other way to change direction. The runners on the bottom slide along the snow."

"Ready?" I asked and gave them a push. Off they went to Claude's squeals of delight.

"We make a good team," Guy said to me after he'd pulled Claude and the sled back up the slope for the tenth time. "But I think it's time to go inside now."

"I not." Claude's protest went unheeded.

"If you don't make yourself sick again, we'll take you for a sleigh ride in a few days," Guy promised.

"Papa, I love you," Claude said as his father tucked him inside his coat while I pulled the sled.

By the time we made it back to the morning room, Monsieur and Madame de Laval had arrived and were listening to the BBC on the radio. A fire blazed in the fireplace, and the room felt hot to me after being outside.

Madame's brow creased as she held out her arms for her grandson. "Guy, are his clothes dry?"

"Don't you trust me, Maman, to care for my own son?"

"Of course I do," she said, while taking off Claude's coat and hat and examining his clothing. "Let me get him out of these things."

"Non, Paulette wants to do it!" Guy said. "We'll take him upstairs to Yvette."

His mother turned her back to us and rejoined her husband. She said something to him, but I couldn't hear her.

The tension between mother and son surprised me. She was generally so gentle and loving to both Guy and Claude. I'm sure she acted out of concern for their best interest. I wished I could make it right with her. Sometimes, her son could be oblivious to the effect of his actions, I knew from personal experience. Yet, I understood that he loved his son and wanted to be with him and make decisions concerning him as much as possible.

Things will be easier for both of them when we are married, I thought.

"Where have you been?" Yvette asked Claude while I helped him into fresh clothing, although the need didn't exist except in his grandmother's mind.

"Ride in snow. Going to go with horse and sleigh."

"You are? What fun. Are you ready for lunch?"

His head bobbed up and down.

Guy and I gave Claude a kiss and a hug before we left them. As we walked down the hall, Guy paused. "Thank you, mon trésor. You're a natural with Claude."

"My babysitting experience helped."

"It's nice to have someone besides Maman who understands children. Of Course, Yvette is wonderful. I know Papa, in his way, cares. But he is focused on his grandson's future, not what is needed now.

"Don't worry so much. Claude gets wonderful care here at Lamont."

"That wasn't my plan. I want my son with me." Guy sighed and gave a shrug. "But that's not possible right now."

Fate had dealt him a lousy hand. I gave him a hug. "I'm so sorry."

He brushed my lips and nodded, drawing me nearer for a moment before releasing me.

"You know I want to help in any way I can. But we do need to spend some time with your parents. Just think how much you care about Claude and know that's how much you mean to them."

"It's different. Have you ever watched birds care for their young, only to push them out of the nest when they're able to fly?"

"Not really, but point well taken. Come on, humans aren't birds. Your parents want to spend time with you."

"I know. What about *your* mother?"

I nodded as I pondered my response. "She didn't want me to leave home, because she no longer had Daddy. Many times she and Daddy left me and traveled to France while I stayed with a nanny."

"Hum. Not something we need to talk about now."

Madame de Laval's face lit up when we returned to the morning room. "Won't you join us for a cup of hot chocolate here by the cozy fire?"

"Sounds wonderful," I said.

"Merci." Guy passed the first cup to me and sat down beside his mother. "We really needed this marvelous Christmas here with you." He kissed her cheek. "I know you and Papa put a lot of time and thought into making it memorable."

"What a nice thing to say. We did want the season to be a joyful one," she said, her eyes moist. "It's wonderful to have you and Paulette here for Claude . . . and for us."

I didn't speak until my emotions were under control. Guy had acted upon my observation about his relationship with his parents, and I loved him for it.

"Paulette and I promised to take Claude on a sleigh ride. We'd like for you and Papa to come along—like we used to do."

Madame looked at her husband. "Well, Mathieu, what do you say?"

"Humph, it's pretty cold out there. I don't know. I suppose it might be all right."

"Papa, it will be."

We waited another four days before Guy and his helper prepared the old sleigh of Guy's childhood memory for the family outing. Mystique, Guy's black Labrador, picked up on our excitement and ran back and forth in anticipation.

"How long has it been since this sleigh has been out of the stables?" I asked.

"Years. At least ten or fifteen," the stable hand said.

I looked at Guy. "Does that mean Claude hasn't been out in it?"

"Afraid so. You have to remember that Claude lost his mother when he was a year old, and I lost a wife."

"How thoughtless of me. I'm sorry." I cleared my throat. I hadn't stopped to think about Claude's first year "Anyway, today's his day."

Guy nodded. "You bet it is." Mystique nuzzled Guy's hand and barked her approval.

The stable hand, Nico, handed me four sprigs of holly and red ribbon for decorations. I appreciated feeling useful and placed the holly and ribbons on the railing on each side of the sleigh in front of the large leather bell straps. After the horse was hitched, we rode to the courtyard. The handy man held the reins out to Guy and said,

"Or do you want me to drive while you're with the family?"

"You do it today. I want to be with Claude and the family."

Claude, Yvette, and Claude's grandparents came outside before the sleigh came to a full stop. When everyone was settled, off we went. Claude chattered the duration of the thirty-minute ride around the wooded paths in the forest behind the stables.

The following week the weather turned warm, and the snow was no more, at least for the time being. Our precious time with Claude was rapidly coming to an end. We tried to make the most of the time we had left. Yvette had taken Claude out to ride on the sled and play in the sun, but the season for rides had ended, at least for the present. Guy suggested we go for a boat ride, which Claude agreed was as exciting as a sleigh ride. He was such an inquisitive child and somewhat needy for his father's attention, so we spent the warm sunny days of that week with walks in the woods, exploring things of interest—birds, squirrels, plants, holly trees.

The day before we were to leave for Paris, we took a picnic lunch and went to the river for another boat ride. We walked along the sand, stopping for Claude to examine anything that drew his attention along the way—a stray leaf on the ground or a hole by a tree trunk—until we reached the boat. I spread our blanket on the sand near the boat and set the picnic basket on the blanket under the shade of a tree. Guy carried Claude on his shoulders part of the way to the boat. I climbed onto the boat, and he handed Claude to me while he sat in front of us and manned the oars. Claude loved seeing the other boats making their way up and down the river—some large, some small fishing boats.

After an hour or so, Claude rubbed his eyes. "*J'ai faim.*"

"I'm hungry too. Looks like its lunch time and nap time," Guy said and brought the boat ashore.

We climbed onto the river bank, and I walked along the sand with Claude while his father secured the boat.

When we circled back around, Guy came to meet us with the blanket and picnic basket. "A change of plans," he said. We walked a little farther and turned into the woods below the chateau. After a bit of a climb, we came into an opening where a small chapel was hidden among the trees. The smell of smoke masked the scent of the surrounding pine trees. A decorative lintel above the Gothic door boasted two elegantly carved warriors. At the point of the arch, an angel appeared to be keeping watch. When Guy opened the door, warm air encircled us. A fire crackled in the small fireplace.

"There's a fire in the fireplace?" Alarmed, I said, "You don't suppose the Germans have anything to do with it, do you?"

"No. I asked Nico to get it started for us."

Guy set the basket on the table and opened it. He unwrapped a sandwich for Claude and set it in front of him. He placed a larger plate of sandwiches and two bottles on one end of the rectangular table, close to the fireplace. "Milk for Claude and Champagne for us."

Claude chattered about what he'd seen during his day until his eyelids drooped. Guy carried him to the sofa, covered him with a blanket, and placed a couple of chairs by the sofa to keep him from rolling off the edge.

He poured Champagne, and I reached for a second sandwich. The fresh air and activity had stimulated my appetite. The bubbly beverage warmed my belly, heart, and imagination. The vignette of the three of us together, intimate and comfortable, approached perfection.

As I have looked back to that day through the years, I have realized my impatience did more harm than good. How could I know I'd put Guy in an untenable position? Each passing day of our three weeks together had brought us closer together. And at that moment, I had Guy's full attention. Heaven only knew how long before another opportunity such as that would open. Surely, the time was ripe to talk of our relationship and marriage.

So I launched into my much-rehearsed pitch. "These three weeks have been wonderful here with you and Claude."

Guy slipped his arm around my shoulder and kissed me. "Oui, I wish it didn't have to end."

"It doesn't. We can get married before we leave for Paris."

He rose and paced. "Non, there's a war to fight!"

"Claude's almost three. He can be with us in Paris. I'll be there for him when you have to be away."

"For God sake, don't you think I'd have him with me now if it were safe? Marriage has nothing to do with it."

Taken aback by his uncompromising response, I rushed outside and sat on a fallen log, devastated by his harsh rejection.

He followed me and said, "I'm sorry, mon trésor. I can no more place you in danger than I can Claude. I love both of you but must be free to follow my conscience as to what I must do in these times of extraordinary circumstances."

"You don't seem to care how I feel about it," I said, wiping a tear from my cheek.

"That's not true. You should know me well enough to know I have rational reasons for my decisions."

"So your conclusion is that I'm safe alone in my little apartment but would not be safe with you in your home?"

"Yes, under the current circumstances."

"What are you doing . . . collaborating with the Nazis?" I asked in frustration. I regretted it immediately.

"That comment from you, who clings to Colonel Dietrich, doesn't warrant a response. We both need time for reflection. I don't have the answers." He left me sitting on the log.

I sat there for at least fifteen minutes longer, hoping he'd return. That didn't happen, so I went back inside to get warm.

Claude still slept on the sofa, and Guy stood at the fireplace with a poker, stirring the glowing embers. He turned when he heard the door close and waited until I drew near. "We'll leave here in the morning. I've thought about how my behavior affects you. It tears me up inside, but I can't do anything about it yet. If you believe in me, you will give me the benefit of the doubt, but if you can't, I won't blame you."

I went to him and put my arms around him. "I do trust you. It's just so hard to be kept in the dark."

He cupped my face in his hand. "I know. Your love is the one stable thing in my life just now. It means everything to me . . . and to Claude."

"Papa," Claude called.

"We're ready to go as soon as I secure the fire," he said to his son and kissed me before stirring the embers, dousing them with water and shoveling sand on top.

Chapter Twenty-Four

Mid-February 1941 – Paris

Members of Resistance Arrested, screamed the headline on the front of *La Monde*.

My heart stood still when I saw the newspaper. After a month away from Paris, Guy should be home. Had he been in the city all the while? No! I wouldn't entertain such thoughts. I had to find out more, but how? The article gave few specifics and no names were listed. The walls of my tiny apartment seemed to mock me. I had to escape—to take some kind of action, to seek answers. I'd cut off all contact with Dietrich, so I couldn't find out from him.

I have to talk to somebody! I grabbed my coat, cap, and scarf and put them on, but then I did not know where to go, did not know where to turn. *Aline? Oui.* She might help me. She had many contacts from her work at the hospital. I dialed her number and prayed she'd answer.

"Allô," Aline's familiar voice greeted me.

"This is Paulette. I need to talk."

"Would you like to come over tomorrow?"

"What about right now?"

"Better give me two hours before you do."

Concerned that I'd interfered with her plans, I said, "Of course. Or if you have other plans, I can come later."

"Two hours suits me."

I'd been to her apartment several times since Guy and I had been dinner guests after we'd returned to Paris. I had two hours to spend somewhere before then, and it wasn't going to be in my apartment. I settled on the Tuileries Gardens, my place for quiescence.

I walked there and sat on a bench facing the reflection pond. Given the cold, windy day, I seemed to have the place to myself, until a stranger approached. He struck me as a Russian Cossack from Siberia. Rather than taking one of the many empty benches, he sat beside me. He wore a heavy black overcoat, the collar pulled high around his neck, and a fur hat pulled low on his forehead. His scarf covered the lower part of his face, like a character out of the movies.

I wondered whether he had followed me and, if so, had he been watching the apartment? Not unreasonable thoughts, given my connection to the Resistance.

I snatched a quick look at him. He turned his stony face toward me. A frozen gaze met my eyes. I looked away, my heart pounding against my ribs.

What if he's an assassin and has a pistol with a silencer?

When I saw two men come our way, I mustered the courage to stand up. I didn't hesitate to fall into step with them but still feared what the strange man might do next.

By the time I reached Aline's apartment and knocked on the door, I was putty-legged, panting like a dog after a fox hunt.

"My word, what happened to you?" Aline whispered, her hand on her chest.

"I'm not sure. I'm jumpy these days. I'm worried that Guy could be one of the Resistance members the Germans have arrested. I don't know where or how to find out."

"Why don't you ask your Chris?" Santoni called from inside.

"What are you talking about?" Aline and I said in unison.

"I saw him a few days ago in a café with two German officers."

Aline ignored him. "Take it from me, Guy is okay." She held the door open, shivering in her light-weight, fuchsia lounging attire. "Come in out of the cold."

"Thank you." I glared at Roberto Santoni. "Aline, you should have told me you had company."

"It's all right. Roberto is just leaving."

"I am?" He ran his hand over the dark stubble on his unshaven face but didn't make a move to get up or leave.

"Yes, you are," Aline said with a firm tenderness, like a mother to a petulant child.

His brows drew together in a feigned expression of anguish. "Out in the cold?"

She behaved as if I weren't there and reached for his hands. He stood and they clung to each other for an awkward moment. "I'll be in touch." She walked him to the door and whispered something in his ear.

I felt like an angry voyeur. "I wouldn't have come if you'd told me he was here."

"Don't look at me like that. Just because I'm married doesn't mean I don't care about my friends."

"I'm sorry. It's just that I know you and he were more than friends."

"And now we are just friends."

"You still love him. I saw it when you looked at him."

"I don't deny that. But you didn't come here to talk about me, so let's get to your concerns. A cup of hot chocolate will do you good."

I followed her into the kitchen and sat at the table covered with a red-and-white oilcloth. She heated the copper kettle and scooped brown powder from a matching canister.

"During the holidays, I believed Guy understood he needed to share his plans with me. So far it hasn't turned out that way," I said.

Aline set the steaming cocoa in front of me. "I don't think I can change that for you."

"I didn't think you could influence him, but you might know something about what's going on. He's been gone a month, and I'm stuck alone in my apartment, worried sick about his safety." I sighed. "Roberto mentioned Chris. Can you believe I don't even know what he's doing, other than ignoring me?"

Aline sat down across from me with her cup. "You're going to have to understand that Guy is descended from a line of warriors. He feels a great sense of responsibility to protect his homeland. Country comes before personal desires. If you love him and want to be part of his life, you're going to have to accept him as he is."

I gave the smooth warm beverage time to sooth my angry stomach and tender throat before I said, "I don't know whether I can bear being left alone in that apartment. I need someone to care about what happens to me."

She tapped a fingernail on the side of her cup and seemed to be weighing her response. "I … can't be here for you or help you with Guy. What I can do is to assure you he is safe at this time. The men arrested were part of the Musée de l'Homme Resistance group. But Guy is not part of that group."

"What if Chris is involved with them? He stayed to work in the Resistance because of me." I paused, trying to keep tenuous control of myself. "I'll be devastated if any harm comes to him."

She placed a hand on mine. "I know you would."

"I can't blame him if he doesn't want to see me. I made it clear I had chosen Guy. I didn't consider his feelings. I don't know what to do next."

"There's nothing to do but go to your classes."

"Aline, you don't understand. I need to do something to help with the war effort, but Guy prevents that."

"Come back to the hospital again. Believe you me, help is desperately needed. They're short staffed, and soon I'll spend most of my time at the Chateau Maille. You could help fill the void when I leave."

"Why are you leaving? Does the marquis demand it?"

"No, it's because of Roberto. I'm pretty sure I'm going to have a baby, and I must not encourage him to count on me. He thinks I'll cast aside my marriage for him. I absolutely will not."

Speechless, I wondered what she'd gotten herself into.

"In case you're wondering, Roberto is not the father."

"No, of course not. Are you happy about the baby?"

"I don't know. At least I'll satisfy my husband's need for another heir. He's restless already."

I nodded. "I think I should quit college and work at the hospital fulltime."

"No, no, you shouldn't!" she said. "You'd regret it later on."

"I can't keep my mind on my classes. None of my friends are still there." I shook my head, not yet trusting my voice. "You, Guy, Chris, and the others."

"Renee is there, isn't she?"

"She's there but has changed after her arrest. She shuns me and most of the other students. The only friend she has is another Jewish girl. She's even cut ties with her own father. I wish I could help in some way. I stop by to visit with him, but it doesn't seem to matter."

Aline cast her eyes toward the floor. "It must be heartbreaking for him." She glanced at the wall clock. "I hope I've put your mind at ease about Guy. He is safe. I'm psychic, you know."

"I hope you are. At least I feel better after your assurance." I rose and put on my coat and hat. "Thank you listening to me on such short notice. Let's get together before you leave for Lyon."

"We will. I'll have you and Guy to dinner as soon as he's home. Maybe one evening next week."

"That's good. I hope we can." I left her home with a modicum of hope that I'd be with Guy soon. I decided to take the Metro, as I should have done earlier, instead of detouring by way of the Tuileries Gardens. At least I wasn't alone. A group of students congregated in the center of the car. Toward the front three German soldiers laughed and talked to each other in their native tongue. I sat a couple of rows behind them.

When I got a glimpse of Chris waiting at the next stop, I moaned, "He's in town." I felt the burn on my cheeks as our eyes met for a moment before he passed by me. As much as I wanted to speak to him, I knew I couldn't acknowledge him with Germans in view.

He disembarked at the next stop, and although risky, I got off too. I hoped to speak to him. "Pardon, monsieur, do you have the time?" I asked when I caught up with him.

He turned and looked me at me for a long moment. "*Désolé*, mademoiselle."

I couldn't read his expression and whispered. "Will I see you again?"

He shrugged and walked away—much as a stranger would have.

Chilled to the bone, teeth chattering, I caught the next Metro, rode the three stops to my apartment, and slowly climbed the stairs. I stared in disbelief when I turned up the last flight and saw Guy at the top, waiting near my door. Before it fully registered, I raced up and found myself enveloped in the warmth of his embrace.

"Where were you? I thought you only had morning classes," he said after a prolonged kiss

"I stopped by to see Aline. What about you, when did you get back to Paris?"

"Last night."

"I'd invite you in, but you might freeze," I unlocked the door and pulled him in with me anyway.

"I'm getting used to the cold," he said and slipped his arm around my waist.

As much as I wanted to bombard him with questions, I held back. I'd test Aline's advice to be patient with him. I left unsaid the question about whether his house was warmer than mine. It wasn't too difficult, because of my joy to have him with me. I knew I shouldn't mention my suspicions about the man in the gardens. I'd just been overwrought about Guy's safety. "May I get you a cup of tea?"

"Sounds good. Or better yet, let's get the tea and a bowl of soup at your favorite café near here."

"D'accord." I slipped on my coat and hat. "Let's walk." Time with Guy motivated my suggestion so that we'd have more time together. During the short walk, I focused on the moment, knowing the evening would end too soon.

After we arrived and took our usual seats, I made an effort to keep the conversation light. "The soup here is always delicious. Remember that time we had their split pea soup, and I wanted you to ask for their recipe?"

Guy smiled. "And I told you they would politely decline."

We laughed, something we seldom did.

"Which they did," I said. "I think they wanted to keep us coming back for more." I fell silent because every time I thought of something I wanted to say, I held back to avoid friction. He'd have to take the lead on the topics for discussion.

"You're in a pensive mood. Is everything okay?"

"No. It isn't," I said. "Sometimes, I think it's better not to tell you how I feel."

Guy reached for my hand. "I carry a burden with me when I leave you and can't speak of my plans. I know it's unfair to you. All I ask of you is to trust me and know that I love you."

I shook my head, tears clouding my vision. "I do believe you, but at times, I can't bear the uncertainty."

"I'm sorry. It must be hard being in a strange land away from family and friends. That's all I can say. It's your life . . . and your decision to make."

"I know. If only I were like you, strong enough to stay the course."

"You give me far more credit than I deserve. I'm conflicted too. I'd like to flee to America with you and forget this miserable war."

He took my breath away. "You would? I had no idea."

"Maybe that's a fatal flaw of mine. For you, my love, I'll try

184

to change."

"Don't stop feeling that way. I know you'll always do the right thing."

Guy laughed. "So do I, or I'll suffer a terrible consequence."

Completely overwhelmed at his revelation, I think I would have agreed to do anything for him. "From now on I'll work on not asking so many questions, and I'll wait for you to tell me what I need to know about your schedule."

It was his turn to be flabbergasted. "Don't promise the impossible." His voice was calm, his gaze steady.

I had to acknowledge that he knew me well. "Of course, you'll need to inform me on a regular basis. Your protective attitude does more harm than good."

"I'll do my best, but there are many plans I cannot share."

"Any improvement will be welcome."

During the intervening silence, I tried to imagine how well our plan would work. Could either of us stick with it?

Guy interrupted the quiescence of the moment. "I spoke to Aline last night. She's invited us to dinner on Tuesday before she and her husband leave for Lyon . . . in a week or so."

I didn't let on that I knew anything about dinner. "Oh, that'll be nice," I murmured. "She'll be missed. One less friendly face in town."

His fingers, tapered and strong, caressed his mug. "Eh . . . I believe time away from Paris would do you good. Claude and my parents would welcome your companionship . . . and I'd be with you as often as possible."

"I'd like that, but I want to do something to help the war effort. I've decided to volunteer again at the hospital while I'm in school. But during breaks I'd welcome time at Lamont."

He nodded. "Good plan." He reached for my hand and squeezed it. "Ready to go?"

I'd dreaded this moment but knew it had to come. "When will I see you again?"

"Let's plan to spend Sunday together. I have things to attend to for the next few days, and you'll have a chance to catch up on your school work."

"Okay, I'll count on Sunday and Tuesday for now."

"Oui, and don't think I won't be looking forward to those

days with you."

On the way to my apartment, neither of us said much. It seemed his thoughts were elsewhere, so I expected he'd kiss me goodnight and leave. However, he surprised me. At my door he looked at me, devilishly handsome, and said, "What about that cup of tea you offered me?"

"By all means, come in, and I'll make good on my offer of hospitality."

We each prolonged the evening by suggesting another round of tea until he said, "Isn't there anywhere more comfortable to sit than on these wooden chairs?" He knew full well that the bedroom contained a well-cushioned loveseat and sofa . . . and the bed.

The prospect frightened me. It wasn't so much what he'd do, but what I'd do. The consequence of such an indiscretion could be horrific. I couldn't chance it.

I stood and took his hands and pulled him up from the chair toward me. "You know I want you more than you can imagine. I just can't take the chance. I'm alone here in Paris, and as you tell me, the time is not right for marriage. I must take responsibility for my behavior."

"Mon trésor, you misunderstood my intentions." He locked eyes with me. "I would never want to place you in a perilous position." He held me against his chest. "But you are right, intentions or not, it was a bad idea. It's just that I don't want to leave you tonight—or ever."

"No, it's not you I'm worried about," I assured him. "I'm weak and find it hard to resist the temptation of keeping you here with me."

"Damn it! We're going to have to wait a while before we marry. Things I'm involved in are critical to the lives of so many people." He shook his head. "I'm sorry. I'll leave now, but we'll have Sunday and Tuesday together."

Careful not to ignite passion, he gave me an affectionate kiss on the cheek and left me . . . unfulfilled, as I'm sure he was.

After a short midday meal on Sunday, Guy and I avoided further temptation by attending a play by a small group of actors. The

Tuesday evening dinner shouldn't encourage any missteps. I think both of us were leery about spending time alone.

Monday and Tuesday in class I found my mind wandering to Guy. I couldn't wait to be with him again.

Somehow, the time passed, and Guy and I arrived at the Maille apartment. The marquis and Aline greeted us. Their swan song to Paris and to us appeared to be an important event. A butler had been hired for the occasion and served smoked salmon hors d'oeuvres.

"What's the special occasion?" Guy asked the marquis.

"Well, as you know, we're leaving Paris and will return to Chateau de Maille. My wife is expecting a baby. My son will need to spend his early years in his ancestral home."

Aline lost no time telling him. Maybe she should have waited to be sure, I thought.

Guy raised an eyebrow, apparently taken by surprise. "Congratulations."

"I might have to sell some of my paintings to ready the chateau for my family."

"You might as well. The Germans will confiscate them if you refuse to sell to them. They covet our art and other national treasures."

"You could be right," Maille said.

"Paulette appreciates art. Perhaps after dinner you'll show her your paintings," Guy said while we enjoyed a delicious veal dish, *blanquette de veau*.

The butler made the rounds, serving Dom Perignon Champagne.

"I'd be more than happy to," Maille said to Guy. "That is, if you'll keep my wife company while I do."

"It will be my pleasure."

So far the evening seemed to pose no temptation to Guy or me. I actually looked forward to seeing the art collection.

Aline said, "Dear, we'll have liqueur in the salon after Paulette has seen your art."

Her husband straightened and smiled at her. "Marvelous idea. Mademoiselle, come this way."

I glanced at Guy. I would have preferred he accompany us. As if reading my thoughts, his eyes met mine. "Go ahead and enjoy yourself."

The marquis loved to talk, especially about art. As we moved down the long hallway from room to room, he explained in minute detail the history of each artist and the provenance of the piece. It became an extended lecture.

"Do you give talks to various groups about art?"

"As a matter of fact, I have and do so whenever I receive an invitation." He sighed. "I'll have to make it known in Lyon that I'm back and available as a speaker. If I sell some of my collection, it will make me sad to think and talk about the ones I had to sacrifice for the good of my family." He paused and looked expectantly in my direction.

What could I say? "I suppose it would. Thank you for the tour."

But along the way back to the others, he couldn't resist stopping and talking at length about the artists again. By the time we neared the dining room, we could overhear a portion of the conversation between Guy and Aline.

Aline could clearly be heard saying, "Those airmen are so brave and remarkable. We have to do everything we can to get them out of the country."

The marquis paled. "Come with me. I want to show you a photo of my new acquisition. It'll arrive any day now."

I didn't budge and strained to hear more while the marquis droned on and on.

"They'll have to stay put until their injuries heal," I heard Guy reply. "If they're rushed, they'll die for sure."

"It's dangerous for all of us. But what choice do we have?" Aline said.

I smiled at my host. "We better join them," I said and sauntered along, in no hurry to arrive.

"Their only hope is to reach a safe house and pray," Guy said.

Safe house? I've heard about them from some of the Resistance workers. Had Aline made up the story about the baby in order to go to Lyon and run a safe house for the Resistance?

I hoped Guy wasn't involved with her.

I felt nauseous. I just wanted to leave but forced myself to wait until Guy finished his glass of amber-colored liqueur. When he sat down his glass, my eyes met his. "I'm not feeling well. Please take me home."

Aline stared at me. "What seems to be the trouble?"

"A little indigestion. I'm sorry to rush off before we've had a chance to visit more."

I wanted as much distance between Guy and Aline as possible. The Mailles couldn't leave Paris soon enough to suit me.

For once the marquis remained quiet.

Guy slipped his arm around my waist on our way to the car. "That was sudden. Did the marquis offend you?"

"Non. To tell you the truth, I'm worried about what you and she are plotting."

He gave me a look of awareness that I'd overheard their conversation but remained silent, his familiar mask in place once again.

Chapter Twenty-Five

May 1941 – Paris

The time of truth loomed before the beleaguered lovers.

Changed from girl to woman within a few months, I no longer viewed the world through the rosy prism of a fanciful youth. I'd taken charge of my life and my expectations of it. After four months of volunteer work at the hospital, I'd learned to anticipate how I could be most helpful to the medical team, and I felt comfortable with my role in helping the war effort.

College classes and work occupied my waking hours, but every evening as I readied for bed, my thoughts turned to Guy. What future might we have together? On the night of May twelfth, I drifted to sleep with the knowledge that in the morning I'd be on my way to Lamont. I tried to anticipate how this visit would differ from the others.

Guy and I were taking time from our busy schedules for a week's hiatus at Lamont to celebrate Claude's third birthday. My outlook had changed about forcing Guy's and my relationship; rather, I looked forward to our time together with his family as an opportunity to evaluate whether I would be a suitable addition to the de Laval family or whether I should return to California at the end of the school term. My work was cut out for me to reach out to Madame and Monsieur de Laval and Claude to be realistic about our compatibility.

Loire Valley

"*À quoi penses-tu?*" Guy asked as we turned off the A-10 and entered the city of Tours.

I started at the broken silence between us. "My thoughts?" And quickly added, "Just about us."

With a quick glance my way, he asked, "What about us?"

"All of us. Claude, your parents, you and me."

"Anything particular?"

"More questions than answers. I want to get to know all of you better."

"Don't you know me?"

"Not as well as I should."

He sighed. "I think I understand what you mean. It's my part in this war. I haven't been free to show you who I am."

"Let's talk about our time at Lamont," I suggested, eager to make the most of the time we had together.

"You're a wise woman. We need to take joy in the time we have."

I nodded. "Every minute counts. I'm looking forward to our time with Claude. He's adorable and growing so fast."

Guy reached over and laid his hand on my arm. "I know. I miss watching him wake up in the mornings, so full of wonder at the world around him."

"Thank God he has Lamont and his doting grandparents when you're not able to be with him."

He took a deep breath and turned from the highway into the winding lane that led to his hilltop ancestral home.

My heart went out to him. In many ways, life had cheated him already. I only hoped the future would be kinder. If fate so ordained, I wanted to be a source of joy to him and Claude.

There I go again, pushing away the present, I thought. "I'm going to take my own advice and make each precious moment memorable . . . I hope you will too," I said to Guy.

His smile widened with approval as he brought the car to a stop in the courtyard. "Deal."

I watched him swing his long legs out of the car and come around to open my door. He grasped my hand and rushed me toward the chateau. "Come on," he said as he dashed inside, dragging me with him. His voice reverberated throughout the cavernous, stone entry gallery as he called, "Where's Claude?"

"Papa!" I heard Claude but didn't see him coming until I felt the impact of his weight against his father's outstretched arm. I dropped Guy's hand so he could hold his son and walked alongside them. Claude looked as though he'd grown another two or three inches. His face was that of a child rather than a toddler. "Pau-ette" he waved at me and burrowed his head against his father.

"Sweetheart, how are you?" I said and tiptoed to kiss him on the cheek.

"Bon. We can go to the river?" He bobbed his head and said, "I'm not sick anymore."

Madame de Laval came from the morning room and kissed us on each cheek. "That little fellow talked about you all day. He's really excited to have you both here," she said and looked at me.

I smiled. *She likes me!* And I found it easy to like her also. She had a delicate, aristocratic beauty and charm that put me at ease and garnered my admiration. Her husband remained another matter. I'd have to work at breaking the ice with him. I planned to ask Guy how to best approach his father. I'd have to use the time wisely and divide my focus on each member of the family.

We found the major in his easy chair, listening to the radio—just as he had been when we left in January. My reaction was to no longer wait for him to speak to me. I drew up a chair beside him and listened as the commentator reported that a *rafle*—round up—of Jews had begun in Paris.

Always the one to welcome me, Madame called, "Come, sit over here. We'll visit while he listens."

"Merci, I'll be there in a few minutes."

Monsieur de Laval threw me a quizzical look. "Damn, I can't believe that General Pétain would allow such a thing. There has to be more to the story."

"Perhaps" I said and at his nod was encouraged to go on. "When I heard they'd created the *Commisariat Général Aux Questions Juives* to suppress the Jews, I feared what would come next."

"My dear, I'm afraid it's not that simple. There has to be a reasonable explanation. You have a good head on your shoulders. Don't jump to conclusions."

I could see he would always defend the general he'd known during the Great War and would refuse to criticize him. I hadn't come to argue with him, but I couldn't agree with him either.

"I suppose you've noticed that my family doesn't share my preoccupation with current events." Under his breath, he said "Nor many other things."

"Monsieur, I don't think that's the case. It's just that they have many responsibilities that demand their attention. Perhaps you could think of things you'd like to share with them, such as chess or checkers or something like that. Time together is important also."

"Just because I complimented you, don't think you can change me. They've already tried. I am a soldier through and through, one imprisoned in a disabled body."

"Please forgive me if I've said anything to offend you."

"Not at all, my dear. You mean well. I don't want to disappoint you, too. God knows, my wife has given up on me, and my son shuts me out of his life."

I'd inserted myself into family affairs further than I'd wanted. "While I'm here I'm going spend some time with you . . . unless you object."

His tight expression eased into a tentative smile. "I'd like to hear your thoughts."

I stood. "And so you shall, but I mustn't neglect Madame de Laval and Claude either."

"Nor my son. He needs someone like you in his life. He may not think I care about his happiness, but I do." He looked up at me with moist eyes. "That little boy over there"—he pointed across the room toward Claude—"gives me a purpose in life."

His comment concerned me. In the last few months, I'd come to realize the danger of expecting others to make one's life worthwhile. Of course they were important, but so much depended on your own expectations. I nodded and started across the room, leaving him to his musings about little Claude's future.

When Claude looked my way, he ran to meet me but refrained from jumping into my open arms; rather, he reached for my hand and tugged on it. "*Ma mamie* wants to ask you."

"Ask me? What about?"

He shrugged.

I picked up the pace, forcing him to run, much to his delight.

Guy and his mother curtailed their animated conversation and waited for us to reach them.

"Do join us," Madame said. "We've been making plans for Claude's birthday party and need your suggestions."

I sat in an armchair across from them. Claude headed for the sofa and wedged himself between his father and grandmother. "What are your plans?" I asked. "I'll see what suggestions I can make."

"We'll keep the celebration simple this year. The war is difficult on everyone. The Germans are depleting our resources.

They skim the cream from the food supply needed to feed our families. An elaborate celebration is out of the question."

I felt at a disadvantage, not knowing the limit of their resources. What could be done and what couldn't? I looked at Guy. "I don't know what is usual or how the celebration needs to change."

"It's really very simple." He recited a list. "Sing happy birthday, eat simple dessert, open gifts, children play with the toys."

"I see. I don't know what I can add."

"That's okay. Maman wants you to feel a part in our plans. That includes five or six boys about Claude's age and their parents. That's pretty much our custom."

"I see no reason to change. Claude's of an age where he'll be happy with any celebration that makes him the center of attention."

"I agree. And we'll serve sandwiches at the conclusion," Madame de Laval said—for my benefit, I believed. "Ordinarily, I'd plan a three-course meal, but times are uncertain these days."

"How well I understand. I'm sure everyone does," I said.

"I do what I can for the neighbors and my family. But to take my mind off the uncertain future, I indulge in my desire to create things of beauty from the lovely fabrics and ribbons I have on hand. I give them as gifts and hope to brighten someone's day," she said.

"That's wonderful."

"Paulette, while you're here, I'd be happy to show you my place of peace."

"Thank you. I'd like that very much." It became evident that I wouldn't be at loose ends on this visit. I looked forward to time spent with Claude, Monsieur, Madame, and, especially, Guy. Overall, things were good as far as my relations with the family were concerned.

Claude lost no time persuading Guy and me to take him to the river and out on the boat, and after that he wanted to go on a horseback ride.

"Paulette, after the boat ride why don't you let the boys ride, and we can visit my retreat?" Madame suggested.

I looked at Guy and Claude. "That's a good idea. What do you say?"

"Papa?" Claude waited for Guy to answer.

"Son, it's a good idea for the women to spend time together."

The boy puffed his chest. "Oui, Papa, just you and me. I wish

Papi could come, too. He's a man and will be sad."

"When we get back and tell him all about it, he'll be happy. He loves you very much."

Claude's lip trembled. "Sometimes, he yells at me."

"You may be too young to understand. He hurts much of the time. You need to do as he asks."

"That's right," Madame said to Claude. "He is the head of the de Laval family and will teach you how to be a de Laval man when you grow up."

Claude cast his eyes downward but said nothing.

Guy picked him up and said to me, "Let's get started. The boat is empty and waiting for us."

I relaxed when I saw that Claude seemed unaware of his future role and clung to the present with his father and the boat adventure.

Most of our time was spent at the river's edge in spite of Claude's attraction to the water. I never tired of Claude's sheer delight when discovering the world around him.

"No, come back here. We're here for a boat ride," Guy called to his runaway son, who had reached the place where land met sea. He grabbed his hand and led him to the boat. After untying it, he set Claude on the seat, and we climbed in beside him.

Guy looked at me. "Do you want to watch him or row?"

"I'll take the easier job. I'll row." I knew Guy didn't want to be on the water for long, because of the threat posed by German patrols along the river. There had been unexpected bombings along the waterfront as well; hence, increased surveillance.

Claude pointed to a large boat upstream. "I want to go see that big boat."

"Too far away. It's just a lot of men fishing," Guy said. "Nothing to see."

"I want to." Claude pounded his little fists against his father's chest.

I took matters into my own hands, so to speak. I pulled on the oars and turned our boat around toward the launch site. This outing had been a frustration for both of them.

On our way back to the chateau, Guy carried his son and said to me, "He's late for his nap, and that's never a good thing. I'll take him to see the horses for a short while. Maybe we can go riding tomorrow."

I left the "men" where the trail branched toward the stables, and I continued toward the chateau. I turned to gaze at the view of the Loire River and breathe in the fresh air before continuing on to spend time with Madame de Laval. A glance at my watch prompted me to get started if I wanted to arrive in plenty of time for the appointment.

I returned by way of the morning room and found Madame seated in front of her husband, but I didn't hear the radio. As I drew closer, I paused, amazed to see them playing checkers.

Madame saw me first. "We're almost finished. I'm letting him win." She chuckled as his king jumped her queen to end the game. She rose and patted his hand. "Same time tomorrow?"

He nodded. "I'll give you another chance."

After we were out of earshot, she said, "Can you believe he asked me to play checkers?"

"Do you and he play often?" I asked before I dared think I'd had any part in his request.

She laughed. "Heavens, no. Not since before his discharge from the army." I followed her upstairs almost to the end of the hall. She stopped one door short of reaching the rounded tower at the end of the hall. I'd wanted to see behind the carved, hunting-scene door with the well-worn brass knob, but instead, she turned the handle on the one next to it.

Although the door had not intrigued me, what lay behind it did. "This is indeed a retreat from the cares of the world," I exclaimed as I viewed the room.

Luxurious silk fabric dressed the windows and chairs. An Empire-style daybed, covered with forest-green velvet upholstery, and a matching desk and chair set, delineated a place for quiet relaxation separate from the creative activities in the rest of the room.

I imagined that she spent many creative hours here with her needlework, which stood at various stages from inception to completion. The elegant fireplace of green marble and its gold firebox reminded me of the colors of the Loire River and the golden-leafed trees along its banks.

Two melon-colored upholstered armchairs invited an afternoon of fireside reading in an alcove. With no thought of Madame, I imagined myself alone on a cold winter day with a cup of coffee, snuggled in one of the two chairs, relaxed and contented by the fire.

Madame slipped her arm through mine. "Come. I'll show you my work in progress."

"Oui, *s'il vous plait*." My face warmed at my momentary lapse of good manners, or had it been from my vivid imagination of the cozy retreat?

Other sections of the room housed three long tables, covered with projects in various stages of completion, destined to become decorative accessories such as doilies, table runners, and wall hangings.

"Wow." I brushed my finger along a bit of teal-colored velvet. "This is beautiful." Lengths of grosgrain, gold cord, tassels, lace, and various other types of fabric were arranged beside each of the items.

I examined one of the tassels and was surprised at its texture and weight. "Is this some kind of metal?"

"Oui. Real gold threads are interspersed with the others."

"It's amazingly lovely"

"Merci, I'm fortunate to have a good supply of materials on hand," Madame de Laval said. "Everything now is in such short supply."

"Indeed, you are fortunate. I'd be contented to stay here every day."

"If you're interested in making something to take with you, I'd be happy for the two of us to work together."

An offer I couldn't resist. "I would. Thank you." I loved the luxurious variety of materials and felt comfortable with Madame de Laval. What a wonderful opportunity to get to know her better and learn more about the de Laval family.

"Good. Tomorrow morning about nine?"

"Yes."

"After I take care of my household duties, I work here for a while then have coffee—over there by the fireplace. Time allowing, later in the day I knit sweaters and blankets for Christmas gifts, before my time with Claude and again taking care of the household."

Reluctantly, we exited the lovely room, and I accompanied Madame to pick up Claude and take him to the morning room.

"While I take care of a few things, why don't you take him to Guy," Madame suggested. "I'll join you later."

"My pleasure." I broke into a rapid trot to catch up with Claude before he dashed too far ahead of me.

Where is Guy? I really wasn't prepared to keep both Claude and his grandfather entertained.

The old soldier turned toward us as Claude stopped short of him. "Mademoiselle Rousseau, just the person I want to see, and with Claude, no less."

"Madame de Laval has been showing me her beautiful fabrics and needlework."

"Before Guy returns, I want to ask that you bring Claude to me each morning that you are here."

I wondered why he wouldn't ask Yvette or a family member rather than me.

His eyes were sharp and assessing. "You're puzzled. Let me explain. In another three years, my grandson must be ready for boarding school in preparation for his future role as head of the de Laval family. He'll be expected to carry on the traditions of his forefathers. It is up to me to prepare him for his responsibilities in that regard. Do you understand?"

What could I say? First, I needed to recover from the shock that a six-year-old would be separated from his family and put in the care of strangers. Such a thing hadn't entered my mind. Had Guy also spent little of his youth with his family? Had he been molded at a boarding school?

I wanted to say that I didn't agree with sending Claude away, but all I said was, "No, I guess I don't understand. My family circumstances didn't prepare me for such a view of life."

"Be that as it may, I'm sure you want the best for Claude."

When the child heard his name, he stopped in front of me. I put my arms around him and met the major's cryptic gaze.

He continued, "From now on, his daily schedule will include time with me for two hours each morning. By the time he's six, he'll have a sense of his responsibilities as the future patriarch of the de Lavals of Lamont."

With no clue of what response, I could make, I waited in silence for him to continue.

He sighed and said, "I hope Claude lives in a better time than Guy and I have." He shook his head. "Sometimes, I wonder whether I failed my son in some way."

"I'm sure you did everything you could," I said with a heavy heart. The de Laval birthright demanded much of them.

"A word of advice while I have your ear. You've brought my family closer to me in the short time you've been here, and I thank you. As much as I would like you to stay with us, I feel compelled to warn you not to wear your heart on your sleeve. Guy is the man I made of him, and he will always allow duty to come before his love of a woman. You must consider whether to return to America or stay here with him. There will be no guarantees for your happiness if you choose him."

"I have no intentions of going home." A lump formed in my throat as I clutched Claude's hand. "Let's find Papa, shall we?" I said and hurried from the room. Deep down I couldn't deny that I believed the old man spoke the truth.

We went outside and started toward the stables—a way to entertain Claude. I thought I heard whistling, and as we rounded a bend, we came face to face with Guy. He slipped his arm around my waist and kissed me on the cheek. "I was coming to rescue you from my parents. At this rate we won't have any time for just the two of us."

"Didn't know you cared," I said, still wounded by the major's confirmation of my fears about his son's priorities.

He drew me to him and kissed me on the mouth with undeniable passion. He'd put aside his guarded behavior toward me. "Well, I do care and have plans to change it. What do you say we take Claude for a short ride this afternoon and plan to leave early tomorrow morning?"

"Why tomorrow?"

"So you and I can have a holiday together and forget the rest of the world for a few days. I owe it to you." He sighed and added, "And I need it myself."

I reached for his hand and gave it a squeeze. "I love the way you're thinking."

"Soon I hope to arrange things so that we'll spend more time together while in Paris. I know you don't like staying alone at your apartment, and I don't want that for you either. But before this vacation ends, the two of us will have the use of a little chateau near Chartres. It's on our way to Paris and won't add any extra travel time."

I drew a deep breath and slowly exhaled. "A love nest . . . near the famous Chartres Cathedral?"

"Don't worry, we'll be guests of a friend of mine and his wife."

I frowned. "Maybe love nest wasn't an accurate description?"

"Does that disappoint you?"

"Maybe."

"They'll respect our privacy. They understand that the demands of my Resistance work preclude much of a courtship."

"That's for sure. I can't wait to meet them. And thank them."

"You're okay with the arrangement?"

"Of course I am. What girl doesn't like an amorous pursuit by her fiancé?" My determination to heed the major's advice began to waver. At the moment Guy seemed ready to wear the mantle of a lover. The thought crossed my mind that, perhaps, his mother had had a heart-to-heart talk with him on my behalf. I had convinced myself that both of his parents felt I could contribute to his happiness.

We said our goodbyes and left Lamont shortly after the noon hour.

"I'm glad your father and mother have begun to play checkers with each other." I wanted to hear what Guy thought about it, and I wondered whether he knew that his father had told me about his plans for Claude.

He took a deep breath. "I don't want you to misunderstand about my feelings for my father. I respect him and know he feels a sense of failure because he didn't have a chance to stay in the Great War and become a general. After he came home with the injury that changed his life, he took out his frustrations on Maman and me. It was especially difficult for her. The man who came home wasn't the husband who had gone off to war to defend France. She made the best of a difficult situation."

I decided now was not the time to confide in Guy about what his father had said to me about Claude or our future together. "Maybe things will get better between them now."

He shrugged. "I hope so."

"Does your father have any interests other than politics?"

"He does. He's an astute student of financial matters. He's made wise investments and is responsible for the financial well-being of our family. My grandfather made unwise investments that threatened our financial stability and squandered a fortune. We were deeply in debt when he died, on the brink of losing some of our real estate holdings. Papa diversified our investments into minerals and natural resources such as Venezuelan oil fields."

"The business aspects must keep him busy," I said.

"It occupies much of his day, and nights when he can't sleep. I hope to do as well financially. But I've vowed not to be the failure he was in his role as father. He determined where I should go to school and whom I should marry. The career training was successful, although I resented not having a say in my future. My marriage was a mismatched failure from the start."

Guy glanced at me and patted my arm. "And now that I have found a woman I can love, outside circumstances have caused me to hesitate. But we know life carries no guarantees, so I've decided to straighten out my affairs with the Resistance so we can marry in the near future."

"Is that possible?" I said.

"We'll soon know."

He had just talked more openly with me than ever before. Content to leave him with his thoughts, I remained silent.

Chartres

Guy surprised me when he turned off the main road before we reached Chartres proper. I'd been prepared for a long journey and had started to read the book I'd brought with me. Now I closed it and took in the scenery as we moved along an unpaved road cut through a wooded area. In a short time a small chateau, nestled in the hills among the trees, came into view. After another twenty minutes Guy pulled to the side of the house and parked the Renault. My keen eye, developed during my work with the Resistance, noted the car was out of sight from the front of the house. I cautioned myself not to let my imagination get the best of me.

"Are you going to get out of the car, or could it be you're having second thoughts about the love nest?" Guy said with a wicked smile as he held the door for me.

"Ah, yes." I gathered my book and purse and stepped outside. "This seems so far away from civilization, but I guess it's not really," I said as I looked all around us.

"Enjoy the magic of the illusion."

I nodded. "The approach to Lamont gives the same feeling until the hills overlooking the Loire come into view. Traffic on the river allows public activity to intrude or, to put it another way, makes it less secluded."

Guy reached for my hand. "You're quite right. Now let's not keep our host and hostess waiting."

The sensation of his fingers linked through mine warmed my heart. I felt we had a real connection and eagerly went with him to a side door. He gave a rhythmic four raps. "Don't guests use the front door here?"

"Aren't you full of deep thoughts today?" he asked but didn't elaborate as the door opened and a good-looking, blond man stood before us. I estimated him to be another ten years older than Guy. Standing a few paces behind was a petite brunette. She stepped forward and greeted us, "Bienvenue."

"Curtis and Chantel, please say hello to Paulette Rousseau, my fiancée."

Curtis leaned close to Guy and said, "Chantel and I will be at a meeting with Jean tonight and tomorrow, so you'll have the place to yourselves after dinner. The housekeeper is here during the day until six to prepare meals and be of service."

Puzzled by the surprise on Guy's face at the mention of Jean's name, I made a mental note to ask him about it when we were alone.

"Come, I'll show you to your rooms," Chantel said. She escorted us upstairs and stopped by a door. "Guy, this is your room. Paulette, yours is the one next door, and it has a separate dressing room.

I smiled. "That's a bonus."

She opened the door to a bright, comfortable room. A settee sat by the window with a small table next to it. And then I noticed the door in the center of the wall closest to Guy's room. *Must be a suite of rooms. Hmmm . . . good idea?*

"Feel free to show Paulette around outside . . . or inside. Dinner's at five," she said to Guy and departed.

I snuggled against him. "Chantel didn't say anything about a bathroom."

"It's down the hall two doors. I'll show you later." He lifted my chin and gently kissed me, his gaze moving over my face and searching my eyes."

Overcome with desire for him, I drew him to me and coaxed his lips to mine. Many a lonely night I had lulled myself to sleep by imagining such a scene. I looked up and saw a smoldering flame in his eyes. I'd started something I knew we shouldn't pursue.

He knew it too and quickly stepped away from me. "It's getting late. I'll show you around outside before dinner."

"Later," I said.

He took me by the hand. "Non, now." We retraced our steps along the hall, down the stairs, and to the door at the side of the house.

"This is a working farm, so you can expect a good meal tonight." He took me down wooden steps that led to a vegetable garden on a lower level. We paused to look at the bountiful crop. After a few minutes, Guy prompted, "Ready? The greenhouse is down this way."

"This chateau comes with everything," I said as I followed him down another level of stairs.

We walked along by the side of the *orangery* and peeked through the greenhouse windows. There wasn't much to see, only a few vegetable seedlings and an orange tree. I went ahead, down yet another flight of steps, and came to an opening where a small door seemed to lead into the side of the hill.

"What's in there?" I asked when Guy joined me.

"An icehouse, I presume. Let's get back," he said.

"Okay. Curtis mentioned Jean. Who is he?"

Guy picked up his pace up the stairs, leaving me breathless.

"A friend of Curtis and mine."

"Would you like to see him, too, while you're here?" I persisted when I reached level ground.

"Non. I'm here to be with you."

I wanted to ask more, but his actions told me he didn't want to talk about it.

☦

After dinner Guy saw me to my bedroom.

"Come in," I told him at the door. "We need to plan what we'll do tomorrow."

"What do you suggest?" he asked as he sat on the settee across from me. I moved next to him before I replied, "I'd like to take a walk in the woods and look for moss and wildflowers. It looked like a world unto itself."

The thought of having him to myself, away from everyone else, thrilled me. I'd seldom been alone with him, and most of those times had been in a car—not the most conducive place for romance. I edged closer.

He didn't resist my invitation and put his arm around me while the other hand found its way under my blouse and along my shoulder. I leaned against his chest. *My husband, I love you.* I unbuttoned my blouse and placed his hand on my breast. The scent of his aftershave and the sensation of a lock of his dark hair touching my skin sent heat waves pulsing through every fiber of my body. When he glanced at me, the clear blue of his eyes had changed to a deep, turbulent-ocean blue.

Whenever we were apart, I'd visualize him as a completed canvas, but now each detail became separate brushstrokes, living and changing. I yearned to meld with him into our unique silhouette, to devour him in every way so that we truly were united as one. How often had I dreamed of such a time and awakened disappointed? Harmless fantasies abounded, but now I confronted a level of passion I hadn't imagined. I unbuttoned his shirt so that my breast lay against his bare chest. I tightened my hold around his neck.

Before I knew it, he'd carried me to the bed.

My mother's voice seemed to penetrate the roar in my ears.

"Men don't respect women with easy morals. It's the woman who is left with an illegitimate child. She's damaged goods!"

I have to stop this. I'll lose Guy's respect. I can't risk pregnancy. What can I do?

Guy's warm breath touched my ear as he murmured, "*Bonne nuit*, mon trésor." He disengaged from my arms and stood.

Disoriented, I mumbled, "Goodnight."

After the initial shock of such a close call, I struggled into my nightgown and got into bed. "In the morning I'll know what to think," I whispered as I wrapped an arm across my chest to the opposite shoulder and tried to sleep.

Chapter Twenty-Six

June - September 1941 – Paris

By the time we started the drive to Paris, I felt confident that Guy's intentions were honorable. Otherwise, why would he have resisted the temptation to make love in Chartres?

"You surprised me that our love nest didn't tempt you a second time," I said. "You must have a will of steel."

His head snapped around toward me. "I hope you didn't think we were playing some sort of game."

"Of course not! Why would you say that?"

"Paulette, you're incredibly naïve. I suspect you haven't ever slept with man?"

"Well . . . no."

He nodded and said, "I thought so. I'm not the stereotypical Frenchman who preys on young virgins. After our marriage we'll consummate our union. Will it be easy to wait? I think you're experienced enough to know that it won't."

"I've never tried to seduce a man before I met you. I'm really not like that. Please know that I tell you the truth. It's just . . . you're different than the others, and now, so are the uncertainties of life."

He rested his hand on my arm. "I know, mon trésor."

His gesture of assurance calmed me. I knew he'd worked his schedule around my classes and hospital commitments so we could spend time together before he left on another month-long mission. But one thing still bothered me—the house on Rue Notre Dame des Champs was still off limits to me.

I took the day off from school and work at the hospital on the day before Guy left for another undisclosed mission. We'd spent over two weeks together, and I dreaded the long separation that lay ahead.

After we finished lunch Guy said, "What next?"

"Let's go to the Tuileries Gardens to enjoy the sun and to talk."

Guy nodded. "That sounds pleasant."

The beauty of the gardens didn't deter me from pressing him to answers questions I guessed he'd rather left unasked.

"Where did you meet the Jean that Curtis knows?"

"Jean Moulin lived in Chartres while he was the *préfet* of the Eure-et-Loir Department before he was dismissed by the Vichy regime."

"Do you see him often?"

"Occasionally."

I got right to the point. "Does he have anything to do with the reason I'm an unwelcome guest at your house?"

"Goodness, no. You're going to have to stop prying into my work and my acquaintances. You know better!" Guy said as we walked past the Arc de Triomphe toward the Tuileries Gardens. "Paulette, I believed you when you assured me of your trust that I would secure my home for both of us. Please don't press for details."

I suspected he indulged my love of nature to enhance my mood, but it hadn't worked this time. I could have kicked myself, because I knew he wouldn't reveal his secrets. All I'd done was waste what little time we had together. I reached for his hand. "I'm sorry. I shouldn't have asked." After a short silence, I said, "I'll throw myself into my work until you're free to confide in me."

He stopped still and drew me to him. "I'm sorry too. We shouldn't have to wait long."

I lay my head against his chest and murmured, "I hope not." I fully realized I'd have to work until I dropped to keep my sanity.

Softly, his breath caressed my face as his lips brushed mine.

After an early meal at the small café near my apartment, we went to my place. Guy left early to allow us to get ready for our return to our separate routines. I hoped this would be our last such heart-wrenching farewell.

For the first week after Guy left, I went to my classes and then directly to the hospital so as not to be alone. My resolve to be unemotional had deserted me. Often, I felt close to tears at the thought that, each time Guy and I parted, I might never see him again. I think that's why I wanted him to make love to me. Of course, that was the worst thing I could have done. My heart overruled my head.

Soon after I had first begun volunteering at the American Hospital, I had learned of a secret portion of the facility. Publicly, the hospital served the citizens of Paris. But secretly, many Allied personnel—mostly British Royal Air Force airmen—were brought in for treatment for a variety of injuries such as burns, lacerations, and broken bones suffered when their aircraft were shot down. Only a handful of the hospital staff knew of the secret facility and most of them spoke only French. Since most of downed airmen didn't speak French, I found myself in high demand to translate. I knew it was dangerous work—and Guy would definitely not approve—but I finally began to feel that I was filling an important role in the war effort, and I made a point to learn something about each of my patients.

One day a young man came in on a stretcher and called to me, "Mademoiselle, *parlez-vous Anglais?*"

"Yes, I do. What can I do for you?"

"The doctor tells me I'll be here a while before I can begin the journey back to England. I'd like to get to know you while I'm here. It'll keep me from forgetting my native language," he quipped, mischief in his eyes.

So young. About my age. My heart went out to him. I knew he'd already been through a lot, but the rest of the journey was in no way assured. Danger lurked at each leg of his trip.

"I'll stop by as time permits," I said. "And we can talk about whatever suits you."

"You're American, aren't you?"

I laughed. "So I don't make you think of home after all?"

He became serious. "The English language makes me think of home."

"I do understand. Friends?" I held out my hand to him.

He gripped it as though it were a life preserver cast to him in the middle of the ocean.

"Friends. My name is John." His closed his eyes and released my hand.

"I'm Paulette." I moved on to the next patient but couldn't stop thinking about John and what a story he could tell.

Somehow, my encounter with John enabled me to take a renewed interest in life. I no longer wanted to leave school. Given my change of heart, I knew I'd have to devote more time to my studies to raise my grades and be prepared to do well in my final exams. No longer did I stay at the hospital after the end of my shift but hurried home. I often stopped for a sandwich on the way when the cupboards were bare.

One such evening I got off the Metro close to a café and bumped into Chris as I entered the eatery. "Paulette, how are you?" he asked. A smile lit his face.

"Well, thank you. How about you?"

He shrugged. "Likewise. Won't you join me for dinner?" He held up a bag."

"Just for a short while. I have to study, but I have to eat, too. Be back in a moment." I placed my order, half expecting he'd disappear while I had my back turned. Much to my surprise, he waited for me.

"Are you in Paris for long?" I asked.

"Not sure. You know how it is. I go where I'm told."

"You must have some idea."

He ignored my remark, instead asking, "Are you still in school?"

"Yes."

"What else fills the hours of your day?"

"School and the hospital."

"How many hours a week at the hospital?"

"Six or more."

He rewrapped his sandwich. "It's good to see you, but I have to run."

I rose when he did. "I don't wonder. Our small talk is guarded like two strangers meeting for the first time."

He hugged me. "Paulette, you are a part of me whether you like it or not." He held me and seemed reluctant to let go, but when he did look at me, my eyes were filled with tears. He looked away and rushed out the door.

I sat down in a daze, trying to stave off the feeling of loss that closed in around me. I thought it strange he hadn't mentioned Guy's name. Nevertheless, I felt guilty about having caused pain to Chris. Our past relationship meant a lot to me.

During the two weeks that John, the pilot, stayed at the hospital, I learned that he'd flown a Spitfire and had been hit by

German fire. Parachuting to a hard landing in an open field, he had suffered a broken ankle and an ugly gash on his arm. He managed with one hand and his teeth to tie two shoelaces together and use them as a tourniquet to stop the blood flow. He knew he had to get to cover as quickly as possible before being spotted by the enemy. After crawling to a nearby farmhouse, he knocked on the door, not knowing whether he'd be welcomed or captured. As luck would have it, a friendly French farmer and his wife took him in and treated his wounds.

John's injuries responded well to our care, and I expected within a week or so he might be well enough to start on the perilous journey to return to England. Until then, I looked forward to our talks.

As I approached his bed, he sat up. "I'm so glad to see you. I didn't want to leave without thanking you for helping me through these long days here."

"Leave. When?"

"I was told to be ready to leave tonight."

"I'm happy for you." I tried to put on a cheerful air. Fear for his safety gnawed at my gut. I'd become attached to him. "I'll wait to see you off."

"You will? Are you sure?" A smile spread across his lips. "Better be careful, I might take you with me."

"That wouldn't be a good idea."

One of the doctors stopped beside me. "Mademoiselle Rousseau, come with me."

I followed him to his small office and wondered whether a reprimand awaited me for spending too much time with one patient.

He sat down and gestured with his hand for me to do the same. "I've noticed you've gained the confidence of one of our patients."

"Well, yes, I speak English with him and . . ."

The doctor raised his hand. "Let me finish. We need your help," he said. "That is, if you're willing."

"I know you are familiar with Resistance work on behalf of English airmen, and others, who want to leave country. The guide who was assigned to help John reach a safe house has been arrested. Will you accompany him tonight?"

The heavy weight of responsibility for another person's life scared me. In the past I had risked my own life, but John's was another matter. Maybe, he could leave tomorrow night with a new guide.

"Take your time. I'll wait," the doctor said.

"I'll do it! Understand, I'll need good instructions, as I've never been a guide." Of course, I would do it.

"My dear, that goes without saying. You'll need to leave within the hour. Good luck."

I returned to the nurses' station and waited for my contact, as instructed by the doctor. The friendly face of a nurse I'd known from my days in the storage room with Aline appeared at the door. She stepped inside and said, "Let's get a cup of coffee."

I followed her to a small room next to the doctor's office. She closed the door and said, "Welcome to our circle," while handing me a piece of paper with the address of the safe house.

She poured two cups of what passed for coffee and gave me one. We sat on two stools along a storage counter that faced the door.

I unfolded the half sheet of paper and almost fell off the stool. The address was Guy's! I gasped. *Good Lord, no wonder Guy didn't want me at his house!*

"What's the matter? You're not getting cold feet, I hope."

"No. It's not that. I won't have any trouble finding this address."

"Alright. Read over your instructions."

I did so and nodded to her.

"You will go back to John and give him an identifying description of this address and have him memorize it. Tell him he will be expected, if he has been spotted, or any other questionable thing has happened, to abort the plan. If that happens, we'll try another time and place.

"After your meeting you'll take the paper from him and destroy it. Then let him read the travel instructions, and again, you're to destroy them before you leave the hospital. You and he will take the Metro to within walking distance—but not too close—to that street. From there you'll walk ahead of him, and he is to follow at a safe distance until you reach the house, where you will pause long enough for him to spot it. He is to stay in the shadows as you continue on. At no time is there is to be any conversation between the two of you or any acknowledgment of the other. Any questions?"

"No."

She hugged me. *"Bonne chance."*

I couldn't afford to think about anything to do with Guy at the moment. I had to keep focused on my first significant mission for the Resistance.

My first assignment went as planned, but I knew the risk of continuing to work as a link with the escapees. I didn't hesitate to agree to do so, however. But I had become personally invested in John's welfare before I'd known it mattered. That had to change, or I'd be dismissed as a danger to the operations. Still, I wanted to learn what I could do to help others I knew would come.

Two weeks later, I delivered two more RAF pilots to safe houses but not to Rue Notre Dame des Champs. I wondered whether our group leader had learned of my relationship with Guy and if that had precipitated the change. This time I felt exhausted and went to bed as soon I arrived at my apartment. I tried to block my thoughts, yet sleep eluded me.

I froze at the sound of a tap at my door. *The Germans?* Had I slipped up some way? Visions of being dragged down the stairs were threatening to overwhelm me when, fortunately, I heard Guy's three distinctive taps. Pulling on my robe, I ran to the door . . . and stopped. *But what if it's not him?* flashed through my mind.

"Paulette, open the door."

My heart leapt at the sound of Guy's softly modulated voice. There was so much I wanted to say to him. I pulled the door open and flung my arms around his neck as he swept me off my feet and carried me back inside. I leaned my head back and gazed into his eyes. "I'm so happy to be with you again."

He set me on the loveseat in the bedroom and sat beside me. "I came back as soon as I could with good news. I've arranged my home so you can visit anytime and stay as long as you want."

I took a deep breath before I dared respond. How could I tell him I knew that he ran a safe house—that I was sorry I'd doubted him and questioned his motives? "You did that for me?"

"Yes. I was harboring fugitives from the Germans, and I

couldn't risk your involvement in such serious offenses."

"Guy, I found out about your safe house while you were away. I, too, am involved in helping people leave the country."

He stared at me in disbelief. "How?"

"I help downed airmen reach the first leg of their journey home."

His features darkened. "Who got you involved? Was it Chris?"

"No! Don't blame Chris. He's been as secretive as you have the one time I saw him on the street."

"Who then?"

I'd never seen Guy so upset. "A doctor at the hospital." I reached for his hand.

He pulled away. "Why did you agree? You shouldn't have done that."

"I wanted to feel as though I can make a difference. You need to understand me."

"Right now, I can't understand you. Good night, Paulette. I'm going to leave."

"Please don't leave this way." I put my arms around him.

"God knows, I don't want to go." He nestled his face in my hair.

Panic set in. Did he mean to leave Paris right away? "Please don't go? I know this displeases you, but I also know it's because you love me and you're concerned for my safety. All I ask is that you know that what I am doing is because I love you."

"Mon trésor, how can I object?" He held me close and gave me a long sweet kiss. "You've been patient with me, and now all you ask is the same from me."

We moved to the bed to be more comfortable and indulge in the nearness of each other, but faithful to his vow, he did not make love to me.

The next morning we went to his house and had real coffee and croissants. I wondered whether his supplies had been obtained on the black market or whether he'd gotten them while out of town.

"Will you have to travel again soon?" I asked.

"Not for a couple of weeks, if my current plans hold."

"Classes will start again in a few weeks. I thought about not enrolling this term."

"There's no reason not to as far as I know," Guy said.

"Maybe not. If I could stay here and keep the safe house open, classes would be a good cover."

He took a deep breath. "I don't think that's a good idea. I went to a great deal of effort to discontinue that activity in my home."

"There's such a great need. I've heard that some of the rescued RAF men have gone home, only to return again to fight the Germans."

"I know. They're real heroes. But they're not the problem—you and Chris are."

"What do mean?"

"Chris has been working from here as a guide. You and he would have to work together."

"I didn't know." I thought about it before I commented. I knew Chris would be jealous if I lived in Guy's house. Of course he'd think it was all right for him to be there. "The airmen are more important than Chris and me. I'd like to try to work with him."

Guy gave a half-hearted nod. "We could try it on a trial basis. Say, for one month. I'll be here some of the time at least."

"Thank you. I know it'll be a good thing."

Chapter Twenty-Seven

October - December 1941 – Paris

I'd wanted a significant role in the Resistance after I'd been what one might call promoted. That achievement, if uncovered, carried serious penalties—perhaps, imprisonment and torture. By all accounts I shouldn't be humming as I packed my bag to begin work in Guy's safe house. I wished the circumstances were different, and I didn't relish the idea of Chris dampening my display of affection for Guy. Still, I couldn't wait to be with Guy for two whole weeks. He'd surprised me when he'd given in to my plea for inclusion in his Resistance work.

Guy arrived right on time to pick me up for breakfast at my favorite café before we continued on to his house on Rue Notre Dame des Champs.

After I was seated in the car and my luggage stowed in the trunk, I said, "It's nice of you to take me out to breakfast this morning."

"I thought it would be easier for both Chris and you."

"You're right. I think after breakfast we should spend a little while at my apartment before we go to your house."

"Did you forget to pack something you'll need today?"

"In a way, I suppose. We need time together to snuggle and talk before sharing a house with Chris. It is a less-than-ideal arrangement, as you pointed out."

"Your point is well taken, but you'll be glad to have Chris there when I'm away." Guy chuckled. "But while I'm here, we may have to make frequent visits to your apartment."

"I think so."

"I talked with Chris about the arrangement, and he agreed to it."

After breakfast and snuggle time at my place, we went on to Guy's house and went inside. Until then I had been confident that everything would work out. Now, the enormity of the plan threatened to make me physically sick. What right did I have to jeopardize Chris's work at the safe house? If we didn't get along, what would I expect Guy to do? My involvement could be disastrous for the three of us.

By the time Guy brought my bag in the house, my head ached and my shoulders were in knots. No matter how stressful a situation I had faced in the past, I couldn't recall such a reaction. I sat down on the sofa and closed my eyes.

"You're flushed." Guy placed his palm on my forehead. "Do you feel okay?" he asked as he sat beside me.

"I don't know. This is all too sudden. My head aches, and it feels like my shoulders are locked in place. I've never before experienced such a feeling. One minute I'm fine, and the next I'm a bundle of nerves."

"Relax. Take a deep breath." He gently massaged my shoulders. "Is that better?"

Gradually, I felt the tension ease. "Thanks . . . feels good."

"Do you want an aspirin?"

"Not now. Ummm . . . don't stop." I slid to a prone position on my stomach, and Guy continued to massage my shoulders. The tension had scarcely left my body when Chris came into view, apparently from the back of the house.

He cleared his throat. "Am I interrupting anything?"

Guy remained calm. "Chris, if you want to be helpful, bring Paulette an aspirin and a glass of water."

"Is she ailing?" he asked with a touch of sarcasm.

"Just do it," Guy snapped.

By the time I sat up, Chris was standing over me with a glass of water and the aspirin. He faced me, concern in his eyes. "I'm sorry, Paulette. It won't happen again."

"Give me the pill, and all is forgiven."

He smiled at me as he placed the glass in my outstretched hand. "I think all three of us need one of these," he said and dropped the tablet into my free hand. "You and I will make a terrific team."

I gulped it down. "I know," I said, much relieved that he had made the best of an awkward situation.

Guy rapped Chris on the back. "I expect you to work well together."

Chris looked uncomfortable. "I have to meet with Tony," he said, which I concluded was a code name.

"I'll show Paulette around here and explain more of her responsibilities while you're gone," Guy replied.

I put my arms around Guy after he closed the door behind Chris. "Do we have to get to work right away?"

He gave me a peck on the lips and said, "Oui, mademoiselle." He took my hand and guided me into his office and toward the window seats. "Remember, I told you what to do if the Germans come to the door." He lifted the fabric-covered cushions, exposing the leather seats, and placed them underneath one of the bookshelves. The seats, when raised, revealed a storage area. What came next wasn't visibly evident until he removed a fabric-covered section of the bottom of the floor to reveal a fold-down ladder into the basement.

"Yes, I remember this," I said like a good student.

"You'll need to practice using this method of escape while I'm still here."

"Okay. Give me a couple of days to get used it."

"Of course. Now that you're living here, you need a room of your own." Guy picked up my bag. "Let's get you settled."

"I like the rose guest room I used before."

"Before you decide, would you like to see the bedroom that awaits the future Duchess de Laval?"

"I want to see *your* bedroom."

"All in due time, mon trésor"

Somewhat flustered at the thought of a bedroom of honor that wasn't mine yet, I replied, "Duchess or not, I want to share your bedroom." I certainly didn't want to be put into the room reserved for his mother. It didn't matter whether or not she came to Paris often.

"Americans. That's what I love about you." He patted me on the back. "You know, your preferred arrangement won't work while Chris is here."

"I suppose not. What I meant was that when we're married, I don't want a separate bedroom. For now the rose bedroom is mine."

During the two weeks while Guy was with us, Chris made sure Guy and I had time alone. I doubted he had as many engagements as he suggested. Could he and Guy have agreed to a schedule that took him out of the house for blocks of time? I loved having the time with

Guy but worried that no airmen had been delivered to us. I didn't want to depend solely on Chris for guidance when the first ones came.

"Why do you suppose no one has been sent here yet?" I said to Guy as we ate breakfast in the kitchen one morning.

"They're probably being taken to other places to lessen the risk to this location. It's important not to be predictable."

"I'd think they'd need to use all places available."

"Remember, I worked hard to take a break from this activity. My initial agreement was that I would make my home available for up to six months at the most. When you wanted to be part of the operation, against my better judgment, I told them I'd keep it open for another four, barring any unforeseen complications."

Our last few days together flew quickly because two pilots had arrived on our doorstep, and I tried to learn everything I could to assure their safety. Chris and I began our teamwork. I'd go to my classes, come home, and take food to our guests while Chris—and a couple of times Guy, if time permitted—went to meet with the team leaders.

Fortunately, a young woman came to escort the pilots on the next leg of their trip. Their success would remain unknown to us. When I closed the door behind them, I breathed a sigh of relief that we'd completed our part without complications. Guy's guidance had been most welcome, and I felt more confident about my role. But still, when Guy left the next day, I didn't go to my classes.

I sat with a cup of coffee and tried to imagine our next guests and how Chris and I would share responsibilities without Guy's leadership.

"Aren't you supposed to be at school?" Chris asked as he went straight for the coffee pot. He turned to face me and sipped from his cup.

"I'm not going today. Why are you over there? You're welcome to join me." I patted the chair beside me.

He walked to the far side of the table and took the chair across from me. He locked eyes with me. "You're going to have to toughen up in this business. You can't afford to sit around moping because your idol's not here."

I wanted to throw my coffee at him. "How dare you say such a thing? As a matter of fact, I was thinking about you and wondering whether we can do a good job on our own."

"You don't have to worry about me. I know what I'm up against. But you better grow up . . . and *fast*."

His words stung and bitter tears threatened to support his point. I rose quickly and left the room. I felt belittled, but was it Chris's fault or did he speak the truth? Unwelcome confusion intruded to threaten my confidence. I paced. *I know what I'm doing, and I won't allow unkind words to trip me up*, I assured myself. I felt better and settled in to await our next guests.

I didn't see Chris again until later that afternoon when I returned from school and had begun to study at Guy's desk. When I heard footsteps, I looked up.

"Paulette, I'm sorry if I upset you this morning," Chris said. "We're a team that has a job to do. You should know that I'm a team player. Given your school obligations, I suggest we keep the same schedule established while Guy was here. Okay?"

I nodded and looked back down at my book. "That's fair."

He turned and left without another word.

Part of me wished I hadn't been so rude, but my emotions were raw and I didn't want him to see my weakness. Without Chris there to bounce ideas around, life would be lonely, only to be replaced with anxiety when our airmen guests' lives depended on us.

True to his word, Chris kept our established schedule, whether we had guests or not. He'd leave the house in the early evening and, sometimes, be gone all night. It wasn't the best arrangement for me, because our guests always arrived after dark, and I was left alone to care for them. It wasn't like him to leave me with all the responsibility, and I wondered whether he'd found another object of his affections.

Why should I care? But I did.

The weather had turned cold, and the trees had lost most of their leaves by the time November arrived. Chris had been missing for three days. I vacillated between thinking he was with a woman or worrying that he was in some kind of trouble. In spite of raw nerves on that bleak Monday morning of November fourth, I'd bundled up and gone to my classes while we had no airmen. My mind wandered during the lectures to thoughts of the stranger I'd seen watching the house when I left for school and whether his appearance had something to do with Chris. I couldn't tell whether it was a man or woman and tried to put it out of my mind. When the professor finished his lecture, I gathered up my books and wrapped up to face the cold. Maybe, Chris had returned or at least left a message for me.

As I reached my bike, I heard my name called. "Mademoiselle Rousseau." It was not an inquiry. It was a command.

"Yes," I replied and looked into the eyes of one of two French gendarmes.

"Come with us. You are under arrest."

"What for?"

"You'll be given a chance to answer questions, and if there is no wrongdoing, you will be released," the spokesman said in a polite, matter-of-fact tone.

"Where are you taking me?"

"*Un commissariat de police.*"

They put me in the cell in the back of a black paddy wagon with a gray bearded man who looked familiar. After racking my brain to no avail, I still couldn't place him. However, I sensed his eyes fixed on me.

"What's a young girl like you doing in this business?"

I ignored him. Good grief, how dumb could he be to speak of his business.

He taunted, "You don't have talk to me. Just be sure you don't sing to these traitors."

The rough ride ended abruptly in front of the police station. I was taken to a holding cell containing five other women. I thought no more of the man and put him out of mind until the questioning began the next morning after a breakfast of mush and watered-down milk. Two guards took me to a small room. One sat beside me while the other, the interrogator, sat across from me.

"You're American?"

"Oui."

"You volunteer at the American Hospital?"

"Oui."

"Who directs your activities there?"

"I work with the nurses and often stock medical supplies or

assist with patients when needed." I answered the next few questions and began to believe I might be released, since they hadn't mentioned Guy.

"After your nursing duties, you serve as an after-hours escort."

I retorted, "I certainly do no such a thing!" *That man must be pimp. They think I'm a prostitute.*

"Mademoiselle, do you deny that you know the man who rode here with you?"

"I have no idea who he is."

"Well, he knows who you are."

"I can't imagine how that could be."

"He's one of the contacts for an escape network. But he's had a change of heart and implicated network members at the hospital, including you."

The two of them took turns questioning me until seven o'clock in the evening. I soon realized they thought I accompanied the downed airmen to various locations, and they intended to get those addresses from me by whatever means necessary. They made that abundantly clear.

When they took me back to the cell, exhausted but not defeated, I collapsed on a mat in a dark corner, but I couldn't sleep. I hoped I hadn't contradicted myself with the answers I'd given. Even more troubling was my suspicion that Chris's disappearance wasn't coincidental.

He's gone, and I'm locked up in a cell.

The following day a rough guard came for me. He pushed me out of the door with such force that I stumbled and fell. He grabbed me by the arm and wrenched it behind my back. In a low, guttural tone, he said, "Don't you try to escape from me." I had done no such thing but knew better than to protest. He kicked my leg with his heavy boot and kept my arm in a vice-like grip until I was inside a room painted a sick shade of green. The door slammed closed.

Two sullen inquisitors had replaced the two from the previous day. The one facing me smirked. "How do you like our facility here?"

I said nothing.

"Not quite the Ritz, huh?"

Dietrich came to mind. Had he arranged my arrest? I

dismissed that possibility because the stranger I'd been caged with on our way to jail had apparently incriminated me. Had he infiltrated our Resistance group, or was he sacrificing me for some other reason?

One of the guards grabbed me by the hair and slapped me across the face. "Answer the question. We don't have time to waste with your games."

By the end of the day, when I was sent back to my cell, I had multiple bruises on my body and face. One eye was swollen shut. One of the women in the holding cell used some cold water and a portion of her blouse to use as a cold compress against my cheek and eye.

The next day I wasn't called from the cell, although two other women were. I didn't know whether the break from the incessant questions and battery would give me enough time to renew my resolve to endure what they had in store for me or whether I would break under their brutality.

Early the next morning the guard I'd seen the first day called my name, opened the door, and led me to a different room. You can imagine my surprise at seeing Colonel Dietrich seated behind a huge desk in a spacious office—the commissioner's, I think.

"Leave us," he said to the guard.

The man turned on his heel and closed the door as he left.

"Be seated, Mademoiselle Rousseau," Dietrich said. "I see you didn't take my advice to choose your companions with care. What do you have to say for your actions?"

When I was sick I'd seen a gentle side of him, and now I wondered how much cruelty he would inflict.

He pushed his chair back and moved toward me. When I hid my face in my arms for protection, he gently removed them and put his hand under my chin. "War is not a wise pursuit. Now that you've interjected yourself, there's only so much I can do to help you, if you won't learn from your mistakes."

He went back to his chair and looked at me for a long moment. "You remind me of a cat that has used eight of its lives and may be too dumb to stop before the ninth one is over. Dare I think you might be interested to know I'll be returning to Germany in a few months?"

"Why?"

"I must warn you my departure will make little difference to you. If you're arrested again, I won't intervene on your behalf."

"Why are you telling me?"

He stood and glared at me, his face distorted with anger. "In fact I may order your arrest myself."

"How can you become such a hateful person?"

"It's a survival defense. We all need one, and you better find yours."

I cowered in the chair as I saw the hard side of him, although he told the truth. Still, I had to wonder why he had given me another chance. He must have liked something about me.

He opened the door and called the guard. "Take this prisoner back to her cell for the day and get her some lunch."

I hadn't said much to him, and now it was too late. When he'd spoken to me, his expression has been somber until I'd tried his patience. At least he'd granted me one day free of abuse. I dreaded the days ahead. How long would it be before Guy found out? Would he come for me? What would he risk to gain my freedom? My hollow footsteps along the stone floor were as empty as I felt.

December 6, 1941, is a date I will never forget. Upon Dietrich's orders I was released from prison and given a ride to the Rue Notre Dame des Champs house. My bicycle stood by a tree in the yard. Who could have brought it? Chris?

As I walked up the drive, the gardener, Hugh, rounded the corner of the house with a wheelbarrow filled with garden tools. "Mademoiselle, you're back." He looked at the green and purple bruises on my face. "They did that to you? How can Frenchmen betray their country so?"

I rushed to him and allowed him to comfort me. "Oui, *les agents de police.*" All my pent-up fears tumbled forth with no censorship on my part.

"Collaborators!" Hugh spat. "Come inside. You're free now. Monsieur de Laval should be here any day."

"I hope so." I couldn't take my eyes off my bike. "Do you know how my bike got here?"

"One of your classmates saw what happened and brought it."

Once inside, Nina showered me with attention. She cooked a nice meal and insisted I try to rest. "If anyone comes to the door, I know how to take care of him. Don't you worry about it."

"Don't let me take you from your work."

"I'll sit up with you tonight, and awaken you in the morning if you insist. That's the least I can do for you and Monsieur de Laval."

"Thank you from the bottom of my heart. I hope our luck holds, and we won't have any visitors tonight."

I think her presence enabled me to relax enough to drift to sleep, but the next morning I awoke with a start. For a moment I wondered where I was. Then Guy's image materialized through the dense fog of sleep. I flopped back on the bed. "Thank God you're here."

He lifted me gently and, cradling me in his arms, carried me to the satin-upholstered settee by the window. "I'm lucky *you're* here," he said and brushed my hair aside to better see my facial bruises. "They gave you quite a beating. I'm going to take you to a doctor to be sure you're healing properly." He dropped a tablet in my hand and gave me a glass of water.

After I swallowed what I guessed was a pain killer of some type, I asked, "How did you know I'd been arrested?"

"Contacts in the police department got word to me."

I could imagine it was hard for him not to say he had warned me about the danger. "Thank you for not saying, 'I told you so.'"

He shrugged. "I'm sure you don't need any reminders."

"You're correct. I don't want to waste a moment of the time we have together. Life is precious . . . especially when I'm with you."

The emotion in his moist, cornflower blue eyes was the most precious gift he could bestow on me.

"I'll get dressed so we can go downstairs and have breakfast. I'm starving."

"I'll wait for you."

"Okay." I moved slowly because my whole body hurt. "I can't raise my arm very well."

"I'm here to help, and we'll see what the doctor says."

I smiled to myself. I didn't have an ounce of modesty left nor did I care what people thought. I only stepped behind the door of the wardrobe and turned my back to Guy while I dressed so that he wouldn't see the extent of my bruises. He already felt terrible about what had happened in his absence. I didn't dare tell him that Dietrich had interceded on my behalf.

The delightful aroma of fresh coffee greeted us before we arrived in the kitchen. Nina turned at the sound of our footsteps. "You shouldn't be down here. I'm preparing a tray at this moment."

"Thank you. That's sweet, but I'm much better now that my love is here." I patted Guy's arm.

"Do sit down. I'll have breakfast on the table in a jiffy."

"Nina, either my nose deceives me or that's real coffee." I glanced at the stove. "And ham too! However did you manage that?" My mouth was watering in anticipation.

Nina smiled and winked, saying only, "Best not to ask."

We sat while she poured coffee and set two places at the table. She went to the stove and arranged several slices of ham and scrambled eggs on a platter and set it beside a freshly baked baguette.

"I'd have brought in flowers from the greenhouse had I known you'd be down for breakfast," she said. She set the platter and bread on the table in front of us and stood back. "If you have everything you need, I'll be on with my chores."

"Merci, Nina," Guy said. "And we'll be off to the doctor's office as soon as we've finished breakfast."

We ate in silence for a while, as though neither of us knew what to say to the other. So much had happened that grieved us both. Guy seemed pensive, and I worried that he might feel he had failed me in some way. I knew I'd pushed him to let me come to his safe house.

But when he said, "I can't believe it's December already. I've been away from Claude too long. I'm no better father than mine was to me," I realized he'd shifted his attention to Claude. "I don't seem able to be a good father and serve my country at the same time. Everything I resented about my father; I've become."

"You're too hard on yourself. You can't be everything to everybody. Your selfless actions are so that Claude will live in a better world."

"Sorry, Paulette, that's not good enough."

"I miss Claude too and so look forward to Christmas with

225

him."

He gave a resigned nod. "You're right. I need to think of the time with him not the time we're apart. I'm blessed to have you at my side."

"I know we're lucky to have each other."

"As soon as your classes break for the holidays, we'll leave for Lamont. By then I'll have closed down the safe house."

"That's not necessary. I wasn't arrested because of that. The betrayal was at the hospital. One of our members reported that airmen were being helped to escape. I don't know how many names were given. Hopefully, none of the doctors or nurses were implicated."

Guy nodded. "All the more reason to step aside from this activity before it's too late."

"I hope you're not doing so because of me. You know I want to participate in the Resistance."

"I won't try to stop you. But you won't do it from this house."

"There's such a great need. Is that your final decision?"

"Oui!"

"I see."

Guy lifted my chin and kissed me. "I am involved in high-level work that is critical to the overall success of a Free France. I won't risk failing my country because of one safe house."

General De Gaulle's group? I could not be involved, I realized. "I understand," I said with finality.

The next morning, December 8, I rose at six o'clock and dressed. I hadn't been so eager to start a day in a long time, but that day Guy and I planned to spend time in the Tuileries Gardens and have lunch afterward . . . just the two of us. Time alone with him was as scarce as steak at the butcher shop these days. Most of the prime cuts of meat were used to feed the German troops, while many French people ate mostly scraps. I knew Nina spent a large portion of each day standing in lines, hoping there was something left to purchase with her ration coupons when her turn came. Often, she came away empty handed or with scraps that would have been fed to the animals prior to the war.

As I started past Guy's office on my way to the kitchen for a morning cup of ersatz coffee, I saw him with his ear pressed to the radio, the volume so low I could not hear it from the hallway. I stepped in to listen, and to interest him in breakfast, and stood a little behind him. So intent was he on the broadcast that he seemed unaware of my presence.

When I recognized the voice of the speaker, I understood the need for secrecy. Guy was listening to the BBC, a dangerous activity in France these days. Eleanor Roosevelt was speaking to the nation on her weekly radio program, "Over Our Coffee Cups."

I am speaking to you tonight at a very serious moment in our history. The Cabinet is convening and the leaders in Congress are meeting with the President. The State Department and Army and Navy officials have been with the President all afternoon. In fact the Japanese ambassador was talking to the President at the very time Japan's airships were bombing our citizens in Hawaii and the Philippines and sinking one of our transports loaded with lumber on its way to Hawaii.

By tomorrow morning the members of Congress will have a full report and be ready for action.

"Oh my God, when did it happen?" I gripped Guy's arm.

He turned toward me. "Yesterday, in the early evening, our time."

"What do you suppose will happen next?"

"America has no choice now other than to enter the war. You know what that means? You'll no longer be a citizen of a neutral country."

The gravity of the situation struck me in the solar plexus. I must have relied on the protection of my American citizenship more than I had realized. The uncertainty of the situation for my American family, friends, and myself frightened me. The thought of the horrors of warfare on American soil were alien.

Guy turned off the radio and held me in his arms. "We have to be hopeful and believe that everything happens for a reason."

"Is that what keeps you going?" I wiped away my tears.

"Without hope we're defeated. You're in shock now, but I

227

know you're a fighter."

I knew that he'd had two years of German occupation of his homeland to soul search and find his own personal answers.

"Thank you for believing me, even when I doubt myself."

He rose and rolled the beverage cart to the settee where I waited. "Wine or brandy?" he asked.

"Wine. I don't usually drink before breakfast, but there's nothing usual about today."

He poured wine for me and brandy for himself and then reached for my hand.

The warmth of his hand around my cold one assured me that he'd be there to help me adjust to my new reality. Leaning back, I sipped a little wine until I began to feel its effects. "Maybe we should have breakfast and then keep to our plans for the day." And that we did.

The streets of Paris gave no signs of the trauma in America. Parisians who had ventured out scurried around as though eager to get back behind the shuttered windows of their homes after waiting in long lines to get food for their tables.

Guy and I spent the afternoon in conversation about Christmas with Claude and ideas for gifts for the family. Shortly after ten, we tuned in to the BBC to get an update on the conditions in America. We learned that the United States had declared war on the Japanese after a rousing speech by President Franklin Roosevelt to Congress and the American people. The President had begun with the opening statement:

Yesterday, December seventh, nineteen forty-one—a date which will live in infamy—the United States of America was suddenly and deliberately attacked by naval and air forces of the Empire of Japan.

The President continued speaking for several minutes and finally concluded by saying, *I ask that the Congress declare that since the unprovoked and dastardly attack by Japan on Sunday, December seventh, nineteen forty-one, a state of war has existed between the United States and the Japanese empire.*

I turned to Guy. "That still doesn't bring the U.S. into the war against Germany and Italy. It won't help France."

"I know, but I doubt we'll have to wait very long. The Tripartite Pact between Germany, Italy, and Japan requires Germany and Italy to come to the aid of Japan if Japan is attacked. In this case, Germany and Italy are not obligated to do so, since Japan attacked the United States. But I rather imagine Monsieur Hitler will do so anyway."

We didn't have to wait long for answers. On December 10, 1941, Hitler and Mussolini declared war on the United States, and the United States reciprocated by declaring war on Germany and Italy. The world was now truly involved in a fearful, full-fledged, global showdown.

Shaken to my core, I clung to Guy. There seemed to be no safe haven left on Earth. I wondered whether Guy and I would ever be blessed with a normal family life and with children who would be spared the evils of war.

Chapter Twenty-Eight

December 1941 – Paris

Guy suggested I contact my Sorbonne professors and arrange to take my term exams early so we could get to Lamont as soon as possible. He anticipated he would face increased demands on his time for work with the Free French and reflected how that would affect his time with Claude.

I had half a mind to forget about school. "Let's go to Lamont right away," I suggested. "I don't want to continue in school. My priorities have changed."

"Paulette, no! You'll be sorry if you don't at least take your exams. You've invested months in this term. Who knows about the future?"

"I know how important it is for you to get to your family, especially, your son. He needs his father at a time like this."

He shook his head. "A few days won't make a big difference to him, but to you it will."

I sighed. "Okay, I'm going." I put on my heavy coat over my sweater and skirt and wrapped a scarf around my neck before braving the bone-chilling wind. The gray sky and leafless trees reminded me of death.

Needless to say, my general malaise affected my perceptions. While pondering how to best make my case to my professors, the answer came: play the American card. They'd think I wanted to try to get back to the States as quickly as possible. I took the nearly empty Metro to get to school, with the hope that I could catch my professors before classes started.

When I first stepped inside the building, it felt warm, mostly because of the windbreak it provided. But gradually, I became aware of how cold it really was. I knew what to expect on days like this one. The professors and students stayed bundled up because the fuel shortage affected everyone—institutions as well as individuals.

I went to the office of my advisor to test his reaction to my request. I needed a success to bolster my confidence before I approached the other two professors.

I was in luck. He was there, sorting papers.

"Bonjour, Professor Beckmann," I said as I approached.

He looked up, clearly surprised to see me—and for that matter any student, I think.

"I need to leave Paris before my final exam. Is it possible to take it this week rather than next?"

"I think it can be arranged. The hard part for you will be getting out of France at a time like this."

"Merci, Monsieur. I'll need luck, but I have to try."

"See me tomorrow at ten, and be ready for your exam."

I succeeded with the other two professors and finished my exams by mid-week.

Loire Valley

We arrived at Lamont five days before Christmas for a much-needed time away from Paris.

Guy parked outside the chateau and turned off the engine, but he didn't get out of the car right away. "You'll find the festivities quite different from last Christmas. Circumstances have changed. The Germans have taken a tremendous toll on our food supply, as you well know. Food is nearly as scarce here in the country as it is in Paris."

"How else will it differ?"

"Many ways, and one in particular."

"What one?"

"There is no longer a reason why we shouldn't marry because of your citizenship status."

Stunned that he would bring up the subject when I had assumed all along that it was a convenient excuse to avoid the topic, my eyes met his to gauge his sincerity. "I guess you're right. What reasons remain?" I asked wary there might be something else.

"The only one I can think of is whether you want to fulfill the role of the future Duchess de Laval."

"I haven't been groomed for such a role. Does that rule me out?"

Guy kissed me on the cheek. "Of course not. But it might limit some of your activities and require things you hadn't

231

expected."

"Such as?"

"As you already know, my family has many traditions that are important to us. Our community is a part of our extended family, and we accept the responsibilities that go with it."

"I love you, Guy de Laval, and will make every effort to do what is best for us. I want to be your partner in every way."

He nodded. "I would like to have more children. Is that something you want too?"

"Yes, I do. Can't you tell how much I love Claude?"

He patted my arm. "You're very good with him. Let's get inside; it's not getting any warmer out here."

When we got out of the car, I was surprised to see the gardener and Guy's black dog running toward us. "There was no holding back Mystique," the gardener said when they reached us. "As soon as she heard that car, she barked at me and took off."

"I'm glad you didn't try," Guy said as he rubbed down Mystique. "That's my girl." He patted her on the head and turned to get our luggage out of the trunk.

"Here, let me give you a hand with those." The man reached for my large one, already on the ground, and walked with us to the door. "Come on, Mystique," he said. "We've got to get back to work."

A chill filled the large entry gallery, but inside the morning room a huge log fire crackled and provided adequate warmth. Claude saw us first and raced to us. "Papa! Pet!"

I'd swear he'd grown at least three or four inches since we'd last seen him. His face had matured into that of a boy. None of that stopped Guy from hoisting his son onto his shoulders and carrying him to Monsieur de Laval.

The major stood with some effort and greeted us. "I think you'll see quite a difference in Claude," he said to Guy. "He'll make a fine military officer." Then he turned and greeted me. "Bienvenue, Mademoiselle Rousseau. We must talk often during your time here."

We all made ourselves comfortable, the major with his wife on the sofa across from Guy, Claude, and me on the loveseat. Claude soon tired of the conversation and ran off to play with his new toy airplanes and tanks.

"I hope you won't be disappointed in our Christmas

activities," Madame de Laval said. "We won't be able to celebrate to the extent we did last year. Our dinner will be less elaborate and include only the overnight guests we can accommodate. People can't risk being out after curfew. The cathedral has cancelled midnight mass for that reason."

Guy frowned at his mother. "What about in our chapel this year?"

"We'll have it. Father Mahoney will be one of our overnight guests."

"Good. Paulette and I will want to talk with him."

Madame de Laval's face lit up. "Are there wedding plans to be made?"

"Madame," the major interrupted his wife. "Let him speak for himself."

Guy stood and went to his mother's side and cupped her hands in his. I followed him.

When she rose and put an arm around each of us, Guy kissed her cheek. "Oui, Maman, Paulette and I are ready to set a wedding date."

By that time the major had joined us. He clapped Guy on the shoulder. "My boy, it's the smartest thing you've done for a long time. This news calls for a celebration. Madame, let's have a glass of Champagne in honor of this joyous event."

"By all means, dear." She poured champagne and we all clicked glasses.

We all repeated after the major, "Santé."

"When will you marry?" Madame asked.

Guy looked at me. "I suggest while we're still here for the holidays. Sometime after the New Year, perhaps? What do you say?"

What did I think? The sooner the better. After all, I thought we should already be married by this time. I still couldn't believe this wasn't just another sweet dream. "Yes," I said demurely so as to temper the eagerness I felt.

"Now that that's settled, if you'll excuse me, I'm going to try to catch up on the BBC's report on the war effort." Monsieur reached for his cane.

Guy handed it to his father. "I'll come with you."

"The Vichy government is increasingly hostile to the Jews,"

Guy's father paused and said, "I suppose you know about the latest edict that forbids Jews from changing their domicile, and the word *Juif* or *Juive* must be stamped in red on their ID Cards. I can't believe that Marshal Pétain allows such a thing." He frowned. "I suppose he was forced to by the Germans to prevent something like a complete occupation of the country."

Guy shook his head. "No telling. Just before we left Paris, the Germans arrested over seven hundred affluent French Jews in the city. Come on. We have a lot to talk about."

I hoped Guy could lure his father into playing a game of checkers or something to take his mind off the terrible state of affairs.

Once Guy and his father had departed, Madame de Laval moved to sit beside me on the sofa. "I'm sorry the war will affect your wedding. I don't imagine your family in America will be present. I'm sure that grieves you."

I held my emotions in check and looked at my hands. "Oui, it does, but I know that nothing is certain these days. Guy's love sustains me. I thank the Lord for each precious day we have together."

She slipped her arm around my shoulder. "We are your family away from home and will do everything we can to make your wedding day a joyful one."

"Merci."

"As you've seen, I have suitable fabrics for a wedding dress. We'll take a look at them so you can make your selection. I'll see that it's ready for your big day."

"I don't know how to thank you. I brought a simple dress with me, but I wouldn't want to wear it for the wedding."

"I'm the one who should thank you. I so wanted a daughter and hoped one day to help plan her wedding."

"With your help, I know everything will be perfect for Guy's and my big day."

"Have you and he made any decisions yet?"

"Only what you heard. We haven't made specific plans."

Perhaps you'll want to be married the day after New Year's. There'll be the civil ceremony and then the religious one. The de Laval family has a time-honored tradition of being married in the chapel here at Lamont."

"I know family tradition is important to Guy. And I can think of no other place as perfect as the beautiful chapel."

Madame's eyes glazed. "How well I remember the day I married Monsieur de Laval in that lovely chapel. We were filled with hope for our future. Not everything turned out the way we hoped, but we are blessed with our son and grandson . . . and soon, we'll have a new daughter, too."

I reached for her hand. "I'm committed to being a loving wife and a loyal family member."

"And I'm sure you will be. May God's grace be with us all. Oh, yes. Have you seen Aline and her baby girl?"

"No. We received an announcement of the birth. I hope that Guy and I can visit her at Chateau Maille."

"That won't be necessary. Aline and the baby will be our guests here for Christmas. They should be arriving later today."

"That's wonderful. I can't wait to see them."

"They should be here any time now." She shook her head. "The marquis plans to go on to Paris for the holidays."

"I'm sorry to hear it but am not surprised. He appears to be wrapped up in his art collection."

"Perhaps you and Aline will help wrap gifts after dinner."

I smiled at her. "What fun."

"I've kept you from my son long enough. Yvette will bring Claude to you after he's finished with his lessons, which should be soon."

"Lessons? But it's the holiday season."

"The season, oui. But his grandfather insists he continue them until Christmas Eve."

"Last year he seemed still a baby and now he's . . ."

"Insists on what?" Guy had slipped in behind us, unbeknownst to either of us.

I twisted around to look at him. "How long have you been standing there?"

His mother didn't give him a chance to answer. "Your father insists that Claude studies with the tutor until Christmas Eve."

"That's Papa. I don't agree with him, because I remember how I felt when it happened to me."

"You didn't walk off just now while your father was talking. I hope."

"Non, Maman. He fell asleep and left me to talk to myself."

"I worry that he feels helpless. He sleeps more than is necessary."

"Maman, I agree." He kissed her on the cheek and reached for my hand. "Let's see the tree before we pick up Claude."

✝

Time alone would give us the much-needed chance to consider wedding plans without interruption. Guy led me down the long hallway, and neither of us spoke until we were out of earshot of his parents.

"I thought we were on the way to the great hall," I commented when he stopped and entered the library.

"We are. Just by way of the library." He closed the door behind us. "I suggest we get married on January seventh."

"You do have it figured out."

"I think it allows enough time after the holidays to get ready for the wedding."

"I agree. Your mother suggested the second, but I prefer your choice of dates. She has offered to make a wedding dress for me. I don't want anything elaborate, and she assured me I have my choice of fabrics and style."

"That tells me that Maman approves of you," Guy said with a straight face.

We'll go to the *mairie's* office and be married in a civil ceremony and then have the religious service in the chapel that afternoon. It's best to keep it simple, just close friends and family. Maman will see to a nice reception for us."

"I have no doubt about that."

"Where's Papa?" Claude's voice carried to us from the gallery.

I smiled. "The whole house knows when he's around."

Guy nodded. "It's okay. He has to be that way sometimes to get attention."

I'd opened the door. "Claude, we're in here, waiting for you. Want to see the Christmas tree with us?"

He scowled. "I've already seen it. I want to go outside."

Guy squatted down in front of Claude and put both hands on

236

the boy's shoulders. "Is that any way to talk to Paulette?"

He looked down at the floor. "Non, Papa."

Guy picked him up. "You can come with us or stay with Mamie until I can go outside with you."

"I'll stay with Mamie." He ran off toward the morning room.

"Claude needs to be around other children more often. I'm going to speak to the tutor about including several other boys in the classroom. It might be different if he had brothers and sisters of his own." A wistful expression revealed his concern. "I know what it's like to be an only child in an all adult household."

"Including other boys in the lessons would go a long way toward solving the problem," I said.

Even if Guy and I had children, the age difference wouldn't offset Claude's need for companionship, so I hoped Guy would follow through right after the holidays. I reached for his hand "Christmas is such a happy time of year. I can't wait to see the tree."

"It's good to be home with you and the whole family."

We dashed to the great hall like a couple to kids. Guy paused on the threshold and looked up. We were standing under the mistletoe and his lips pressed against mine. My heart skipped a beat. I didn't want the divine ecstasy to end, and I clung to him.

He released me and took a deep breath. "We better take a look at the tree."

"Do we have to?"

"Oui, mon trésor. I promise I won't forget where we left off."

"It's torture!"

"How well I know."

Arm in arm, we made our way to the tree. There was no fire in the fireplace, and many of the ornaments in boxes awaited their places on the fragrant branches.

"Let's hang some." I took a box of bells, climbed the ladder, and placed half of them on the top branches while Guy hung silver ornaments on the bottom half.

We worked until the mantle clock struck the half hour then Guy set his box on the table. "Claude is waiting for me." He took my box and extended his hand to mine as I descended the ladder.

Voices drifted toward us as we approached the gallery. A baby cried.

"Do you think Aline is here?"

"I don't know."

As we drew closer, I saw Aline, holding her baby, Madame de Laval, and the two other couples from Bordeaux whom I'd met the previous Christmas. A boy and girl stood nearby. The marquis stood at the far end of the room and talked to the priest. Guy stopped to greet the two men, and I rushed to say hello to Aline. Her haggard appearance shocked me. Dark, half-moon circles emphasized the golden color of her eyes, but her face had little color, not even on her hollow cheeks. She looked as if she'd lost a lot of weight since her marriage. How could she possibly breast feed her baby? Had the Germans taken most of their food?

Claude ran forward and grabbed my hand.

"Here's your Papa. Come, let's greet your guests," I said to him.

The three of us made the rounds and welcomed everyone. Then the butler escorted the other two couples to their rooms while Madame talked at length with Aline and her husband.

"I'll show you to your rooms after we've had a glass of wine. I'm sure the other guests will join us soon," Madame said to them.

The marquis raised his hand. "I'll have one glass, but I have to leave for Paris right afterward."

Madame blinked in disbelief before she recovered her voice. "You'll miss the holidays with your family?"

"Afraid so. It can't be helped."

"If I may be so forward," Madame de Laval held his gaze. "I suggest for appearance sake, if for no other, you at least spend the night and leave early in the morning."

"Madame, since you put it that way. I accept your kind invitation."

When Guy hugged Aline, she laid her head on his shoulder for a long while before either of them said anything. I didn't know what to say to her, so I listened to their small talk, nodding occasionally.

"May I hold little Martine?" I held out my arms for Aline to give her to me. "It's hard to believe she's three months old already." She looked so peaceful for a short time, until she started to fuss and her face reddened as she shifted into a full-fledged wail.

Aline took her from me and laid her in a wicker portable bed. "I'm going to have to feed her in the library. Come with me where we can talk freely," she said.

I followed mother and daughter and closed the door as they settled down on a swivel chair. Aline sat with her baby and unbuttoned her blouse for her to nurse.

Baby Martine suckled with gusto for quite some time and then began to whimper.

"You must have your hands full with the baby and the chateau," I said softly.

Aline sighed. "Yes. It's been hard for me since the difficult delivery. Not only has my health suffered, but so has my marriage." She lifted the baby to her shoulder and patted her back until Martine burped a couple of times and began to cry again.

Aline moved her to the other breast. "This baby is ravenous most of the time. It's hard to produce milk with the food shortages we have these days."

"Well, she certainly looks well-nourished at any rate. It has to be hard on you." I couldn't imagine what sort of complications she had gone through; it surely must have been awful. Guy had seemed to sense that something was terribly wrong with Aline and had gone out of his way to comfort her.

"Martine was a breech birth baby and the doctor did everything he could to save her, but in the process I was torn up inside and an infection set in. My life hung in the balance for three days." She lifted the baby and held her against her shoulder, gently patting her back. Her eyes met mine. "I won't be able to bear any more children."

I gasped. "Oh, no. I'm so sorry."

"I guess every pregnant woman prays to have a healthy baby and to be able to care for them. Most of them look forward to other children to complete their family. But they don't expect their husband to reject his child and his wife."

I couldn't believe the man was that shallow. "Included in the marriage vows is the promise to love in sickness and in health."

"Apparently, some men don't take their vows seriously. After the doctor told the marquis and me the sad news, my husband announced he had business in Paris and would leave in two weeks. By that time I was stronger and began to prepare for the trip. He confronted me and asked what I thought I was doing. I told him I was getting ready for Paris. He glared at me and said the baby wasn't up to the trip—that the two of us would have to remain at home. To tell you the truth, I was relieved. I didn't argue with him about it."

My heart ached for Aline. I shook my head. "I can't imagine how awful that made you feel."

"For the sake of my daughter, I had to stay at the chateau and make a home for her the best I could. A month later, he came back, only to see if I had taken care of the chateau. Then he announced he'd return to Paris in two days. By that time there was no question that both Martine and I were well enough to make the trip, so I suggested that we accompany him. He said it wouldn't be possible because the bedrooms were needed for his art connoisseur partners. That's when I realized our marriage, in the true sense of the word, was over. I'm lucky he brought us to Lamont for the holidays. What really hurts is how he ignores his own child."

"Maybe, when Martine is older, he'll come to value his family," I said.

"He has my dowry, but he'll have no son from me. I'm of no more use. It's final in my mind. I'm sorry to burden you with all my troubles. I stay busy at the chateau but have no confidante. I miss you and my friends in Paris."

"Madame de Laval is a loving person, and she is fond of you. I know she and I are here for you."

"Bless you, my dear Paulette. In some ways Guy is more like his mother than his father. He's always been good to me."

"Guy and I have set our wedding date for January seventh. I hope you will stay at Lamont and be my matron of honor."

After she placed the sleeping Martine into her portable bed, Aline hugged me. "I can vouch for him. You're getting a good man."

"I know," I said as tears rolled down our cheeks." I cried for joy at my good fortune and for the pain that Aline suffered. I think she felt the same.

By December twenty-third the chateau was filled to capacity with invited guests who would celebrate the holidays with us. Guy and I had little opportunity to spend time with Claude because he and the other children played inside and outside from dawn to dusk. Madame had planned various indoor activities for them, and the men took turns with the youngsters during the outdoor adventures.

That afternoon, while the children were outside, Madame took me aside and asked whether Aline and I would help wrap the many gifts she'd made for the children. Aline agreed and the two of us joined Madame in the craft room.

"I can't believe you made all these things this year. It's like Santa's workshop," Aline said as she set the baby on a vacant spot on the gift-wrapping table. Madame de Laval worked in the center of the table between Aline and me and distributed gifts to be finished with ribbons and nametags. The time flew quickly as wrapped gifts were stacked to precarious heights.

"I need to get to the kitchen to see how the cook is getting with her two new helpers," Madame said at last.

I put the tag on a completed package. "If you need me to help there, let me know."

Madame nodded. "I'm confident you'll be able to continue here without me, and we'll manage in the kitchen." She gathered up as many packages as she could carry. "I'll have Yvette place these around the tree. She knows how I want them arranged. By the time we host the wedding reception, the other girls will know their jobs too. But this is their first day here."

After Madame left, Aline set aside her work and pulled up a chair beside me.

"Are you okay?" I asked.

She nodded. "I need your help," she said in a whisper.

"What is it? You know I'll do what I can."

"One of the reasons I'm exhausted is that I'm involved with the Resistance."

"No, you can't risk your life now with a baby who depends on you."

"All the more reason to work to defeat the Germans."

"You're only one person. There are others who will carry on."

"I don't have to leave the chateau. I take care of the medical needs of downed airmen until they are well enough to make the long trek across the border to Spain to return to England. But I really need your help with the nursing duties. Your hospital experience has prepared you for that work."

"I know it's dreadful for those airmen in that situation. If

241

they can make it back, they'll return and fight again. I've helped them in many ways, but I've decided to stay at Lamont after I'm married."

"What about the Sorbonne?"

"Claude needs me. In another year or so, he'll be ripped from his childhood. It's already begun. His grandfather has secured a tutor to prepare him for boarding school in a couple of years."

"The de Laval men are heir to an honored tradition, continued from generation to generation."

"Claude needs balance in his life, and his grandfather isn't sufficient. How will he know how to love a woman?"

"Trust Guy to know."

"Yes, I do, and I give his mother all the credit." I paused and changed the subject. "You haven't told me whether you'll stay with us for the wedding."

"Nor have you said whether you'll help me with the airmen."

That's when I began to lose my resolve. "Maybe I can divide my time between you and Claude while Guy is away. When he's home, my place is with him."

"Merci, *mon amie*. I'll be able to stay for the wedding, if you and Guy will take me home and spend a few days with me," Aline said. "My husband didn't say when he'd return for us."

"I'm sure Guy will agree, and Madame de Laval will want to provide a dress for you, as she is for me. She'll insist on doing so. Come, we have tell Guy about our plans."

Claude ran to meet us as we entered the morning room. "Paulette, where have you been?" The tone of his voice demanded an acceptable response. Had his military preparation progressed so quickly?

Aline laid the baby in my arms. "Claude, we've been helping get ready for Christmas. What would you like for Père Noël to bring you?"

Claude frowned and Martine bawled. Claude's nostrils flared as he pulled on my arm. "I don't like her."

"Why do you say such a thing?"

She's a crybaby. A coward."

"No. She's not big like you." I returned Martine to her mother.

"She's pink and has a round belly like a pig." He stomped his foot.

"Claude, come here. You know you're my man, don't you?"

He didn't respond but ran across the room to his grandfather.

I looked at Aline. "I'm sorry. I must work at gaining his confidence. I love that boy so much. It hurts to see his grandfather curtail his childhood."

She nodded. "I should have been more sensitive to his situation."

I wondered whether Guy would object to my getting involved with the Resistance again. If so, I wouldn't blame him.

Chapter Twenty-Nine

January - March 1942 – Loire Valley

Minutes before midnight on New Year's Eve, under the mistletoe, I slipped into Guy's arms. At the stroke of twelve, his lips touched mine, caressing, more than a kiss. We were at the dawn of the New Year—a time which promised happiness and prosperity, according to traditional folklore.

Our wedding, set to take place a week later, filled me with hope of a blessed union. I pushed grim thoughts of war from my mind and savored the well wishes of the guests at our small celebration.

Brother Roger embraced Guy. "*Bonne Année*, my friend. And congratulations on your upcoming nuptials." He turned to me. "Take good care of him," he said before he stepped aside so others could wish us well.

Aline toasted us, saying, "Guy and Paulette, may you have many happy years ahead of you and remain as radiant in each other's company as you are today."

Guy gave her an affectionate kiss on the cheek. "Thank you for agreeing to be Paulette's maid of honor. It means a lot to me."

"Paulette is like a sister to me," she said. "And Guy, I'm eternally grateful for your friendship."

Curtis and Chantel from Chartres waited some time before they congratulated us. "Chantel and I are happy for you," Curtis said when they finally approached. "But may I borrow your man for a moment?"

"I suppose, if you're sure it's only for a moment."

"Ladies, please excuse us," Curtis said.

"I hope you'll visit us again," Chantel said and triggered my curiosity when she gave me an enigmatic smile after the two men stepped away.

I could see them speaking to Brother Roger. I wanted to know what they said but could not hear because they talked so quietly. Brother Roger left them and cornered the Tours cathedral priest. The two of them looked our way as Brother Roger gestured with his hands while he bent the other man's ear.

Sometime after two o'clock in the morning, the houseguests, as well as the rest of us, retired for a few hours' sleep before gathering again for the mid-morning New Year's Day breakfast buffet. Most of the guests planned to stay at Lamont until the day after the wedding, so we could pretty well plan our schedules until then. Local friends of the family wouldn't arrive until time for the afternoon religious ceremony in the Lamont chapel.

Wedding plans and arrangements filled my days when I wasn't with Guy and Claude. Palpable excitement filled the household. Guests and family worked to make our day special.

The day after New Year's, after breakfast, Madame approached Aline and me. "Let's go. It's time you make decisions about your dresses."

"Thank you. I feel like a princess. A wedding dress for me to marry my prince."

"You're most welcome. I don't have a daughter of my own, so I didn't dream I'd ever have this pleasure. Aline, I've known you, although not well, since your childhood. I'm happy to do this for you, too."

When we arrived in the crafts room, Madame de Laval went to an armoire and removed a white, satin-lined lace gown. "This was my wedding dress, made from lace given to me by my Grandmother Ligne. You're welcome to wear it, or you may select fabrics of your choice and give me an idea of the style you'd like."

"It's beautiful, but perhaps you'd rather save it for a future granddaughter."

"Ma chérie, if I wanted to do that, I wouldn't have shown it to you."

After my remark, I realized that, if she were to have a granddaughter, I would be the child's mother. It seemed reasonable that I be married in the family heirloom. "I'd be honored to wear your beautiful gown."

"Don't do it for me. If you like, I'll alter it for you. But I understand if you prefer something else. It's your wedding."

"There's no question about it. Your gown is my choice."

Madame de Laval appeared to be convinced and turned to Aline, "Now to your dress. When I show you fabrics, it's because I want you to choose one. You don't have to ask whether I want you to use the material."

"I understand and promise to stick with my decision."

Aline chose a gold lamé before responding to her fussy baby. "I'll go and tend to Martine. I shouldn't be gone long."

Madame waved at her. "Take your time, I'll be here."

I noticed that Aline's choice of fabric accentuated her golden eyes.

Madame waited until Aline disappeared from view before shaking her head. "Marriage doesn't seem to have been kind to her. Arranged marriages often lead to heartache." She sighed. "I'm happy that my son will soon be married to the woman he loves." She closed her eyes and appeared to forget my presence for a moment. "Paulette," she said after a few minutes. "Let's get you into this dress to see what alterations are needed."

An inner glow warmed my spirit. Madame de Laval had given me her seal of approval once again.

While she slipped a few pins into tucks around my waist, she said, "We have flowers in the *orangerie* for a beautiful bridal bouquet, and there are snowdrops in the garden. I suggest a nosegay of white and blush-pink roses. Have Guy go with you to take a look at them later."

At dinner the evening before the wedding, Major de Laval rose and rapped on the table before the meal began. "Thank you, each of you, for helping us prepare for Guy and Paulette's wedding. I know we will cherish this time together now when unity of purpose is so important."

"Hear! Hear!" the guests responded in agreement.

And as a measure of my sincerity, I've delayed the resumption of Claude's studies for three more weeks."

Laughter followed the remark, and after his father sat down, Guy stood. "Paulette and I look forward to greeting you at our wedding reception on what will be the happiest day of our lives."

Shouts of "*Santé, Santé,*" echoed around the room.

Although the hour was late, Guy took my hand and led me to the deserted petite salon. We kissed and snuggled on the loveseat.

"I don't want to let you go, but it is getting late," he said.

"It doesn't matter how late it is. I'm lonely when you're not with me."

Guy held me close to his heart. "It's a good thing we're getting married tomorrow. After that we'll have time for just the two of us. That reminds me. We still have a few decisions to make."

I breathed in the woodland scent of him. "Well, we better talk about it now. What are they?"

He kissed the tip of my nose. "I recall you said you wanted to sleep with me in my bedroom, but I must caution you that it's a small room . . . not a honeymoon suite. Of course, Lamont has a spacious one available for such an occasion. Mademoiselle, what is your pleasure?"

I chuckled. "I want you and your bedroom, Monsieur."

"Your wish is my command."

"All right, there are some things I need to ask you," I said.

He leaned back and studied my face. "I'm listening."

"I want the two of us to visit Aline at Chateau Maille. May we do that?"

He nodded. "And what else?"

"I'd like for us to take Aline home after she spends a week here with us."

"That should be all right." He frowned. "But I thought you might want the two of us to go away to a little cottage for a honeymoon of sorts."

"That sounds wonderful for another time. Aline has asked me to help her nurse downed airmen on the escape line, and you know how much I want to contribute to the war effort."

He stared at me as if I'd lost my mind. "I thought you wanted to spend time at Lamont with Claude."

"I do. I intend to divide my time between Lamont and Maille."

"What about the Sorbonne?"

"I'm not going back. You and I need to spend as much time as we can with Claude. He's growing up so fast. We have to do it before he's sent off to boarding school."

"Don't you think I know that? It keeps me awake at night."

"I know," I said. "That's why it's so important that we're with him as often as possible."

"I'll have to go to Paris for periods of time to assure that the house is owner-occupied and not declared abandoned. The Vichy government would use that as an excuse to seize it. I've arranged for Hugh and Nina to be fulltime staff there. I had thought you'd stay there and go to school, but I like your plan better." He sighed. "Now

I know how you must feel when I'm away. We both know the risks involved in our work and must make some tough choices."

I shall never forget awakening on the morning of January seventh—Guy's and my wedding day—and pinching my arm to be sure I wasn't dreaming. "Ouch" I muttered. It wasn't a dream. At least if my arm had bruised, the sleeve of my bridal gown would cover it.

A glance at the clock routed me out of bed. I had less than two hours to dress, have breakfast, and meet Guy and our witnesses at *la mairie* for the civil ceremony, which would be performed at City Hall and which was required to be legally married in France. Guy told me that the civil requirement had to do with separation of church and state. So, after that ceremony, we would be legally married before our wedding in the chapel at Lamont. Although not required, our religious ceremony held great significance for both of us.

A knock at the door threatened to delay me. I ignored it.

Madame de Laval called, "Paulette, open the door. I have a surprise for you."

"Just a minute." I fumbled with a button on my robe then scurried to the door and opened it.

"I waited as long as I could to deliver this." She handed me a beautiful maroon velvet dress and matching jacket.

"For me? Thank you. How did you know?" I'd admired that lovely velvet when Aline selected her fabric. "It will be perfect for our civil ceremony today."

"That's what I thought. Is there anything I can do to help you get ready?"

"Yes, Please help me into my dress without mussing my hair."

We arrived at the Tours City Hall at ten o' clock, the appointed time for our civil marriage ceremony. How ironic this cut-and-dried ceremony was the one that legalized our marriage. The five-minute ceremony required that the mayor and the secretary read from a script written and approved by the National Assembly in Napoleon's time. No deviations! Guy and I were entering into a legal marriage contract.

The mayor, a friend of the de Laval family, wore the required official sash of the mayor's office, the tricolor, same as the French flag. He welcomed us before the brief ceremony began. Aline served as my witness and Brother Roger, the monk, for Guy. Monsieur and Madame de Laval waited with us for the completion of the marriage certificate, a requirement for presentation to the priest prior to our religious ceremony.

The ceremony itself was brief and to the point, lasting only a few minutes. When he finished speaking, the mayor inscribed his signature with a flourish and handed the marriage certificate to Guy. "Congratulations, Monsieur and Madame Guy de Laval. I look forward to attending your afternoon ceremony."

By the time we returned from Tours—we were delayed by a German checkpoint along the highway—we had just enough time for a light lunch and to change for the ceremony in the chapel.

Guy and I couldn't keep our eyes off each other, but we managed to keep our hands to ourselves while having a bowl of vegetable stew. As the clock crept toward two, we made time to be alone before changing clothes. We returned to our favorite hideaway in the petite salon, and as soon as Guy closed the door, I put my arms around his neck. "Kiss me," I whispered.

He picked me up and carried me to the sofa. "You don't have to ask, mon trésor." He nibbled on my ear, kissed my forehead and cheeks, and then his lips, warm and sweet, were on mine.

A soft tap on the door intruded at a critical moment. I sat up and brushed my hands along my hair.

Aline stepped in and moved back against the door. "I'm sorry to disturb, but it's time for Paulette to get ready."

"Madame, ask you not permission of Paulette's husband before you whisk his wife away?"

Aline smiled and came forward to hug him. "No, Monsieur, she is one of the few lucky ones with a husband who indulges her." She laid her head on his shoulder for a long moment before she straightened with dignity and looked at me, her tear-filled eyes shining like newly minted gold coins.

I wanted to comfort her but was uncertain whether my effort would have the opposite effect. She and Guy seemed to have a deep connection on some level.

"Be off with you," he said to me. "I don't want to be left waiting at the altar."

Aline had recovered her composure and replied, "I'll see that she doesn't."

He kissed Aline's cheek and brushed my lips with his before we left him.

"He won't need much time to get ready, but you will." Aline put her arm around my shoulder. "Madame de Laval arranged for Yvette to take care of Martine all day. She said I needed the day off. All I'll have to do is nurse the baby before the wedding reception. I didn't produce enough milk for two feedings."

Grateful for her friendship on this special day, I gripped her hand and we ran towards my bedroom.

I walked down the aisle to Guy in his mother's wedding dress—which fit perfectly after a couple of alterations. I carried a bridal bouquet of white roses, edged in blush pink, and ferns. Guy wore the blue suit he'd worn at the civil ceremony, the one that drew attention to his cornflower blue eyes. His smile warmed my heart and led my eyes to one of the stained-glass windows that commemorated the union of his fifteenth century ancestor, another Guy de Laval, who had united two great estates. I felt a part of a surreal pageant while I passed by twisted stone columns and saw my Prince Charming waiting for me in front of the altar and stained-glass windows. The elderly priest led us through the traditional Catholic wedding ceremony. Our wedding vows were interspersed among the three rituals of the sixteen-step process.

My heart sang with delight as Guy said, "I, Guy, take you, Paulette, for my wife, to have and to hold from this day forward, for better, for worse, for richer, for poorer, in sickness and in health, until death do us part. With this ring I thee wed and pledge thee my troth."

Not until now had I felt we were truly husband and wife.

Strange how the religious ceremony seals the sacred sense of two becoming one.

Reception dinners usually go on until all hours, but ours was shortened so that guests could get an early start the next morning. There were the traditional toasts and the food, although limited by necessity, was, I am sure, delicious. But I heard little and tasted even less, wanting only for the dinner to end so I could be alone with my husband . . . at last.

✝

Yvette showed me to Guy's bedroom. "This room is too small for the two of you. What were they thinking of to ask me to bring you here?"

"I requested this room."

The scent of Guy's woodland aftershave hung in the air. I wanted to be alone and look at every detail of the room. I didn't want to discuss the room. It felt warm and inviting, minimally furnished with a bed, armoire, and small table and chair in the elegant style of Napoleon III, all placed on a large rose-and-brown Aubusson rug.

"Whatever for?" Yvette exclaimed. "A man's room is not usually large enough or elegant enough for a lady. Men can get along with little space." She helped me out of my wedding dress, hung it alongside Guy's shirts, suits, and sundry other garments in the armoire, and brought my bag to me.

I stood before her in my bra, panties, and slip. "That will be all, thank you," I said with a smile. "I can manage the rest."

She giggled. "I'll bet you can."

Little did she know of my lack of experience in such matters. How I wished I could be as confident as she. I looked around the room a second time then went into the bathroom and stared into the mirror. I wanted to understand my new husband. What was important to him? I felt sure his room would reveal new things. I tried to make sense of what I saw so that I could become an important part of him. I'd imagined this night many times but still felt shy as it approached.

I stared into the mirror and wondered if my breasts were too small as I fumbled with the bow at the neck of my nightgown. *No.*

It's not a suit of armor. I left it loose. I wanted to please my husband and to adequately meet his needs. What did I know about a man's expectations? I had to push myself to leave the security of the bathroom to await Guy's arrival and was surprised to see him already in the bedroom.

He came to me and held me against his chest. "I know this is a new experience for you. We'll take our time." He carried me to the bed and was gentle and patient as I clung to him, my nails pressed on his flesh. His tender caresses and kisses calmed me. "That's better. We have all night to get this right," he murmured in my ear.

I awoke before he did in the morning. Rather than awaken him, I watched my magnificent husband sleep. His chest rose and fell with each life-giving breath. I resisted the impulse to kiss him so that he'd hold me in his arms again; instead, I lay still so as not to disturb him. Too many nights he'd been without adequate sleep. I'd do anything I could to protect him but had little power to do much.

He sighed and extended his hand until it touched my chest.

Chateau Maille, near Lyon

Early the next morning—Monday—we said our goodbyes to the de Lavals and climbed into the Renault for the drive to Chateau Maille. Aline and the baby were in the back, and I sat in the front with my husband.

After we got underway, Guy draped his arm around the back of my seat. "Claude has changed a lot since he started lessons with the tutor. My friends were impressed with his desire to participate in our outdoor activities."

"What sorts of things did you do?" I asked.

"Archery, for one. He wanted a turn shooting at the target. So we set about making a slingshot for him to use. He agreed only after I promised I'd get him a bow and arrow."

"I'm not surprised. I've noticed how he has matured since our last visit. He needs someone to keep an eye on him. A companion. Do you suppose your father could do that?"

"I spoke to our gardener about overseeing him when he gets his bow and arrow." Guy shifted his position. "I envy him. I'll miss that special time with my son."

"It's heartbreaking, I'm sure," Aline said. "I'm fortunate not to have to choose between my child and work, although, I do put her in danger of losing her mother should something go wrong."

My heart skipped a beat. What a terrible dilemma they experienced, and I'd be faced with the same if we had a child before the dreadful war ended. What could I say to them? Our work was for the good of the whole, not just ourselves.

Guy placed his hand over mine. Was he thinking about our future children too? He'd been hesitant to marry because of his divided loyalties. And with our marriage, future innocent children could be affected.

"Aline, how much have you told Paulette about the work you want her to do?" Guy asked.

"What do you think I told her? I simply asked her to help nurse injured airmen at the chateau until they were well enough be escorted into neutral Spain. You know what I do!"

Guy gripped the steering wheel with both hands. "Nurse injured men to wellness. Is that all?"

"You know in this work everything is uncertain. We do what the situation requires."

"I want your word that only in an emergency would you ask Paulette to do anything other than nursing."

"You know I can't promise that. I don't know what will happen."

Guy fell silent, as did Aline. I dreaded a confrontation with my husband, and yet, I couldn't retreat to the safety of Lamont. I worried that my safety would be a constant distraction for him. No wonder he'd been reluctant to marry.

I closed my eyes. There was no single correct choice to be made. My angst triggered a splitting headache.

I slept until we stopped along the way for lunch. Later, at Aline's request, we detoured for another meal to see us through the remainder of the day. After that Aline and Martine slept. By the time we bypassed Lyon and drew closer to the Chateau in the less populated region of the Auvergne-Rhone Alps, gone was the weak sunshine of the Loire Valley. Threatening clouds hung heavy in the dark sky.

I shuddered and hoped its dismal welcome wouldn't prove prophetic for our time at Maille. This was not the place for our honeymoon. How could I have been so shortsighted? I glanced at Guy and shivered. He looked tired, yet, he drove on.

"I'll drive for a while so you can get a little rest," I offered. I felt as hollow as my voice sounded.

He shook his head and looked at me, his usually bright eyes dimmed with weariness. "It's all right."

Was there anything I could do to make amends? "Will it help if I look at the map with the flashlight?" I asked when the sky opened up and dumped sheets of rain on us, obscuring the view of the road.

"I don't think so." He flexed his shoulders. "I'll let you know if I change my mind. It's getting hard to see the landmarks."

"Have you been here before?"

"Oui."

"Often?"

"Often enough."

"You don't want to talk about it?"

"Non, I don't." He ran his hand through his hair.

I began to worry. I didn't know what I could do to help. So I retreated into silence and decided I'd confess later that I'd made a mistake and was sorry. I'd tell him that I wanted to stay just long enough to see how she ran her safe house and that the two of us should spend the rest of our time together alone at the cottage, if we still had the option.

After another fifteen minutes or so of driving, Guy pulled the car to the side of the road. "Aline, wake up. We're getting close to the turnoff to Maille. I may need your guidance as to the road conditions into the house."

Guy and I both turned to look at her as she sat up, rubbed her eyes, and checked the baby. "Martine is still asleep. It must be the hum of the engine."

"We're almost to the turnoff to the chateau," Guy repeated. He edged the car onto the highway. "Keep an eye out for it."

"Okay." Aline straightened and leaned forward, watching out the windshield as best she could.

A short time later, she said, "Slow down. It's right ahead of you. I hope the creek hasn't overflowed onto the road."

"We'll cross that bridge when we come to it." Guy sighed. "No pun intended."

"We better hope it hasn't," she said in a whisper.

"At least it'll probably slow down the German motorcycles."

She didn't respond, and I kept my thoughts to myself, although I didn't think it was funny. "How much farther is it?" I asked

"Half a mile," Guy said. He took his time along the muddy, rough road until we approached the still-visible log bridge that saw us safely to the other side. The headlights revealed the old chateau set in an open space of tall grasses and large trees. It was hard to see much else.

When Guy switched off the engine, Martine began her whimper that transformed into to a full-blown wail—as usual. Aline's full attention turned to her daughter. She bundled the baby into her arms and made a dash toward the house. Guy leaned over and kissed me. "Good thing I know my way around here, or we might have had to sleep in the car tonight."

What a ghastly thought. I shivered and a general malaise overtook me. "I'm glad you're in a forgiving mood. I need to apologize for suggesting we come here instead of going to the cottage. Let's leave tomorrow after Aline shows me around. I don't want to squander our time together."

"In the morning, we'll leave for the cottage. I brought the key with me . . . just in case you came to your senses."

"Do you really know me so much better than I know myself?"

He nodded and I hugged him. "I'm ready to go inside and call it a night."

He yawned. "Me too." Moving quickly, he removed the luggage from the trunk and opened the car door for me. Then he ran up the steps to the chateau and held the door.

A man with salt-and-pepper hair met us inside.

"Maurice, I'd like you to meet my new wife," Guy announced proudly.

"Pleased to meet you, Madame de Laval."

After I murmured a greeting, Guy said, "Maurice, please show us to our room. We've been on the road all day." Guy impressed me with the tact he used to forestall what could have been a long evening with Aline.

The house wasn't warm, but the bedroom was beyond cold. I expected that my husband had gone to sleep as soon as he lay down. I watched his chest rise and fall with each deep breath. I couldn't resist curling into the curve of his warm body. When he turned toward me, his nearness overwhelmed me as my heart pounded an erratic rhythm. I had awakened the sleeping giant.

Early the next morning we had our bags packed and in the car before Aline made an appearance. Maurice, however, joined us in the kitchen for a cup of the coffee that Guy had made. "*Les enfants?* Children here now?" Guy asked.

The question puzzled me but not Maurice. "Two," he said. "I expect to take them across the border before the end of the week."

Guy refilled his cup. "RAF?"

Maurice nodded.

I began to understand. Maurice escorted downed airmen out of the country. Well, that would be a good thing since I wouldn't be back until April to help her. My little family—my husband and Claude—were my first priority, whether or not Aline had more *les enfants* sooner rather than later.

Aline hadn't come downstairs by ten o'clock. It wasn't easy for me, but after Guy and I talked about it, I wrote a note to her that we were going to honeymoon, and she could count on my help during the entire months of April through June.

Chartres

Upon our arrival at the cottage, I dubbed it Sunnyside because of its pale yellow hue against the cerulean sky. The scene reflected in the nearby pond. The fluffy clouds were as inviting as soft down comforters. My heart sang—such a magical place for my husband and me. I had him to myself!

"Aren't you going to get out of the car?" Guy stood by the

open door.

"By all means." I accepted his outstretched hand. "I wish we could stay here forever."

"That would be nice." He nodded and broke into a satisfied smile. "Next best would be to return often."

"Yes." I stepped into his arms and relaxed against his muscular body. "Guy, words cannot convey how much I love you."

He kissed the tip of my nose. "Wherever I am, I'll carry you in my heart always."

I dashed off toward the pond with my husband in pursuit. It didn't take him long to catch me. We rolled on the thick grass at the water's edge. I laughed until my sides hurt and panted to regain my breath. "Let's take a picnic lunch with us tomorrow. And a blanket to while away the afternoon."

"Your wish is my command."

The next morning I awoke at nine and lay quietly beside him until I could no longer contain myself. "It's almost ten o'clock. Come on, get up. It'll soon be time for that picnic lunch I packed last night."

He rolled out of the bed and stretched. "I haven't slept so well since I was five years old."

"Maybe I shouldn't have awakened you."

"It's okay. I don't want to miss lunch. You better hurry up and get dressed; I'll be ready in five."

After a cup of coffee and a slice of bread and cheese, we saddled up two of the four horses in the stables that Guy had pointed out as we drove in to the cottage. I chose the gray Arabian mare, and he chose a larger, chestnut-color horse.

"What breed of horse is that?" I asked as I drew up beside him.

"It's a Selle Francaise."

"Pretty fancy—French breed, I gather."

"*Precisément*. You're correct."

The breeze whipped my hair into my face. I turned the mare toward the pond. "Race you to the pond."

Guy won and waited for me, the blanket spread near the

water and the basket open for lunch. I set out slices of Gruyere cheese, grapes, a baguette, macaroons, and wine. We filled our plates and glasses.

"Claude would like it here," Guy said as he refilled my glass.

"Of course, he would. You know how he loves horses, and it seems so far from everyday life."

"I think Papa's too overbearing when I'm not there to call him out. I wish I could spare Claude what I had to go through with Papa, but I can't be in more than one place at a time. Sometimes, I deeply resent my father and think of placing Claude somewhere else with friends. And then I realize that Claude has a unique role to fill in the family, which he has to learn from either Papa or me. My hands are tied until we can make a home for him in Paris." He sighed. "Come on, let's take a walk until I snap out of this mood."

We walked in silence halfway around the pond, soaking in the sunshine and breathing the fresh air.

Guy stopped and held me close to his heart. "I'm sorry to spoil a beautiful day, talking about something that can't be changed yet. I won't do it again."

"It's on your mind. I'd rather you put it into words that let it fester inside. You can talk to me. I understand."

He kissed me. "My sweet Paulette, what would I do without you?"

His mood did change, and we raced back to our spot on the blanket and dozed in the sun until we rode back to the cottage.

The days flew by in a similar way—sans any down moods—during our month-long honeymoon.

On what I believed was our last day at the cottage, we were once again in our favorite place by the water. My head pillowed on Guy's lap, I looked up at him. "I'm not ready to leave. I wish we could stay here forever."

"I feel the same. Guess what?"

I shook my head. "I can't."

"We're going to stay here until the end of March. It belongs to us."

I sat up and kissed him. "I'm so hap . . ." I stopped and stared at him. "Can you take so much time away?"

"Yes. I can and I will! We lose our freedom when we leave here. As you Americans might say, 'The honeymoon will be over.'

It'll be hard to find time for each other once we're back in Paris."

"No, we won't let it happen."

"As long as this war is on, your work with Aline and mine with de Gaulle will be our masters. There are no guarantees for what our future holds."

I threw my arms around him. "Don't be negative."

"I'm not, my love. I'm realistic."

"Each day with you is precious. Let's not waste them."

Two days later, I woke up with flu-like symptoms, much like the bout I'd had in Paris when Dietrich brought me medicine. But this time the nausea that had plagued me for the past week intensified. I felt exhausted.

Guy brought me a glass of milk and a slice of bread. "You need to eat something." His hand brushed mine as he felt my forehead. "You're fevered. I'm off for the doctor. I shouldn't be gone long."

I nodded. I'd had bronchitis and knew how quickly it could go into pneumonia. I prayed that I hadn't infected my husband and that I could throw it off in a few days.

Why, God? Why now, when we're so happy together?

I must have dozed, because Guy and the doctor surprised me at the bedside. "What time is it?"

Guy glanced at his watch and back at me, his brow furrowed. "Ten after ten."

"Good morning, Madame de Laval," the doctor greeted me. "Congratulations on your recent marriage." He opened his bag, took out his stethoscope, and listened to my heart. He prompted me to take a deep breath and hold it while he listened to my lungs. He stuck a thermometer under my tongue and took my blood pressure.

"You have bronchitis and considerable congestion," he pronounced. He dug around in his black bag, retrieved a bottle, and set it on the bed stand. "Here's some sulfa drug. Take this twice a day, morning and night."

"Prontosil?" I asked.

"Related, yes. You're certainly up on the latest treatments."

Guy frowned. "That's the German name. How do you know about it?"

"I had bronchitis last year while you were away."

"Eh. I see."

"With bed rest, plenty of fluids, and your medicine, you'll be fit as a fiddle in no time, if you follow orders." The doctor closed his bag. "I'll stop by to see you again tomorrow."

The next day I was breathing easier but was still plagued with bouts of nausea.

On March fourth Guy turned on the radio, looking for music for me while he rode the gelding around the property and I rested in the sunroom. The radio was still tuned to the BBC.

Yesterday and today, the Allies bombed Boulogne-Billancourt, the suburb of Paris where the Renault factory is located.

Forgetting all about his proposed ride, Guy sat in a chair next to me and looked down at the floor. "My God, I know it was necessary. The Nazis manufacture their weapons of death there." He shook his head. "But civilians will have been injured, if not killed. It's insane!"

I knew I had to rally myself out of whatever ailed me. Guy needed a good and strong wife.

I guess I did have some control over my health after all, because each day I felt better, and at the doctor's fourth visit, he announced, "Miraculous recovery. Of course, you're young and in love . . . a good tonic."

"My wife still doesn't have any appetite," Guy said. "She needs to eat more."

The doctor looked at me. "How long has this been going on?"

"Couple of weeks, I guess?"

He looked at Guy. "Did it occur to you that your wife might be pregnant? Often, morning sickness occurs in the early months of pregnancy."

"No, it didn't. Paulette had bronchitis."

"Strangers things have happened." He gave a good-natured chuckle and patted Guy on the back. "Time will tell."

Guy sank into the chair beside me. "Whoa, I didn't see that coming. It's a wonderful idea, mon trésor, wonderful . . . if it's true." He frowned. "How do you feel about it?"

"My darling Guy, I pray it is so."

He took me in his arms, kissed me, and whispered of his love and hope for our family.

Chapter Thirty

The morning of April 1st, Guy wanted to get an early start from the cottage back to Chateau Maille, but he humored me by agreeing to my request to take one last horseback ride around the property— through the woods and back around the pond—before we left. I was feeling almost normal, although the nausea still affected me first thing in the mornings. However, we could delay our departure no longer, because of my promise to Aline.

Guy hadn't mentioned anything about a baby since the doctor first suggested it. I had expected he'd ask me, but he didn't, so I brought my horse beside his to talk.

He glanced at me. "Do we need to go back?"

"I'm pretty sure I'm pregnant. I've missed two monthly cycles."

He frowned and held my gaze. "Why didn't you say so when the doctor was here?"

Not exactly the reaction I sought. Disappointed, I broke eye contact. "I wanted to be sure before I said any more."

He brought his horse ear-to-ear to mine. "It sounds pretty sure to me. We'll need to stop in Tours to see a gynecologist. You'll need regular obstetric care."

Why should I be surprised that he knew my needs? He'd been through this with Claude's mother.

He reached over and patted my arm. "Don't look so disappointed. It's awe-inspiring, the thought of a new life."

"You didn't seem pleased when I told you."

"Believe me, I am. I also have to be sure that you're well cared for while I'm away. When I'm with you, I'll see to it."

I pursed my lips, not convinced myself. "I'll be all right."

"I would prefer we be together more often than will be the case." His eyes met mine. "But we'll have to make the best of it."

As we headed back to Sunnyside, I realized there was no going back for either of us.

✝

I turned for one last look at the cottage as our car looped around the graveled circular driveway. "Maybe we'll be back as a family . . . with Claude and the baby."

Guy kept his eyes on the road. "I hope so."

"Would you like a boy or a girl this time?"

"Do I get a choice in the matter?"

"Well, no. But if you did?"

"A boy, I suppose. I have experience."

"I'll bet a little girl would be Daddy's little darling."

"In that case, I'll welcome either." His smile broadened in approval. "What about you?"

"I'd thought a boy for you, but I'll love any child that's yours."

"You'll be an amazing mother. Lucky baby."

We traveled in silence, lost in our own thoughts, until we reached Tours. The appointment with the doctor confirmed that we could expect the arrival of the baby in October. He instilled confidence in both of us that he would take good care of me.

After we left the doctor's office, Guy insisted we stop at a small café for lunch. When we were seated, he said, "Keep in mind, it's confirmed that you need to eat for two."

I wasn't hungry but ordered chicken soup and crackers to satisfy Guy, and because I might not get anything more until we reached Aline's.

As we got underway for the long drive, my thoughts turned to my Resistance work. "I hope nothing terrible has happened to Renee."

Guy cleared his throat. "She's safe in New York."

"How do you know?"

"After the Germans began to hound Mr. Greenberg because of her, she hid at my house until Chris could arrange her escape. That's why I insisted you stay at your own apartment."

"Where's Chris now?"

"I don't know."

"He's not working in your network anymore?"

"No."

"I hope he didn't leave because of us. He just disappeared and left me alone at the house."

"I'm sure Chris had a good reason for leaving without an

explanation. He loves you too much to do that unless it was necessary."

"What makes you think so?"

"He spoke from the heart of his love for you. He told me he accepted that you didn't feel the same about him."

"I never wanted to hurt him. Did he know that?"

"I believe so. He asked if I loved you. I told him I did. He congratulated me and said, 'If you promise to make her happy, I'll give you my blessing, but if you hurt her, I'll bust your chops.' Whatever that means."

I didn't bother to explain the American slang.

Chateau Maille

In the late afternoon sunlight, Chateau Maille didn't seem so ominous as it had on our first visit. The sun slanted through a curtain of trees and shone on the moss-covered stone. But the chateau still looked as though it could be an abandoned relic from centuries past, with its oversized yet dumpy round tower. *Will that impression be enough to protect us from German patrols?* I wondered.

Guy linked arms with me as we approached the wide bank of steps leading to the heavy-duty oak door. "I can't stay."

"Stay a little while."

"Better not. I'm going by Lamont to see Claude before I leave on assignment."

"I know. You've sacrificed time with him already on my behalf. I promise I'll make it up to you and Claude next month."

He knocked on the door and gave me a quick kiss. "Take care of yourself and the little one," he whispered and took the steps down, two at a time.

That separation didn't feel right. "I will. You too," I said, a lump in my throat as I watched him get into the car.

Aline opened the door at the thud of the heavy metal knocker. "Thank God you're here. Last night we received another patient. He's going to require a lot of attention over the next few days."

That's when the full impact of my decision hit me. I doubted the wisdom of it. I couldn't deny that I was not only putting my own life at risk, but also that of our unborn child.

"You look tired. Would you like a cup of hot chocolate before you get to bed? It'll help you sleep."

"Thank you, no. We started early and it was a very long day in the car. I doubt I even have the strength to unpack tonight."

Aline had spent more than an hour showing me around the main wing of the chateau and then we ate a quick meal in the kitchen. Now she and I were climbing the stairs to the room Guy and I had shared. It was still as cold as I remembered, and now I wouldn't have Guy to warm me. I couldn't risk another bout with bronchitis. "Do you have an extra blanket or two for the bed?"

She rummaged around in the wardrobe and pulled out a threadbare patchwork quilt that had seen better days. "Here's something."

"Good night, then." I spread the extra cover on the bed.

"Bonne nuit." Aline started for the door and looked back over her shoulder. "I'll get you started with the nursing in the morning."

I waited for the door to close, kicked off my shoes, and crawled into the bed fully dressed.

I slept until the sun peeked through one of the windows in my room. The queasy feeling, I was becoming accustomed to drove me into the old-fashioned washroom. I dipped the washcloth into cold water and wiped my face—a warm bath would have to come later. I brushed my hair and went downstairs to the kitchen. "Good morning." I looked over Aline's shoulder as she mixed a pan of oatmeal.

"Help yourself to a cup of coffee. Then I'll introduce you to our patients when we take down their breakfast."

"Not now. Do you have a piece of bread I can have?"

She spun around and stared at me. "The usual order of things here is to check on the patients and take them breakfast. Then we eat."

"That won't work for me." I didn't move.

"I didn't know you thought of yourself first."

I glared at her. "I need something for morning sickness."

She continued with her drill-sergeant stance. "Oh my God, you're pregnant already?"

Irritated and in no mood for a lecture, I retorted, "Is that surprising?"

"Here, here, let me get you some bread." She opened a tin breadbox on the counter and sliced a piece for me. "I thought you and Guy would take precautions, given your involvement in the Resistance. A child will make it much more difficult. Believe me, I know."

I ignored her and nibbled on the bread.

"Let's not get off to a bad start. I'm sorry. I've been so busy and not sleeping well."

"Let's get on to the patients," I said, wondering how I'd survive here for a month.

She set a large tin tray on the chipped, yellow-tile counter, and I filled bowls of cereal while she poured coffee into a pewter carafe. "By the way, you'll be called Andrea while you're here."

We departed the kitchen through the pantry and down two flights of stairs into a large room. Five beds seemed to protrude from the gray expanse of the far wall, and shelves of medical supplies stood beside an old icebox. "We do the best we can with our infirmary." She directed me to the patient closest to us. "Andrea, let me introduce you to Captain William Tillson, an American pilot. He's been shot down a second time during his many missions over France."

My code name—I'd have to remember to respond. "Good morning, Captain."

He gave me a bright smile. "Good morning. It's good to hear American English." He winced and closed his eyes.

"Andrea will take good care of you," Aline said as she cranked up the bed. She handed me a small tray. "See that he eats a little something. He arrived here last night and has an ugly infection in his leg."

265

He waved his left hand. "There's nothing wrong with my appetite."

Assured that the captain could feed himself, Aline led me to the medical supplies. "Twice a day, he'll need sulfa and his bandages changed. It goes without saying that you'll need to monitor his temperature and administer pain relief at his request, if within reason. It's not just his leg; he has a simple fracture of his lower right arm as well."

"All right." Impressed by the sophistication of the infirmary, I asked, "How do you manage to restock your medical supplies?"

"The American Hospital sees to it when they bring new patients by ambulance. They delivered more supplies last night with the captain. He may be here the entire month before he can make the trek to the border. He knows what he's in for."

"How often do they come?"

She shook her head. "No set schedule. Just when conditions allow."

"Quite the operation."

We left the American to eat breakfast while we went to the other two men, British RAF—one a pilot, the other a gunner—for introductions and their breakfast.

Our daily routine continued about the same until two weeks later. The two British airmen were scheduled to leave for Spain, and I helped Aline prepare them for what lay ahead. We explained how they would be passed from one small Resistance cell to another, that the need for secrecy was paramount, and that it would take about ten days to reach safety. That they must never reveal our location was left unsaid but it was definitely understood.

Later that evening, the escorts for the first leg of the long journey joined us for dinner at the kitchen table. I could tell that Tillson dreaded the loss of their companionship. At Maille the days grew long for the airmen because the Germans made routine visits to homes to search for anything out of the ordinary. Some neighbors alerted them about things they deemed suspicious. In the case of the airmen, they were confined to a dark cellar most of the time, having to stay out of sight.

We cooked a good meal, and I insisted that the American join us at the table, as did the two husky escorts.

"You'll get a little respite now," the younger of the escorts said.

"I don't think so. There'll be more any day," Aline said.

The older one nodded. "Sad, but true."

✝

Three days later, four men arrived by ambulance. The doctor made the rounds, stopped near Tillson's bed, and said to Aline, "Madame de Maille, I think you can handle up to eight men when you get the additional beds."

Aline stared at him. "Not the seriously injured. They'll have to stay in the hospital longer and be in better shape before they come here."

"Doc, how much more time before I can leave?" Tillson asked after the doctor thoroughly examined him.

The medic shook his head. "It'll be at least another month before your leg is strong enough to make the trip, maybe longer."

My heart broke for the American. I knew how eager he was to leave. Once the four new airmen left—all of whom were only slightly injured—he'd be bored to tears again without companions to help pass the hours.

The four men left two days later, but Tillson didn't have to wait long for additional company. A few days later, we received three more airmen, who stayed with us about a week before leaving with their guide.

Given our nonstop routine, time passed quickly. I had hoped to leave for a week or so the first of May for Claude's birthday at Lamont, but our workload increased as the war intensified and I knew I couldn't leave with a clear conscience. There was simply too much for Aline to handle on her own. I wrote to Guy and asked him to visit me at Maille at his earliest opportunity.

The following week the ambulance driver delivered a response which hinted that Guy was in Paris. Guy himself arrived at Maille three days later and stayed with me for a week. He teased me about my expanding waistline when were alone in the bedroom. I think he did it to take our minds off how thin I'd become. I placed his hand on my tummy, as the baby seemed to have awakened. "Did you feel her move and kick?" I asked him.

"I did. She must be eating well. She has quite a kick. But maybe, *he* will make a good football goalie." He kissed me on my belly.

"I don't know about that."

"We'll have to wait and see."

"There is something I'd like you to do."

"Ask."

"I'd like for you to meet the American pilot who's been stuck here for weeks. The isolation is really hard on him."

"I wish I could, but that wouldn't be wise. You know the danger—if he's captured and tortured, he may talk. You never know how much a person can take until after something like that actually happens. Always remember, they can't tell what they don't know."

"That's true. He knows me as Andrea, by the way. It's how Aline introduces me to all the patients."

During the week that Guy visited, he took over my outdoor responsibilities, freeing me to rest after lunch. He stayed out until dark one evening to repair a section of rotted boards that had tumbled down from the vegetable garden fence. Aline had asked me to take care of it, but I didn't have the time, much less the strength for it. Every day the opening remained we'd lost much-needed vegetables and plants to rabbits. On Guy's last two days with us, he harvested apricots from two trees. Aline had been saving sugar all summer and she was able to make enough jam to last through the long winter months. Guy's work was definitely augmenting our meager provisions.

My afternoon rest periods did wonders for my energy level but at the cost of time with my husband.

The week drew to a close much too soon. Guy and I cuddled and talked into the wee hours of the morning on our last night together.

"In the morning I have to get an early start to Lamont. I've been away from Claude far too long."

"You know how I wish I could be there for his birthday, but I just cannot leave now. And I already promised Aline she could count on me through the end of June. After that, I'll go to Lamont, I promise. In the meantime, give Claude a hug for me."

"I will. I'll try not to disturb you when I get up."

"No! Wake me. I want every last minute possible with you.

Promise me you will."

"If that's your wish, I promise. Now go to sleep, mon trésor."

☩

As the time passed and airmen came and went, I began to worry about Captain Tillson. His outgoing personality seemed less apparent than when I'd first met him. Each week that passed found him more withdrawn. Something had to change.

I went to Aline. "I'm worried about Captain Tillson. I think he needs something to keep him from brooding about his situation."

"What do you suggest?"

"I'd like to take him outside in his wheelchair. He needs a change of scene."

"Tell me how you'd go about that."

"I'd wheel him up the supply ramp from the back of the infirmary for an hour a day and sit with him while I peel vegetables or mend. I'd try to get him to talk about his situation."

"All right, give it a try and see how it works."

"Thank you. I think you'll see a vast improvement."

"The doctor has spoken," Aline said.

When I went to see Tillson in the infirmary, he looked up at me with little expression. "You're off schedule, Andrea," he grumbled.

"No. For the next hour I'll enjoy the sunshine out back while I peel potatoes."

"Why torment me about it?"

"How would you like to get in that wheelchair and join me for some fresh air?"

"That's a cruel question. You know how much I would."

"Let's get you into the chair, then, and we'll be on our way."

He gripped my hand. "I can't believe this is happening."

"We'll do it every day, weather—and German patrols—permitting."

My plan worked well. The captain and I engaged in small talk about the chateau, my duties, the birds, the trees, the vegetable garden, or whatever came to mind."

"May I ask you a question?" the captain asked.

I looked up from my sewing. "I suppose so."

"A while back your husband was here for a short time, I heard." His eyes slid to my belly. "You're pregnant, aren't you?"

I couldn't give him any personal information. I shook my head. "I haven't been eating the right kinds of food. You know, too much bread and not enough meat."

"I'm sorry. I hope I haven't offended you."

"Bruised ego, that's all."

"Was I right about your husband's visit?"

"Captain Tillson, you must know I'm not going to talk about that. I'll listen to you talk about yourself."

"I've been through this before, so I know what's ahead of me. The last time I almost didn't make it—and that was with *two* good legs. What can I expect this time? This leg isn't healing like it should."

It was my turn to reach for his hand. "It's healing slowly, but it *is* healing. I know you're impatient to get this behind you, but the only way you'll have a chance for success is if your leg is strong enough to make the trip. You'll just have to trust us to do everything we can to prepare you."

"I suppose you wonder, 'What the hell is his rush to get back in the sky with the Nazis?'"

"What type aircraft do you fly?"

"Mostly B-24 Liberator bombers."

I grew silent because I didn't want him to dwell on the fate of his crew. The Resistance cell that found him had reported that they had all perished in the crash.

As the days continued, the captain seemed much more positive in his outlook, and I was thankful for the positive effects of the sunshine and change of scene. When I spoke to Aline about it, she agreed to continue his outings after I departed at the end of June.

Guy's work schedule in May twice brought him to Lyon. He visited me a couple of days each trip before returning to Paris. Other than his brief visits, life at the chateau was a continual blur of nursing.

Paris

On June twenty-eighth Guy and I departed from Maille on our way to the house on Notre Dame des Champs in Paris. We would have a few days together before he left for work with the Resistance and I settled in to await the birth of our baby at Lamont.

I'd agreed to do one more assignment for the Resistance while in Paris and was filled with anticipation while I waited. The plan was for me to accompany two seriously injured airmen from the American Hospital to Chateau Maille then continue on to Lamont. When the day came to depart Paris—another separation from my husband—I rolled over on my side and kissed him. "Less than a month and we'll be with Claude again. I'm more than ready."

"I'll say. You've slept most the time you were here."

"Sorry. I'm tired all the time, it seems."

He placed his hand on my tummy and encircled its increased girth. "Are you sure that's all the baby?"

"You tease, you know it is."

"I know. Aline works you as if you were three people. You can't keep it up."

At ten o'clock, Nina brought us breakfast in bed.

I glanced at Guy. "What's this?"

"Breakfast."

"You're trying to fatten me up." I turned to Nina. "How did you know when to bring it?"

"Madame, just following orders."

"It's wonderful to be spoiled once in a while."

She nodded and slipped out of the room with as little fanfare as possible.

At seven o'clock that evening, my suitcase sat packed and ready to go as soon as my driver arrived with the airmen. Most of the evening, Guy and I waited on the sofa, careful not to say anything to remind us that our time together was drawing to a close. Restless, he rose and moved around the room. The clock struck the half hour, and we looked at each other. Why the delay?

The driver arrived twenty minutes later. "Sorry I'm late. I had to wait to be sure the German patrol I'd seen earlier had cleared out of the area."

Guy's shoulders tensed. "You have the two children from the hospital with you?"

"Oui."

"Did you see German patrols near the hospital?"

"No. Besides, I'm not driving the ambulance. I have one of the doctor's personal car."

Guy insisted we wait until he'd taken a quick check around the block on his bike. He returned in ten or fifteen minutes. "I didn't see anything. You better get out of here while it's quiet."

"Oui, Monsieur," he said and edged forward from the curb.

About the time I'd relaxed my head against the back of the seat, we encountered a roadblock. We were hemmed in with no way to change course.

A swarm of solders surrounded the car and demanded we exit. By the grace of God, the injured airmen somehow managed to comply. One of them spoke German in a vain effort to protect the other who, I guessed, spoke neither French nor German.

They were quickly arrested, along with our driver. Then the Germans turned their attention to me.

"You're under arrest." A husky soldier pushed me into the back seat of one of their cars and climbed in beside me.

"Where are you taking me?"

"Not far." A guttural sound of satisfaction rose from deep within him. "I'm sure you know of Fresnes Prison."

I was struck with fear. Of course, I'd heard of it. Who in Paris hadn't? Members of the Resistance had, for sure. Many of their friends and team operatives were held there and tortured, and some died.

My arrest created a dreadful dilemma. If they found out I was pregnant, they'd use that knowledge to break me. I'd be confronted with betraying my network or losing my child.

They mustn't know!

I had to destroy my fake Andrea ID. I slipped it out of my purse, hid it under a fold of my wide skirt, and slowly, ever so slowly, tore it in half and then again. I wadded the piece with the photo on it and slipped it into my mouth, chewed, and swallowed it. For certain, my purse would be searched at our destination. The best I could hope for was that I'd be questioned as an American married to a Frenchman, rather than a nurse companion.

I was taken to a local police station where, about 9:30 that night, my interrogation began. Although not wearing a French uniform, the man sounded like a native Frenchman. I judged my good-looking interrogator to be in his late twenties—a young officer willing to betray his countrymen for advancement with the occupying forces.

The officer had searched my purse and removed my identification. "You are Madame Paulette de Laval? Is that correct?"

"Oui."

He handed my ID—my real one—to me. "Take your time. Is the information correct?"

"Oui."

"Does your residence shelter Jews or other enemies of the French Government?"

"For heaven's sake, why would you even ask such a thing?"

"Madame, I'll ask the questions, and you better answer them."

I waited for the next question, and he waited for my answer to the previous one.

"What's your answer?" he demanded with irritation. "Do you or do you not run a safe house at your residence."

"No," I said. My conscience was clear—at this time we were not. "I thought you understood that."

With a smug demeanor, he replied, "That's not what your neighbors say."

"In that case, they are mistaken."

He motioned to the officer stationed outside the door to come in. "Take Madame de Laval to her cell. She needs time to improve her recollection of events."

The two of them snickered as the guard grabbed me by the arm and pushed me into the hall. He looked like a teenager who needed a good paddling.

Early the next morning I was transported with two women and four men to Fresnes Prison. The facility sprawled across a large, relatively open area. From a distance it didn't betray its purpose or reputation as a Nazi prison.

As we were being led into the building, I overheard one of the men say, "At least this is better than being held at Montluc Prison in Lyon."

How could it be? I wondered.

As I was taken down a long hallway, we passed row after row of cells on both sides. I ended up in a cell with five other women. The women looked me over as I looked around the room. The accommodations exceeded my expectations. The cell contained a toilet in one corner, a water tap with a small sink below it, and a fold-up table. A small oil-burning stove sat against one wall.

"Where are we expected to sleep?" I asked.

A tall woman with red hair and a bruise on her face pointed to a pile of rolled up mats. "The floor."

I nodded. "I see."

My previous arrest experience had shown me an example of prison routine. I expected to be taken for extensive questioning. I'd better be as alert as possible. A single slipup could be disastrous. I lay on a mat on the floor in our cramped quarters beside another woman, about my age by the look of her. I thought of Guy. I hoped he knew of my arrest. If so what could he do about it? I stayed there until our dinner of broth, dry bread, and watered-down coffee substitute arrived.

Pssst, pssst.

The sound came from my mat mate.

I feigned sleep by slowing my breathing to a steady rhythm and actually went to sleep soon after.

Early the next morning a scar-faced Goliath of a man came, grabbed my arm, and dragged me out of the cell.

"You don't have to pull me. I'm not resisting you."

"Get a move on it, then." He laughed and broke into a gallop.

I raced along beside him, determined not to give him the satisfaction of humiliating me. He slowed as we got closer to an office door where he punched me in the back with his fist, sending me hurdling through it. I barely recovered my balance in time to avoid crashing into the table where two officers sat.

One of them gestured for me to sit in the chair across from him, and they took turns asking questions about my "crimes."

On the third day a kind female guard came for me. "Let me know if there's anything I can do for you," she said as we walked along the hall."

My mind blanked. I needed many things that she couldn't get. "Merci, I will."

On the fourth day I planned to ask her for a toothbrush and a cup of coffee when I was returned to the cell. Much to my disappointment and dread, the sadistic scarface came for me while I lay on my mat. "Get up, whore!" he commanded and kicked me in the stomach.

The pain took my breath away. He jerked me up by my hair and dragged me into the corridor. I almost blacked out but managed to regain some of my senses by the time we reached the door to the now-familiar interrogation room.

Scarface stopped and knocked on the door. *What restraint he shows*, I thought. When a voice from inside called, "Come in," the guard opened the door, shoved me inside, and retreated.

"Come in," the voice repeated.

His hair had grayed and his eyes had dulled since I'd last seen him. I took a double take and asked, "Do you come here regularly?"

He stood and walked around the table. "Here, let me help you to a chair."

"Thank you." The room began to spin as I stepped forward, faltered, and stumbled into his arms. He held me close for a long moment. It was as though the world stood still for a time. In a strange way I drew hope from his presence, as I had once before when I had felt alone and he'd brought medicine for my bronchitis.

He guided me to a chair, his eyes confirming my pregnancy, and sat across from me.

"Have the guards mistreated you?"

"Oui, one of them, a stocky man with a scar on his face kicked me in stomach this morning and roughed me up the first day I was here."

"I'll see to him." Dietrich sat still, a faraway look in his eyes. The tick-tock of a wall clock was at odds with the thump-thump of my heart.

He held my gaze. "Your fate is in my hands. There is sufficient evidence that this is not the first time you have aided the escape of enemy airmen." He looked toward the door. "You must realize that, with the stroke of my pen, you will end up in a work camp in Germany."

Too shocked to respond, I lowered my eyes to my protectively positioned hands across my belly and nodded.

He shook his head and stood, his torment evident. "You'll be released in the morning." He rose and opened the door. "Guard."

The female guard who'd been kind to me yesterday stepped into the room. "Yes, Colonel Dietrich?"

With pen in hand, he said, "Have a nurse examine Madame de Laval before you return her to the cell."

"Yes, sir." The guard noticed that I swayed as I stood, and she steadied me with her hand. "Is the prisoner quite well?"

"She is not. Give her your arm to lean on." Dietrich didn't stand or stop writing at the table.

I held onto the hope that he wouldn't change his mind about my release. The guard supported most of my weight as we made our way to a room where a nurse rubbed salve on my bruises and cleaned my scrapes and cuts. "That's about all I can do," she said. "Just try to take it easy and you should recover in a few days."

When we got to the cell, the kindly guard said, as she closed the door, "I'll bring you some broth and bread."

I hadn't slept more than an hour when she returned. At my questioning look, she nodded, a faint smile on her lips. "Gather your things. You'll be released today."

An hour later all the paperwork was deemed to be in order, and she led me out to meet Guy by the gate.

I relaxed into the cushion of his embrace as he whispered into my ear, "Thank God, you're free. Let's go home."

"Yes, my love, yes." I tried to tell myself that the cramps weren't as bad as earlier, although they were. When a particularly painful one hit, I couldn't help but hold my midsection.

"Is it the baby?" Guy asked.

"No, my stomach just hurts, like the rest of my body." I prayed that was truly the case.

"Let me know if it gets worse."

By the time we returned to the house, the pressure and pain in my abdomen was almost unbearable. As soon as we got inside, I dashed to the bathroom, Guy right behind me.

"I'll wait outside the door," he said as I pushed the door closed out of a silly, ingrained sense of modesty. "Let me know if you need help."

I sat on the toilet and tried to catch my breath. "I will." That's when I saw blood on my panties. The cramping wasn't getting better either. Whether I wanted to or not, I hadn't any choice other than to tell Guy how bad the pain was and admit that I'd been kicked in the stomach. I called out to him. "Come in. I'm bleeding."

He seemed to appear instantly. He saw the blood and placed his hand on my abdomen. "You're in labor."

"I'm not sure. One of the guards kicked me in the stomach."

He rushed me to the American Hospital where, two hours later, our baby boy was born on July eighth, two and half months premature.

Lucien died that same day, another victim of the dreadful war. I blamed my hardheaded refusal to listen to Guy's wishes for me to leave the Resistance and await the baby's birth at Lamont.

A week later, in our bedroom at Lamont, I placed my hand on my lifeless belly and continued to mourn my son. I'd held him in my arms right after his birth; Guy hadn't been afforded the chance. Our loss overwhelmed me as I clung to Guy and looked into his eyes. "I'm so sorry." My voice broke as tears streamed down my face. "I should have listened to you."

"It's not your fault. We all make decisions that might turn out badly, but we can't let it paralyze us into inaction."

I sobbed and gulped. "I am lost. My heart is broken. I loved and wanted our baby so very much."

"I know. I did too. You have to forgive yourself. At the time you did what you felt needed to be done."

He cradled me in his arms and kissed me on the cheek. "We have each other's love to carry us forward. To think,"—his voice broke—"I could have lost you, too. When the time's right, we'll have other children."

"I will always grieve for my little boy lost." I sobbed.

"Of course you will. As time passes, however, it will hurt a little less."

"I don't know what I'd do if you weren't here to listen to me and give me hope."

"I've been thinking about how we can spend more time together."

I shook my head. "I can't ask you to change your plans."

"I'll be at Lamont with you and Claude until the end of this month. In August we'll bring him back to Paris with us for a holiday before his lessons start again in September."

"And after that, I'd rather stay in our Paris home alone while you go . . . wherever you go," I said.

"What if you weren't alone, but with me?"

"But you're gone so much of the time."

"I'll work out of the house most of the time and take short trips to Chartres. I won't go far from Paris, I promise. Some of the time you could go with me, and we could stay at the cottage."

I threw my arms around him. "You mean like a real family?"

He kissed me. "Oui, mon trésor. A year from now Claude will be ready to go to a preparatory school in Paris."

"He's so young," I said. The thought of such a change for the little boy added to my sadness.

"No, he'll be five years old."

"That's what I mean."

Guy was quiet for a while and then said, "This is the second time Dietrich has come to your aid. Why does he take such an interest in you?" He looked at me as if waiting for an explanation.

I knew Guy suspected that Dietrich's interest in me was more than casual—I did too—but neither of us would put that into words. Instead, I said, "I don't know why. But he does strike me as not having lost every shred of humanity, as most of his comrades have."

"What can I say other than I'm indebted to him for returning you to me."

Guy didn't bring it up again, for which I was grateful.

If not for Guy's love and attention during the months following my arrest, I wouldn't have recovered my zest for life. But by the first of November, he was again away from home more than he was there. I was most grateful that he'd arranged for Hugh and Nina to accept living quarters in our Paris house. Their companionship and presence carried me through the tense times as the Allies battled the Axis troops in North Africa. Things changed so quickly that I listened to the news every night.

On November eleventh, after dinner, Guy seemed

preoccupied.

"Want a glass of wine while we listen to the news?" I asked while I massaged his tense shoulders.

"Sure. There's no shortage of that," he said with unusual pessimism. "I'll need to get an early start for Lyon tomorrow."

I turned on the radio.

There is no longer a free area in France. The Germans have occupied the formerly unoccupied zone of France, stating that they could no longer preserve the armistice and that all measures must be taken to 'arrest the continuation of the Anglo-British aggression.' All foreign-born Jews are now being arrested. This comes on the heels of the Admiral Darlan's call for all French forces in North Africa to lay down their arms. This is truly a dark day for our glorious nation.

"Did you anticipate this move by the Germans?" I asked Guy.

He chewed his bottom lip. "There have been indications that they're getting more ruthless. Truth be told, nothing they do surprises me."

The fighting escalated during the next two weeks, and Guy's assessment of the situation was confirmed.

On November twenty-seventh, the French Vichy Government scuttled its naval fleet at Toulon to prevent a Nazis takeover after the Allied invasion of Morocco and French Algeria in Operation Torch. Hitler dissolved the Vichy army, calling their actions a "betrayal" and stating he could no longer "trust French admirals and generals."

I supposed my father-in-law thought that General Pétain had demonstrated his loyalty to France.

Although the Axis had suffered some defeats, our fate remained uncertain. In some ways the Germans were more dangerous now than at the beginning of the war. That's why I worried so about Guy's work with the Free French.

Chapter Thirty-One

January - July 1943 – Loire Valley

After the traditional New Year's Day brunch at Lamont, Guy and I decided to go outside for fresh air and to walk off the excess of our larger-than-usual meal. Neither of us ate much during those times of food shortages across the nation, and our indulgence sat heavily in our stomachs. After trekking through the woods to the edge of the Loire River, Guy said, "I think we'll begin to see the Allies win a number of strategic battles this year. I pray to God that the war will be over before nineteen forty-four dawns. At least I won't need to travel as often this year and will be able to spend more time at home—our home in Paris."

"Really?" I threw my arms around his neck. "I'm so glad." I wondered whether he knew of something that would turn the tide of the war.

"So am I. We'll be able to celebrate our first anniversary in our own home and begin to live a somewhat normal life."

"I hope so." I reached for his hand as we walked along the sandy trail.

"This year I'll carry out most of my responsibilities from Paris or Chartres, and that won't require long absences," Guy continued. "That way we'll have our own home for Claude when he comes to boarding school in the city. He can be with us on weekends and holidays."

As he spoke, I visualized scenes of our family life and felt as much joy for Claude as I did for Guy and me. Suddenly, I shivered, I don't know whether from the chill of the wind that carried threatening clouds our way or what.

He slipped his arm around my shoulder. "Cold?"

"A little bit," I said, my voice husky with emotion.

"Looks like it might snow." He took off his jacket and put it around my shoulders over my trench coat. "We better start back. It's always easier coming down the slopes than going back up. But the climb will warm us."

"Sounds good to me." Dead leaves crackled and crunched with each step along the tree-lined path past the boathouse.

"Let's stop here for a little while before we start back," I said, wanting to prolong the precious moments when I had Guy's undivided attention. I could broach the subject of my working with the American Hospital again.

He chuckled. "I'm not in any hurry to get back to the house either." He pulled the key from his pocket, unlocked the door, and pushed it open. Soon, we gathered around a crackling fire in the stone fireplace. Although still cool inside, especially when we stepped away and sat on the leather sofa, it felt good to be out of the wind that swept storm clouds our way.

"We might have to spend the night here if it snows," he said.

"That would be fun. It's a romantic thought." I snuggled against my husband. "I wish we had more times like this. It's been a beautiful day together."

He drew me close and kissed me. "This is how it should be. We'll make it happen."

For a time we remained silent with dreams of the future until Guy spoke again. "It's not just wishful thinking. We have a home of our own now. The Paris property belongs to us."

An unwelcome thought intruded. What if the Germans aren't defeated? What kind of life would we have?

Stop! You can't think like that and win.

"I plan to help at the American Hospital again."

"What brought that to mind?" His arm tightened around my shoulder in a protective gesture.

"Nothing. I've been thinking about it but waited to bring it up. There's no better time than now."

"Well, since you put it that way, I guess there's no need for me to object." He smiled and nodded. "Actually, I'm proud of you, and if possible, I love you more every day."

In spite of the uncertainty of the war, I prepared to leave Lamont, filled with gratitude that the three of us would be together. We would begin the next chapter of our life together with Claude—and another baby as soon as possible, God willing. For the first time I felt secure in our marriage.

Claude seemed to share my enthusiasm and, in his haste,

rushed to the car without a goodbye to his grandparents.

"You forgot something." Guy caught the boy by the arm.

Claude frowned. "What?"

"Papi and Mamie."

"Oh." After hesitating a moment, he ran to them and gave his grandparents a hug, "Bye," he said and dashed back to the car.

"Have him back next week in time for his lessons," his grandfather told us.

My husband stood by the open car door. "Oui, Papa."

I suspected there would be trouble ahead when Claude came to live with us and entered a private military preparatory school in September. The major had made it clear that he wanted control of Claude's education. He had given his half-hearted approval to Claude living with us only after his wife insisted that Guy's and our nuclear family residence would be at the de Laval Paris mansion.

"Why can't I have a tutor in Paris now?" Claude asked.

"It's better to finish the next few months with the tutor you have. You, Paulette, and I will spend much of the summer with Mamie and Grand-Papa. They're going to miss you very much."

"All . . . right." A precocious child, Claude seemed resigned to his fate and opened the book about stars he'd requested for Christmas.

The Renault rumbled along the nearly deserted roads. Most people were staying close to home with family for the holidays.

Paris

We arrived at the city limits late in the afternoon.

"Claude, we're in Paris," Guy said to the drowsy child.

"Papa, will you get me a gun?" Claude asked in a flat voice.

"Before you start the military academy, I'll teach you how to shoot with one of mine."

"Non, I need to know how now. It's dangerous in Paris."

"No more than anywhere else."

"Grand-Papa said that Paris is crawling with les boches."

"Can't deny that, but so is all of France."

Claude squeezed his eyes shut. "I'll kill them all."

282

"Son, don't let anyone hear you say that."

"Why not?"

"You can't trust everyone. Some people would tell the Germans."

When we exited Boulevard Saint Germain onto Rue Boulevard Raspail, Claude tapped his father's shoulder. "Are we almost there?"

"Why do you ask?"

"Because you let out your breath and slowed down."

"Aren't you quite the detective?" Guy took a deep breath. "Oui, we're close to home. What do you want to see while you're here?"

"Stop! Stop! Germans ahead." Claude pointed at the soldiers ahead of us.

"Calm down. I see them."

"Turn around," Claude said, fear in his voice.

"Claude, it's all right, we've done nothing wrong." Our car came to a stop at the German checkpoint. It was manned by armed soldiers.

I shared Claude's dread of an encounter as I counted five uniformed German soldiers, their rifles in clear sight.

Two of them approached Guy's open window. "Bonjour. What are you doing in this neighborhood?"

"Returning to our home on Rue Notre Dame des Champs."

"Family outing today?"

"A visit with grandparents."

"Monsieur, Madame, your identification papers." The shorter one held out his hand, his eyes resting on Claude, who ignored him.

Guy and I complied.

The soldier kept our ID papers for what seemed an eternity, looking at them and consulting with the other man before he handed them back and waved us on. In the meantime, several vehicles waited behind us. As we drove through the checkpoint, I turned to Claude. "See, it's okay."

"This time it is," Guy said. "But if you're doing something they don't allow, it's not all right. So be careful."

✝

Although not yet past the dinner hour, darkness blanketed Rue Notre Dame des Champs. Blackened windows gave little evidence of whether the houses were vacant or occupied. There was no trace of the festive lights of the city that, during peacetime, never slept.

Claude strained to see the house as Guy pulled into the courtyard. "No gate?"

"The gate was removed twenty years ago, after the end of the Great War, the one that Grand-Papa served in until his injury. In those days everyone believed that war ended the need for wars, and I suppose, gates."

Claude frowned.

"Do you think we need to get another gate?"

"Oui." Unlike his usual behavior, Claude waited for his father to open the car door. He stepped out and stayed close to us as we walked to the front door.

A stream of light poured from the house when Hugh welcomed us inside. Nina opened her arms wide. "This must be Claude."

He didn't advance toward her, and he ignored her gesture of welcome. Instead, he straightened his shoulders and held his head high. "I am Claude de Laval."

Not to be discouraged, she said, "I met you when you were much younger."

"I don't recall."

"Never you mind, we'll get reacquainted while you're here. In the meantime I'll rustle up some dinner. A boy of your age needs a good meal." She turned and went to the kitchen.

"Papa, The Great War didn't keep the Germans away. Is that why I'm going to be a soldier when I grow up?"

Guy nodded. "You come from a long line of warriors, and I expect we'll need brave men in the future, as we do now."

By the time we had shown Claude to his room and returned downstairs, it was dinnertime and Nina summoned us to the dining room. "It's wonderful to have a family here again," she said, setting a small platter of ham and potatoes on the table between two bottles of wine. "I'm sorry I don't have any garden vegetables for you this time of year. We're lucky to have this ham for the holidays. I got up at four-thirty to stand in line at the butcher's shop with the hope for more than just a ham bone. I got the last quarter ham!" she said with satisfaction. "It took all my meat ration coupons. We're only allowed twenty-five grams of meat per person a day now. I would have left the ham for the family next in line if Claude weren't going to be here. I know it's important for him to have a hardy meal."

I quickly converted the grams into ounces. I knew an ounce was a little over twenty-eight grams. That meant, basically, an ounce of meat a day per person! How could we be expected to work and thrive on that?

"You have a generous heart, Nina. I'm sorry so many families suffer so," Guy said, but he was unable to stifle a yawn. "The meal is wonderful, but you'll need to excuse us for tonight. We've had a long day and need to go bed early."

"Do I have to? I'm not sleepy," Claude protested.

Guy nodded. "Tomorrow we'll show you around the city. What would you like to see first?"

"I need to see the stars outside tonight and, tomorrow to be ready to go to an observatory. You told me you would take me."

Guy patted his head. "That I did. Come on, we'll star gaze in the garden."

I watched father and son leave for the garden. The night was perfect, with few clouds in the mandatory, blacked-out city sky. As tired as I was, I followed them out because the stars shone brightly in the moonless night sky.

"There's the Big Dipper." Claude pointed to the sky.

"Where's the Little Dipper?" Guy asked him.

Claude pointed and moved his finger. "There's the North Star."

"Yes. Did you know that sailors used to use it as a navigational aid?" Guy patted his shoulder. "Time for you to get to bed."

On the way into the house, I said, "Take a look at the Milky Way."

After Claude had gone to bed, Guy said, "Claude asked me for a telescope."

"Are you going to get him one?"

"I'll be able to tell you after we've been to the observatory."

The next morning an urgent knock at the bedroom door awoke me. "Who could that be?" I mumbled to Guy's side of the bed. No response. Another knock.

"Paulette, breakfast's ready," Claude called. "We have a busy day."

"Merci, I'll be there in five." I splashed my face, brushed my hair, and slipped on the first dress I took from my still unpacked suitcase. Luckily, it was respectable enough to join my family for breakfast. Real coffee would do wonders, but I had no assurance that Nina had a supply. When I arrived I found she did not. But bless her heart, she'd found eggs somewhere and served them with a freshly baked baguette, butter, and strawberry jam.

"Nina, where were you able get eggs? And real butter?" I asked as soon as I saw them.

"I bartered two jars of strawberry jam, made last summer from our own kitchen garden strawberries. My sister's brother-in-law has a small farm outside the city and has managed to keep a cow and several chickens hidden from the German patrols."

Inquisitive, Claude's ears perked up. "Where's the kitchen garden?"

Nina laughed. "Just outside, near the kitchen. I'll be glad to show it to you. There not much there now in the dead of winter, but in a few weeks, we'll plant lots of good spring vegetables."

"Don't spoil him," Guy said. "You have your hands full with us here. Paulette and I will show him around."

"It's fitting for his parents to do the honors," she said, but her expression was a bit crestfallen.

I sympathized. She wanted to win the affection of Claude—as did I.

"We better get started," Guy said to Claude. "I have work on my desk that needs to be taken care of before our adventure this afternoon."

The three of us went out to the beautiful formal garden in the back the house and stood along the balustrade that separated the upper and lower gardens. Water trickled from the artichoke atop the three-tiered fountain.

Claude dashed down the wide stairway to the lower level where Hugh was pruning the yew hedge. "Where's the kitchen garden?" he called as he rushed to Hugh's side.

Guy slipped his arm around my waist and turned toward me. I couldn't resist giving him a kiss.

After an ardent response, he said, "I love you." And under his breath he added, "Maybe too much."

"I heard that. There's no such thing as too much love," I said.

He shrugged. "Non, of course not, mon trésor. We better rescue Hugh from Claude's incessant barrage of questions." With a faraway look in his eyes, he continued, "It's nice to exist in the protective prism of childhood, free to seek gratification."

"For sure. Claude is curious about everything." I squeezed his hand.

"At least the kitchen garden shouldn't take a lot of time. But knowing our son, he'll have lots of questions." As we approached Claude, he added, "I'll ask Hugh to spend an hour or two with him tomorrow to answer any other garden questions."

The wrought iron gate into the kitchen garden stood open. Claude took a look around and quickly lost interest in the barren but neatly cultivated rows awaiting spring.

Guy said to me, "This garden has been a nutritional life saver these past three years since the occupation."

"Does Hugh plant it every year?"

"Oui, Nina insists, and I wholeheartedly agree with her. It's not only convenient but essential in times like these."

During lunch, Claude spent more time talking about the heavenly bodies than he did eating the delicious stew flavored with beef broth and herbs.

As promised, after our meal we set out for the *Observatoire de Paris*, not far from the house. It was a little too far to walk, so we took the Metro to its first stop and walked the rest of the way. The site was at the original geodetic meridian in France and had been used when making weather maps. I learned, along with Claude, that not until 1884 did an international convention adopt the meridian of Greenwich, England, as the prime meridian, the zero degree point of the Earth's three hundred and sixty degree circumference. It was at that point the time zones around the world began and ended.

When we paused in the Cassini Room—named for the first official director of the observatory by a Royal brevet in 1771—to view the stones set in the floor tracing the Paris Meridian, Claude said, "I want to see the telescopes."

It soon became apparent that Claude wasn't interested in anything but getting to the domed observatory. Guy leaned in close to my ear. "I don't dare tell him there's an even larger telescope at the Meudon location, where observations by the Greek astronomer Eugène Antoniadi helped disprove the Mars canals theory."

"When was that?"

"Umm . . . about nineteen ten, I think"

"I thought you knew everything," I teased, half in jest.

"I know it was before the start of the Great War," he replied.

I smiled at his earnestness. He really was a wealth of knowledge, and Claude seemed likely to be also.

"Where do you want to go next?" Guy asked as he gripped his son's hand.

"Grand-Papa said I should visit my boarding school."

"If you want, we can take the train tomorrow to visit."

"That's what I want, and Saint Cyr, too."

I'm sorry, son, Saint Cyr military school disbanded last year after the Germans invaded the Free Zone. I'm working hard to ensure that it will be open when you're ready for it."

I had a hard time filling my days while Guy worked in his office and traveled to Chartres for various meetings and Claude returned to his studies with his tutor at Lamont. I hesitated to return to work at the hospital for fear I'd be at work on the days my husband was at home. I felt we needed time together to work on making the house a family home.

By mid-January Nina and I had become well acquainted, as I spent hours in the kitchen, asking her questions about running the house.

One day she took pity on me and said, "You must miss your family in America. Tell me, what was Christmas like at your house?" She gave me her full attention while I pondered what to say.

"What do you want to know?"

"Such things as traditions, food, gift exchanges, decorations."

"I'm an only child, so our celebrations were limited. On Christmas Eve after I went to bed, my parents put up the Christmas tree and decorated it—that is, when they weren't traveling. When I got up in the morning, I opened my gifts. Later in the day, we would go to my uncle's house for dinner with his family."

"Did you and your mother bake cookies?"

"Strange you should ask. We didn't when I was a child, but when I was a teenager, we did. That was after my father died. We made anise and peanut butter cookies to take to my uncle's house.

"My dear, why don't we make a cake today? My sister just brought me six more eggs and I have a little butter left. We can make enough batter for two cakes—one will keep until your husband is home, and we can have the second one for our dinner tonight."

"I'd like that. I want our family to have wonderful traditions, and I want our children to be involved in those traditions. The whole family should decorate the tree together."

"I agree," she said.

They do that at Lamont."

"That's nice. Madame de Laval used to decorate here as well."

Some weeks later, when Guy was again away, Nina and I sat at the table with a cup of chicory in lieu of coffee.

"It must have been dreadful when Claude's mother died. Tell me about her," I said.

"Monsieur de Laval, your husband, asked Hugh and me to stay after he took over this house to establish his own family. His wife had refused to live anywhere other than Paris and made selfish demands about their schedules."

"What was she like, Guy's first wife?"

"Nicole was a party girl, plain and simple. There's no other way to describe her."

I sipped the last of my chicory. "Didn't she change when she became pregnant?"

"During her pregnancy, she became moody and disagreeable." Nina shook her head. "I saw the collapse of their marriage at that time. She was an only child, used to getting her own way."

"Guy is an easygoing man. He's not a demanding person to live with."

"You're not taking into account that he loves you, and I'm sure you want to please him. I think he lost patience with Nicole's lack of compromise. My hunch is that the only time her father stood up to her was when he arranged her marriage and that she blamed Guy rather than her father, although it was evident to me Guy was reluctant to marry as well. It broke my heart to be in the house with them."

No wonder my husband was marriage shy, I thought. "I'd have thought she'd settle down after Claude was born."

"Within a year of their marriage, the baby was born, and after one week, she hired a nanny and a wet nurse without a word to Guy. She all but abandoned them. She hung around various nightspots and took up with a musician who drank to excess. The musician was driving when the accident occurred. Both of them were killed."

"So Guy tried to be father *and* mother to Claude."

"Apparently so. I didn't see Claude again until he came this month." A fleeting smile rippled across her lips. "I think the boy will be just fine. The three of you together are a joy to behold."

After a three-day absence, Guy arrived home in time for a leisurely dinner. After we ate, he reached for my hand. "I'm sorry to have spent so much time away from you already this month. January is about over and we still haven't had time to get down to specific plans for the house or taken much time just for us."

"You look tired. Are you getting enough sleep when you're in Chartres, or is Curtis keeping you up too late?"

"They're not the problem. You remember meeting Jean Moulin?"

"Wasn't he associated with the socialist or communist resistance?"

Guy cleared his throat. "Well, now he's working on a resistance unification project for General de Gaulle, and I'm helping him as much as I can."

"Oh," was all I could say. Chills ran up my spine. This was more serious than I had imagined.

"More wine?" he asked as he refilled his glass.

I nodded, near tears. I didn't trust myself to speak.

A loud knock sounded on the front door as we sat in candlelight, the house darkened since the dinner hour. Our eyes met. I shook my head, fearful that the Gestapo intended to arrest my husband.

When the knocks became more insistent, I froze, but Guy

rose. Looking down at me, he said, "We have nothing here to hide. And there's nothing to be gained by having the door battered down."

I figuratively held my breath until I heard Aline's voice. "Let me give the best-looking man in Paris a hug. How are you?" she said as she clung to him.

"Not as well as you seem to be," he said, disengaging from her. "I've had a long day. What are you doing here? Where's your daughter?" he scolded.

"She's in good hands . . . with your mother. I'm in Paris for a while until it's safe to return to Maille."

Guy said, "I've heard things are getting rough in Lyon."

By that time I'd gathered my wits and was able to ask, "Won't you sit down and have a glass of wine."

"I'd like to spend a few days here with you," she said. "I'll be driving an ambulance for the hospital." She stared at me. "I thought you might give me a hand while I'm here."

Guy stood. "Aline, you may stay tonight, but you'll need to find somewhere else in the morning. It's too dangerous for us, and you, for you to be here."

"Oh, never mind, then. I'll intrude on my husband and his mistress." Aline didn't look at Guy; instead, she looked at me. "Think about my proposal. I'll check back with you in a day or two."

"Goodnight," I said and showed her to the door.

The next morning when I awoke, Guy was still sleeping beside me—most unusual. I'd learned to expect to wake alone, whether he was at home or not, but this particular morning I worried about his level of exhaustion. I was deeply concerned that he felt it necessary to share with me the seriousness of the work he was involved in. Aline's visit had further complicated things. I worried about her but was annoyed with her attempt to override whatever decision Guy wanted me to make.

He stirred, and mumbled. "The bastards . . ."

I moved closer and cuddled against him. He took a deep breath, opened his eyes, and blinked. He stretched and put his arms around me. "What time is it?"

"About six thirty."

He rolled over and kissed me. "You know I love you, mon trésor."

"Yes, and I love you more."

No more words were spoken as we advanced to physical expressions of our affection for one another for quite some time.

Afterwards, Guy appeared relaxed, and I thought he was dozing, but he began to speak again. "Aline's visit underscores how complicated the Resistance operations have become. I suspect there is a traitor in her group, and I don't know how many other groups might be infected."

I gasped. Now I understood why he was so angry at Aline. Had the mole followed her to our house? "I can't believe Aline risked coming here," I said.

"I question the wisdom of your staying in Paris while I commute. We'd be safer together at the cottage in Chartres . . . at least until we learn more about the leaks."

"The sooner the better. When do we leave?"

"This afternoon."

The cottage at Chartres

On the first of February, Guy and I arrived at Curtis and Chantal's house in Chartres.

Curtis opened the door. "You just left yesterday."

"I know, at least it seems like it."

"What are you doing back so soon?" His face clouded with concern as he led us to the kitchen. "Don't tell me you couldn't stay away from my wife's rabbit stew."

Guy slapped him on the back. "How did you guess?"

"Easy. And this time you brought Paulette. I suppose you think it's time she learns how to cook a hardy meal for country men. None of that Paris rations slop."

"My wife's baked desserts rival the best of them," Guy said in my defense.

Chantal stood at the stove, stirring a large pot of stew. "Curt, leave her alone. Guy's wife isn't one of the fellows."

He took one look at me and said, "All kidding aside, I'll bet you'd cook us a mean American steak. The fatted calf, no less."

"I don't know about that. I'll stick to my specialty . . . dessert."

"We're on our way to the cottage for an extended stay," Guy said. "Aline's Lyon operation suffered a security breach, and she's complicated things by going to Paris."

Curtis nodded. "I'd heard about some of the arrests. We can't consolidate the efforts of the Resistance groups soon enough." He turned to his wife. "Let's warm the bellies of our friends here."

"We have our work cut out for us." Guy said.

Their hospitality warmed my heart. In addition to the rabbit, the hardy stew contained onions, carrots, and potatoes. I planned to try it sometime while at the cottage—if Guy would clean the rabbit for me.

While Guy and Curtis stood by the door as we prepared to leave, Chantal handed me a picnic basket filled with a large jar of stew, bread, and a bottle of wine. "A little something to tide you over until you get supplies."

"Thank you." I gave her a hug. "We brought a few things with us, but nothing to compare with your delicious stew."

"While you're in the neighborhood, let's plan a weekly dinner. I'll provide the stew and you the dessert. We need the strength of friendships."

"That's a wonderful idea. Thank you again, my dear lady," I said.

As Sunnyside appeared on the horizon, the weight of the Paris situation dissipated with the knowledge that Guy and I would be together most days and nights. True, he'd have occasional meetings that wouldn't include me, but I hoped our time at the cottage would turn out to be the closest thing to a normal life we'd yet had. I wanted our cottage to be a place where he could restore his body and soul between meetings with de Gaulle's committee, chaired by Jean Moulin in de Gaulle's absence. Guy had told me they were trying to hammer out an agreement among diverse Resistance groups, most of whom fiercely guarded their independence. The Free French Army needed the support of a national council of resistance.

Our days were filled with work and play. We slipped into a routine of breakfast and a morning horseback ride. The daily chores included care of the horses, a few chickens, rabbits, and a milk cow, and work in the small vegetable garden. The evenings when Guy was home, I prepared a stew or soup from simple recipes Chantel had shared and always one of Nina's dessert specialties—usually Guy's favorite, a light angel food cake, with jam when fresh fruit wasn't available. Guy kept our table supplied with wine.

I healed and thrived in the idyllic life, and we seemed to be keenly attuned to each other's emotions. I wasn't sure to what extent Guy's work detracted from his peace of mind. One thing was for sure though; our nights together validated our union and strengthened our love.

By the first of April, I'd missed my second monthly cycle and I felt confident that I was pregnant again. Everything had to be perfect when I told Guy. I baked an angel food cake and prepared a baked chicken to complete the best dinner possible, given the supplies at hand.

After dinner I followed him into the sitting room and turned on the radio to my favorite music station—we didn't need to hear the news. While we sipped wine, I tried to think of a clever way to tell him about my pregnancy, but I drew a blank as to how to interrupt while he read the newspaper.

He seemed to sense my need for his attention and set the paper aside. "You're mighty quiet. Is everything okay?"

"Oh, yes. We're going to have a baby!"

"You're sure?"

I nodded.

He smiled and moved beside me on the sofa. "That's the best news I've heard in a long time."

"I just need the doctor to confirm it."

He held me in his arms and sought my lips for a slow, prolonged kiss while the soft strains of "Blue Moon" played in the background.

He laid his head on my lap. At the end of the song, I wondered whether he'd gone to sleep, but he said, "Let's plan on going to Paris to see your doctor as soon as I can arrange it."

"For a medical opinion?" I teased. I knew he hoped for a baby as much as I did."

"Yes."

"I could see the local doctor."

"No. Your doctor in Paris knows your medical history, and you need to be under his care."

We returned from Paris in mid-April with the happy news

that the baby had a due date of November seventeen.

"What a Christmas present!" Guy said, his face aglow.

As we drove back to Chartres and approached the city, the verdigris green roof and stone spires of the Cathedral of our Lady of Chartres dominated the view and seemed to float above the surrounding buildings.

Guy turned off at the exit and drove to the church.

"Can't you wait to tell Curtis and Chantal about the baby?" I asked, eager to get to the cottage.

He didn't answer until he parked the car. "I need to go inside. Come on, you too." He held my hand as we walked along the path. "I want to pray for you and the baby."

I didn't comment but wondered why he wouldn't include himself in the prayer.

We entered through the Royal Portal and passed by the well-worn, paved labyrinth. I wondered, if I walked the labyrinth, would I contact the mystical power of my inner self?

I sat beside Guy and offered my own silent prayer of gratitude. I asked that God see us through whatever lay ahead. My heart filled with love for my husband and the coming baby. Just when I thought I couldn't be any happier, I found that I was. On our way to the car, I said, "I'm glad you thought to stop at the cathedral."

"While you were still in Paris, I started attending mass here," he said. "It gave me the faith to go on after especially difficult days."

"You didn't tell me."

"I didn't want you to worry."

"I don't want you to keep things from me. But I think sharing with a higher source is a good idea for both of us. Let's attend mass on Sunday and the next week, as well. That's Easter."

"I'd like that," he said without looking at me.

My life changed the first day of May. The blissful time with Guy had come to an end. A coverlet of yellow daffodils blanketed the meadow, save the trail taken on our daily horseback rides, and gave no warning of what awaited our return home.

"What's a strange car doing by the house?" I asked.

"I don't know," Guy said in an even tone.

Immediately, I shifted to danger mode. "What are we going to do?"

"You stay here in the stables. If I'm not back in ten or fifteen minutes, take Betsy and ride to Curtis's house. Stay there until you get further word from me or until he finds out what's happened."

I tried, without success, to swallow the lump in my throat. "Okay," I whispered above the loud thud of my heart.

Those were the longest minutes I've ever experienced. I had no choice but to wait a reasonable amount of time—but what was reasonable? I lost all sense of time as I sat on a bale of hay toward the back of the building, waiting to hear Guy's voice.

"Paulette?" He paused. "It's safe. Come out."

I ran to his open arms. "Who was it?"

"Jean Moulin is here to see me. He has serious decisions to make and wants my advice."

Although his arm was around my waist on our way to the house, I couldn't shake a kicked-in-the-gut feeling of dread. Only a dire situation would have brought Moulin to the house. Their group had regular meeting times. And it wasn't at our home.

I carried on like the dutiful wife and served wine to them in Guy's small study. I took a quick look at Jean, a still good-looking, middle-aged man with dark hair and intelligent brown eyes that I guessed didn't miss much of anything.

They stayed closeted for more than two hours, while I puttered in the vegetable garden. I picked peas and shelled them, pulled and cleaned radishes and green onions. After that I pulled any weeds I could find. I brought the vegetables inside and popped the loaf of bread that had been rising into the oven. Soon after, the bread was ready, and almost at the same time, the study door scraped open. Guy's and Jean's expressionless faces gave me no clue as to what to expect.

"Won't you join us for lunch?" I said to Jean.

"Merci, I wish I had the time, but I don't."

"At least take a sandwich with you. I'll have it ready in a

jiffy."

He nodded. "I'd like that."

I'd already sliced cheese for lunch, and I had his sandwich in his hands within two minutes.

After Jean left I set our lunch on the table and waited for Guy to say something—anything—to enlighten me about their meeting. When he took a bite of his sandwich and set his plate aside but remained silent, I asked, "Aren't you hungry?"

He took a deep breath. "You know that I'm now involved with Jean to bring the various Resistance groups together as one united effort on behalf of the Free French Movement. General de Gaulle wants to establish the *Conseil National de la Resistance*, organized under his leadership. Last October Jean managed to unite three groups from the *Unis de la Resistance* . . . the MUR. That's when Jean and others returned to London and returned home again with orders to form the Conseil National . . . the CNR.

I'd listened without interruption, but when Guy grew silent, I asked, "Did you go to London?"

He nodded but wouldn't meet my gaze. "Paulette, you must understand this is a critical time for the Allies. We must be victorious against the Axis powers. Our future hangs in the balance."

"I need to know what your part in all this is."

His voice grew stronger. "And you know I can't tell you."

My brain knew he was right, but my heart felt rejected. I swiped at a salty drop perched on my cheek.

He stood and took my hands. "Come here," he said. He drew me to my feet and held me in his arms.

A self-loathing threatened more tears. "I can be brave when I'm making the decisions, but when there's nothing I can do, I . . ." My voice broke.

He rubbed my back. "I understand. I feel like a pawn in this war. But that doesn't change what I must do. I'll be away from you more than I have been recently."

I felt the vise tightening around us. Nothing was certain. What could I say? I slipped from his embrace. He didn't try to stop me. The next thing I knew I was in a fetal position in bed. I dried my eyes and willed myself to feel nothing. I tossed and turned without the promised security of my husband's arms, "You better get used to an empty spot in the bed," I scolded myself.

I must have dozed, because when I awoke, Guy sat beside me, his face etched with emotion.

I gave him a small smile. "I'm under control. Come on, lie down beside me."

He hesitated. "Are you sure?"

"Yes, please, come here." I opened my arms.

He didn't move. "Have you recovered from the shock?"

I nodded.

"It's best that you be at Lamont, for the rest of the summer at least. I'll be there when I can, and with luck we'll be able to return to Paris in September with Claude when he's ready for preparatory school."

"Maybe you're right. And I'll be able to spend time with Claude," I mused. "He'll be away at school so soon." I got up and sat in the chair next to Guy. Reaching for his hand, I continued, "We'll treasure whatever time we have with you."

"We need to close up the cottage and leave here by the end of next week." His eyes met mine. "At least we'll be able to attend mass at Chartres tomorrow."

"Right. It might be the last time for a while," I said. "And afterward, let's have lunch in that charming café in the old town. I forget its name."

He nodded. "I know the one you mean. On Monday I'll plan to go to Paris. And after that we'll be busy getting ready to leave here. I'll alert Curtis that we'll need to have him take care of things while we're away."

I worked diligently to be ready to leave Sunnyside within a few days. I didn't press Guy about his Paris trip. He'd tell me if he wanted me to know. While he was gone, I determined to make each moment together a special one.

I was pleasantly surprised when my husband returned before sunset. I had prepared a soufflé and baked an angel food cake. I planned to serve it with whipped cream and some of Chantal's strawberry jam.

Guy opened the bottle of Dom Perignon champagne he'd brought for me from Paris. "I remembered," he said. "Your favorite."

I kissed him. "What a good memory. Thank you."

After dinner we sat on the sofa in the living room and shared another round of the Dom Perignon.

I tuned the radio to a music station while he refilled our glasses. Again, my favorite song, "Blue Moon," played softly in the background.

"Did you miss me today?" he asked.

"What do you think? I was lost without you." I snuggled against him, happy to have him home.

His kiss was long and searching—not like usual. "I thought of you all the time I was away."

"I must be growing on you," I said with a giggle.

Suddenly, he was all business. "I have some things for you," he said. He picked up his briefcase from the side of the sofa, reached inside, and handed me a sheet of paper. I stared. It was the deed to the cottage—in my name only.

"Why isn't your name on here too?"

"Because I want it to belong to you." He gave me a large envelope in which there were shares of American and Argentinean oil stocks, and a New York bank account, again in my name. "And these as well."

"But why all this now?"

"I want to be able to sleep at night and know that you have sufficient funds for yourself and our child. I'm not concerned about Claude. Provisions are already in place for him."

"Does this have to do with Jean's visit?"

"Not really. I admit I was moved to action because of it. I should have done it sooner but let it slide. As the war ramps up, we all face greater danger. Try not to worry. Now that this is done, I've done what I can."

"I'm glad, if it gives you peace. I don't want you to worry about me or the baby."

We talked into the night and at midnight went to bed, contented, in each other's arms.

Loire Valley

Madame de Laval met us in the entry hall when we arrived at Lamont a week before Claude's birthday. "Your father will be happy to see you," she said to Guy as she walked with us to the morning room. "He's concerned about the latest turn of events. He's lost confidence in General Pétain, although he blames Prime Minister Laval for the dreadful things that are happening."

The major sat in the study, his head down. He appeared to be reading a book. The room seemed strangely silent without the usual sound of the radio in the background.

While still some distance from the major, Guy asked, "Is Claude still with his tutor?"

"Oui, your father decided he needs additional hours of study. He'll be free at three o'clock. Now that you're here, perhaps an exception can be made so that he can be with you."

Guy's shoulders tensed. "Claude is *my* son, and I'll determine his number of study hours."

"Oh, I didn't mean it that way. Don't get into a disagreement with your father. You know he can be unreasonable, but he does what he thinks is for the best."

"I'm sorry, Maman. I can't ignore him anymore. I'm his son but not his minor child."

Madame looked to me, her eyes pleading for help.

I reached for Guy's hand. "I'm sure the major understands that things are different for Claude when we're here."

He dropped my hand. "I'll get Claude and bring him down. The family needs to be together on the rare occasions it's possible." He looked at me. "Are you coming?"

Pleasantly surprised that he'd asserted his parental authority, I said, "I am."

Her brow creased, Madame shook her head. "I'll let your father know you're here."

Upstairs, Guy and I stood outside the door of the classroom and listened for a few minutes.

"My papa's going to get me a telescope for my birthday," Claude announced.

"That's next week, isn't it?" the tutor asked.

"Non, it's *this* week."

"When you get your telescope, we'll be able to study the stars at night. What do you think of that?" the tutor said.

"It'll be more fun than staying inside all the time."

Surprising both tutor and child, Guy spoke from the

doorway. "In that case, you'll replace your morning classes with a night class."

"Papa, Paulette, you're here already," Claude said as he climbed onto Guy's shoulders. "Does that mean in the mornings we can go boating and horseback riding?"

Guy hugged his son before setting him back on his feet. "Until August, and then you'll finish up your summer studies before starting boarding school."

"I'll make sure you're ready," the tutor said to Claude.

À toute à l'heure," Guy said before we started out of the room to return to the morning room.

Claude persisted and called after us, "And I can go back to Paris with you?"

"That's the plan. Paulette and I will be here all summer with you."

As we started down the stairs, Guy said, "I'm not in a mood for Papa to tell me what Claude can and cannot do."

At the sound of our voices, the major stood and welcomed us with an air kiss to each cheek.

Nothing seemed to have changed at Lamont. The daily routine continued on pretty much as usual. Monsieur and Madame de Laval were at odds about the motives of the Vichy Government. The major discouraged discussion of the topic. I think he found the Vichy administration's behavior indefensible but didn't want to admit it and lose face. His way of coping was to become short tempered and turn his full attention to Claude's education and the glorious future he wished for him.

The bickering didn't help Guy's mood. He appeared tense and introspective. I wondered whether his father's behavior or the increased pressure on his role in the formation of de Gaulle's resistance council was the primary cause.

I found myself seeking the companionship of Madame de Laval that often included time with Aline's two-year-old daughter, Martine, who was prone to tantrums when she didn't get her way.

On the day of Claude's birthday, Madame de Laval and I

were setting the table for dinner. Martine whined and pulled on Madame's apron. "I want a cookie."

"No. It'll ruin your appetite"

"I want it," the child screeched.

"Young lady, sit down and color your picture." Madame led her to a small table with a picture of a birthday cake to color."

At least Martine was quiet while we finished setting the table for the celebration.

"She's being such a good girl. I don't think one cookie will ruin her meal," Madame said as she took a small cookie from the plate.

I didn't think she should give in but kept my thoughts to myself. When I heard Madame scold, "Look at what you've done!" I turned to see what the child could have done to elicit Madame's ire.

Martine had scribbled on the wall with red and black crayons.

"I should have known you needed a nap," Madame muttered.

Martine ran to the table and poked her finger into the birthday cake. Madame carried her, kicking and screaming, from the room as I took the frosting spreader and repaired the cake as best I could before I started scrubbing most of the crayon off the wall.

A half hour later, my mother-in-law returned. "I read to her until she went to sleep. You know it's hard on a little girl, not to be with her mother."

I didn't respond."

"I best get to the wall," Madame continued.

"I took care of it while you were gone."

"Merci, you're a sweetheart." Her gaze lingered on my face and moved to my tummy. "You're pregnant again?"

"I am. How did you guess?"

She put her arms around me. "You have a telltale glow about you."

I didn't tell her it was from the exertion of scrubbing the wall. "Guy and I plan to wait until after Claude's special day to mention the baby. Can I count on you to respect our wishes?"

"Of course, ma cherie. It's wonderful news. I'm so happy for all of us."

✝

Guy, Claude, and I had a perfect two weeks with the family, stargazing in the evenings with the new telescope, horseback riding and boating in the mornings.

Guy and Claude took up archery, while Madame de Laval and I spent hours in the craft room, working on personal projects and Christmas gifts for the children at the annual community Christmas event at Lamont. I even had time to make myself a beautiful table runner of turquoise, pink, and, beige velvet lined with linen and with tassels made of large, gold metal threads.

Toward the end of the month, Guy said to me when we'd retired for the evening, "You need to see your doctor in Tours while I'm here to go with you."

"Does that mean you'll be away again soon?"

"Oui. I'll leave for Paris on the twenty-fourth. The first meeting of the CNR is on Wednesday, the twenty-seventh, in Paris."

"Do you know when you'll be back?"

"I hope to be back within a week. But you never know in this business."

I was thrilled when Guy returned within the week, just as he'd said. During the next two weeks, he traveled to Lyon once a week but always returned in a few days so we could resume our activities with Claude. At the end of the third week of June, Guy changed our routine. His mornings would be reserved for the two of us to take long walks and ride our horses, and his afternoons would be spent with Claude."

As much I looked forward to time with Guy, I ended up disappointed because he didn't talk to me about our future together or other things of importance.

"Talk to me," I begged one day.

Guy ignored my plea. "I think I'll groom the horses myself today. You don't need to wait with me."

"But I want to. It'll be fun for me learn more about them."

"Not today," he said. "I'm not very good company. You deserve better."

Later that evening, when we retired to our bedroom and sat on the sofa in front of the cold fireplace, he seemed in a better mood and laid his head on my lap.

"Would you rather we weren't going have a baby so soon?" I asked.

He sat up and put his arms around me. "You know I love you, and I do want this baby." He lay back down and stayed still, his eyes closed. "Hell of a world he'll live in if we don't win this war." His voice was so low I had to strain to hear.

I gripped his hand. "We will win! But we better get to bed if you're going to leave at seven in the morning."

He stood. "I'm going to sleep in my study tonight. I don't want to keep you awake."

"I sleep better when you're with me. Please stay."

"Don't ask me tonight."

"Okay, for the price of a real kiss."

His kiss was so passionate that I thought he'd changed his mind, but he moaned and abruptly left.

Almost three weeks after Guy left for the meeting of the CNR in Lyon, I had a puzzling dream about a stadium in which I observed a dark-haired man sitting alone on one of the benches. He turned his head toward me, lips moving, but no words sounded. I awoke and thought, *What an odd dream*. I couldn't get it out my mind, so I went outside and sat under the ancient cedar tree, its protective arms, spread wide, affording a place to ponder without distractions. Guy's dog, Mystique, slipped up behind me and nuzzled me before lying down beside me.

After I gave up on trying to understand why the dream stayed with me, my thoughts turned to Guy—a pleasant interlude. I counted the days until Guy and I would share the elation of lovers reunited once again—before the whole cycle of togetherness and separation repeated. My ears pricked at the sound of a truck motor. *Guy's home!* My heart leapt with joy. I stood and watched the truck cross the drawbridge. The door opened.

I ran into the courtyard. Guy didn't rush into my open arms; rather, Brother Roger emerged from the cab of the truck. "Madame de Laval, I have news of Guy."

I crossed my arms. "Yes, what is it?"

"He and seven other council members, including Jean Moulin, were arrested as they gathered in a private home for their meeting two weeks ago in Lyon." He paused. "I imagine you knew about his activities."

I nodded and tried to control the panic I felt. "Where has he been taken?"

"To Montluc Prison in Lyon."

I nearly fainted at his words. Everyone knew the prison was controlled by the Gestapo. Few if any left its walls untouched—and most never left at all. I wondered if the dream of the man at the stadium had in some way been trying to prepare me for the news of Guy's arrest.

"There's no telling how long he'll be kept there," Brother Roger continued. "We've planned an escape attempt. Pray God it succeeds.

Chapter Thirty-Two

July - mid-October 1943 – Loire Valley

A little after midnight I awakened from a deep sleep. In the haze of semi-consciousness, my husband appeared as youthful and handsome as the first day I had fallen in love with him at the Sorbonne. Or was it just the dream of a distraught wife?

In the light of day, I told myself that a dream is just a dream. That I must believe the rescue effort would be successful. From the day Brother Roger informed me that Guy had been arrested, I had agonized over the depraved brutality he faced. If the escape succeeded, he'd be a hunted man and an easy target because, knowing him as I did, he'd go right back to work for the Resistance. But God forbid, if the escape attempt failed, he'd be tortured within an inch of his life before being tossed onto a train destined for a German concentration camp.

I joined Madame de Laval at breakfast for a cup of coffee. "Bonjour, Madame," I said, making an effort to sound cheerful.

She looked up, the strain of uncertainty etched in her face. "*Ma petite fille chérie*, you need to eat something." She buttered a piece of bread and spooned a small bit of scrambled egg onto a plate before setting both in front of me. "Eat what you can."

I slid it to the side. "I'll start with coffee."

She readjusted the plate as it had been. "Guy would want you to think of the baby." Her voice quavered as she spoke. She seemed to have taken on the role of my caretaker. I knew she wanted this pregnancy to be successful. I appreciated her consideration and concern but found it smothering at the same time.

"Merci, I know he would. We both need a cup of coffee," I said and filled our cups with a shaky hand. I realized that she, as well as I, was deeply concerned about Guy and neither of us was behaving in our usual way—not a good mix.

She seemed pleased that I ate breakfast and that she'd succeeded in encouraging me to do so. "I'm going to work on the Christmas gifts for the children. Why don't you join me?"

"And how about you coming with Claude and me to the dock. He wants to go out on the boat, and I want to spend time with him before this afternoon when he'll be with his tutor."

"Oui, I should spend more time with him too. I'm afraid since Martine has been here she has taken time away from him. I'll have Yvette care for her today while we're with Claude and in the sewing room."

It was true that Madame had spent most of her days with Martine while I'd been here. She seemed to love indulging the little girl and had sewn several dresses for her already. I hadn't paid much attention to her while Guy and I had taken every free minute to be with Claude.

After our picnic lunch of cheese, fresh bread, grapes, and lemonade, I stretched out on the blanket and dozed.

"Claude and I are going to take a short walk along the river before we have to leave," Madame said. "He needs to collect a few plant specimens to take back to class."

"Ooh. I'll go too." I struggled to get up.

"No need. We'll stop back for you."

I stayed put and drifted with the mesmerizing warmth of the sun. For a short time, I escaped the soul-wrenching thoughts about my husband's fate. When I could no long maintain the peace of the moment, I stood and folded the blanket in readiness to return to the house. I walked along the sand in the direction Madame and Claude had taken and watched for them along the bluff.

I thought about Claude as I went. He shouldn't be late for his studies if we wanted to keep peace in the family. The major tolerated little deviation to the boy's routine. I disagreed with him. For goodness sakes, the man wouldn't bend a little, even under these circumstances. Claude knew his father was in harm's way, and he needed the love and reassurance of his family rather than a rigid study schedule. Since word of Guy's arrest, the major seemed to direct his energy into finding fault with his grandson.

I didn't see Claude coming as he dashed down the slope, but I heard him call, "Paulette, here we are."

"I'll wait down here."

Madame took her time navigating the perilous terrain. "Oh, dear, that took longer than I anticipated," she said.

We scaled the hill until the ground leveled as we passed the chapel, and we continued on to the front of the house in time to see the door open on the produce truck, the same truck that had brought the news about Guy earlier in the week.

My heart skipped a beat. Where was Guy? He wasn't in the truck. What did that mean?

Brother Roger climbed out of the passenger side of the truck, came forward, and leaned down to speak directly to Claude. "Claude, I'm Brother Roger. It's been a few years since I first met you." He nodded at Madame and me. "So good to see all of you." He tilted his head toward Claude but addressed us. "Is the Major inside?"

"Why, yes, he is," Madame said. She turned her attention to Claude. "You better get those plants to your tutor right away, while I escort Brother Roger in to see your grandfather."

Claude took his cue and ran inside, and I led the monk into the morning room.

The major looked around when we entered and stood and greeted Roger, his expression masking his feelings. "Do have a seat." He gestured toward an armchair and took the vacant one beside him. I noticed the color had drained from Madame's face. I took her arm as we sat on the sofa together across from the men.

Brother Roger focused on me and shook his head. "I'm sorry to have to tell you that our attempt to rescue Guy failed. He was shot during the escape attempt."

"How?" My voice sounded like it was in a tunnel. I knew of the atrocities practiced by the Gestapo. Barbie's goons would stop at nothing to get information from him. Perhaps, Guy had lacked the strength to escape after life-threatening injuries at their hands.

"The Gestapo must have been tipped off. They shot him as he climbed down the rope we'd managed to get to the window of his cell. He survived and was taken to a hospital, but it was too late."

I felt as if all the air had been sucked out of my lungs. I gasped and lowered my head between my knees so as not to faint. So long as Guy had had a breath of life left in him, there had been hope he'd return to us. Now, the finality of death could not be denied. I realized I couldn't afford to wallow in despair, for I had an unborn baby and Claude to consider. I had to go on and do everything in my power to make sure their world wasn't the hell their father gave his life to prevent. I had to have faith that God would watch over Claude, the baby, and me in a free France. I had to believe, or Guy's sacrifice had no meaning. When I raised my head, all eyes were on me. Madame sat beside me and held me in her arms, tears welling in her eyes as she gently rocked me back and forth like a baby.

Even the stoic major blanched and batted his eyelids as if cinders irritated them.

"Guy died a hero," Brother Roger said softly. "He was a real soldier, so unlike many of our countrymen who have chosen to collaborate and benefit from the spoils of their betrayal. I'm honored to have been his friend, and I grieve with you."

"We had an inside man at the hospital who released his body to us. It's here now. You'll need to bury him as soon as possible, but it must be a closed casket ceremony. I took the liberty of contacting a priest at the cathedral. He'll be here at ten o'clock tomorrow morning."

"Merci, I understand," the major replied. "Your presence today and tomorrow will be a great comfort to the family and me."

"Paulette, Claude must be told right away," Madame said to me.

"I'll go get him."

"It's about Papa, isn't it?" Claude said as we made our way back downstairs."

"Yes."

Claude gripped my hand, his shoulders military straight.

His lack of questions surprised me, and the major's reaction did as well. He spoke softly to Claude. "Your father died for France. You have every reason to be proud of him. He was a brave man who fought for his beliefs. I know you'll be a soldier who will make him proud."

"I will," Claude said, his voice solemn.

After a light supper, when everyone else had retired for the night, Brother Roger and I made final plans for the service the next day and talked long into the night.

"What hymns would you like?" Brother Roger asked.

"'Amazing Grace' and 'You Are Near.'"

"Do you have a preference for scriptural passages?"

"From the Old Testament I would like Ecclesiastes Three, verses one through eight. I memorized some of them. One in particular speaks to me." I quoted, "To everything there is a season, and a time to every purpose under the heaven," and softly, I spoke the other verses:

A time to be born, and a time to die; a time to
plant, and a time to pluck up that which is
planted;

A time to weep, and a time to laugh; a time to
mourn, and a time dance;

A time to love, and a time to hate; a time of war,
and a time of peace.

I fought my tears and said, "I'm sorry, I can't think clearly
tonight. I'll let you know in the morning about passages from the
New Testament and Gospels when Monsieur and Madame de Laval
also meet with you to plan the service." I paused and then added,
"I'd like to see Guy one more time."

He shook his head. "Remember him as you last saw him."

"It's hard, you know. Thank you for bringing him home to
us."

"The least I could do."

He seemed eager to allow me to grieve in private, but I
couldn't let him go while I still had so many unanswered questions
about Guy's role in the war. "Can you believe there's so much I
don't know about my husband—there was so much secrecy
surrounding him. Tell me about him. How did he come to be doing
the work he did? I need to know."

He took a deep breath. "All right. I must preface my remarks
by reminding you that the Resistance involves teamwork and that
each member is put at risk if one member has information that
implicates the others. Yet, because of the pain I know you feel, I will
speak of him"

"Did you know that his father insisted from a young age that
Guy was to enter the military?"

"Yes, I guessed as much. There were little things that Guy
said. He and his father often disagreed on Claude's studies and free
time."

"Well, at any rate, in nineteen thirty-nine, Guy graduated
from Saint Cyr as a major in the Army of the Third Republic of
France."

I raised my hand to my lips. "I didn't know."

"When you met him at the Sorbonne, he was there as an
undercover agent for the Third Republic. I think you can begin to

understand the secrecy that plagued your relationship. After General Petain's Vichy Government came to power, the French State replaced the Third Republic. Guy continued his work with the Free French, which ultimately led to membership on the steering committee of de Gaulle' Resistance Council. It cost him his life.

"I've said more than enough. But I can assure you that he cared deeply for you and Claude. He looked forward to a bright future with you and many children.

"God works in mysterious ways. We don't always understand why things turn out as they do. But you must have faith that he will comfort and care for you."

I nodded. "Thank you so very much. I don't know how I could have faced tomorrow without you. Bonne nuit."

He stood. "Guy was my best friend for fifteen years."

Three days after we laid Guy to rest, I wandered aimlessly along the long approach to the drawbridge, lost in the haze of grief. I resented the interruption of a motor vehicle that grew louder by the moment and stepped to the side of the road to allow it to pass. An ambulance came into view, and I caught a glimpse of Aline at the wheel, her long black hair twisted into a bun on top of her head.

None too happy to see her, I muttered, "Now what?" and followed her into the courtyard.

She opened the door, jumped to the ground to hug me tightly, crushing against my swelled belly. "I came as soon as I could after I heard about Guy's arrest . . . and death." She took a step back, tilted her head, and stared at my nonexistent waistline. "Oh my God, not again! You poor thing."

"Stop right now. This baby is all I have left of my husband, and I can think of no greater gift from God than this new life."

"It won't be easy without Guy. Take it from one who knows about absentee fathers."

"Your situation is entirely different than mine." I said, none too graciously.

"I'm saying all the wrong things. I'm sorry," she said. "And if you're happy about it then so am I."

"I'm not exactly my charming self either," I said. "Right now my head is muddled."

"Let's go inside, shall we? I need to see my Martine."

"She was in the sewing room with Madame when I left them. Madame dotes on your little girl. She's like a surrogate grandmother to her since you've lost your mother. Madame loves having a little girl in the family, so much so that she told her to call her Mamie."

"Who knows, maybe you'll have another little girl for Martine and Madame."

I scoffed because I felt sure I'd have a de Laval son for Guy and Claude. "Could be."

We went upstairs to find Martine.

"Ma-Ma!" Martine ran to her mother.

Aline lifted her up until they were face to face. "Little one, you're growing like a weed." She turned to Madame de Laval. "I'm so sorry for your loss. Guy meant the world to me."

Martine giggled and struggled to get down. "Look at my new dress. Mamie made it for me."

"It's beautiful on a beautiful little lady," Aline cooed.

"Oui, and I've made three more." Madame went to the wardrobe, removed the dresses, and handed them to Aline.

"Merci, Madame, they're beautiful."

A tap at the door interrupted us. "It's time for Martine's nap," Yvette said.

Aline picked up where she left off. "Guy was always there to quell our fears, even when the future seemed hopeless. He never doubted that good would prevail."

I couldn't have agreed more. "You've said it well."

Aline and I left Madame at work on Christmas stockings. On the way to the sitting room, Aline looked at me and asked, "How is Claude taking it?"

"He puts on a brave face, but I know he's at a loss about his future. Guy wasn't always physically here with him, but they'd made plans for the future that would have brought them closer and made a dramatic difference in Claude's life." My voice broke. "And now it's up to me to try to implement Guy's plans for him."

"In what way?"

"Claude's home would have been in Paris with his father and me. He's enrolled in a preparatory school just outside the city, from where he could have easily come home for weekends and holidays."

"He'll be crushed if that doesn't happen. I'm so sorry."

"Fortunately, Guy encouraged Claude's interest in a wide range of subjects and was able to participate with him while we all were together, in Paris and after we returned here."

"What sort of things is he in interested in?"

"He requested and received a telescope for his birthday. We spent a lot of time stargazing, and we visited the Paris observatory. I wouldn't be surprised if you received an invitation from him to stargaze tonight and, perhaps, identify some of the visible constellations."

"Oh, I don't know how well I'll do."

"How are you at archery, boating, or horseback riding?"

She shrugged.

✝

Unlike me, Madame de Laval handled her grief by planning activities for Aline, the children, and me. There were games, tea parties, trips to the boathouse, walks along the shores of the Loire, and of course, stargazing.

One morning when Aline, Madame, and I lingered at the table and talked about the holidays, Madame said, "Guy and Paulette's baby will be with us for Christmas. I've always wanted a houseful of grandchildren, and now I will have it." She stared into space. "How I wish Guy could be here with us."

I felt as if a dagger had been driven into my already bruised heart, and I tried to keep a tight rein on my emotions. What purpose would my life serve while I waited at Lamont for the birth of the baby in November? Claude, who would soon be away from Lamont at boarding school, wouldn't need me.

Aline put her arms around Madame de Laval. "So do we all."

A few days later, while Aline gathered flowers for one of Madame's daily tea parties, she said, "I don't know why I didn't realize that I might draw attention to you and Guy when I visited you in Paris the last time. I want to apologize and assure you that I left Maille as a precaution, not because I knew of any breach in our security there."

"But there had been a betrayal. That's why you should have

known better. However, I accept your apology. We best let go of bygones."

She snipped another red rose and placed it in the jar we'd just about filled. "That does it for flowers. Now for a few ferns and we have the makings of a beautiful bouquet."

"So we do," I said, with little enthusiasm.

"I'll leave next week for Lyon," Aline said.

"Is it safe?"

"I just told you there is no known danger."

"Ummm."

"The need for me to return is overwhelming if we're going to win this war. I'm desperate. I need you to come back with me."

"It's out of the question. End of story. Claude and I are going back to the house in Paris. In September he'll attend the boarding school that's already been chosen. For holidays and weekends, I intend to respect Guy's wishes that Claude have the home we planned for him."

"Some of the wounded heroes, who have been unfortunate enough to be shot down or otherwise injured in service, will die if they don't get the care they need. They'll never return to the battlefield to defeat the enemy. It's a matter of life and death for us all. It's the cause Guy sacrificed his life for. Surely, you don't want his death to be in vain. All I ask is that you give it thoughtful consideration." Aline picked up the jar of flowers and strode toward the house.

I went in the opposite direction, to my favorite cedar tree, and flopped down on the grass to clear my head. I knew the situation was as she outlined it. What would Guy's advice in the circumstances have been? He'd leave it up to me but hope I'd make the right decision. But what was the right decision?

Claude could be enrolled in a boarding school in Tours and still have Lamont as his home base. I didn't have to occupy the Paris house yet. I could wait until after the baby was born—or another year for that matter.

I had my answer for Aline. I'd stay at Lamont until the end of August. From September to November I'd be with her at Maille, after which I'd return to Lamont to await the birth of my baby.

By the time I appeared, all that was needed for the tea party to begin was my presence. Aline and Madame hid behind their chairs. Martine squealed in delight when she caught sight of them.

"Where's Claude," I asked, feeling relieved that maybe I hadn't been the culprit who kept them waiting.

Madame waved her hand in dismissal. "He's with the tutor. They're hunting for daisy and other wildflower seeds. Or some such thing. That boy is growing away from us."

"I wouldn't say that. I don't suppose he'll be expected to attend many tea parties at preparatory school."

"That's the very reason I wanted him to be here today."

I hugged her. "I know he means a lot to you. Your days are filled with plans for him. Maybe we should include some games such as dominoes or Battleship."

"Martine wouldn't be able to play those games."

"And Claude shouldn't be expected to want to play tea party or dolls."

She nodded. "I suppose you're right. Boys have different interests than girls. If your baby is a boy, he won't want play with Martine for very many years. Maybe until he's three or four."

"I certainly hope not. Shall we girls be seated and have our tea?"

"I can tell Paulette will take good care of Guy's boys." Aline pulled out a chair for Madame de Laval and then placed Martine at the table.

Madame's lips ruffled as she sat in silence.

I poured tea and she passed bite-sized baguettes squares filled with cheese and slivers of precious ham. On another plate the squares of bread contained jam and butter.

"The flower decorations are beautiful," I said to Aline with a sense of having shirked my responsibility.

"Merci." She grabbed Martine's hand as the child reached for one of the red roses. "After we finish, I'll give it to you," Aline said.

Martine pouted. "I don't want this one. I want that one," she said as she pushed away the ham sandwich and reached for one with jam.

"No, Martine, not now. You eat this one this first."

The little girl rolled her eyes at her mother and said to Madame, "I want that one."

At least Madame de Laval had the grace not to go against Aline's wishes.

"Aline, I'll go to Maille with you for two months, September and October," I announced. Madame gasped, and Aline stared at me as if not sure she could believe what I'd said. "I'll return to Lamont for the birth of the baby. After that I can't promise you anything."

"You talked about being in Paris with Claude and being there on weekends with him," Aline said.

"Since I said that, I've considered Monsieur de Laval's suggestion that Claude attend preparatory school here in Tours." I didn't go on to say that I had disagreed with him at the time.

Madame's face brightened. "That's a good idea for Claude." She sobered and shook her head. "However, you shouldn't put yourself and the baby in harm's way. Aline, what have you done!"

"Don't blame her," I said. "It's my decision to make."

Madame stood and picked up Martine. "It's time for her nap," she said as she bustled away.

Aline looked at me. "Merci. If the need weren't so great, I wouldn't ask."

"I don't have to be convinced about the need. At least I'll feel useful."

"I'll be leaving for home tomorrow and plan to be back in time for your birthday to take you back with me."

✝

Aline left as planned, and Martine stayed on with Madame de Laval. The arrangement seemed to be agreeable with both women.

One morning a few days later, I stopped by the morning room to talk with the Major. "Is this a good time to discuss your suggested change of plans for Claude?"

He gave me a quizzical look. "I'm surprised you brought up the subject. You didn't seem to think much of it."

"Times and attitudes change. All in all, I think it's for the best for him. He needs a sense of stability in his life, and this is the home he knows. If all goes according to my plans, I'll return to the Paris house with Claude and the baby next year in September so that Claude can attend the boarding school his father selected for him."

"We'll see at that time what is best for him."

I didn't like his take on it, but there was no need for

confrontation now. At least we agreed about the immediate plans for Claude. "I'll let him know about the changes."

"Don't bother, just send him to me. I'll inform him, man to man."

I didn't mention my immediate plans about working with the Resistance. It might complicate the plans for Claude. "I'll check back with you later," I said and took my leave.

✝

The first week of September found Madame de Laval and me busy making Christmas stockings for the annual holiday event at Lamont.

Taking a break, Madame set aside her work and looked at me. "Where did August go? I can't believe that Claude will leave Lamont for boarding school in just another week."

"I can't either. As soon I've seen him off to school, I'll have to leave to work with Aline."

She put her hand on my arm, "I wish you wouldn't."

"I know, but I feel it's what Guy would want."

"At least wait until after you have the baby. I could take care of him . . . or her if you still wanted to go."

"I gave my word. I'll be all right. Don't worry. I'll be back in a couple of months to await his arrival."

Madame got up, went to the armoire, and returned with a black dress. "This is to wear on special occasions—a birthday present. We'll have a little celebration for you tomorrow in honor of your twenty-second birthday." I stared at the beautiful silk dress.

"Here, let me help you into it," she said.

I gazed into the mirror and saw that the elegant silk dress fell discreetly over my rounded belly and expanded waist, yet the high Empire waistline emphasized my full breasts, and the rounded, delicate, ruffled neckline drew attention to my face. "It's wonderful. I can wear it now in my condition and also after the baby's here." I kissed her. "I feel better already."

"You look beautiful," she said with a smile. "Now, excuse me. I must see to Martine."

"You go ahead, I'll tidy up here."

I was happy to see her joy at my reaction.

The next day I made an effort to look my best for the

birthday dinner. Fourteen guests were expected to join us. I curled my hair rather than my habit of twisting it into a bun on the back of my head as I had since Guy's death. After applying a touch of red lipstick to my lips, I opened the case that Guy had given me in Paris for our first anniversary—just a short, yet seemingly very long, eight months ago.

The ruby ring and pendant completed my party-perfect outfit. I looked in the mirror and scarcely recognized myself.

Oh God, how I love you, Guy . . . and miss . . . and need you.

At that moment my intense need propelled me down the hall into his bachelor-days bedroom, the mystical room where I'd insisted we spend our wedding night. And, weeks before his death, when tensions mounted, where he'd slept when he came in late from Lyon and didn't want to disturb me.

Our large bedchamber wasn't uniquely his, but this small room was. I went inside and stood transfixed. His boots, a shirt ready to wear, and a cap on the foot of the bed from the last day I'd seen him, all remained as he'd left them. A faint scent of his sandalwood after-shave carried me back to our wedding night. In that room I could capture his essence. Without awareness, I drew strength from cradling my rounded belly in my hands. I sighed, tiptoed to door, and closed it before I started downstairs to dinner.

Chateau Maille

On the way to Lyon, I passed a great number of German convoys traveling in both directions. Although not hungry, I stopped along the way and ordered a bowl of soup. The sandwiches I'd packed in the ice chest to keep me going while driving didn't appeal to me, and the need to replenish my water supply, not to mention the use of a toilet, outweighed my inclination to keep driving.

When I was ready to resume my journey, I could see from where I was seated that a truck filled with German soldiers was pulling in next to my blue Renault. Seven uniformed men poured out of the truck like oranges tumbling off a conveyer belt. Two of them circled my car and appeared to be in animated conversation. The other five came into the café. I suppose it was because I was the only patron in sight that the tall, skinny one said to me in strongly accented French, "Is that your Renault outside?"

My heart thumped so hard I was afraid he might hear it. I willed my voice to be steady. "Why do you ask?"

"Give me the keys."

"Please don't ask. I'm on my way to deliver a baby … I'm a midwife," I added quickly as soon I realized I'd revealed my vulnerability. I held my breath and hoped he hadn't guessed the truth.

"Too bad. If we didn't have to keep going, I'd accompany you. I'm a medic."

The other soldiers broke out in laughter and elected to sit at tables by the front window.

When the waitress brought my watery soup, I asked for a cup of coffee. "It's just chicory, is that okay?"

I nodded.

She went on to their table and took their order. The medic asked her, "What kind of meat is in the stew?"

"It's carrots and potatoes cooked with a ham bone."

"Seven large bowls. And bring some wine," the driver of the truck said. "Next time we come in you better have some meat to feed us and some real coffee."

They devoured the thin stew in record time and went on their way—without my car, thank God.

After all that time and excitement, my bladder felt as if it would burst. After I'd been to the toilet, I got into the Renault and drove nonstop to Maille, constantly watching the rearview mirror for German trucks.

After a week back at Maille, I had adjusted to the business of survival. The number of airman had been pushed to the limit, filling the small infirmary in the cellar as well as the new, makeshift hospital in the huge old silo attached to the chateau at the end of one wing. The silo could be entered from the infirmary or from the outside.

The responsibility for keeping things going fell almost solely on Aline and me. A local woman and her daughter volunteered when they could take time from their other responsibilities. Other than that, it was just us and we rarely managed to take even a few free hours for ourselves.

I typically rose at four o'clock in the morning to care for the patients while Aline prepared breakfast. I also took over the responsibility for the vegetable garden. At its peak of production, the fresh vegetables were the mainstay of the meager meals we served. My presence allowed Aline time to stand in ration lines for additional items we couldn't produce ourselves. I managed to carry out my responsibilities during September, but it became more difficult as each week passed.

By the first of October, I worried that my endurance would falter before I returned to Lamont at the end of the month. I'd lost weight in spite of carrying a child, and I only managed to get five or six hours of sleep a night.

One evening when Aline and I stayed up late to make pumpkin pie, I said, "You need to find someone to do the outdoor work. I'm exhausted and can't continue at this pace another month."

"I know I'm asking a lot from you, Little Momma." She patted my tummy." I'll see what I can do. If I have to take over the animals and the garden, I'll be tied down here. I don't know who'll get the supplies we need or be a runner for pamphlet distribution. I wouldn't want to ask you to do that in your condition."

I resented her apparent lack of planning for finding my replacement. "You'd better make it a high priority."

"I will. Tomorrow while I'm in town and make my run, I'll make inquiries. Don't worry."

The following day when the nursing and breakfast duties were done, Aline left for town, and I remained at the chateau to take care of everything until our part-time help arrived.

I wanted to sit down, but I went outside to feed the chickens and rabbits and to gather eggs. I had no time or energy for the weeds in the garden. So far, the minor repair work outside had fallen to me because so few men were available in the community. The loss of men during the three years of war had decimated their numbers. An old garden chair tempted my weary body to rest awhile.

The sound of motorcycles carried to the backyard. I stood and slowly made my way toward the front of the chateau. The sound grew steadily louder. I ran back and went into the kitchen. I knew that trouble was about to announce its presence. I dashed to the basement to pile the bales of hay against the opening to the infirmary as Aline and I had rehearsed on a regular schedule. The problem was that it took the two of us to get the disguise into place. Could I do it alone? I thought not.

The motorcycle sounds stopped, but immediately, loud banging sounded on the front door. I don't know where I got the strength to hoist the last bale to its top position, but I did. Then I took the stairs two at a time to answer the door, calling out, "Just a moment," and panting to fill my lungs with air.

I opened the door and found two German soldiers, wearing immaculate uniforms, complete with tall, polished black boots, ready to pounce if I put up any resistance.

They took a step back when I appeared in the doorway. "Madame de Maille?" the taller one asked.

No, I'm a friend of hers, here for a visit."

"Show us to the salon, and tell her we're here to see her."

"I can't do that."

"You have no choice."

"I'm sorry, I can't tell her because she's in town, standing in the ration lines to see whether we'll have broth or stew for the next few days."

The shorter one snickered. "That doesn't sound like much fun. What time do you expect her home?"

"No telling. By dark I hope."

The taller one took a deep breath. "Well, you'll have to do. We have reports that you have enemy airmen here as guests. Don't bother to deny it. My men and I will see for ourselves." He pushed his way into the entryway and said to his companion, "Call the men. We're doing a complete search of this place, even if it takes all night and all day tomorrow."

He grabbed my arm. "Where does this go?" He walked toward the kitchen, his boots clicking on the stone flooring with each step he took. "What's the general layout of this place?"

"The kitchen and dining areas are at this end, the formal salons and library are in the other direction. The upstairs is mostly bedrooms."

By the time I told him what I wanted him to know about the house, there must have been fifteen or twenty Germans inside. The one in charge continued to bark orders, and soon soldiers were spread out in all directions.

There was little I could do to keep them from searching the

place. Angry voices called out their positions, stating that they'd found nothing. Finally, they all clattered down the stairs into the cellar.

I sat down, deciding to save what little energy I had left. I shuddered when I heard noises in the cellar and things being thrown against the walls and floors. I had no idea how we'd survive after such a thorough search. And then all was quiet until the sound of boots on the stairs echoed. Everyone crowded into the salon.

The tall one said to me, "We need a look around in that silo in front. How do we get in?"

"I don't think it's locked. All that's there is hay from the days the Mailles kept horses."

"Come on," he motioned to his henchmen. "We'll take a look around in there. And Madame, you look for where your friend keeps the keys, in case we need one."

I stood and breathed deeply. I knew where to find the large key to the tumbled-down barn door. I'd seen it earlier and asked Aline about it.

I gathered my courage and ran to the silo entrance. The door stood open, and much to my relief, hay was piled up against the wall. The only thing I could think was that Aline had sealed off the outside entrance to our little hospital, hoping I would be able to take care of hiding the entry to the infirmary, should the Germans arrive during her absence.

I turned around, went back into the house, and sat at the kitchen table before the Germans noticed my shaking knees. The soldiers, led by their commander, crowded into the kitchen behind me.

"I told the men about the pumpkin pies stored in here," the commander said. "What are they for?"

"To give to the neighbors and to freeze for later. You know they have to be made when the pumpkin crop ripens."

The men grabbed kitchen knives, cut pieces for themselves, and threw the rest against the walls, in frustration that they had failed in their mission. One of them pointed and cursed at my belly. "Another damn French baby," he said to the accompaniment of catcalls from the others.

The soldier next to him snickered. "Or a German baby." His comment was met with hoots and wolf whistles. Before things could progress in the obvious direction, the commander snapped, "Get out of here. We don't have time to play around."

The next thing I heard was the roar of motors as the Germans started their engines and rode into the last of the daylight.

I was trembling. It had been a close call. If they had come an hour later, they would have been present when the guide arrived to pick up some of the airmen for the trek to the Spanish border and freedom.

Three days later, October sixteenth to be exact, I awoke in the night to a pressure in my groin and a wet sheet. I went to the toilet to relieve myself and was overcome by cramps radiating around the lower half of my body. My back ached and my stomach was rock hard. I slipped to the floor and lay there until the worst of it passed, then returned to the bed and lay there until the waves of pain started all over again. The pressure was agonizing. When the torment subsided, I went and woke Aline. "Wake up. Something's wrong."

"What?" She rubbed the sleep from her eyes. "What is it?"

"I woke up to a wet bed and went to the toilet. That's when I had horrible pain all around my lower body."

"How much fluid was in bed?"

"I don't know. Maybe I wet . . ." I moaned and held my pelvic area.

She placed her hand on my abdomen. "You're in labor."

When I could breathe again, I said, "How could I be? I'm not due for another month."

"I hope this is a false labor. Such things can happen. We'll time your contractions."

I didn't respond, but I tensed and began a moan that slowly built into a groan as the next wave struck.

Aline squeezed my hands and prompted me to breathe and pant. She left for a moment and returned with cool washcloths, patted the perspiration from my face, and placed a cloth across my forehead. When the worst had passed, she stood and laid a baseball bat next to me. "Grip this if you feel another contraction. I'll grab some chloroform and see how it goes."

"Please hurry."

"I will. If this baby holds off until morning, the housekeeper will be here to help with the birth."

"I've given birth, and it wasn't anything like this. I haven't had any spotting."

She turned and looked at me, her face pale, brow furrowed—unusual for the unflappable Aline. "Each one is different," she said as she hurried out of the room.

And then I recalled that her labor had been difficult and had torn her up so much that she couldn't have other children. "Ohhh, what am I in for?" I moaned as I gripped the bat.

Chapter Thirty-Three

Late October 1943 - June 1944 – Loire Valley,

My precious son, who had the dark hair of his father, and I left Chateau Maille by ambulance after a new group of injured airmen were brought there. I'd been overjoyed when I delivered him at a healthy six pounds, three ounces. I named him for my daddy, Jean-Paul Rousseau, since Claude carried the traditional ancestral family names. Guy and I had not talked about names, but I'm sure he would have wanted to honor my family.

For the first few days, Jean-Paul eagerly nursed at my breast, but by the third day his healthy pink skin had taken on a slightly yellowish tinge. By the time the ambulance arrived, his color was a jaundiced-yellow. He often fell asleep while nursing.

"Paulette, the baby is too sick to be at home," Madame de Laval said the day after our arrival. "We have to get him to the hospital right away."

"No! He needs his mother, not strangers, to care for him." I didn't want to let him out of my sight. I'd waited all these months for my baby. He was all I had after Guy's death.

"You don't understand, we'll lose him if we don't act quickly."

"Are you trying to frighten me?"

"After Guy was born, I lost my little girl at birth. She was jaundiced, also. Get Jean-Paul ready and let's go."

I'd never heard of such a thing. Frantic, I rushed to get ready.

Because of my emotional state, the doctor arranged for me to sleep on a cot beside Jean-Paul's bassinet and to feed him. "A baby needs his mother's milk," he said. "We'll do everything in our power to save him."

On the second night, the doctor came into the room with a priest and told Madame de Laval and me that Jean-Paul would have to be cared for by a nurse in another location. He gave me a sedative. "Your son isn't likely to survive the night. His acute respiratory problem hasn't responded to treatment. I'm sorry to bring such bad news." He took a deep breath. "The priest is here for Jean-Paul."

Tears streamed down my cheeks. I turned to the priest.

"Please perform the last rites for him before the nurse gets here."

Madame's eyes glistened as she blinked back tears.

I awoke at dawn when the nurse came into my room with another sedative.

"My baby. How is he?"

She shook her head. "He is with God."

"And with his brother and father. That's where I should be," I said between sobs.

She held my hands. "My dear, I'm so sorry."

"Where's my mother-in-law?"

"She'll be here first thing in the morning to take you home after the doctor sees you."

Home? *Where is home*? I wondered. I don't have a family anymore or a home.

I awoke to emptiness too dark to describe the next morning. I'd lost both my son and my husband within three months' time. How was I going to bear such grief?

Breakfast, I assumed when I heard carts and trays rattle along the corridor.

"Bonjour. You'll be going home today," the nurse said in a cheerful voice. She set my breakfast of scrambled eggs, toast, and coffee on the bedside tray. "I'll be back to help you dress."

Maybe because my body was still in milk-production mode, my ravenous appetite took me by surprise. I'd cleaned the plate long before the nurse returned.

She rolled a cart into the room and removed the dishes before she helped me out of the hideous hospital gown. Next she removed long strips of cotton from a tray. "First, we'll bind your breasts to discourage milk production, and we'll send home a breast pump for you to use if they become painful. Only remove enough milk to relieve the pressure, or you'll keep up the production." She laughed. "I doubt you want to be a wet nurse, do you?"

She hummed all the while she helped me into my clothes and assisted me to the wheelchair she'd placed beside the bed.

"I don't need to sit in that thing, I can walk."

"Hospital policy requires I take you to the doctor's examination room."

I acquiesced.

We rode the elevator to the first floor and down the hall to the doctor's office.

"Madame de Laval, are you feeling a little better today?" he asked.

I shook my head. "No. There's a hole in my heart."

"I'm sorry. I'll rephrase. Do you have any concerns about your health?"

"I feel well other than my breasts are tender."

"That'll clear up in a few days. Just to be sure you're healing well, let's you get onto the examination table." He pressed all around my abdomen and pelvic region and asked that I tell him if I felt any pain. "Hmmm. Good. Hmmm. You're healing nicely." After he helped me sit up and get back into the wheelchair, he asked, "Do you have any questions for me?"

"Why did my baby die? Was it something I did or should have done and didn't?"

"I doubt it was your fault. I don't know for sure, but I suspect the cause. There is ongoing research on what is called the Rh factor. It has to do with a blood antigen. Some people carry the antigen in their blood, and the ones who don't are labeled Rh negative."

"If a Rh-negative woman carries a Rh-positive baby, her body develops antibodies in response to the Rh-positive factor of the baby. The antibodies increase with each pregnancy, and that increases the risk for each subsequent pregnancy.

"That might be the explanation. But much more research is needed before we'll understand how to offset the effect.

"The good news is that you're healing well. I see no reason why you shouldn't be able to have more children."

I rose out from the wheelchair. "No, I won't be able to have more children! My husband is dead."

"I'm sorry, Madame. I didn't know."

"No, I don't suppose you would. Please forgive me."

He frowned. "My remarks were about your physical ability to have other children. I understand you're distraught. I'll send some sedatives home with you. Take one at bedtime for a week. See me on December twentieth for your final checkup." He patted my hand. "The nurse will see you to the lobby to meet your mother-in-law."

☦

327

Madame de Laval's concern for me warmed my heart. She suggested we have breakfast together each morning and then spend as much time as I'd like working in the craft room. "Aline calls me by my given name, which is Lucia," she said. "There's no reason you shouldn't also. I think of both of you as friends as well as family."

"Merci, Lucia." I glanced around the sewing room but didn't see the baby blanket she'd been working on for Jean-Paul. "What will you do with Jean-Paul's blanket now?"

"It's yours to do with as you like." She reached for a beautifully wrapped package and handed it to me.

I opened it and found two blankets inside, one blue and one yellow. I held the blue one to my face and said, "They're so soft and beautiful. I'll treasure them always."

She hugged me. "I'm happy that you're pleased. If you'd like, we can make larger ones for the older children."

"That's a good idea." I wasn't sure how many I'd complete before early December, but at least it would keep me busy while I recuperated physically and emotionally. High on my list was to make several of the beautiful table runners while I had Madame's guidance and materials available. When Claude and I began to spend more of our time in Paris, I might not be able to continue with such a time-consuming craft.

"Lucia," I said. Such familiarity did not come easily, but I would try. "This room, away from everything else, is wonderful. Thanks for sharing it with me." I meant every word. I knew I would need it after I confronted the major about my intention to honor Guy's wishes for Claude's education, many of which were out of line with those of Monsieur de Laval.

"Ma cherie, spend as much time here as you like, whether I'm present or not. Consider it your retreat. And feel free to use any of the fabrics that you'd like."

"Are you sure? I'll ask before I do."

"Sometimes, I take my knitting and sit with my husband. One positive outcome of the evil France is enduring is that it has brought us closer together. We need to comfort each other about the state of affairs, especially now that Guy is gone. My husband won't admit it, but he's devastated. He keeps his pain pent up inside. But every so often, in a moment of weakness, he tells me how much having me with him keeps him going. I know he doesn't want to let go of

Claude but knows it's inevitable, and that will leave just the two of us."

"I'm happy to hear of your renewed companionship. It's important to have someone who cares."

"It's not easy to have Claude at boarding school." She lowered her head. "At least he's close enough to come home on the weekends."

"You seem to be fond of Martine and enjoy watching her grow up."

"Oui, I am. No question about it, she fills a void."

I nodded. "I'm happy that Claude has you. You're a wonderful grandmother. He knows he can count on you to love and care for him."

"He's a special boy. Guy loved him so much and valued our family time."

It was my turn to fight back tears.

I wavered about confronting the major about Guy's wishes for Claude after Madame's comments about the void they felt without him. They had lost a son when I lost my husband. I should try to understand how I must appear to them—an outsider who wanted to step in and tell the family how to run its affairs. Had I stopped to consider what Claude wanted? I rationalized that he wanted what his father had planned for him and decided to have a talk with the major. I found him dozing in his armchair and started to tiptoe away.

"Paulette, I see you're up and about. How are you feeling?" His voice carried a tender tone I hadn't heard from him in the past.

I put my arms around him. "I'm all right, trying to carry on. It's hard sometimes." I straightened and faced him.

He nodded. "I know it is. I'm sorry you've had to bear such heartache."

"I know it hasn't been easy for you and Madame de Laval either." At that moment I couldn't bear to bring up my plan to take Claude to Paris for a week or so before Christmas. But I'd have to do so soon to give them time to adjust. I couldn't wait until the week before we left.

Each morning after Lucia and I worked on our needlework, I made it a point to visit the major. By the end of the week, all traces of tenderness had vanished. Still, I hesitated to bring up the subject of Claude. Finally, the week before Claude's school recessed for the Christmas holidays, I approached him while he listened to the radio. "Good morning. You seem to be back to your normal routine," I said.

He turned his head in my direction and looked me in the eye. "I'll never be back to my previous routine. I've lost a son, and my grandson is all I have anymore." He raised his eyes to the de Laval coat of arms on the far wall. "But for his good and the good of France, I have sent him to preparatory school, as I did my own son. It breaks the bond, but we de Lavals have to look beyond our personal preferences and meet our noble obligations to country." He turned back to me. "I don't expect you to understand."

"I do know what Guy planned for Claude's education. And I intend to carry out his wishes to the best of my ability."

"What is that supposed to mean?"

"Claude needs to get acquainted with Paris, as he will attend school there come next September."

"Not if the fighting continues."

"Time will tell, but in the meantime Claude and I will spend two weeks in Paris before the holidays, and then we'll be back with the family."

The major rose to his feet and shook his finger at me. "Are you saying you plan to keep him from his blood relatives for most of his Christmas holiday?"

"Non. I think he should be here for several days before we go to Paris."

"You are not his guardian. If you don't respect our ways, you should return to America."

"I represent Guy's wishes, and you must know that I have nothing to gain by doing so."

"Leave my presence. I don't wish to hear any more about this."

Unexpected footsteps preceded Claude's entry. "Stop it! Neither one of you is right. I'm going to spend the holidays with the headmaster and Pierre. They're going to teach me how to ski."

I was speechless, while the major found his voice. "I won't tolerate insurrection from you, young man. You'll ask for my permission when you want to change our family plans."

Claude stomped out of the room. I followed but didn't call to him.

The major lost no time contacting the headmaster and telling him that Claude had misbehaved and would be unable to accept their invitation.

Claude sulked in his room and made everyone else miserable. I don't know whether Madame persuaded her husband or he decided to suggest that Claude and I go to Paris the week before Christmas; nevertheless, arrangements were made and Claude and I departed as planned.

Our week in Paris was not the idyllic one I'd imagined. Claude blamed me as well as his grandfather for his lost opportunity to learn to ski. That's when I most missed Guy's steady hand with his son. Of course, the boy longed for congenial male companionship—which I could not provide.

The day before we left Paris for the holidays at Lamont, Claude came inside from helping Hugh trim shrubs. "Paulette, Hugh told me I should tell you about how I feel and why I don't want to spend Christmas at Lamont."

"I'd like to know. Please tell me."

He sat cross-legged on the floor, facing me. "All right. I don't like everybody arguing about me. It was different when Papa told Grand-Papa what we were going to do, but you aren't a real de Laval and don't know how to teach me about it."

"Oh, Claude, what you say is true. I'm not a de Laval by birth. I don't pretend to be an expert on the family role in history. I am simply trying to do what your father planned for you."

He looked at me with his big brown eyes. "You can't. You don't know how."

"I felt I had to try, but if I can't do what is needed, that changes things."

"It doesn't mean I don't want to come to Paris and visit you or visit Grand-Papa and Mamie at Lamont. But most of the time I want to be with the headmaster and Pierre. I'll learn from them how to be a man and a soldier. That's what Papa wanted."

Chateau Maille – 1944

As soon as Claude returned to school after the New Year, I returned to Lyon to care for downed airmen at Aline's not-so-safe safe house. The tension at Lamont overcame my reservations about working for the Resistance. I no longer felt confident that my actions were beneficial for Claude. Without Guy, and now Claude, I served no positive purpose for the de Laval family. My vision of a happy family life in France quickly unraveled.

"Why so quiet?" Aline asked as she cracked eggs to scramble for breakfast.

"Don't you miss Martine?" I asked. "By the time she comes home to you, she might think of Madame de Laval as her mother."

Aline chuckled. "I'm not worried. She'll think of Lucia as her grandmother. I'm there often enough for her. Besides, I think of Madame as my mother. She's been incredibly good to me."

"She's been kind to me too. My concern is that the major doesn't want me to have a say about Claude. I know Guy wanted me to see that Claude be given more freedom than his grandfather allows. Guy said so."

"I understand the problem. The major follows strict de Laval family traditions established many centuries past. You won't win that battle."

"I have to do what I can for Claude. I owe it to Guy. But I don't think Claude trusts me to do so."

"Well, you can't change it today, and we have hungry airmen waiting. Let's get them their special Sunday breakfast. I've even opened one of our last jars of jam for them." Aline handed me a tray with scrambled eggs, bread and jam. "I'll bring the pot of what passes for coffee as soon as I finish up here."

As I made my way down the musty back stairs to the underground infirmary, I felt numb. I'd lost my grip on the purpose of my life. Mother would say, "You don't want to put all your eggs in one basket." Metaphorically, that's what I'd done, and the basket had fallen. At the moment, I lived in limbo.

As soon as I stepped into the hospital area, I put aside my troubles and thought of the men and the sacrifices they and their families were making to secure freedom from tyranny.

"A good Sunday morning to you," I said as I served them, all except those who couldn't feed themselves. Aline and I made the rounds and fed them; there were a few who required a liquid diet.

Our routine remained much the same as it had been before my baby was born. I stayed at the chateau while Aline continued her Resistance activities, weather permitting. Because the number of patients had increased, I managed the activities of four volunteers. On the other hand, gardening work wasn't excessive during the cooler weather. Frequent snowstorms kept outdoor work at a minimum, and often, we had time to listen to the BBC on the radio.

On March 6 we heard a brief newscast that the U.S. had launched a large-scale air attack on Berlin and that many casualties had resulted. Aline and I looked at each other, knowing full well what that meant for our workload.

"I wonder how many of them we'll have," Aline said.

I shrugged. "I wish them luck wherever they're taken." My American patriotism had resurfaced. I wanted to help them and then go home to the United States. When the first five men were brought to us, I found a renewed purpose and loved talking with them and hearing their American accents.

Two weeks later, I rode Aline's bicycle and stood in the ration lines for hours—and had one hambone to show for it at the end of the day.

When I got back, Aline said, "Three more airmen arrived while you were gone."

I shook my head. "I'm exhausted and going to bed."

"You can't until you greet our new arrivals." I couldn't understand why she acted like a kid at a birthday party.

I stood with reluctance and followed her. She led the way with a spring in her step that I hadn't seen for a long time.

When I entered the room, my eyes met his. I ran to his bedside. "Chris! What are you doing here?" I thought he must have come back to the Resistance. I put my arms around his neck and kissed his cheek.

"Lady Luck must have been sleeping on the job."

"Don't say that." I thought of Guy and his work.

"It was a lucky shot for them. The boche nabbed our bomber."

The pieces began to fall into place. "You can't mean in Berlin?" His injury wasn't visible, as he lay covered on the cot, one arm tucked inside.

"That's what I mean."

I turned to Aline and mouthed, "What's wrong with him?"

"It's his right leg," she said. "We have to go. He's sedated and needs rest."

"I'll see you in the morning," I said with mixed emotions. A shadow of doubt remained about his story. I questioned whether he'd done anything to put Guy in danger before his mysterious disappearance from Paris and my life. When Aline and I were well out of earshot, I asked, "Chris, an airman? How do I know he's telling me the truth?"

"I thought you might ask such a question, so I have an answer. I'll show you when we get upstairs. Chris and I had a long talk about you and how you might feel about seeing him after all this time," she said as we walked along. When we reached the kitchen, she removed a large bag from behind some canned goods and handed it to me.

I pulled out one boot, a compass, and lastly, Chris's dog tags. "What did he say about what happened?"

"I'd rather let him tell you in the morning—and that will come soon enough. Bonne Nuit."

Physically tired, I climbed into bed as soon as I got to my room. I wanted to sleep, I needed to sleep, but my mind raced through all sorts of explanations, and sleep eluded me until well after midnight.

I managed about four hours before I awakened. I rushed to get dressed to make my rounds on time. Aline already had breakfast prepared for the men but needed me to get it to the patients. My ambiguous feelings toward Chris bothered me. My first reaction had been disbelief, followed by a rush of affection. I couldn't shake the guilt that plagued me. It seemed a betrayal to Guy, who had died less than a year before. What kind of woman would react that way? I determined I would serve the other men before I went to Chris.

"There you are," Aline said with a knowing look in my direction. "Didn't think you'd want me to serve breakfast without you."

I hoped she didn't see evidence of the heat that warmed my cheeks. "I'm sorry if I'm late. I didn't sleep well."

"No excuses. Let's get to it."

At least I had enough self-control to serve the other men first, and I spoke with each one before I even glanced in Chris's direction.

I have to admit it was difficult. I questioned whether my motive was to spend a little extra time with him. When I reached his cot, his back was turned toward me. "Good morning, Chris," I said in an upbeat voice.

He turned slowly. "Bonjour, Madame de Laval."

"How's your leg today?"

"It could be better." His eyes started with my face and traveled the length of my body. "You're too thin."

"Aren't we all . . . these days?"

"Most of us, anyway." His expression hardened. "I'll wager the de Lavals still eat well."

"Chris, why on earth are you talking like that? They've had to cut back like everyone else during this war."

"I'm surprised your husband allows you to go hungry. Why aren't you with him, anyway?"

"Don't you dare say anything more!" I felt like we were back in high school. Choking back tears, I said, "Guy died in July."

"Oh my God. I'm sorry. How?"

"What do you care?"

He shook his head. "I care more than you'll ever know."

"You suggested Guy ate well while his countrymen starved. You know better than that. He gave his life for the Resistance and Free France." I went off in a huff and took the trays to kitchen, still fuming. I remembered how much Chris irritated me at times.

"What's with you?" Aline scolded as she rinsed the trays in a pan of sudsy water.

"Chris! You or someone else will to have tend to his injuries. I can't be around him."

"What did he do?"

"He had the gall to pretend he didn't know you told him Guy was dead."

"I didn't tell him."

"You said he asked about me and that you had a long talk."

"I told him you were here. That's all."

"Now I feel foolish."

"The best thing to do is to explain the misunderstanding. If you didn't already do so, you better go down and change his bandage, at least."

"All right." Back in the infirmary, I stood by his cot for a few moments before leaning over to speak to him. "Chris?"

He gave me a drowsy glance. "Paulette, you're back."

"Yes, I've come to change your bandage . . . and to apologize. I thought Aline had explained to you that Guy had been killed at a group meeting of Resistance leaders."

"No, all she told me was that you came back to work after your baby died." A long silence followed. "Two losses so close together must be dreadful. I'm truly sorry."

I reached for his hands and held them. "Am I forgiven?"

"I suppose." He closed his eyes.

I released his hands. "Now let me see that injury of yours."

Chris lifted the blanket from his right leg and folded it across his body. A large area of his leg was bandaged above a cast on his lower leg.

"Tell me about this," I said, tapping the plaster.

"A fracture . . . taken care of in Paris." He pointed to the bandaged area. "This got infected as I searched for help after the crash. A farmer and his wife took me in and bandaged it. But I didn't get any sulfa drugs for a week, not until I arrived at the hospital in Paris."

I looked at his chart and saw the care prescribed. A notation in red ink alerted me to keep an eye on the deep wound on his right thigh and, if any sign of infection appeared, to start him on sulfa drugs. When I unwrapped the bandage, I could see the long gash in the red-and-purple flesh that ran along the side of his leg, miraculously missing the artery.

I had to quell my emotional response to how close he'd come to death. It frightened me to realize how strong my feelings were. I'd seen all manner of injuries to other airmen, and yet I had remained detached enough to do my job. I wasn't ready for another emotional rollercoaster ride, worrying about someone near and dear to my heart.

After changing his bandage, I asked, "Would you like an aspirin for the pain?"

"No. But can you spare a few minutes to talk to me?"

"I'm sorry, not right now. I have to get to the other patients." I dashed off without meeting his gaze. As soon as I finished my rounds, I hunted for Aline and found her in the kitchen, preparing a medical supply list.

"Aline, you have to add Chris to your patient list. I'm not ready to handle what he asks of me."

"Do you realize that he's as vulnerable as you are? He'll be here for a few weeks and then on his way." She looked at me as though I were some kind of monster. "Don't you have it in your heart to help him heal?"

"That's just it. I don't want to talk to him about how it used to be when we were dating in high school. I'm a widow, still in the first year of grieving for my husband. Of course, you don't know what that's all about." I paused, fighting the urge to cry, before I spoke again. "If you insist he's my patient, I won't stay here."

"You're making a mistake, but you win. I'll have his cot moved to my section."

That evening, when I returned to the hospital, I avoided looking at him. I went straight to work with my patients and then scurried away like a guilt-ridden thief in the night.

My behavior continued for five more days, until I saw Aline rush to the medicine cabinet and get additional supplies. I wondered if she needed my assistance and saw that she ran to Chris' bed. I ran to his bedside, my heart pounding. "What's the mat . . ." My voice broke.

The answer lay before my eyes. His leg had red streaks running from his wound. "Start sulfa treatments right away," I shouted.

"That's what I'm doing. Would you like to take over for me?" Aline shot back.

I grabbed a glass of water and a tablet and handed them to him. As I applied a sulfa ointment to the wound, I told him, "You're going to be okay. I'm going to see to it."

Our eyes met.

"Now I know I am," he said.

I smiled. "And what do you mean by that?"

He shook his head. "I know better than to tell you."

"You'll tell me later?"

He shrugged. He knew me too well. When we were dating, I'd never been satisfied with just a shrug.

"Right now you better sleep on it." I shook my finger. "I'll be back to check up on you."

I was worried when I saw him at the evening meal. His

temperature was elevated and he didn't eat.

"Eat a little of your dinner," I coaxed. I scooped a spoonful of broth from the stew and held it close to his mouth. "Here, swallow this so you won't have to take your medicine on an empty stomach."

He started to push my hand away.

"For me, Chris."

He opened his mouth and swallowed, a faint smile gracing his lips.

"Thank you." I squeezed his hand and gave him a tablet to swallow while I held the glass for him. After I removed his bandage, the red lines radiating from the wound still looked ugly. While I changed the bandage, I offered a silent prayer that the sulfa would heal his leg. I didn't want to lose him.

I spent a restless night, afraid of what morning would bring. If the medication worked, he should show some improvement, but if not, what hope was there?

I arrived in the kitchen early the next morning, just as Aline began preparations for breakfast. "Let me help you. We can do our rounds a little early, and goodness knows, there are enough other things to be done around here."

"I can always use an extra pair of hands." Her intense gaze didn't go unnoticed. *Is her sixth sense at work*? I wondered.

I walked into the hospital and went straight to Chris. His eyes looked brighter than I had seen them since his arrival. I placed my hand on his forehead. The fever seemed to have broken. Hope filled me as I served his breakfast. "Will you eat this, or do I have to feed you?" I asked.

"I don't know. Why don't you get me started?"

"Just the first few bites. I have other patients waiting."

"Swell. That is, if you promise to stop and talk for a bit before you leave."

"Agreed."

When I'd finished with the other men, I returned to Chris to give him his medication, take his vitals, and dress his leg. "You're doing remarkably well. Your temperature is down to ninety-nine degrees. The sulfa is doing its job."

"You won't believe this. I dreamed about you last night," he said.

"You did? I hope it was a good one."

He nodded. "We were at the drive-in theater in my old Ford."

"Just like our high school days. I remember the long summer evenings and going to the soda shop afterward. Those were carefree days."

"And happy days." He started to say something more but held back.

"They were," I said. "I don't know whether it was because we were so full of life then or because we were both too young to realize how harsh life could be. I don't know where that girl is anymore."

"Paulette, you're still that girl. It's the world that's changed."

I sighed. "Oh, Chris, I wish I could believe it."

"It'll take time. But you will."

"I hope so." I smiled, something I hadn't done recently. "I remember our senior prom. We were the king and queen and danced the jitterbug until dawn. Then we went out and had a hamburger and soda. Momma was waiting when we got home and forbid us from dating for month. That could be when I decided I'd go to college as far away from her as I could—where she couldn't tell me what to do."

"Your dad always wanted the best for you. I remember when he took me to work with him at Douglas Aircraft Company. I told him I wanted to be a pilot one day, like he was in the Great War."

"Are you saying you were the pilot of the bomber you were in?"

"Yes, thanks to your dad. When I left France, I wanted to come back and fight the Nazis the best way I knew how."

"And now you face a new challenge, to recover enough to make the arduous trip to the Spanish border and get back to England."

"That's right. I want to get back and, with better luck next time, take on the enemy."

"Chris, why would you want to go through that again? You've served your country."

"It's a challenge for a good cause."

"You always did have a hero complex. But if that's what you want, I'm here to help."

"With you by my side, I can't lose."

"I didn't say by your side. That has connotations of a lifetime commitment. I'm still crying myself to sleep at night because I lost Guy. I can't think beyond that right now. I have to think of my stepson, Claude, and follow up on Guy's wishes for him. Please understand, I value your friendship and the memories of our dating years. That's all it can be."

"I'm sorry if the way I worded it upset you. You misinterpreted my intentions. I'm disappointed that you think I'm that much of a jerk to intrude on your period of mourning."

Over the next weeks I did everything I could to help Chris recover, but the damage was done. He didn't mention our past again and was guarded in what he said to me. I blamed myself for overreacting to his choice of words that day. He was alive, as was I. We both needed a connection with a close friend with whom to share our hopes and dreams, but whenever I tried to tell him that, he blocked me like he had the opposing team on the football field.

In spite of our setback, Chris continued to improve and began rebuilding the strength in his right leg for the tough journey over the Pyrenees to neutral Spain. As the time drew closer, I watched over him with concern. But if he noticed, he didn't let on. When one of the doctors from Paris accompanied a patient with serious injuries, he gave Chris the go ahead to seek freedom with three other airmen.

As we waited in the darkened house, I tried to tell Chris that I cared about him.

He stopped me with a finger to my lips. "Paulette, please don't say any more. Don't worry about me. Believe me, I'm going to make it."

"That's the spirit. I know you will."

He looked at me with an intensity that disconcerted me. "It's you I'm worried about."

"What do you mean?"

"When you spoke of Claude, you didn't seem to recognize that you can't replace his father, no matter how well intentioned. The more you alienate his grandparents, the more you'll drive Claude away. He is a de Laval. What do you think you're going to do, uproot him and take him to America if the going gets rough with his family?"

"No, we'll live in Paris . . . that's what Guy wanted."

"You've acknowledged that he's being prepared for a military career. God only knows where that will take him. He has a special heritage in an old French family. You don't connect him to that at all."

His words stirred up the self-doubts I'd already experienced. "I'll think about what you've said." I hugged him. "Thank you for caring. You'll be in my prayers."

He took a deep breath and kissed my check. "Thank you."

I'll never forget that dark rainy time, shortly after midnight, when the guides came to lead the men along treacherous mountain trails, two and a half months after Chris had made a brief entrance into my life again. Against the pitch-black sky devoid of moonlight, ideal conditions for the men to leave undetected, any collaborators at their windows or in their yards couldn't detect their silhouettes. I stood with them outside, and when they were ready to go, I hugged Chris. I had tears in my eyes and saw that his eyes were moist too.

He quipped, "You must care a little about what happens to me."

The weeks flew by after Chris left. No one told us whether or not he made it safely back to England, and I planned to ask the guide who'd escorted him.

The guide, who returned six weeks later to pick up another group of men, assured me that Chris had made it safely into Spain and that he had no way of knowing what happened afterward. We could only assume that Chris had made it to safety.

Aline and I worked late into the evenings, canning garden vegetables, before I left for Lamont to be with Claude during the summer and to make a home for him in Paris. He would attend a school about twenty miles out of the city, close enough that he could spend weekends at the Paris house.

We received reports that the Allies were going to attack Axis strongholds along the French Atlantic coast. Each evening we listened to the BBC, anxious to know when and where such attacks would take place. We knew the number of injured or killed airmen would be overwhelming and wanted to be as ready for them as possible.

The thought that Chris might already be back in the air disturbed me. "I know this sounds crazy, but I hope Chris isn't flying again." I wiped the perspiration from my brow on the tip of my apron.

Aline placed a jar in the boiling water. "No, it's not crazy. I know you try hard to suppress your feelings for him. But when I watched you and him interact, there was no doubt about the extent of your feelings. Don't think you're betraying Guy in any way. He wouldn't want you to spend the rest of your life sad and alone."

"I don't think he would either, but what bothers me is that I no longer cry myself to sleep because he's gone and I'm alone. Now I worry about Chris. He does mean a lot to me."

"How many years did you date Chris?"

"Three, while we were in high school."

"Did you think you would eventually marry him?"

"Yes. But that changed when he followed me to Paris. I needed time away to be sure of what I wanted—it wasn't about what Mom and Chris wanted."

"You were infatuated with Guy. He appealed to you because *you* chose *him*, not the other way around."

"Well, yes, he was different, aloof at first. He didn't want to tell me what to do."

"It was so obvious you were infatuated with him, while he was still disillusioned about women, and marriage in particular. I know you and he came to love one another and would have had a happy marriage. It's tragic that you lost him and your babies."

"I have to confess that I didn't have a chance to get to know him as well as I wished. He kept his thoughts to himself and remained a mystery. We were just getting to the point where we could be open with each other when he was killed. But he loved me, and God knows I loved him passionately."

Aline put her arms around me and whispered, "I know. I know."

We turned on the radio, as was our habit before we made patient rounds. The words we heard stopped us in our tracks: *The Allies have landed, wave after wave, on the beaches along the coast of Normandy. There have been many casualties.*

342

"June sixth. Exactly three months since Chris was shot down," I said and started to shake uncontrollably at the awful images that sped through my mind. He wasn't a cat with nine lives. *Please God, spare him.*

Numb with fear, I became aware of Aline's voice. "Are you okay?"

My body shook as if clothed in a summer dress during a blizzard.

Aline placed a light shawl over my shoulders. "I'll bring you a cup of broth."

"I don't know what's wrong with me," I said apologetically as I struggled to regain my composure.

Aline sat down beside me. "There's nothing wrong. Your concern about Chris is normal—a good thing. Maybe, in time, you'll feel free to embrace it. Perhaps, you and he will have a family. I think you have more of a future in the United States than you do with the de Laval family. I don't say that lightly."

"Do you know something I don't?"

Aline hesitated for a moment. "I get impressions about people and situations that are often quite accurate."

"I know. Guy mentioned it too. So tell me, what are your impressions?"

"Your motives are misguided when it comes to Claude. His grandparents are in a much better position than you to prepare him for life. If you persist, Claude will rebel and resent you."

"I won't leave France until I'm sure I've done everything I can for him. I owe it to Guy."

"I understand. Now's not the time. You'll know when it is. You've given a lot to France and had your share of grief as a result. You deserve to be happy. And I don't think you'll find it here."

"I can't make any decisions now. I'm still grieving over the loss of Guy and our boys."

"I understand." She patted my hand and repeated, "You'll know when."

"Strange thing is, Chris said the same thing."

"You see?"

"I'll think about it," I said, with every intention of doing so.

Chapter Thirty-Four

June - September 1944 – Lamont

On a bright mid-June morning, I drove from Lyon, having concluded my Resistance work there. Mile after mile, I debated whether I should return to work at the American Hospital in September after Claude's new school term began. Well aware one of my toughest conflicts awaited me at Lamont, I focused on life in Paris with Claude. We'd leave Lamont by the end of July and, perhaps, stop at the Chartres cottage. In any case, he would have a month with his grandparents during his summer vacation. Of course I'd steeled myself to face strong opposition from the de Lavals, but I knew success hinged on Claude. If he wanted to come with me, I'd face the major's wrath with a clear conscience that I'd followed Guy's plans for his son.

By the time I'd reached Lamont, it was almost night, but I hoped to have dinner with the family and have a little time with Claude before I went to bed in Guy's room. The thought gave me the strength to be prepared for whatever the future held. The morrow was uncertain, and I needed to have regenerated and reviewed my plans afresh.

As soon as I stepped out of the car, Guy's dog, Mystique, tail wagging, barked and nuzzled my hand in greeting. A lump formed in my throat as I recalled how overjoyed she had been to see Guy the first time I'd been there and each time thereafter. I leaned forward and patted her head. She lay down, her head on her paws. "Good girl," I said, misty eyed. "I miss him too."

"Bonjour, Madame." The gardener was leaning on his shovel. "She missed you, and that cedar tree in the garden looks like something is missing when you're not there."

"Thank you. How are things here?"

"Like usual."

"You keep the gardens beautiful. Many days I've wished I could relax in my favorite spot," I said as I removed my luggage from the back seat and went to the house.

Madame de Laval met me as I entered and embraced me. "I'm relieved that you're safe and sound. How's Aline?"

"She's well and keeping busy. The number of airmen increases each week. Since the Normandy invasion, the Germans have become even more brutal, if that's possible."

"Yes, we hear the reports of the atrocities they have committed in retribution."

"It's frightening, because they've been trained to fight to the death, although I saw much activity heading east. I don't know where they're going next."

"I don't like the thought of Aline there with little protection," Madame said as we entered the morning room.

"Bonjour, Monsieur de Laval." I smiled in an effort to disarm the major.

"Are you ready to acknowledge that I am the patriarch of the de Laval family, and as such, Claude is my responsibility?" It was plain he was going to be antagonistic from the start. "You understand ours is an ancient family that can be traced back to the time of Charlemagne."

"Where is Claude?" I asked, ignoring his challenging words. "I've come to assure him that I will take him to Paris as planned."

The major grumbled, "He's not here now. Boys will be boys."

I glanced at Madame. "Where is he?"

"Visiting with Pierre, the headmaster's son, for a few days."

I wasn't pleased with that development. "When will he be back?"

"Next week sometime. Because the boys worked hard in school this term, the headmaster promised them a fishing trip, among other things."

I was disappointed at my stepson's absence, but kept my remarks simple. "I'm glad Claude has made friends and is doing well at school. Guy would be pleased."

"Martine is with Yvette in the garden. How I love that little girl," Madame said, trying to take us away from the sensitive subject of Claude's future.

The major turned to his wife. "It's fortunate you have her, dear. Goodness knows, we'll have to wait for Claude and Martine to add to our family."

His comment hit its target. I felt as if my heart had been pierced when I thought of Guy's and my dead sons. Cruel fate!

Maybe, I was too sensitive, but I felt sure his remark was directed at me.

I pondered his meaning about Claude and Martine. Was an arranged marriage on his mind? An unhappy marriage such as Guy's dutiful one to Claude's mother, all to please his father? I'd have to ask Aline about my suspicions.

Madame said, "After that long drive, I suppose you'd rather rest than visit. Or if you feel up to it, you're welcome to join me while I work on Christmas blankets."

"What a delightful luxury. At Aline's there's no time to rest during the day. Or half the night, for that matter. I'm going to indulge myself and lie down for a while." Not only physically tired, I was emotionally drained. I just wanted to surround myself with pleasant memories of Guy. My thoughts turned to Mystique and how she must miss him, and I went outside to take her with me to his room.

Mystique and I climbed the stairs and returned to the honeymoon room. I'd been incredibly happy then. Guy's familiar woodland scent still lingered there. His boots and cap sat near a chair. A glimpse of the reflection of my thin body and flat belly propelled me back to the last time I'd been here. At that time I still had the full breasts of a nursing mother and a less-than-flat profile.

Mystique settled near Guy's boots and closed her eyes, and I pulled back the covers and got into the bed. I dozed, my mind filled with images of Guy's arms around me as he whispered passionate words in my ear. My mind burned with memories as I curled up and cried myself to sleep.

The first thing I heard when I awoke was the repetitive tick-tock, tick-tock of Guy's alarm clock. I had napped longer than I intended and had little time to dress for dinner, but I managed to make an appearance on time. I don't know how I made it through the meal and small talk. Afterward, we made our way to the morning room and listened to the BBC. The death toll and a tally of infrastructure losses continued to increase daily in staggering numbers as the Allies overtook, one by one, the German strongholds in Normandy.

✝

The week dragged on while I waited for Claude's return and the opportune time to confront Monsieur de Laval—before Claude's arrival.

Friday morning, after breakfast and time with Mystique, I stopped by the morning room and engaged in small talk with the major. But while we were expressing caution about the success of the Allied attack, Claude rushed into the room. "Grandpa, Pierre is going to the same school in Paris that Paulette arranged for me."

"Do you know what he's talking about?" Monsieur gave me a scathing look. "What do you have to say for yourself?"

I took a deep breath and pictured Guy beside me. "It's true I have enrolled him in the school in Paris that Guy selected. I informed you of my intentions."

The major ignored me and addressed Claude. "I make the decisions about your education while you're a minor. With the dangers in Paris heightened now since the Allied invasion of Normandy, the city is no place for you. I don't suppose you've heard the news, young man. I won't hear of you leaving Lamont."

Claude scowled and turned to me. "You promised to take me to Paris like Papa wanted."

"I know, and I'm going to do it. I'm sure Pierre's father wouldn't allow him to go if he felt it wasn't safe."

The major stood, his face flushed with outrage. "I forbid it!"

Madame went to her husband's side. "Calm down. This isn't good for your heart." She gave me a piercing look. "Guy would not want you to create friction in our family," she said to me. "Claude, while you're in this house, you will obey your grandfather. Go to your room now."

The major stared at me. "You've been disloyal to this family. Isn't it enough that you share responsibility for Guy's death? If he hadn't worn himself out and risked traveling back and forth here and to Lyon to see you, he'd be alive today."

Seldom reprimanded, the indulged boy did as he was told. I excused myself and went outside. I walked aimlessly, ending up at the cedar tree, where I sat down to take in what had just transpired. Mystique ran up and licked my face before she lay beside me. I rubbed her back. "You're the only one here who understands."

My mind was too jumbled to come up with any solutions. I began to walk with Mystique along the garden paths while I decided how to handle the impasse with the de Lavals. I decided I'd compromise by spending August in Paris with Claude. If things improved, he could start classes at the Paris school, as long as the Tours headmaster held a place open for him if conditions changed. I felt sure Claude would agree, since his friend Pierre faced a similar dilemma. Much relieved, I started toward the house and met Claude running in my direction.

He stopped when I called his name. "I hate him. I'm going to run away."

"You don't need to do that. I have a plan. I need to talk to Pierre's father and then to your grandfather."

"It won't do any good. Grand-Papa won't change his mind," Claude said and ran into the woods.

When he didn't come to dinner, Madame went to his room. A short time later, she returned. "Claude is on a hunger strike and refuses to open his door."

After four days of this stalemate, I telephoned the headmaster and told him what had happened. He liked my plan and agreed to talk with the major. The next morning the headmaster came to Lamont and met Monsieur de Laval. I waited in the courtyard until his return to the car, as we had agreed.

"How'd it go?" I asked.

"Major de Laval had reservations, but I convinced him that I'd monitor the conditions in Paris and would not allow the boys to attend school there if I felt the conditions were unsafe. He asked that I give my word to watch out for Claude as if he were my own son and wanted my assurance that I'd reserved space in the Tours school for the two boys, should they need to return."

"Does that mean he agreed?"

"Oui. I assured him I would drive the boys to Paris, stay several days to take them for a visit to the boarding school, and escort them around the city for an educational sightseeing adventure."

"That's wonderful."

Events happened quickly when Aline arrived at Lamont the next day during lunch.

Madame rose, arms positioned for a hug. "Ma cherie, what a pleasant surprise. You're just in time for lunch. Your little sweetheart is asleep."

"Merci." Aline sat across from me.

One glance and I knew something was dreadfully wrong. Her shoulders sagged and, since I'd last seen her, the area under her eyes had darkened. I waited for her to speak.

Madame rang for Yvette. "Set a place for Madame de Maille."

Yvette scurried away and returned with another place setting. She poured a glass of wine and set a bowl of the chicken stew in front of Aline.

Aline lifted her spoon but held it poised above the stew. "I plan to stay with you for a few days before going on to Paris, if that's all right."

My first thought was, what about the airmen? "You found reliable help to care for your guests at Maille?" I asked.

She lowered her eyes and shook her head. "The chateau has been compromised. It's no longer safe. I don't know how or who. As far as I know, none of the airmen who left have been arrested. But someone pretty well acquainted with our operation betrayed us."

"Does anyone come to mind? One of the guides, maybe? Or what about the new volunteers?" I asked.

"I have no suspects in mind, and I haven't heard of any arrests in our group. But as you are well aware, anyone may break under torture and tell what they know." Her brow crinkled. "Ida had been helping in one of the other safe houses in the area. When it was compromised, she came to me and asked whether I needed help. She said that the need for help at Maille was expected to increase greatly. And now this . . ."

She paused and her hand shook. "Oh, you may not know, after Dr. Jackson was arrested at the hospital, his wife and son were arrested by the *milice,* Pétain's secret police. The police loaded them into the back of their Citroen and headed south. No one seems to know where they're being held."

I felt as if the breath had been knocked out me. I gasped. "Nooo."

"I don't have any reason to think there's a direct connection to my problems," Aline said, eyes downcast.

"The Jackson family lived right across the street from the Gestapo's house of horrors, where they took high profile prisoners and stopped at nothing to break them."

"It seems nowhere in France is safe these days." The major locked eyes with me. "That's why I want to keep Claude close to his family here at Lamont."

I ignored him and looked across the table at Aline. "You're welcome to stay with me while you're in Paris."

"That's most kind of you, but I have my apartment."

"You do? How can you afford it?"

My husband agreed to pay the rent, so that he and his mistress wouldn't receive unwelcome interruptions when I came to the city."

"That's good news."

"Yes, and I'll be able to have Martine with me there some of the time. Of course, I know Lucia likes to have her here too. When things settle down, I'd like to spend more time at Lamont."

"Well, I should hope so," Madame said. "You're an important part of our family."

Paris

On the first of August, the headmaster slipped into the driver's seat of my blue Renault and drove Claude, Pierre, and me to the house on Rue Notre Dame des Champs.

Darkness had fallen by the time we pulled into the front courtyard and were out of the car. Claude and Pierre caught sight of the gardener and ran toward him.

"Monsieur Hugh, this is my friend Pierre," Claude called.

The headmaster shouted, "Boys, leave the man to his work and come inside with us."

I had been much relieved when Pierre's father had offered to accompany his son to Paris and stay a few days with us before taking a train home. It was a real sacrifice, considering the unreliable train schedules.

Nina met us at the door, a broad grin on her face. "And here's Monsieur Claude, but who is his friend?"

I noticed she looked at him with interest and wondered whether she thought he was one of the Jewish children at risk of arrest.

I introduced her to the headmaster and his son as the boys clamored up the stairs. She appeared relieved that Pierre presented no danger. It took some of the pressure off me to see the boys together. They couldn't have been closer if they were brothers— something that Claude was not destined to have.

"Hugh and I've been rattling around in this huge house while you were away," Nina told me. "It's a good thing you've returned. We got pretty tired of looking at each other."

I shook my head. "I doubt that, with all the work there is around this big place. Everything looks well taken care of."

"Thank you, Madame. I'll see what I can find for dinner."

"Before you go, please show our guests to their rooms. Monsieur will be with us until Saturday."

"Come this way, Monsieur," she said.

The next day while the headmaster and boys gallivanted around Paris, I called Aline and invited her to lunch and asked Nina to prepare a nice lunch for us in the back garden under the shade of a large chestnut tree.

"I need your thoughts about something," I said to Aline when we were seated at the table.

"Since when do you need my opinion?"

"I'm serious. Claude needs me."

"What does that mean?"

"I'm trying to tell you that since I heard about the arrest of Dr. Jackson and his family, I've questioned whether I know what is best for Claude. It's quite a different thing for Guy and me to decide Claude's future together. For a time I thought I would be able to fulfill Guy's wishes, but with the headmaster here, I can see that Claude needs a man in his life—one who can set a good example for him of how to be a strong, responsible man."

She nodded. "You may be right. His grandfather is obviously the next man in line to guide him."

"Yes, I know that. But I sometimes question his plans for Claude, and . . ." I paused to think how best to continue. "I want to be a part of Claude's life, but I'm wondering whether I have anything to offer him."

Aline brushed a fallen leaf from her dress "I don't know, but I do know you and I have sacrificed time with the children so that their future is brighter. I often wonder whether Martine would miss me if something happened to me. No matter what you decide to do, I think Claude will be well cared for."

"Recently, I've felt as though my work is done here and that I should go back home to California."

"I'm not surprised. You've lost your reason for making France your home. Of course I'd miss you, but I know your memories of your time here are painful."

"It's true that my purpose for being here is gone. And I know Claude would be better off not drawn into disagreements between the major and me. I don't want him to be conflicted because of it."

"Do you recall when we were students at the Sorbonne, and I told you that I didn't foresee a future for you with Guy? You didn't want to hear it, and I have to admit I was surprised that he married you. Nevertheless, the feeling persisted that somehow it wasn't real. I tried as hard as I could to suppress the impressions I received, especially when you were pregnant. I prayed that I was wrong and that you and he would find the happiness you so richly deserved. I wanted the best for you and still do."

"But you don't understand. I wouldn't have had it any other way. The happiest hours of my life were those I spent with Guy." I brushed a tear from my cheek. "I admit he's still a mystery to me. There's so much I didn't get to know about him. He didn't often share his thoughts. If we could have grown old together . . . maybe."

"He loved you. That's something I don't have. I envy your sweet memories."

"What about Roberto?"

She shrugged. "I doubt he knows how to love just one woman. He wants women in a superficial way."

"No, I think you're special to him."

"I'd like to think so." Her mouth curved into a smile." I can dream, can't I?"

"We both can." I emptied the bottle of wine into our glasses. "Why don't you stay here while the headmaster entertains the boys? It's only for two more days, and with Pierre's father here to keep Claude entertained, I'll have time to make all the necessary arrangements to go home. I'll need your help."

"I don't see any reason why I can't stay," Aline said. "I'll go home to pick up a change of clothes and my night things before dinner."

After the boys and the headmaster returned, the headmaster read while Claude and Pierre played checkers, and I worked on a list of things to be done before I left Paris.

Aline returned wearing a stylish linen suit and carrying a small overnight bag. She and I retired to Guy's office to make plans for the next day while the boys again explored Paris with the headmaster.

When I closed the door to the office, Aline drew up a chair and looked over the list I had made. "You really intend to go through with it, don't you?"

"Yes, my mind is made up. The more I think about it, the more convinced I am that it's the right thing to do."

"By the look of this list, you've thought of almost everything . . . except how you're going to get out of the country."

"I hoped you'd know how to arrange it."

She sighed. "As you know, it's dangerous, but I'll make some inquires and do what I can."

"Aline, I can't believe you'd let danger interfere. You never have before."

"You make a good point. As I've already said, I'll do my best."

"Thank you. That's all I ask . . . just find a way. Tomorrow, I would like for you to come with me to see Guy's attorney and go to the bank."

"I'm here to help."

"You probably know that this house is in Guy's name and will be passed to Claude when he comes of age. But Guy bought the lovely little cottage outside of Chartres where we stayed so often. He transferred the title to my name when his work placed him in greater danger. He also bought oil stocks in my name while I was pregnant last year. I know he wanted to be sure the baby and I were financially secure." I sighed. "Things didn't turn out quite the way we expected. Now, I want to set up a trust for Claude and for you to serve as trustee."

"What about your expenses?"

"Guy thought of everything. He set up a generous bank account for me. I'll be fine."

"You must know that Claude doesn't need the oil stocks. I'm sure he already has some set aside for him. He stands to inherit everything from his grandparents. Guy intended for you to have money. You say that you respected his intentions for Claude, and yet you want to undo his wishes for you."

"He didn't make the changes until I was pregnant."

"Not because you were going to have a baby. It was because he knew the odds were against his survival. I'll only agree to be trustee of the cottage for Claude. I'll manage the property and sell it after the war."

"Aline, I'll keep the stocks on one condition. That you compromise and accept at least half of them."

"No, that wouldn't be right."

"Of course it's right. I know you don't have a lot of money. For example, can you tell me how much money your husband has?"

"I don't know."

"How will you pay for the upkeep of Chateau Maille?"

"I don't dwell on it. It's not the most important thing in my life."

"What if the marquis stops paying for your apartment?"

"That might happen. It's not that I don't care, but what can I do about it? He's not in the best of health and probably won't live much longer. Then I'll see what happens—whether he's provided for Martine and me, what debt is owned on the chateau. I plan to stay in Paris and work at the hospital as long as I can and also spend time with Martine and Lucia. I'm sure I'll always have a home at Lamont as long as I need one."

"I don't want you to live that way. We have to share the stocks. I know Guy would approve. Say you will so that I can get ready for dinner."

"All right, anything to shut you up about my dismal situation."

"I still want you to keep the cottage for Claude. It's the only place where Guy and I had a chance to really be relaxed and happy. Maybe one day Claude will find the same joy there as his father did." I started to cry, "Oh, God, you don't know how I loved to see Guy happy."

Aline put her arms around me. "He was the happiest around you that I've ever seen him. Rest assured, you brought sunshine into his rather bleak life."

With a sniffle, I said, "Thank you for being a good friend." I blotted my eyes with my handkerchief. "There's one more thing. My engagement ring is in the safe. I want you to return it to Madame de Laval. It was her grandmother's ring." I twisted my wedding band. "This one is from Guy to me." I took it off and handed it to her. "See, it's declares his love for me."

Aline held the gold band in her hand, peered at it, and read the inscription out loud. *Mon trésor, my love for you grows stronger each day.* She stared at me. "I had no clue that Guy was a romantic. No wonder he wanted to marry you."

I glanced at the clock. "It's almost dinnertime. I'll have to hurry to be ready. Meet you back in the salon." I tucked my list into my pocket and rushed out of the office door before my emotions overwhelmed me.

I wanted our dinner to be a memorable occasion for Claude and for me to reminisce about later back in the States. I selected the black dress I'd worn to dinner with Guy at the d'Argent restaurant. My hair upswept into a French roll, red lipstick, and a touch of rouge completed my look for the evening, as it had with Guy that night so long ago. The red lipstick brought out the blue of my eyes and the blue scarf I wore. It worked. I felt better about life in general and looked forward to dinner with my French family.

The headmaster rose when I entered the salon. "I'm sorry, I didn't bring appropriate dinner attire."

"You're fine just the way you are. It is I who needs to apologize for my last-minute urge to dress as if we were going out to dinner."

I called to Claude and Pierre, "Boys, dinner's ready in the dining room."

"How come the dining room? We never eat in there," Claude asked.

"Because it's time we did. It's a beautiful room."

Nina served a simple stew and salad and outdid herself with a delicious apple cobbler with cheese and the use of our fine china. I think she suspected I wouldn't stay in France after the loss of my husband.

Claude said, "I took Pierre and Monsieur to the observatory and guided them. We went to Luxembourg Gardens and sailed boats on the water and then had a *bateau-mouche* ride on the Seine. There were a lot of cargo boats on the water."

Pierre piped up. "We went to l'Arc de Triomphe and Avenue des Champs-Élysées.

"We ended up at the Eiffel Tower and had lunch," Claude added.

"Boys, where are we going tomorrow?" the headmaster prompted.

"Notre Dame Cathedral, Louvre, and military museums."

"Shakespeare bookstore, and our new school in Paris."

After dinner, when the boys were asleep, we went to the basement and listened to the BBC on a small radio. It was disguised as a large planter, a precaution in case the Gestapo interrupted us and decided to search the house. In those days they were desperate to control what the French citizens heard, but everyone knew the Allies were drawing closer to Paris. Talk of the liberation of Paris abounded.

The commentator spoke with optimism evident in his voice.

I have it from a reliable source that within a week or two, the Allies will reach Paris. There's no telling how long the fighting will last. General de Gaulle appears to be confident in victory and has plans for when he arrives in the city. I wish I had a crystal ball to prepare you for the coming weeks, but I do not. What I do advise is to plan accordingly.

"I'll be right here when Paris is liberated," Aline said, a look of excitement in her eyes. "I wouldn't miss that for anything."

I had mixed feelings but knew Claude and Pierre shouldn't stay in the city.

The headmaster cleared his throat and said, "If you will excuse me, I'll leave you now."

"Of course. Good night," I said and turned to Aline. "Let's get some sleep. We have a busy day planned for tomorrow."

As I climbed the stairs to the bedroom Guy and I had shared, I felt compelled to justify why I planned to leave our home. I closed the bedroom door and tried to put into words the emotions I felt. "Guy, if somehow you know what I'm going to do, I want to tell you why I'm going to leave Paris and the life we thought we had. It is because I loved you without reservation, and now that you're gone, the pain is unbearable. I would have stayed for Claude, if he needed me. I know now he will be better off at Lamont, the only home he's known. I believe, if you could hear me, you'd understand why I've decided to return to America."

I folded back the bedspread, climbed into bed, and slipped into a dreamless sleep.

☨

Nina seemed to like an excuse to use the dining room. As people appeared in the kitchen for their morning meal, she said, "Breakfast will be served in the dining room at eighty-thirty."

It worked because we all had plans for the morning. Many a day it would not have worked. She served scrambled eggs, ham, jam, butter, and a fresh baguette.

"Where did you get butter?" I asked.

"I went next door and bartered eggs."

"And the ham? I'm surprised the Germans haven't confiscated it. They would take the food from our mouths if we let them."

"When the war started, I had Hugh dig a storage pit in the garden. The entry is hidden and I only go out at night to get something. So far, we've managed to keep the Germans from finding it."

"You're priceless," I said.

When our plates were clean, the headmaster said, "Madame de Laval, I want to speak with you and the boys in the salon. Madame de Maille may be interested in what I have to say as well."

Claude and Pierre moaned in unison but dutifully followed us and sat down.

"The news from the front lines suggests that the war will be at our doorstep by mid-month," the headmaster said. "It's good news that the Allies are gaining ground and expect to liberate Paris in a few weeks. But if there should be fighting here, I have no choice other than to take the boys home and prepare them for school with me in Tours. I know you are disappointed, but Claude's safety is my responsibility." He turned to the boys and continued, "Claude, I promised your grandparents that I would take care of you. They've put their trust in me."

Pierre pulled a face.

"What about our plans for today?" Claude asked.

"We'll make it a short day, but we won't need to visit the

new school. We'll use that time to be ready to leave on the train tomorrow morning."

I had already come to terms with what must be done for Claude, so I was relieved that the headmaster laid it out for the boys. "Take the car. The train is unreliable." I knew I wouldn't be using the car anytime soon, so it didn't matter if they used up our entire gas ration.

He hesitated before he asked, "Are you certain?"

"I couldn't be more so." I glanced at Aline, silently asking for her opinion.

"In Paris the Metro still runs." She nodded at the headmaster. "We'll be fine."

"All right, boys, you know the plan. Let's get started," he said.

The next morning after Claude and Pierre left the house with the headmaster for their last visit around Paris, Aline and I lingered over a second cup of coffee.

"As I see it, we'll have time to stop by the bank and have lunch before our appointment with the attorney," I said.

"Good. That'll give me time this afternoon to begin work on a plan to get you out of the country."

"Thank you. After dinner this evening, I'll explain to Claude that I'm going home to California. I have to be sure he understands that I wouldn't do so if he needed me." I sighed as I realized I didn't know when—or if—I'd ever see him again.

Aline shook her head. As if reading my mind, she said, "It makes me sad that things didn't work out as we all expected."

"I know. I'm trying to make the best of it. I'll write a short letter to the de Lavals and explain that I am relinquishing Claude's care to them. Later, I'll write a more detailed letter. Will you deliver it in person, along with my engagement ring?"

"I will."

By three o'clock, half of my oil stocks had been transferred to Aline, and the trust had been set up for Claude. All that remained was for Aline and me to sign the documents before the attorney submitted them to the Office of Records. All in all, it was a good day's work, but I still needed to explain to Claude that I planned to return to America. And it needed to be done in such a way that he didn't feel abandoned or rejected. I would do it this evening, as there wouldn't be time in the morning before they left for the Loire Valley.

When I got home Claude met me at the door. "I'm sorry you'll be alone in Paris, but I have to go back to Grand-Papa's and to school in Tours until the war is over."

He sounded so serious and mature that I did not tell him I already knew his plans. "That's a wise choice, and maybe, the only one you have, because the school in Paris will probably be in the path of the fighting when the Allied troops come to liberate the city."

"I know. The headmaster told Pierre and me."

"I'm glad he did. I need to explain my plans to you, as well."

"What plans? Are you going to the country with Aline?"

"No, I'm going home to America, where my family lives and where I went to school when I was your age."

"You've been away a long time, haven't you?"

I nodded and struggled with my emotions. "When I married your father, we wanted to make a family for you, but . . . our plans didn't work out. Claude, I love you and always looked forward to our time together, but it's best if I let you go."

"Like the mother bird lets the baby bird fly away?"

"Yes, sort of. Of course, you'll always have Lamont with your grandparents, and Aline, too. They all love you very much, as do I. Please know I wouldn't leave if you needed me here."

He put his arms around me. "I know. I'm growing up now and will be leaving home anyway."

"You know you can return to Lamont when you're not in school or even afterward, when you're a military officer like your father and grandfather. You know your father loved you with all his heart. You were never out of his thoughts."

"Papa was friends with Pierre's papa, and Pierre is my best friend. He's like a brother to me."

"I know you'll make the de Laval family proud."

I didn't see much of Aline the first weeks after Claude left for Tours with the headmaster and his son. I used the time to reassure Nina and her husband that I wanted them to stay on and care for the property for the de Lavals, as they had in the past. Aline had promised to spend some of her time in the residence and keep Monsieur and Madame de Laval informed of any matters that needed their attention.

Every day the radio reported on the fierce fighting as the Allies made their way across Normandy toward Paris. Each day that passed without an escape plan from Aline, I feared I might get caught up in the fighting and be unable to leave the city.

One afternoon I could contain myself no longer. I relinquished my self-imposed seclusion and went to the Tuileries Gardens to escape the walls of the house that seemed to close in around me. I listened as an excited group of men talked among themselves about General de Gaulle's army and their belief that he would be the one to liberate the city. Their excitement was contagious. Somewhere along the way I'd lost hope but now found a burgeoning sense of it lifting me up. Could it be true after all these years? Would Paris again belong to the French? I took a deep breath and walked home by way of the Sorbonne, where I'd first seen Guy and had been filled with fanciful dreams of a happy evermore.

Only time would tell whether I would find happiness in America. But I felt ready to begin the rest of my life. A trace of my optimism of old had returned. I made a silent vow to get back to the United States, regardless of any delays that might arise.

When I arrived back at the house, Nina opened the door as I fumbled with my keys. "You had me worried, you were gone so long."

"I'm sorry. The time got away from me. The fresh air and jubilant crowds inspired hope for the future."

Apparently hearing our voices, Aline came from the direction of the kitchen. "I've prepared a surprise dessert for dinner."

I laughed. "I hope it's not one of your oatmeal specialties."

She kept a straight face. "Oatmeal cookies."

Nina tilted her head and nodded. "You and Aline sit and rest while I set the table so we can have dinner."

Aline sat down beside me. "Your escape plan is complete. You and I will take the train to Tours on September first and drive to Brother Roger's enclave, where you will be picked up in one of the

Free French's Westland Lysanders. I'm sure you know it's a small plane and the quarters cramped. The good news is that the flight to Britain will only take about two hours."

"To Brother Roger's?" I wondered if I'd heard correctly. "We leave Paris in about two weeks?"

"That's right. You'll wait at the enclave until September eighth, when you'll be picked up by the Lysander. In London you'll be met and given instructions for continuing on to America at a later date."

"I had no idea that the monastery had a field suitable for landing an aircraft."

"It's just a grassy field, but the Westland Lysander was designed for such challenges," Aline assured me. "You'll need to make sure you're ready the minute the plane lands. It can't afford to be on the ground any longer than necessary. You never know who might be watching and betray us to the Germans."

Aline's words implied that the plane would likely be delivering some sort of supplies to the Resistance and that the mission was a risky one. But I was ecstatic at the idea of leaving France, and I uttered a silent prayer for success."

"Have you noticed that people are returning to Paris?" Aline asked me. "It's all the talk about the liberation of the city any day now. The Germans are being attacked from the east by the Soviets and from the west by the Allies. They're in need of fresh troops. So the Resistance plans to approach German General von Choltitz at the Maurice Hotel about an agreement for peace in the city. You know there are citywide strikes by the railroad workers and others."

On August 25 Aline and I were among the throngs of Parisians as the Second French Armored Division marched past us along the Champs Élysées in the western part of the city. We learned later that Paris had been declared an open city, meaning the Germans agreed not to fight for possession. General von Choltitz had signed a formal act of capitulation to representatives of the provisional government of France in the presence of General Philippe Leclerc and the commander of the French Resistance. Teams of French and German officers circulated copies of the document to the scattered groups of

Germans still in the city.

The 6 foot, 5 inch General de Gaulle made an impressive figure as he addressed the French nation from the Hôtel de Ville:

I wish simply from the bottom of my heart to say to you: Vive Paris! We are here in Paris – Paris which stood erect and rose in order to free herself. Paris oppressed, downtrodden and martyred but still Paris – free now, freed by the hands of Frenchmen, the capital of Fighting France, France the great eternal.

Later that day, we joined the crowds gathered to watch and cheer as French and Allied troops triumphantly marched together as the French Generals de Gaulle and Leclerc paraded from the Etoile along the Champs Élysées to the Place de la Concorde. Occasional gunshots—which we assumed were celebratory rather than confrontational—rang out from rooftops. General de Gaulle went to the Cathedral of Notre Dame, where a mass of celebration and thanks took place before an overflow crush of people.

Nina and I had finished gathering vegetables for lunch when I picked up the basket and said, "I see you're busy with those weeds. I'll take these inside and get them washed."

She looked up at me, her straw hat shading her eyes. "I won't be long."

I had just come into the kitchen and set down the basket when I heard an urgent rap at the door. I had a mind not to answer it, but I smoothed down my hair and opened the door. I couldn't believe my eyes.

"Madame de Laval, I won't take much of your time. May I come in?" Colonel Dietrich asked.

"Come in. I'm surprised to see you."

"I'm sure you are, and I wouldn't be here if it weren't important. I'll get right to the point. I've been well aware of your involvement with the French Resistance for quite some time."

I nodded. "You always seemed to show up when I was in trouble."

"Although most of our troops have left the city, there are some renegades who remain and intend to fight on in their own way. You believe that your former classmate and friend, Ida, has your best interests at heart. You are mistaken. She is a double agent for the Reich."

"No, not Ida. How could she?" I said, hoping he would explain how it happened.

"Her loyalty lies elsewhere. She's married to a German officer. She reported the suspicious activities of your friend, Madame de Maille, and many others as well."

"Why didn't you tell me before?"

"Because I was a German."

"You still are. Why warn me now?"

"There's no longer a German cause to fight for. All that remains is madness." He lowered his eyes. "I must leave now. Beware of Ida. Recall the Picasso painting."

Ida had been responsible for the theft of the Picasso! Mystery explained. But, of course, she worked with one of her German friends who collected fine art and had coveted it while at Guy's dinner parties for the German officers. She had stopped by while we packed to leave Paris that day in June 1940.

"Colonel Dietrich, thank you. I'll remember your kindness when others can only think of the dreadful things that happened during this occupation."

He turned and left without looking at me. I noticed that his shoulders slumped, his hair was more gray than blond. I couldn't imagine the internal struggle he must have faced each day.

Orléans

A little past midnight on September eighth I waited with Brother Roger and one other man under the dark sky, ever sensitive to any sound as I strained to hear the hum of an aircraft overhead. I noticed the patterns formed by the few clouds that slipped past the black dome over our heads. They covered or distorted the familiar constellations that Guy, Claude, and I had watched on similar nights, the silence palpable as I sought sensate diversion. I squinted my eyes and was amazed when starlight broke behind one of the clouds to form an infinity symbol. Was it a lesson about life—that life goes on whether here on Earth or in another form in another dimension? I longed for it to be so.

My musings ceased when I heard the Lysander's engine as it drew near, the full moon its only guiding light. I felt alone in the universe. The moment of truth had arrived—a matter of life and death.

Chapter Thirty-Five

October 1998 – Claremont, California

D'un costé Dieu poingt, de l'autre il vingt
(God who gives the wound gives the salve ~ Old French Proverb)

"Mom, I'm here to help you get ready for dinner," Anne-Marie says as she comes into my bedroom.

"I'm dressed, but I need your help with my hair. My chignon never looks right when I do it myself." I smile at my only child, who is now a widowed, middle-aged woman.

This is not a sad occasion, but one of celebration of the upcoming marriage of my granddaughter, Claire Bennett, to Marc-Claude de Laval, although it does bring back memories of the joy and pain, I experienced during World War II while in occupied France.

Anne-Marie takes my hand as I get up from my chair by the window and pause to look at our lemon groves, the ones that had replaced most of the orange groves when Chris and I came to live with Mama and care for her after his discharge from the Air Force in 1945.

"Your hair is a pretty shade of gray and looks elegant for this evening." Anne-Marie fluffs my bangs and gazes at our reflection in my dressing-table mirror.

"Thank you, dear." My eyes meet hers. I notice an unconscious gesture of my hand over the small gold heart I wear around my neck at all times. I remove my hand and hope she hasn't noticed.

"Must be all this talk of Claire and Marc-Claude's wedding. Take your time, Mom, and hold the heart as long as you want. Dad and I understand when you're reminded of so many memories of Guy."

Tears of appreciation threaten to undo my composure. I nod. "Please know that your father is the best thing that ever happened to me. I love you both dearly and wouldn't change a thing."

"We know. You've proved it over and over."

By way of explanation, I say, "After Guy was killed by the

Nazis, I wore my wedding ring until your father and I married in December nineteen forty-four."

"I know, Mom."

Shortly after our wedding, Chris suggested I have a memento made from the ring because he knew I still grieved for Guy. I think that gesture on his part cemented our marriage over the years. His love for me had matured since our high school-sweetheart days, and I truly meant the words when I vowed to love him for better or worse, in sickness and in health. Over the years he has filled my life with joy and meaning. The strength of our union allows me to look forward not backward.

I hold my head high and allow Chris to seat me at the table beside him. Anne-Marie sits beside her son, John Bennett. Our good friend, Colonel Tillson, and his wife, Mavis, are across from them. "Did you know that Mav and I were attendants at your grandparents' wedding?" the colonel asks John.

John frowns. "No. I didn't."

"I knew. Mom and Dad told me when I was a child," Anne-Marie says. "They'd show me pictures of their wedding party and explain that Mom had cared for you at Aline de Maille's safe-house infirmary during the German occupation. Aline was part of the French Resistance that helped you escape from France back to England."

Chris nods. "Those were the days when we didn't know whether we'd live to see the sun come up again. Your mother cared for me there, too, and gave me a reason to get well. Those years influenced her to become a nurse instead of a school teacher. I couldn't believe my good fortune when she agreed to marry me while we were still in England."

Mavis smiles as if she has a secret. "I can scarcely believe you'll celebrate fifty-four years of marriage this Christmas."

"Speaking of Aline de Maille, you may not know that Marc-Claude's mother is Aline's daughter, Martine," Anne-Marie holds my gaze.

"I did not. But it shouldn't surprise me. Claude and Martine spent much of their childhood with Major and Madame de Laval at

Lamont."

"Tell us about Claude, Mom," Anne-Marie urges. "You didn't talk about him when I was growing up."

"At the time there was no point. I felt they were ghosts from the past, better left in peace. But now things have changed. You'll be there with the family that I knew so well. I loved Guy's son, of course, but after his father was gone, Claude's grandparents were best suited to prepare him for his role as a French aristocrat."

"He's done very well. He's a general in the French Army," John says.

"Indeed, he has," I reply as chills course through me. Guy gave his life for future generations. I pray that Claude will not be called upon to do the same.

Chris notices my shivers and rises to close the patio door. "This time of year, you never know what the weather will bring."

"I found it puzzling that Marc-Claude didn't follow in his father's footsteps as a military man," John muses.

"Why don't you ask him yourself while you're there for the wedding?" Chris says.

John ignores him. "During my research, I saw that Guy de Laval posthumously received the French Legion of Honor for his service during World War Two."

I hadn't known that and worry that my emotions might overflow.

Anne-Marie speaks as she looks at me. "I hope Claire and Marc-Claude will be here to celebrate with us on your anniversary next month. Then we can all ask any questions we have. Mom, I'm sure there's so much to interest you, since you've been away from France so long."

"Just think, they'll be married two weeks from today in the beautiful St-Gatien Cathedral in the Loire Valley, not far from Chateau Lamont," I say, a wistful note evident in my voice.

Chris reaches for my hand, "Paulette, I'm sorry our health prevents us from making the trip."

"No, my dear Chris, don't be sorry. Remember when you piloted that little Westland Lysander to that remote, wooded field near Orleans, France, so many years ago to rescue me? You requested that assignment even though it was considered quite dangerous.

"That's when I gave my heart and dedicated my life to you. I'm the luckiest woman in the world to have had the love of two heroic, wonderful men in one lifetime. I reflect on how things have come full circle and wish our young couple as much joy as you and I have known."

Chris reaches for my hand and kisses it.

"Dad, your love for Mom always set the standard for the kind of man I wanted to marry," Anne-Marie says. "I was pretty lucky. You know, my John gave you a run for your money as the very best."

I smile and say, "My mother used to tell me that happy is the marriage when the husband loves the wife more than she loves him. In my case, it's not possible."

"Nurse Andrea wasn't the only one to be rescued in a Lysander operation," Colonel Tillson says with a smile.

I lock eyes with him. Of course, Colonel Tillson couldn't have made his escape on that leg that hadn't healed properly. Why hadn't I put two and two together before now? I'd accepted Aline's news of him without question. I suddenly realized that the U.S. must have arranged to fly him out. After all, he had been an agent of the OSS. It would have been disastrous for a great many people had the Germans captured him.

"So Madame de Maille arranged a joy ride on a Lysander," I say to him. It is more of a statement than a question.

"More than that, she accompanied me to the airport—a clearing in the forest near the chateau."

John frowns. "Are you speaking of Madame Aline de Maille, by chance?"

I wink at him.

"Enough of this Lysander reminiscence." Chris waves his hand. "Wouldn't you know, we've been offered a huge sum of money for our citrus groves, now that we're too old to spend it all."

"Will you sell?" Colonel Tillson asks.

"The suburbs are encroaching now, and eventually, they'll surround us. So yes, we probably will."

"I'd stay as long as possible. It's beautiful here," Mavis says.

After the others retire for the night, I ponder what I've learned in this long life of mine. When I left for France in 1939, I was like a rudderless ship—adrift. But in the intervening years, I learned to accept things I couldn't change and to change those things I could. I feel I brought love into Guy's difficult life, and he taught me to believe I was worthy of his devotion.

As I look back, I realize that many of the decisions I made paved the way for others to have a better life. I smile and think about Claude and the man he has become. And not in my most fanciful dreams would I have thought Guy's grandson would marry my granddaughter, Claire. I feel confident that Guy would say to me, "Job well done, mon trésor!"

SOURCES AND FURTHER READINGS
ON OCCUPIED FRANCE

—Non-fiction

Peter Grose, *A Good Place to Hide*, (2015)

Stephen Harding, *Escape from Paris*, (2019)

Alex Kershaw, *The Few*, (2006)

Robert Gildea, *Marianne in Chains,* (2002)

Alex Kershaw, Avenue of Spies, (2012)

John Misseldine with Oliver Clutton-Brock, *Survival Against All Odds*, (2010)

Jeannine Lemoine Etheridge with Hugh Keller Wood, *Soldier Without Uniform*, (1994)

Helene Berr*, The Journal of Helene Berr*, translated from the French by David Bellos, (2008)

Paige Bower, *The General's Niece: The Little Known De Gaulle*, (2017)

Charles Glass, *Americans in Paris*, (2009)

Ronald C. Rosbottom, *When Paris went Dark*, (2014)

Russell Miller and Editors of Time-Life Books*, The Resistance*, (1979)

Ann Sebba, *Les Parisiennes*, (2016)

Stephen Harding, *Escape from Paris*, (2019)

Sarah Rose, *D-Day Girls*, (2019)

Angela Horn, *Phantom Seven*, (2015)

Airey Neave, *Little Cyclone*, (2013)

Agnes Humbert, *Resistance, Memoirs of Occupied France*, translated from the French by Barbara Mellor) (2008)

Rene De Chambrun, *Mission and Betrayal 1949-1945, My Crusade for England*, (1993)

—Fiction

Lucinda Riley, *The Lavender Garden*, (2012)

Kristin Hannah, *The Nightingale*, (2015)

Regine Deforges, *The Blue Bicycle*, (1981)

Kristin Harmel, *The Room on Rue Amelie*, (2018)
Charles Belfoure, *The Paris Architect*, (2013)
Alan Furst, *Red and Gold*, (1999)
Alan Furst, *A Hero of France*, (2016)
Judithe Little, *Wickwythe Hall*, (2017)

Did you miss Book One of the French Connection series?

Silk or Sugar

A Novel

Elizabeth Pye

FOR AN EXCERPT, TURN THE PAGE

Upon their arrival at the Tuileries, guests paused to watch fireworks light the sky while cannons boomed in the distance. Janine stood beside Lenoir near a window, observing elegant coaches deliver France's military elite and their companions to the festive front lawn. The military *soirée* had begun. Many men wore uniforms—what woman could resist a man in uniform—some of whom would be honored for their bravery during the ceremonial celebration.

Ladies made the most of their grand entrance, posturing to show off their gowns and themselves to best advantage. Brimming with pride, Janine felt equally as elegant as any of them in her beautifully designed gown made from Lenoir Frères silk. Tonight she'd bask in the enchantment—for tonight was make-believe. Tomorrow, the spell would be broken.

Glimpsing General de Bernay and Minette across the room, Janine slipped her arm through Lenoir's, hoping to gain his cooperation. "Come, let's greet the de Bernays. Over there." She gestured with her free hand. Lenoir wrapped his arm around Janine's waist along the way and she shuddered at his possessive familiarity—her peace offering had worked too well.

As they approached them, Minette's husband stepped aside and huddled in conversation with another man. Janine noticed Minette's rouge-covered cheeks failed to conceal the pallor of her skin; her lack of vitality was accentuated by her dark blue gown.

"Good evening, Lieutenant . . . and to you, Janine. You're absolutely gorgeous in your *magnifique* silk." Minette turned to Lenoir. "Would you be so kind as to bring us a glass of champagne?"

After he left, Minette stepped closer, her hand trembling as she slipped a small envelope into Janine's hand. "Keep this safe. Read it after the gala," she whispered. She wrapped her arms around Janine and clung to her for a moment before stepping back. "Have a wonderful time tonight. In this sea of humanity, I may not get to speak with you again," she said, her eyes filled with sadness.

Janine tucked the paper under the linen handkerchief inside her pearl-encrusted evening bag and watched Minette vanish into the crowd. She briefly puzzled over the written message until Lenoir intruded on her musings.

"Where's Madame de Bernay?" He glanced around, passing

one of the glasses to Janine and staring at her as if she were to blame for Minette's behavior.

"I don't know." Janine gestured to the champagne. "I guess it's yours now."

"Why would she leave after asking for it?" he said in a peevish tone. "At least she could have waited and taken it with her."

"Perhaps she needed to join her husband."

"Forget about her. There's a good crowd here already. Shall we make the rounds?"

"There's no better time," Janine said, wanting to escape Lenoir's questions and hoping to meet acquaintances of her parents.

Her escort paused to introduce her to people who seemed to hold him in high esteem and who lavished praise on Lenoir Frères silks. Did he hope to impress her sufficiently to change her mind about him? She needed no convincing about the prestige of his silk business. His military achievements were another matter, and his prospect as a husband dismal. She'd already formed her opinion of him and grew weary of his efforts.

She searched the crowd for Etienne until she found him. Her heart skipped a beat. There he was in full military dress—sky blue uniform with silver buttons on the jacket, the scarlet collar and cuffs with a single row of silver embroidery delicious next to his bronzed face. For the first time she saw the military hero in his element. An air of authority and purpose emanated from him. No longer was he the gardener's son with the mesmerizing eyes. He was a man to be reckoned with, like Bonaparte.

And of course Mademoiselle La Roche stood at his side and watched his every move. He seemed unaware of her as he and Bonaparte stepped aside, engrossed in deep conversation. A burning resentment toward the girl threatened Janine's composure. Her dear, brave Etienne deserved a wife of his own choosing—not one to serve Bonaparte's political purposes. And what about her own contribution to his decision? She must tell him she loved him and valued him so much more than fame or fortune.

The lieutenant saved her from gawking when he gripped her arm rather too tightly and led her to the center of the room, away from Etienne and Bonaparte. Just as well, because she didn't want to further displease Bonaparte. He already knew she'd gone back on her agreement to marry Lenoir; besides, Josephine had warned her to stay away from Etienne. She'd have to be more discreet when she told Etienne of her decision not to marry Lieutenant Lenoir.

By the time Janine saw the First Consul again, *sans* Etienne, he was close enough to reach out and touch her.

Bonaparte stepped closer, looked her in the eye, and said in a low growl, "Your decision to deny a union with the great house of Lenoir Frères is foolish." His tone lightened as Lenoir tilted his head toward them. "It's the perfect place for your talent to blossom among those who appreciate the finer things of life." He waved a dismissive hand and shrugged. "I don't understand women." Janine was left speechless as the First Consul moved away.

Musicians assembled at one end of the room and Bonaparte and Josephine led the way to the dance floor at the first musical strains of a minuet.

"If you wish to dance, we should do so now, before the floor gets too crowded." Lenoir stepped toward Janine.

"Let's do," she said to fulfill her dancing obligation. As they moved around the floor, Janine watched a bevy of waiters, carrying trays filled with glasses of champagne and various hors d'oeuvres, weave their way among the guests.

As the music faded, a cotillion was announced as the next dance.

"I need to rest and would like to sit," Janine said.

"That's fine. Champagne?"

"Non, merci."

Lenoir located a chair for her and went to get champagne for himself, stopping to greet the disagreeable lieutenant general she'd met at the de Bernays' dinner party. She watched the Bonapartes leave the dance floor.

Josephine seemed to float toward her on clouds of white organdy. Her dress contained yards of the fabric, and a garland of pink roses adorned her dark hair. "I saw you dancing. How is your ankle holding up?"

"Very well, thank you."

"Are you enjoying yourself?"

"Very much."

"Is your escort being a gentleman?"

She has an ulterior motive, Janine thought. "He is." She forced a smile.

"Good," Josephine said. "Please excuse me. I must circulate among the guests."

While Lenoir made the rounds, Janine watched for her chance to speak to Etienne.

Clusters of military officers gathered together, if not otherwise in the company of beautiful women. As guests continued to arrive, freedom of movement diminished and small groups began to congregate around the room. Waiters circulated among the cliques and kept the champagne flowing.

Janine searched the crowd until she saw Etienne. Bonaparte was to his left, a short distance away, greeting others. *This is my chance.* She stood, her legs unsteady. She'd have make it fast.

She inched forward, every fiber of her being taut with anxiety while her eyes darted back and forth between the two men. People moved in front of her, forcing her to go around waiters and guests alike, her heart pounding as if it would explode.

A man turned abruptly, colliding with Janine and spilling his champagne. *"Pardonnez-moi."*

Ignoring his apology, she pushed past him and caught sight of Etienne and Bonaparte within a few feet of each other. She'd have to wait until Bonaparte separated from him.

Janine froze in place at hearing a loud clatter, followed by the sound of shattering glass. Had a waiter dropped his tray? Time seemed to stand still. What was the waiter doing? A flash of steel betrayed the blade in the waiter's hand as his arm raised and began its descent toward Napoleon's chest. Janine watched in horror, her breath caught in her throat, expecting to see the First Consul fall. She'd seen just such an exotic Persian dagger in Bordeaux at the Duprés' home. There was no mistaking the ornate, hilted, undulating blade.

Etienne reacted quickly and deflected the Khanjar dagger into his own arm. The crowd gasped in unison at the sight of his blood-soaked sleeve. Etienne thrust his right fist into the assailant's face, the blood-stained weapon now in his left hand. Hushed voices rose to a loud buzz, indistinguishable as few listened and many vocalized their questions. Both men disappeared from Janine's view, but not before she recognized Charles when his white wig tumbled from his head.

Great God, how did he get in here?

260

People jockeyed for position. A woman next to Janine dropped her hand from her mouth. "What happened?" she asked her companion.

Janine and others pushed to get closer to the crime scene. She stifled a cry when a man's boot landed on her foot. Her only thought was to get to Etienne. She watched the palace guards merge into the scene and escort Bonaparte and Josephine from the room. More guards swarmed and kept onlookers at bay, preventing Janine from seeing Etienne or Charles. She looked for Lenoir but didn't see him either.

Janine's head throbbed from worry about Etienne—and uncertainty as to whether she might be implicated by association with Charles. She searched the sea of faces for Minette to no avail. *The envelope. Charles.* No, it couldn't be. She leaned against the wall, her head spinning. Had Charles passed the note to Minette? Surely not . . . what if . . . she must get rid of it at the first opportunity.

After the chaos subsided, the guards positioned themselves around the room, ordering no one leave unless they had express permission or until dismissed.

It seemed an eternity before she overheard General de Bernay say, "There's been an attempt on the First Consul's life. He's unharmed. The perpetrator has been subdued and taken away. No, I don't know who he is. Or how he got in here."

Lenoir rushed up, out of breath. "The First Consul is unhurt."

De Bernay gave him a smoldering look. "How do you know?"

Lenoir squared his shoulders and gave him a smug look. "I took Madame Bonaparte to her husband."

Another general remarked, "I saw it all. If it hadn't been for the quick action by Colonel Tremeau, Bonaparte would have taken the blow. Tremeau saw it coming and pushed Bonaparte to safety with his left hand and deflected the knife with his right arm. The blade went into his arm and still he drove his fist into the man's face." The officer pantomimed the action as he spoke. "Stunned, the assailant tried to run, but the colonel subdued him until the guards took the prisoner away."

Another officer said, "The unfortunate fool won't live to see dawn."

"Any accomplices?" a man asked.

Janine felt like a caged animal, confined as she was with the other guests. The more she thought about the note, the more agitated she became. She feared it as much as if she carried an explosive in her handbag. In her misery her eyes wandered to Mademoiselle La Roche, who clung to her father, wailing at the top of her lungs. Janine walked over to them, reached for the girl's hand, and spoke with an assurance she didn't feel, "Don't worry so, I'm sure the colonel is not seriously hurt."

The young woman turned to her, hope in her eyes. "You think not?"

"Of course I do. He's a skilled and brave soldier. He knows how to take care of himself." *And others,* Janine thought, as wistful memories tugged at her heart. "He'll soon be as good as new. You just wait and see."

Monsieur La Roche patted his daughter on the shoulder. "She's right, you know." He turned to Janine. "Thank you for comforting my daughter. I just don't know what to say to her at a time like this."

"It's been a terrible shock for all of us. It's especially frightening for a young woman who hasn't been exposed to such violence."

He nodded. "That is so. Still, I am indebted to you for your compassionate response. If there is ever any way I can return the favor, please call upon me."

Janine swallowed and hoped the lump in her throat would subside. "You are most kind." She wondered on whom she could call after Charles' identity became known.

Mademoiselle La Roche looked up at her father. "When can I see him?"

"I don't know, dear."

She turned to Janine. "When do you think?"

The girl's innocence touched Janine. "I suppose it depends on Colonel Tremeau."

"Oh. What about you? Will you come to visit with me?"

"Perhaps I can." Janine felt a strange sympathy for her in their common concern for Etienne. She edged away and looked for a place to sit. Finding none, she stood by a wall and waited with everyone else.

✣

The First Consul's personal doctor worked feverishly to stop the bleeding from the ugly gash on Etienne's arm. After more than twenty minutes of compression on the wound, the flow slowed to ooze. While bandaging the arm, the doctor said, "You're lucky the knife didn't hit the bone. You'll need to stay here until morning in case the bleeding gets heavier. Keeping still is important, too."

The immediate danger past, Etienne's thoughts went to the breach of security. The royalists had come too damn close to succeeding in their mission. How had Charles Dupré—the pompous man he'd met on his recent trip to London—been cleared as a waiter in the Tuileries? It had to have been instigated by a trusted authority—but who? He drew a blank. He must get to the interrogation of Charles as quickly as possible.

Now that the rush from the emergency had subsided, Etienne struggled to stand. "There's a pressing matter," he said. "I'll be back as soon as I can."

The doctor raised an eyebrow. "You've lost a lot of blood. You know the risk."

Ignoring his lightheadedness, Etienne reached for the clean, oversized shirt the doctor offered. The other man guided his arms, shaking his head all the while.

Hearing voices in the outer room, Etienne listened.

Bonaparte stuck his head in the door. "Thank God, you're able to stand. It must be your peasant stock." He laughed and then turned serious, staring at the bandaged arm. "I want to talk to you . . . over here." He motioned to the medical supply room and closed the door behind them.

"The situation is serious. I have no doubt that Cadoudal and the Bourbons sent Charles Dupré here to murder me. Dupré has implicated General de Bernay's wife in this plot. The palace and grounds have been searched, with no trace of her. He insisted she was his only contact within these walls. A contingent is fanning out in the city, searching for her."

Minette! She had made a fool of all of them. *What about Janine?* "Does General de Bernay know?" Etienne asked.

Etienne chastised himself for missing clues that must have been there. With Minette's involvement, everything fell into place. It explained Dupré's movements in Tours, at Cadoudal's campsite in the Orleans woods, and at the Tuileries.

"Not yet."

"I don't understand how she was able to deceive everyone."

Bonaparte shook his head. "In light of this, I must ask, do you wish to revise your report on Mademoiselle de Fleury?"

"Non. Her troubles began most likely when Minette told her royalist contact about Janine being in Tours. The imposter at Chateau Fleury may have seen the disguised Dupré as an opportunity to denounce Janine, persuading others to do so as well. After the sworn statements were signed, I did a thorough investigation. I found no evidence of conspiracy on Janine's part. To the contrary, her accusers conspired against her with well-rehearsed statements, some of which were outright lies. As for the pre-revolutionary marriage contract between Janine and Dupré, the terms were not met." Etienne gave Bonaparte a sly look. "You must have known that when you selected her as a suitable wife for Lenoir."

"That's true. Dupré was in England and she in New Orleans. Josephine and I did look into that aspect."

Etienne sank onto the cot. "If you need more convincing, consider that Janine has no authority to make palace staffing decisions. Besides, she was lame and incapacitated while her ankle healed, right here under the watchful eye of your household. She wasn't at liberty to conspire with anyone."

Bonaparte rubbed his temples. "I see your point." He took a deep breath. "This is the second time you've saved my life. I want to thank you for your loyalty. Within a year I'll be crowned Emperor of France, and I want you appointed as my *Intendant General de la Grande Armée*. If you still refuse to marry Mademoiselle La Roche, you will find yourself a traitor to the Republic. Think long and hard about it. You have a choice—share in the future glory of France or face a court-martial."

Etienne clenched his teeth and nodded. *If I do as I'm told.* Consul-for-Life should satisfy Napoleon. But no, he planned a Bonaparte dynasty to dictate to the citizens for generations. *No different than the royal Bourbons.* Etienne saw his fight for the rights of man failing right before his eyes. "I'm honored to know of your confidence in me," he said, buying time to get his affairs in order before he left the country.

Did you miss Book Two of the French Connection series?

Return to Chateau Fleury

Elizabeth Pye

FOR AN EXCERPT, TURN THE PAGE

Paris, September 1998

Slightly disoriented after her long flight followed by an uneasy first night at Michelle's apartment, Claire wondered whether she looked as haggard as she felt. She hoped the brisk walk and fresh air on their way to breakfast at Michelle's favorite sidewalk café would revive her. At least no dreams had kept her awake during the night. Maybe she was too tired to dream, or maybe—and wouldn't that be great—she'd left those annoying interruptions on the other side of the Atlantic. *Don't count on it*, an inner voice warned. She sighed.

Ostensibly, she was here in Paris on a leave of absence to conduct research for publication and to rub shoulders with members of an esteemed international organization. However, she knew deep in her heart that she'd returned to pursue Chateau Fleury and the marquise.

By the time they reached the café along the bustling Champs-Élysées, Claire felt refreshed and ready to start the day. She noticed the sunlight dance across strands of Michelle's sleek raven hair in rhythm with the saucy toss of her head. Even in the unforgiving glare, her friend had not visibly aged a day in the decade since they had been students at the University of Paris.

"*Bonjour,*" a serious young waiter greeted them. "What will you have?" He looked at Claire.

"A cheese omelet and *café*."

"Okay." He turned to Michelle, *"Et vous?"*

"Can't you guess what every French girl eats for breakfast?" she said with a good-natured smile.

"Non, mademoiselle," he said.

It was now they noticed he spoke French with a definite German accent.

Michelle seemed to take pity on him. "A croissant and café, *s'il vous plaît.*"

Her friend's lighthearted banter carried Claire back to her carefree days as an exchange student. She and Michelle Laval had developed a lasting friendship, although at the time an alliance seemed unlikely—their backgrounds were so different—Claire an ambitious middle-class American and Michelle a fun-loving French aristocrat.

257

"Forgive me. I've been doing all of the talking." Michelle's head bobbed in time with her expressive hand gestures. "What plans do you have for your time here, other than visiting with me?"

"Now that my students are settled on campus, I'll work on my research and take care of a few other things." Claire adjusted her chair to escape the glare of the morning sun.

"What other things? I have plans for your time."

"I'm not sure when Professor de Motte will want me to visit with her committee. It's for the UNESCO Report on Higher Education for the Twenty-First Century. You do remember that Professor de Motte mentored me while I studied here?"

"*Oui*. How could I forget?" Michelle pushed aside her half-eaten croissant. "Claire, you work too much. You need to get away."

Michelle's words struck a responsive chord. She did need to unwind. Could time in the French countryside rejuvenate her? "Oui . . . right after the first committee meeting."

"The UNESCO committee or another one?" Michelle sipped her coffee.

"UNESCO. The one I want to discuss with Marc-Claude. Thank you for arranging an appointment with him."

Michelle nodded and smiled. "You and he are alike—always working, too busy to have fun. You'll be old before you know it and still not have lived life as it should be."

Claire glanced at her watch—no time to pursue that comment. It was time to leave for her meeting with Marc-Claude. Michelle's brother was an attorney whom she hoped would help her with her Chateau Fleury project. To that end she needed a quiet walk along the Seine while she gathered her thoughts before they spoke.

Most likely the aristocratic attorney would be put off by any suggestion of impropriety of members of his social circle. She'd have to select her words with care. The nobility of France had protected one another since suffering persecution during the French Revolution. An attack on one was considered an attack on all.

Claire touched Michelle's sleeve before she stood and picked up her handbag. "I really appreciate staying with you while I'm here. I'll call before I start back to the apartment."

Michelle rose and brushed an imaginary strand of hair from her cheek before she and Claire exchanged the obligatory *la bise* to each cheek. "*À la prochaine*. See you soon. No need to plan where to go for dinner. We'll stay in while I persuade you to come to Lamont with me."

Marc-Claude Laval closed the folder and shoved it so hard it flew off his desk. "Blast Michelle and her meddling," he mumbled as he got up and walked around his desk to pick up the scattered sheets of paper. His kid sister couldn't resist worrying about his social life. He knew he shouldn't let her get to him. But she did. She had asked if he would advise her *college friend* about Gypsies or some such thing, to which request, he'd pointed out that his specialty was international business law.

His sister seemed to have no appreciation for the demands of his practice and his responsibilities to the European Union—probably because she only worked part-time . . . and only when she felt like it. He wished she would stop urging him to date more often. She did it for their parents rather than for him.

Marc-Claude was of the opinion that his father criticized him because of his own unhappy marriage. His parents used to argue a lot until General de Laval learned that silence kept the peace. After that they managed to maintain a sham marriage and lead separate lives in opposite wings of the sprawling chateau. *If I can't expect a better marriage than theirs, I'll remain single.* Regardless of Madame de Laval's wish for him to marry Felicity de Fleury, he wasn't motivated to do so. Felicity was too much like his mother—she always had to have the last word.

Claire walked along the Champs-Élysées toward the Place de la Concorde. Michelle was a gem to broker a meeting with her brother, a successful international-law attorney who served on a committee of the European Union. She'd tried to rationalize that she needed his opinion about the legal hurdles faced by third-world-nation women who sought a higher education. But her underlying motive was to gather information about Chateau Fleury—the ancestral home of Marquis Andre de Fleury's family since the sixteenth century.

She'd first read the Marquise de Fleury's diary as a child and since then had fallen under its spell. The words on the pages tugged at her heart. She couldn't seem to distance herself from them. As irrational as it might appear, she felt compelled to find out more about Chateau Fleury and the secrets buried there. She wondered if somehow the essence of the marquise remained in the stones of the chateau. Would it bring her closer to Marie de Fleury to be in the physical location where she had spent so many hours? Sometimes, she felt as though Marie was trying to break through the time barrier that separated them.

Claire intended to seek Marc-Claude Laval's advice about the chateau, but he had no knowledge of her intentions. She had no right to take up his time with what would seem to him a frivolous pursuit. She tried to assuage her conscience in that she hadn't revealed her primary desire to Michelle. Her ancestors' estate had been seized during the Revolution in 1793 and later reclaimed on behalf of the family by an imposter using the de Fleury name—an injustice Claire seemed unable to ignore, try as she may.

Claire's pace slowed when she reached the Place de la Concorde—the site of the 1793 Place de la Revolution, home to Madame Guillotine. She felt dizzy and sank onto a nearby bench as a gray cloud engulfed her. *What is happening to me?*

Dazed, she looked around. She saw nothing through the ominous fog but she heard phantom-like sounds of jeering crowds, creaking cart wheels and horses' hooves striking stone.

She struggled against the pull into darkness. She looked behind her and to the sides but saw nothing out of the ordinary. Raising her hand to her throat, she clutched her heavy gold locket. The buzzing in her head grew louder. She staggered to her feet and began to walk, arms outstretched, feeling her way through the mist. A raw, searing pain sliced through her neck and shot through her head. Disoriented, she heard tires screech and felt a rush of air before her hands connected with something solid—a man's rough hands.

"Why don't you watch where you're going?" After screeching to a stop, the black-haired man had climbed out of his cab, slamming the door shut. "Are you okay?" he asked as he peered at her.

"Oui, monsieur." Seeing no one inside, Claire pulled open the back door of his taxi and flopped onto the seat.

The cabbie got into the driver's seat and looked at her in the rearview mirror. "Where to?" he said, fiddling with the radio dial.

"*Vingt-cinq* Rue de Victoires." Claire sank into the shabby back seat. "Drive around for twenty minutes or so before getting me there. And please stop at the first place you see where I can get some coffee. I desperately need a cup." She closed her eyes and stilled her mind, although true meditation was out of the question just yet.

The lurching ride suddenly changed as the cabbie turned into a McDonald's and screeched to a stop. "Coffee time," he said, exiting the car without waiting for her.

Claire shrugged her shoulders to relax her tense muscles.

I shouldn't have come here.

She went inside, ordered a coffee to go, and went out to wait for the driver. Some minutes later he returned and soon they were traveling along the Rue de Rivoli. She kept track of their location by noting the familiar landmarks they passed. They'd gone by the Tuileries Gardens and the palatial Louvre Museum before they picked up their coffee. Now out of the window she saw the Hotel de Ville for the second time.

Before they reached the Banque de France a second time, the cab turned onto the Place des Victoires, rounded a corner, and stopped by one of the historic Mansart-designed buildings that housed Laval and Associates. The driver turned to face her. "Ninety francs, mademoiselle."

Claire gulped and handed over one precious Paul Cézanne portrait—a 100-francs note. Somewhat intimidated by her surroundings, she knew she faced another challenging encounter inside. She couldn't let that aristocratic Frenchman Marc-Claude Laval deter her from her personal mission. She'd keep their conversation formal and try to maintain her dignity at all cost.

She reexamined the pros and cons of broaching the subject of Chateau Fleury at all. The stakes were high. After all, she hoped to become associated with people at UNESCO, people with whom he interacted. However, at the moment her desire to find out about the fate of the chateau and the descendants of those who had stolen it overrode her pride and professional aspirations.

"Bonjour, mademoiselle." The Laval and Associates' receptionist studied her with a quizzical expression.

"Bonjour. I have a ten o'clock appointment with Monsieur Laval."

"May I get you something to drink?"

"*L'eau,* s'il vous plait."

The trim woman ushered Claire to a tapestry-covered Louis XV-style chair and soon returned with a glass of water. "I'll let Monsieur Laval know you're here," the receptionist said before returning to her desk.

"Thank you." Claire sipped the water and studied the elegantly appointed reception area. Three matching, tapestry-covered walnut chairs and a sofa upholstered in a nubby brown fabric completed the seating arrangement. Laval's office was in the high rent district—outside her budget. She wouldn't be there if this were not a complimentary consultation.

Like a mother hen, the receptionist kept an eye on her. "More water?"

"No more, merci." After waiting for what seemed an eternity, she glanced at her watch. Forty-five minutes had passed.

I'll never get used to the French attitude toward time.

As if reading Claire's mind, the receptionist stood. "Mademoiselle Bennett, come with me." Claire followed the slender suit-clad blonde to a spacious office at the end of the corridor. "Mademoiselle Bennett is here for her appointment, Monsieur Laval," the receptionist said before she turned to leave.

The tall, dark-haired Frenchman approached and took Claire's hand. "*Enchanté.* I'm Marc-Claude Laval. Please be seated." With a light touch to her arm, he guided her toward an overstuffed, maroon leather chair and sat on a nearby matching loveseat. *He's smooth as satin.*

Claire was not prepared for his suave good looks. She had pictured him as a stuffy, nearsighted older man. Michelle's reference to him as her learned older brother, a Rhodes Scholar at Oxford, had misled her. Contrary to her preconceived notion, the man was vibrant—simply put, handsome.

Like a jaguar—sleek and muscular. Those alert golden eyes won't miss a thing—always one step ahead of his prey.

"Thank you. It's nice to meet you."

"Dr. Bennett, Michelle often speaks of you. She tells me you teach French at Boise State University."

Leave it to Michelle to make the introductions. "Yes, that's correct. And, please, call me Claire."

The warmth of his smile carried over to his voice. "Likewise, call me Marc-Claude." His eyes held hers for a brief moment before he spoke again. "Do you come to Paris often?"

Claire relaxed in his presence in spite of herself. "Not often enough," she replied, resisting the distraction of his easy manner.

"Do you enjoy your work at the university?"

"Very much. I enjoy teaching. And of course my research keeps me busy."

"Research, oui. My sister said you're completing some research while you're here and have appointments at UNESCO. What is the topic of your research?"

"It involves a group of university exchange students. They've taken my training workshop and now they're here to practice what they've learned."

An easy smile played at the corners of his mouth. "Training, eh? What kind?"

Had she imagined a teasing tone in his voice? She dismissed the thought. "Cross-cultural training. The idea came from some of my faux pas while I was an exchange student."

"Cultural misunderstandings are quite embarrassing," he said. His English accent was such that even the Queen would approve.

"You admit to such experiences?" Claire responded in her best French.

He smiled and looked her in the eye. "*Une fois n'est pas coutume*. Just this once."

Seeing the amusement in his eyes, she laughed. "My workshops address cultural shock and misunderstandings."

His expression grew thoughtful. "Ummm, that idea has merit . . . for businessmen *and* women." When she nodded, he continued, "I believe you have questions for me about human trafficking of women."

"That's correct."

"I don't know how helpful I'll be. What information would you like?"

She sensed his steady gaze, feeling a warm flush rise up her neck to her face, but she kept her eyes lowered and fumbled with her notes, hoping he wouldn't notice—not likely, given his keen perception.

What's the matter with me?

She inhaled the subtle bouquet of his woodland aftershave, determined not to respond to it. "The EU has sponsored research on trafficking under its Sexual Trafficking of Persons program. Various agencies keep statistics and records on the cases." Claire paused. "However, problems remain. How familiar are you with the issues?"

Marc-Claude leaned back in his seat. "I have no firsthand experience with such cases."

"There is an acknowledged problem for these women," Claire said. "They become just a number on a piece of paper with few options open to them." She jotted a note on her pad before she looked up, her eyes meeting his. What are France and the EU doing about it?"

"Europol reports are compiled from information supplied by member-state national law-enforcement agencies. The statistics are only as good as those provided by the local or regional law-enforcement offices."

"To your knowledge, are there any services to assist women who come to the attention of the authorities here in Paris?"

Marc-Claude picked up a legal pad and pen from the coffee table and made a few notes. "Not that I'm aware of. But I'll see if I can gather more information for you and let you know what I find."

"Thank you." Claire took a deep breath and slowly exhaled. "I do have another matter I'd like to discuss . . . if time permits."

He raised an eyebrow. "*Certainement.* What is it?"

"It's more of a historical question than a legal one." Claire cleared her throat.

"Eh . . . of course." Marc-Claude glanced at his watch.

"I'm sorry. I should have mentioned it to Michelle, but I wasn't sure whether to bring it up with you."

"What's the question?" He regarded her with somber curiosity.

"My family members are the legitimate direct descendants of the Marquis and Marquise de Fleury, owners of Chateau Fleury in the Loire Valley before the Revolution."

A fleeting look of astonishment crossed his face. "You must be mistaken."

She pulled a small book from her purse and handed it to him. "This diary belonged to Marquise de Fleury. Janine, the Marquise's only surviving child, added some brief notes at the end of her mother's diary."

Marc-Claude's eyes focused on a mille-fleur paperweight on his desk. "Janine . . . *beau prénon*. Beautiful name."

"Janine wrote of the horrors of the French Revolution. Her parents were guillotined in 1793." Her voice breaking, Claire paused and pressed her hand to her throat.

Marc-Claude placed his hand over hers for a brief moment before getting up. "*Excusez-moi*." Taking two bottles of Perrier from the small refrigerator by his desk, he returned, handed one to Claire, and sat, placing the other on the side table.

"Merci." Claire nodded toward the Perrier. "After their death, Comte Louis de Fleury, planned their escape from France. But before they could get away, Janine saw him killed."

"By the revolutionaries?"

"Non, stabbed on the chateau grounds by a stable hand who then stole his identity."

Marc-Claude tapped his fingers on the side of the loveseat. "During that time our society collapsed around us."

"Janine recorded that some years later an imposter, calling himself the Comte de Fleury, returned to France and laid claim to the family assets, including the chateau."

Marc-Claude's brows drew together in a frown.

Undeterred, Claire removed the gold locket from around her neck. "This is a family heirloom." She opened the large, ornately engraved, heart-shaped locket and handed it to him. As their fingertips met, a bittersweet yearning touched her.

"The Marquis and Marquise?" He cupped the locket in his hand while lightly running his index finger along the elaborate raised design. His expression defied interpretation while he studied the miniature painting of the young bride and groom.

"Yes." For an uncomfortable moment, Claire lowered her head and fought the urge to cry. She wanted to grab the locket from his hand and change the subject before she fell apart in front of him.

Marc-Claude looked from the miniature painting to Claire and back again. "Remarkable resemblance. Your features are similar to those of the Marquise."

"You think so?" She reached for the locket.

He ignored her outstretched hand and remained silent for a

moment before he returned it. "Tell me more about Janine's escape."

"After her uncle's death, Janine feared she'd be next. She went to Bordeaux with the help of the gardener's son."

Marc-Claude's expression stilled and grew serious. "To help her would have meant risking his own life."

"Yes, he was a brave man, a very special man."

Marc-Claude's voice softened. "Where did she go after she reached Bordeaux?"

"To her betrothed's family. She accompanied them to New Orleans."

"Thank God. Eh . . . did she return to France and lay claim to her family property?"

"She did return to France some years later but ran into difficulties when she tried to challenge the fraudulent claim."

He nodded. "Returning émigrés often faced drawn-out legal proceedings when challenging ownership of property."

"It was more complicated than that. Janine finally gave up on the property but wanted the family history recorded. That's why she added notes to her mother's diary."

Marc-Claude remained silent, his expression unreadable.

Why doesn't he say something? Claire closed her eyes and stroked the book cover. "While I'm in France, I want to pick up where Janine left off and add to the notes in Marquise de Fleury's diary."

"How can I help you?" Marc-Claude held her gaze.

"What were the legal requirements for returning émigrés to reclaim their property?"

"The established social structures, including the legal system, were in disarray during the revolution. Afterward, many fundamental assumptions underlying the entire legal system changed."

She grimaced. "Was there any clarification of the conflicting laws over the years?"

"The Napoleonic Code of Eighteen-Ten, the French Civil Code, sought to mix aspects of revolutionary law with pre-revolutionary law and is the foundation of our laws today."

Without thought Claire blurted out, "What about the provisions in the new Nineteen Ninety-Four Code?" She froze.

Where did that come from? If I believed in ghosts, I'd think I'm possessed.

"I thought you needed to ask me questions," Marc-Claude said, his mouth tight and grim. "It seems this is an unnecessary consultation, since you have already researched it yourself, you should know it doesn't apply." He glanced at his watch and stood.

Apparently, she had been dismissed. Had she ruined everything? How stupid—she needed to keep his goodwill.

www.ingramcontent.com/pod-product-compliance
Lightning Source LLC
Chambersburg PA
CBHW070354260626
47161CB00001B/140